THE LESS WE TOUCH

OTHER BOOKS BY STEVE DUIN

Oil and Water (graphic novel), 2011

The Amazing Love Story (with Mike Ashburn, Young Life Series), 2005.

Father Time (stories), 2004

Blast Off: Rockets, Robots, Ray Guns, and Rarities from the Golden Age of Space Toys, (non-fiction), 2001

Comics: Between the Panels (nonfiction), 1998

THE LESS WE TOUCH

Steve Duin

Based on a TRUE STORY

First Print Edition
2015

Copyright © Steve Duin

stephen.b.duin@gmail.com

Produced and Distributed By:

Library Partners Press
ZSR Library
Wake Forest University
1834 Wake Forest Road
Winston-Salem, North Carolina 27106

library partners press
a digital publishing imprint

www.librarypartnerspress.org

This is a work of fiction.
While the novel is inspired by real events, the names,
characters, places, incidents and institutions either are
the product of the author's imagination or are used
fictitiously.

For my daughters, Lauren and Christina.

THE LESS WE TOUCH

before

He was so much better than this. The lumbering air conditioners and the piss-poor cable service. The industrial-strength pillows and 40-watt light bulbs. The meth addicts at the front desk. The garbage that came with the territory.

He shut the water off and reached for one of the skinny dishrags that the white trash dropped off each morning. He wiped his face and tossed the towel into the wicker basket with the plastic bottles of shampoo and body lotion. He liked the body lotion. The stuff came in handy now and then.

He glanced in the mirror, assessing the weathered stare. He'd seen worse. The dents and scars didn't mar the impressive cut of his jaw. His hairline was holding firm. Still the lone chin. If time was tightening the screws, he could still see the outline of the face he carried into his 20s. He could pretend the college girls at the downtown jazz clubs downtown could see it, too.

In this back-alley light, the mirror did him no favors. He was staring at the laps he'd run, the sacrifices he'd made, the sweet Js that rimmed out at the buzzer. A coach had to rise above the bitter memories in the scoreboard lights. You couldn't sweat the miles you drove, the hours of sleep you gave up, the slights you ignored for the sake of the girls. *For the sake of the team.* Most of your best work never registered. You couldn't let that bother you. You couldn't expect parents, much less the pampered prima donnas they'd entrusted to your care, to realize you were irreplaceable.

He ran his left hand under his chin, massaging the rough edges. The stubble, uneven as it was, added to the look. Careless bad-ass. Prince of thieves. He reached for the T-shirt hanging from the hook on the back of the bathroom door. Still reasonably fresh. He could use a few new T-shirts. Nike and adidas didn't deliver the freebies the way they used to. Something with a novel message, like the beaut he'd seen last night in the parking lot, taut across the 34-inch chest of an off-duty cocktail waitress: "If your dick was as big as your mouth, I'd be interested." He was laughing all over again.

He was surprisingly relaxed. The hot water had taken the edge off. You had to bear down when you traveled with the girls. If the weekend started feeling like vacation, they wouldn't refocus when the bracket dragged them out of bed for an 8 a.m. game. So, he played the Grinch, the Drill Sergeant, the Bad Cop. Not that the roles were a stretch.

He slipped on the sandals, dropped a condom into the pocket of his sweats and cracked open the door to his room. The hallway was empty, the air tart and thick. He could hear the labored breathing of the ice machine down the hall, just past the elevator doors. He always asked for the room by the elevators, to better track the girls' movements. Most of the team had left for dinner 20 minutes ago. He hadn't heard Molly's voice in the careless babbling at the elevator doors.

He walked slowly down the hall, listening for the rattle of a door knob. Not that it mattered. He was a coach, out on patrol, checking on his players. He was the concerned father figure, sweating the details. Nothing out of the ordinary. At the end of the hall, he rapped lightly on the door of room 311. His mouth was dry. Expectation had a way of stringing him out. He stared at the peephole until the shadow passed behind it. He was lifting his hand to knock again when the door opened to the length of the chain.

In the dim light, it was hard to read the expression on Molly's face. She looked lost. He wondered if he'd interrupted a nap. He wondered if her mouth was dry, too.

"How ya feeling, baby doll?" he said.

"OK. I guess." She lifted her brown eyes to his. "Everyone at dinner?"

He nodded. After a beat or two, Molly pushed the door closed just far enough to free the chain, then stepped back out of the way. She knew the drill.

He stepped into the room, quietly shutting the door behind him. The drapes were closed and the back-burner Best Buy TV turned to "Boy Meets World," though the volume was off. The twin beds were a pitch and toss of sheets and pillows.

Molly stood at the corner of the bed closest to the window, nervously pushing her hair behind her right ear. She was almost as tall as he was. As hard as he worked her in practice, she was still 10 pounds overweight, most of it, unfortunately, in the hips. Damn if her breasts weren't flattened beneath one of those damn sports bras that stole the shape from a girl.

"You weren't hungry?" She shook her head. "When's the last time you ate?"

She was trying to remember. "An energy bar. I think. After practice."

"Practice." He could hear Allen Iverson, far in the distance. Sweet ol' AI. He remembered being caught up in the flow, the electricity so intense that every packed-house game felt like practice, and practice against the punk-ass scrubs who didn't have a clue. AI. Why Iverson made it and he didn't was hard to understand but he guessed this much: AI didn't have to go down the hall. In AI's world, the talent delivered.

"Practice," he said again. "Waste of time." His eyes swung from the unmade bed back to Molly. "My time, at least. Couldn't even concentrate. Couldn't stop thinking about you."

"I sucked bad," Molly said. "Afraid you'd notice."

"Notice everything. Don't want to give nothing away. But it's hard, girl. Sometimes, I just have to close my eyes."

She allowed herself a brief smile. She was so awkward, standing there. She didn't know what to do with herself. They rarely did at this age, when they were growing an inch every three months. She knew her body served her well on the basketball floor, but it no longer fit her clothes or her sense of herself. She'd probably already gotten the idea – from the crude remarks at school – that she wasn't going to get anywhere with a boy who fit under her chin. That's where the coach came in, of course. Mr. Understanding. Coach Empathy. He dripped the damn stuff. Not on the court. He ran her butt off on the court. But afterwards, in room 311, he had a different act. He was the victim here. A helpless, rock-hard victim of her charms.

He sat on the edge of the bed. He was restless. Patience was a losing strategy. Someone got sick at dinner. Someone got curious. Some Baja refugee arrived with chocolate mints for the pillow. He reached for the edge of her sweats, his fingers rising under the T-shirt. Damn. He loved this age. Fourteen and ripening on the vine. Clueless as to what to do with that raw talent. Timid, usually, and dumb as a post. In a few months, maybe a year, they'd stop listening. They wouldn't be so desperate for attention that they'd surrender everything for it. They'd skip along to high school, gain some balance or, more likely, fall apart. But right now, they were perfect. Coachable. That was it. Completely coachable.

"C'mon, baby doll, before I lose it. C'mon now." He had one hand at her waist, one hand at his belt. In the dim light of another weekend away from home, Molly looked resigned. Whatever. He had her trained. She knew the drill.

2005

1 2 15 21
3 9 16 22 2
4 10 17 23 30
11 18 24 31
12 19 25
13 19 2

T he back road from Lake Oswego to Oregon City ran roughly parallel to the Willamette River, though the water rarely fluttered into view before you veered onto the narrow Oregon City Bridge, a span encased in gunite to shield it from the sulfur dioxide pouring from the paper mills. The back road covered the dozen miles in 20 minutes, not counting the stop at Starbucks on State Street. Alex Blessing and his daughter, Layla, talked most of the way and the conversation rarely varied. She was tired. She was nervous. Her stomach hurt. She didn't want to play.

"Are you serious?" Alex asked once again, fumbling with his seat belt. He had a section of Kashmir white granite countertop in the back, so Layla's travel bag was jammed beneath her feet. "You don't mean that."

"Yeah, Dad!" Layla said. "I'm sick of basketball. I don't want to do this anymore." Her hair was bound into a ponytail, her nose peeling, the only flaw in her Italian tan. She had not yet laced her Nikes.

"You want to play soccer full time?'

"I don't want to do that, either."

"Sweetheart …" Alex said, but she was reaching for the radio. Z-100 rap. Heavy on the bass.

The back road to Oregon City, Oregon 43 cut across the breadth of the middle class in Clackamas County, linking country club and country common. Lake Oswego was a lush, green community of the brick mailbox and three-car garage. Oregon City was the frayed end of the Oregon Trail, a working-class town forever down on its luck. By all appearances, Lake Oswego was pampered flower baskets, lake views, designer boutiques and Springsteen's first wife, and Oregon City antique stores, chiropractic clinics, and Tonya Harding. Lake Oswego was addicted to its SUVs, Oregon City to its F350s. The towns had little in common but their peevish distaste for one another.

In the heart of LO, Alex swung off State Street into the Starbucks' lot, pulling into the first open slot and ignoring the sign that thanked him for keeping the space free for customers of the veterinary clinic. "What do you want?" he asked Layla.

"I don't care. Leave the radio on."

Alex popped the keys into the Durango ignition and brought Coldplay back to life. "Lock the doors," he said.

The line was eight deep, the baristas dressed like salsa dancers and barking out the orders with falsetto enthusiasm. The perky *senorita* behind the counter was crushed Alex only needed a grande coffee and a slice of banana bread. When he returned to the parking lot, a gleaming white Suburban was parked two spaces down from the Durango and a 40-year-old baroness in spandex and heels was hoisting a yelping fur ball out of the backseat. She glared at the coffee cup in his hands, even as she nodded at the sign. "The rules don't apply to you?" she asked.

"I know," Alex said. "Where's a cop when you need one?"

He had to knock on his window before his daughter unlocked the door; she was totally absorbed by the puppy. "What's wrong with her?" Layla asked as Alex settled in.

"The lady or her dog?" Alex asked, passing the banana bread.

Layla pursed her lips. "Why can't we get a dog?"

"Because we have you. One mongrel is the house limit."

In truth, the Blessings – Alex and Olivia – had two. Layla's brother, Graham, was 15, submerged in lacrosse and internet poker. He wasn't all that interested in his parents.

When Alex turned left out of the lot, a loop of water flared into view, then disappeared behind the austere brickwork and stucco of the homes fronting the east end of the lake. Even if you lived in town, the lake was private, a world all its own. Lake Oswego had its share of strip malls, deadbeat dads and Junior Leaguers who believed a disheveled Shih Tzu entitled them to a reserved parking place. But the lake – Oswego Lake – was a different deal altogether, a dramatic departure from the river that caught its spill-off. While Portland riverboats, Gresham drunks and lonely fishermen toured the Willamette, water cops patrolled Oswego Lake, guarding against similar intrusions. The lake was the ultimate gated community. Access was reserved for those with a boat slip or the millions necessary to buy lakefront property. Oswego Lake suffered neither tides nor trespassers. The murky water was a breeding ground for an obnoxious lime-green algae, and nothing moved across the surface without the express consent of the Lake Corporation. Most of the lots were decorated to the water's edge, a tableau of exquisite lawn, bark-dusted flowerbeds, slate patios and Adirondack chairs. Everything was perfectly detailed. The lake was Disneyland.

Oregon City? Central Florida.

The banana bread had sparked Layla's first enthusiasm of the morning. Her stomach wouldn't sit still for a decent breakfast on game days, even off-season games like this one at Gardiner Middle School, but the banana bread settled her down. When the lake was two miles behind them, she cautiously asked, "Do you think we'll win?"

"Yep," Alex said. "But I always think that. We're better than they are."

"They don't know that."

"No, they think we're soft because we're from Lake Oswego."

Layla picked several brown crumbs off her Navy blue shorts. "How come?"

Mick Hilton, his partner coaching Lake Oswego's traveling basketball team, was better at this speech, Alex thought. When they'd coached their sons, Graham and Derek, in Junior Baseball, Mick could unload like no one else on the latte-sipping, tennis-playing, Subaru-driving, Black Butte-hanging, silver-spoon sportin' New Boys on the Block who gave LO a bad name.

"A bunch of reasons," Alex said. "There's a lot more money in Lake Oswego."

Layla glanced at him with practiced exasperation. "Any under *your* mattress?"

"Why?"

"Everyone but me has been to Hawaii. That is so unfair."

"You're right. I don't know how you deal with it. And I'm betting all the 7th-graders in Oregon City are wondering, too. You grow up in Oregon City and …"

He stopped. They were crossing that steel-arch bridge into Oregon City's cramped downtown core, dropping toward the courthouse and the empty hobby stores, and Alex felt the dark, cold weight of the house at the south edge of town. Lake Oswego was every spoiled child who had romped through the Blessings' kitchen, digging through the cupboard for Sun Chips and fruit roll-ups. Oregon City was Ashley and Miranda.

The back road from Lake Oswego to Oregon City delivered you to the weary, mill side of town. To reach the middle school, you crossed the railroad tracks and climbed the 10th Street hill, passing within several blocks of the old high school gym where Oregon City's girls won all their state championships in the 90s. In the early days of that run, the Pioneer coaches recruited the state's best players to fill out their roster; now, the talent from Newberg or Roseburg naturally gravitated to Oregon City, hoping to register on the radar screen of the college coaches in the crowd.

Given the endless flow of basketball vagabonds, there were never enough seats on the varsity bench for the girls who grew up near Gardiner Middle School. Gardiner was deep in the back pocket of a forgotten neighborhood, surrounded by parched athletic fields, a utility substation and a cemetery. The signboard at the entrance to the parking lot read "Home of Future Champions," but the champs' middle-school holding cell was bathed in a flat, marigold stain. Each time Alex returned, he remembered Linda Virden, the teacher who once stood by the main entrance and watched, appalled, as Ward Weaver pulled up in his van with Ashley Pond and placed a loving kiss on her mouth.

Ashley was 12, Ward the father of one of her best friends.

Ashley disappeared first, Miranda Gaddis two months later. Because Weaver lived at the top of the hill by Newell Creek Village, where the two girls hung on to their mangled families, he was interviewed several times by the police. He toyed with the cops and exploited the celebrity by leading TV reporters on guided tours of the house and the freshly poured cement patio in the back. It was months before the cops decided to dig deeper into Ward's affairs. They found Miranda's body beneath the slab and Ashley's in a barrel inside a backyard shed. One of the girls was legally drunk when she died, the other's body still wrapped in her unfastened bra.

That wasn't the worst of it; there was no end to the worst of it. Several days after the bodies were found, Eddie Alvarado, a reporter at the Portland paper, wrote a piece suggesting you could hardly blame the girls for not recognizing the malevolence in the low-life who would eventually kill them. Their mothers, between them, dated three convicted sex offenders, two of whom sexually abused Ashley or Miranda long before they sought refuge with Ward Weaver. When Ashley was 7, she went looking for her biological father, and found him. What happened during their weekend visits over the next five years eventually produced a 40-count indictment, including ten counts of first-degree rape and another ten of first-degree sodomy.

You grew up in Oregon City under that shadow, Alex imagined in those nights when he couldn't sleep, wondering when such harm would come looking for Layla. Behind its bay-windowed façade, Lake Oswego had its own share of middle-class calamity, its roll call of tortured marriages and failed adoptions, two-bedroom apartments and dead-end jobs, anorexic teenagers and neighborhood sociopaths, Amway hustlers and Ponzi schemes, but they all took shelter beneath the community's illusions of grandeur. Oregon City didn't have that luxury. For one long, terrible spring, Oregon City clung to the possibility that something evil, something foreign, crept in just before dawn and spirited those girls away, someone who might never return. All the while, Ward Weaver was watching "American Idol," joking with reporters, mixing cement.

Alex drove the rest of the way to Gardiner in silence, Layla nibbling on the banana bread. Twenty cars were parked by the back entrance to Gardiner's gym, including Mick's 4-Runner and the Team Chelsea Volvos. Chelsea's grandparents, still a relatively robust foursome, attended each of her games, always arriving in used Volvos off her father's lot in Wilsonville. Jack Lider had a weakness for Swedish engineering. His wife, Annika, was 5-foot-11 and blond. Alex guessed Chelsea would clear that height before she hit high school. She was their best player. She had that fabled mid-range jumper and a passion for attacking the basket.

Alex pulled the ball bag from the back of the Durango. Layla was dragging, a listlessness that would persist until Mick's daughter popped into view. Lisa was Layla's Adrenalin shot. The morning could use one, too. The cloud cover had burrowed in for the long haul. As Alex reached the door, a dirty German Shepherd skirted the parking lot, low and feral.

"Why can't we have a dog?" Layla whined anew, lingering at the open door.

"Chiaro would have a cow," Alex said. Chiaro was Layla's two-year-old hamster. He was already showing his age.

They crossed 40 feet of hallway to reach the gym. Like so much of Oregon City, Gardiner felt like the Fifties: the wide halls, the ancient lockers, the lack of doors on the restroom stalls. Nothing about Gardiner was state of the art ... except the gym. It wasn't Cameron Indoor Stadium or Freedom Hall -- it wasn't even the new high school – but it shared their stage presence. Unlike the compact skating rinks at most of the area middle schools, Gardiner's gym was high-school regulation. The floor was genuine hardwood. The scoreboard worked. The girls sat on plastic chairs, not the front row of the bleachers, with the moms and Team Chelsea breathing down their necks.

The scoreboard clock was ticking down from 24 minutes when Alex dropped the ball bag at the visitors' bench. Chelsea and Mattie were warming up with their flat Naismith-era men's balls, so Alex sent the regulation Wilsons rolling onto the court. Layla plopped down next to Lisa, who was lacing her white-and-blue Nikes. Alex stared at her until Layla, wholly relaxed at last, glanced sheepishly up at him. "Two minutes," he said, "then I want you warming up."

Jeff Reisler, the Oregon City coach was at mid-court, watching his players stretch out in a loose circle around the foul line. He sold paint at the Home Depot. He was 6-foot-1, with a lean look and a Marine Corps crew cut.

"How you been?" Alex asked when he reached his elbow.

Reisler allowed himself a tight smile. "Just fine. Thanks for coming out."

"We missed you guys. Three Rivers League wasn't the same without you. How'd the year go?"

Reisler shrugged. Alex didn't know if he'd fallen asleep with a cigarette the night before, but his sweatshirt had. "Won a few tournaments. Ran into the Black Tornado at a few others. You beat Wilsonville in the finals?"

Alex nodded. "Could have gone either way. Melinda had one of those games."

Reisler offered nothing back. The start of the regular fall season was five months off and he already had his game face on. Alex retreated to the far end of the court, where Mick was lazily feeding rebounds to Mattie and Rachel, both of whom were throwing up jump shots well outside their range. Chelsea was floating out there with them, but her stroke was natural and pure, her shots hitting the bottom of the net or the back of the rim.

"How's our man Jeff?" Mick asked.

"Mr. Hospitality. He asked me to tell you that Mrs. Reisler said hello."

Mick laughed. When the girls were playing a Reisler-coached team as sixth graders, the woman keeping the official scorebook twice told Mick he should be ashamed of the way he was berating the refs. When Mick's annoyance got the better of him, he wheeled on the woman and said, "Shut up, lady."

Mary Beth Reisler, it turned out. Her husband still nursed a grudge.

"They've picked up some players," Mick said, as 15 Oregon City girls ran the three-man weave. "Some height, too."

"I told Jeff we'd missed 'em."

"Like a colonoscopy."

They didn't take the back road from Lake Oswego to Oregon City during winter ball. After winning the post-season tournament during the girls' sixth-grade year, the Pioneers dropped out of the league, complaining about the lack of competition, and hit the road each weekend for tournaments from Seattle to Medford. Reisler had called two weeks earlier, suggesting a scrimmage, so the coaches could grade their girls' improvement and finalize their summer plans

"I'm thinking we've been set up," Alex said. He turned back to the unruly scrum at their end of the court. "Let's get into it, girls!" he barked, directing them into their lay-up lines. "How many do we have today?" he asked Mick.

"Eight, I think. Everyone's here 'cept Jody."

Jody had two lesbian moms, neither of whom owned a GPS system. "Eight ain't enough," Alex said.

The LO girls were curiously apathetic, blowing layups, spacing on rebounds. With six minutes showing on the clock, Mick collapsed in his plastic chair while Alex gathered the girls together and asked where they'd gotten the impression this game didn't mean anything. He'd just begun the "This is Oregon City" pep talk when the door opened at the far end of the gym and Jody shuffled in, looking angry and self-conscious.

"Where you been?" Alex asked.

She winced. "Mom got lost." Jody's mother, Lizbeth, the more congenial of her two parents, lost her bearings in the drive-thru lane at McDonalds. "You feeling alright?" Alex asked.

"I guess." Her head was pointed at the floor. Jody had an issue with eye contact. Jody had so many issues.

"Damn," Mick growled at his left. "Not these clowns." Alex turned to see the game refs canter up to the scorer's table. Burt and Flossie DeMars. They wore matching black-and-white striped shirts and black shorts that accentuated Burt's scrawny legs and Flossie's hefty hindquarters. They stood at the scorer's table, tightening belts, adjusting whistles, primping one another like an old married couple. They *were* an old married couple. They were also the league's two worst refs, lazy, aloof and determined to remind players and coaches alike that traveling basketball wasn't nearly as important as they thought it was. Moving screens, lane violations and blown calls weren't a big deal in Burt and Flossie's universe.

Burt asked the girls at the scorer's table to sound the horn. Jill's mother, Margaret, who kept the LO scorebook, was copying the names of the Pioneers onto her visitors' page. "Who's starting?" she asked.

"The usual suspects," Alex said. "Mattie and Chelsea, Layla and Lisa … and Rachel, I guess." Jody normally got the call but Jody was running on

Anchorage time. Margaret returned sullenly to the book. An attorney at Miller Nash, she had sullen down pat. She wasn't interested in the starting lineup; she was pissed off Jill didn't have a starring role. She'd tracked her daughter's stats since third grade. She claimed she was current on the running tally of Jill's career assists.

"I can believe that," Mick once said. "She's yet to hit double figures."

Alex was looking for enthusiasm, and he couldn't find it. Chelsea was searching the stands for her father, Rachel tightening the hair bands that kept her pigtails in place. Lisa and Layla were playing hard to get.

"This is nothing new. We've been here before," Alex said. "This is Oregon City. They think they invented the game. They think you won the league title because they took a siesta. They were up late last night, dreaming about how much fun it will be to kick LO butt. Well, let's keep 'em up again tonight, trying to figure out what went wrong. Run Spider-Man on offense. On defense, 1-3-1 with Lisa up top. Okay? Chelsea? What are we doing on defense?"

Chelsea was pouting, embarrassed to be singled out. She had Angelina Jolie's lips. "1-3-1," she said.

"Right. You're in the middle. Everyone together now." Alex extended his fist. "Lakers, on three: One, two, three: Lakers!" Three of the girls joined him. They weren't lathered in teen spirit.

The starters wandered listlessly to mid-court, where Flossie was waiting with their game ball. Behind her, 60 or 70 parents were camped in the bleachers. The vast majority, clustered at mid-court, were the pride of Oregon City: laid-off mill workers, Christmas tree farmers, car dealers. The LO parents were scattered in a half-dozen separate cliques, which wasn't unusual. Five of the nine parental units were chewing on the cud of a divorce. Three marriages had crashed and burned in the last 18 months. Ray Tripp wearied of Margaret's frenzied scorekeeping and bailed out the previous summer. Sharon left Mick over the Jewish holidays, and Rachel's parents, Carter and Melanie, separated with the biggest splash when Melanie returned from a high-school reunion and announced she'd finally made up with her senior-year boyfriend. Carter was still drinking that off in his unfurnished house at the south end of the lake.

"You gotta hand it to Team Chelsea," Alex said.

Mick gave him an uneasy sideways glance. "You do?"

"In this crowd, they're the all-American family."

"Jack's psychotic," Mick said. Alex shrugged. In Lake Oswego traveling basketball, whack-jobs had a voting majority. At center court, Flossie tossed the ball up at a 45-degree angle, directly over the Oregon City center's head, who slapped it back to her point guard as Mick lurched to his feet and bellowed, "Burt!"

Burt DeMars yawned. This was seven-grade hoop. Jump balls weren't a big deal, either.

The Oregon City guard sized up the 1-3-1 and backed the ball out. Generally, the zone gave teams fits, with Lisa supplying the pressure up front, pushing the

22

ball handler into double-team traps on the wings with Layla and Rachel. Bad teams tried to force the ball into their wide body at the high-post, a girl who was typically no match for Chelsea. Good teams looked for quick passes and 12-foot jump shots from the baseline.

Like that one. Nothing but net. As Oregon City rolled into a full-court press, Mattie inbounded the ball to Layla, who dribbled straight into a double-team and lost it. Two quick passes and a lay-up and Mattie was taking the ball out again.

Mattie Dawkins' best sport was softball. A killer whale of a right arm. This time, she winked at Lisa and Layla, making their press-break cuts, and threw the ball over the trap, 65 feet on the fly, hitting Chelsea in stride. Chelsea had nothing but open court between her and the breakaway, but she stumbled at the foul line. Once she gathered herself, she was under the basket and her layup attempt clanked off the bottom of the rim. The Pioneers turned the rebound into a 3-on-1 break. Oregon City got the basket, lonely Mattie the foul …

… and Mick came out of his chair snarling. "Asshole son of a bitch!" was the exact quote, delivered just loud enough to float the length of the bench and no farther.

Tourette syndrome. That's how Alex phrased the explanation when he apologized to refs and wounded parents after one of Mick's verbal grenades exploded inside the family circle.

"You know what Dean Smith used to say," Alex said as Mick turned back toward the bench. "Never stop the game before the first TV timeout."

"We aren't televised. Flossie! Time!"

"Full or 20?" Burt demanded.

"You choose," Alex said.

"Full or 20?" Burt barked again.

"Twenty," Alex said. "Life is short." The girls limped to the bench. Mick didn't let them sit, stepping 10 feet onto the court and willing them into a loose semi-circle. No one would look him in the eye. He took a deep breath. "You know what I love about this game? When you mess up, you don't have to wait a week to make it right. It's not like soccer, where you might wait 30 minutes to set your foot on the ball again. Here, you have five or six chances each minute to make a difference: set the screen, hustle back on D, step into the passing lane. When something goes wrong, you can't pout or put your head down because you might miss your next chance to ..."

Tweeeeeeeee!! Burt blew his whistle 10 inches behind Alex's ear. "Let's go!"

"Girls," Mick barked, afraid to release them yet: "Right away, the chance to do something right. Right now. In the next ..."

Tweeeeeeeee!! Burt let fly again. "Time's up!"

" ... 10 seconds. So, let's do it. LO: on three."

When Mick sat down, Alex leaned in. "I would have gone with the gutless losers approach."

"They're not morning people. What else is new?"

It was 40-14 at the half. Oregon City's dominance was so overwhelming that neither Burt nor Flossie was a factor. Like the Laker defenders, they were breathless spectators, trying to keep up with the Pioneers. Nor could the coaches stop the bleeding. Alex called one time out to send in reinforcements, then let the rout unfold, curious to see which girls would fight to the bitter end. Not many did. There wasn't much overlap in the priorities of 13-year-old girls and the fantasies of their coaches and parents. Parents might be jazzed by the prospect of college scholarships and the WNBA draft. Their daughters were focused on piercings, cell-phone tones, and the abs on the wall at Abercrombie. They didn't fantasize about seeing their name in lights. They were trying *not* to be noticed. When parents tried to motivate them by imploring them to practice harder so they could rise above their peers, it was a self-defeating message. They weren't fixated on the marquee. They were lemmings, comfortable in a crowd.

They'd certainly disappeared over the cliff against Oregon City. They were beaten on the boards, beaten to the loose balls, beaten on the break. Everyone broke down, including Chelsea, who missed 9 of 10 shots and four free throws. When the second quarter ended, Mick left the gym without a word. Alex stayed long enough to tell the girls to get water, then hit the rest room. Jack Lider, Chelsea's father, was straddling the next urinal, the sleeves rolled up on his button-down blue Oxford, his elbows atop the porcelain. He was 6-foot-3 and 70 pounds over his playing weight when he started at linebacker for Oregon State. His hair was short, his nose too big for his face, his body language petulant.

"Could you believe that?" Alex said wearily as he unzipped. "Total meltdown."

Jack shook his head. "It gets old."

Alex hazarded a glance his way. "What gets old?"

"You clowns think about calling a few timeouts?"

Alex feared Lider was serious about this, but decided to give him the benefit of the doubt. "Yeah, but we also thought about going Four Corners for those last 10 minutes. Cooler heads prevailed."

"With Mick on the bench? Right. Thought he was gonna have a stroke when Chelsea missed that lay-up, the jackass."

"Believe me, Jack, I too regret Mick doesn't share your commitment to keeping things positive."

Jack grimaced, grinding his teeth. He rearranged his equipment and left the room without stopping at the sink. Alex returned to his plastic courtside seat, subdued and depressed. Somewhere on the back road from Lake Oswego to Oregon City, the personality of the parents changed. Entitlement surrendered to fatalistic serenity. The dads in Oregon City, Alex guessed, had the same warped expectations, the same irrational investment in their daughters' athletic careers. But the Oregon City High School program was so extraordinary, so inaccessible to mere mortals, that it kept their worst instincts in check. They could not wish their little superstar through the well-guarded gate of the varsity program. The degree of difficulty kept them humble, a reticence that was rare in Lake Oswego. As the head coach at the high school once told him, LO parents were Machiavellian little shits, sucking up to coaches, hiring personal trainers, campaigning against anyone who stood between their princess and her preordained berth in the high school's starting lineup.

Chelsea and Mattie were shooting leg-weary jumpers, Lisa and Layla whispering beneath the basket, the rest of the girls slumped on the bench. "Ran into Jack in the boy's room," Alex said to Mick. "He's ticked we didn't call more timeouts."

"No kidding?" The muscles in Mick's jaw tightened. "He say anything about Chelsea shooting one for 9?"

"One for 10," Margaret piped in.

At the start of the second half, Alex benched their daughters and subbed in Jill and Jody. He tried to remain positive as he sent the girls into the teeth of the wood chipper, but he didn't fool anyone. Jody took the inbounds pass and dribbled for 15 seconds before catapulting the ball over Oregon City's 2-3 zone. The Pioneers' moon-faced off reserve guard intercepted the lob without leaving her feet and cantered downcourt, pulling up at the top of the key and launching a rainbow jumper that banked in off the glass.

Mick was frantically signaling for Burt's attention. "Time!" he screamed.

"What are you doing?" Alex asked. The girls seemed equally mystified. Mick shrugged. "I'll show Jack time outs," he said. "Chelsea, take a break. Natalie, you're in. Girls, let's go with the 1-3-1 half-court press. Get in their face. Wonder Woman on offense. Two bucks for the girl who scores the most points the rest of the way … and five bucks for whoever has the most assists."

"Five dollars?" Natalie gasped. "What's an assist?"

Given that three of their best players were on the bench, the girls needed a few minutes to get into the spirit of things. As Reisler had also begun clearing the Pioneer bench, LO's half-court trap pushed the Oregon City subs into the double-teams and turnovers that sparked the break. This time, more often than not, the girls made the extra pass and the ball went in the basket. When the clock finally ran down, Oregon City had a 63-50 win but had lost its swagger.

Both teams lined up, the Lakers muttering congratulations, the Pioneers slapping at their upraised hands, anxious to dash off into the rest of their Saturday. Mick was equally anxious; he had a 1:30 p.m. tee-off time at Pumpkin Ridge, and was gone before Alex gathered the girls at the end of the bench. Parents were hovering behind the baseline, weary and impatient.

"Final thoughts before we call it a summer?" Alex asked. The girls glanced at one another. They didn't have an official spokesman. "We sucked," Lisa finally said, encouraged by her father's absence.

"Yeah, we did," Alex agreed. "We sometimes do. We mail it in. We go in the tank. We play like it doesn't matter. I don't want to make too much of this …"

But Jody was stuffing sweats into her shoulder bag, Layla tightening the rubber band at the base of her pigtail. Jill was editing her stats and Chelsea searching for her dad in the crowd of restless chaperones. "Never mind," Alex finally said. "Go home. Enjoy the summer. Forget about basketball for awhile."

The girls wasted little time. Long before Alex had the team balls back in the bag, everyone had disappeared except Lisa and Layla. "Burgerville?" Alex asked. They nodded, then dismissed him. They didn't want to talk basketball. Alex headed for the parking lot. Jack Lider was leaning against the driver's door of his Volvo, which was parked at a haphazard angle across the handicap spaces by the door. Alex barely glanced at him before Jack stepped into his path: "Hey, *Coach*."

"Jack." Alex was distracted by his size. How did he wrap a tie around that neck?

"Got a question for you," Jack said, working his lower jaw. "Think you can win without my daughter?"

Alex stared. Hadn't Lider's silver Volvo been parked at the other end of the lot before the game? "I don't know, Jack. We just got our butt kicked with Chelsea shooting one for 10 in the first half. What's really bothering you?"

"I'm tired of this shit." Lider had been rehearsing. Getting this ticked off took practice.

"Today's game? This is July, Jack. Hot fun in the summertime."

"You guys aren't committed."

"To what? Your daughter? Laker basketball?"

"I don't see much effort out there. Or coaching."

Alex heard the door open behind him. Layla and Lisa had caught up. Alex dug the keys out of his jeans and tossed them to Layla. "Wait for me in the car," he said.

"Will you hurry?" she said. "I'm really hungry."

He waited for the girls to pass. Jack smelled like he'd spent too much of the day on the back lot in Wilsonville. "How many games did you miss last year, Jack?" Alex asked.

"What difference does that make?"

"How many times did I give Chelsea a ride home from practice?"

"I don't know, Coach, you tell me."

"Twenty. Minimum. What is this 'committed' bullshit? Who's been 'committed' over the last three years? Who's in the gym with Chelsea three times a week while you're at the car show? You didn't even make the last Seaside trip. Where do you get off?"

"I don't like what I see out there."

"That makes two of us."

"It's not helping Chelsea."

"Well, helping Chelsea ain't Job One."

"I've noticed. She's the best you got."

"No kidding. She loves the game. The only one on the team who defines herself by it. You've done a heck of a job with her. And Mick and I have eight other players who need a lot more help. What should we do with them?"

"None of 'em but Chelsea will ever play varsity." Lider reset his jaw. "Well, your daughter, maybe."

"Gee, thanks. I'll pass that on. I can't believe I'm hearing you say this stuff. You're better than this, Jack."

The balding linebacker opened the Volvo door. "That's what you think."

Alex stared after him until the Volvo ducked behind Gardner's sign board – "Home of Future Champions" – and out of sight. Machiavellian little shit. Layla and Lisa were waiting by the car, silently gauging his approach. "What's wrong?" Alex asked. "Lose the keys?"

"Too hot," Layla said. "What's wrong with Chelsea's dad?"

"Nothing," Alex said, opening the trunk.

"Why was he mad?" Lisa asked.

"Frustrated by losing, I guess. Hop in. I'll get the air conditioning going."

Layla had Z100 tuned in before they were left the lot. Two 5th graders had a rickety lemonade stand set up two blocks from the school. Old men were working on their pickups on the dirt of their front lawns. A 6-year-old was riding a pink bicycle down the street, oblivious to the traffic flashing by. In the summer sunlight, the Fords and delivery vans at the Plaid Pantry wore a sullen layer of dust.

Yet the traffic on the drive home was light. On the back road from Oregon City to Lake Oswego, you had the calming sense you were moving in the right direction.

T he six beach towels were lined up in perfect formation at the end of Rachel's dock. As always, Emily's purple towel was closest to the boathouse so she could roll quietly into the shade beneath the eaves whenever the sun turned cruel. None of the other girls was the least bit concerned about the heat. The end of the August tanning season loomed. Jessica, Laura and Layla had brought double-digit sun block at the insistence of their moms, but only Laura was using it. Lisa's No. 4 Hawaiian Tropic was the oil de jour, the high-gloss finish on girls who'd been browning on the lakeside grill since lunchtime. Several of their parents – the anti-tanning salon lunatics – would have gone bonkers if they'd known how many cosmic rays the girls were ingesting, but that's why the girls always landed on Rachel's dock. They never had to worry about her dad wandering down from the house, sunscreen or melanoma lecture in hand.

There were nine water bottles scattered around the dock and several inches of lukewarm water in Jessica's cooler. A half-baked breeze would have kicked them off the dock and into the lake, but the last hour hadn't seen a hiccup of wind, just the low, chaotic screams at the swim park and the rise and fall of outboard motors dragging skiers and inner tubes. Rachel's dock and boathouse was at the southeast end of the lake, a mile from the town center and the best views of Mt. Hood.

"Get ready," Rachel said. "Here comes the Nautique."

Everyone rotated onto their stomachs except Emily, who already had her chin on her hands and her nose in a paperback copy of *Bridge to Terabithia*. With a full-bodied rumble, a Ski Nautique was bearing down on them like the end of summer.

"How can you always tell?" Layla asked. Painfully embarrassed by the play-school numbers her mother brought home from Target, she was wearing one of Lisa's second-tier Trina Turk suits, along with Coppertone 30 and a straw hat.

"Best boat on the lake. And it sounds like it," said Rachel, sounding very much the nautical expert on the lake fleet. The boat belonged to the McCays, who lived 200 yards away in a colossus of golden stucco. Wild Bill McCay was a rising senior, and his parents organized Lake Oswego's annual spring-break invasion of Palm Springs. When Rachel came back the previous

March, she reported that Pam McCay, Wild Bill's mom, had danced atop the table at the Blue Coyote in a canary-yellow sun dress, kicking over a pitcher of beer and two baskets of tortilla chips in the process.

Lisa squinted into the high afternoon glare. "I think that's Deion skiing."

"Deion?" Layla hooted. "Ya think?" All of the girls laughed, even Lisa. Deion Jackson was the starting point guard at the high school after transferring from Madison, one of Portland's dilapidated inner-city schools. He was easily the best known of the 11 African-Americans at LOHS – one percent of the student body – and, thus, the one most likely to be parked in the wake of a Nautique.

"Will you look at that guy?" Rachel said. "My tanning hero."

Like she had any reason to complain, Emily sighed, wiping a bead of sweat off the end of her nose before it crossed the bridge into Terabithia. Rachel was 5-foot-8 with outrageously long, milk chocolate legs. Dolce & Gabbana and Godiva would be locked in a bidding war for her modeling services before she graduated.

As the ski boat passed, Deion bounced outside the wake and one of the USC song-girl spotters stood up and cheered, one hand raised high over her blond hair and red bikini. "Isn't that Darcy Spillane?" Lisa asked, one hand over her eyes to shield the sun.

"You'd think that was her only suit," Laura said.

"That's us in two years," Jessica said, her voice more wistful than confident. They all had their heads up, staring as the boat passed.

"Whose boat are we going to steal?" Layla asked.

"I'll have my license by then," Rachel said. "Dad will never miss the boat."

No one said anything, though Lisa sighed and flipped onto her back. Jessica waited as long as she could, then sneaked a quick glance at Rachel, who had already dropped her head onto her Carolina blue towel and closed her eyes. There was little difference in their dads, except that Rachel's father was the MVP at the Mountain Park liquor store and Jessica's did his binge drinking in Arizona. Whenever they were dropped off at Rachel's house, her father answered the door with vodka tonic. If Rachel didn't roll out of her room in a hurry, he invariably found some dumb-ass reason to wrap his free arm around Jessica's shoulders, check out her fledgling boobs, and ask some embarrassing question about her mom.

"She's fine," Jessica always wanted to say, "because the alcoholic asshole in *our* family is nursing his six pack in Flagstaff." Jessica didn't have a father anymore, just the memory of the thug who knocked her mother into the Jenn-Air after they got home from the 10 a.m. service at Rolling Hills, and the voice that called once a month, bitching about the $200 he sent back to Oregon to keep her in Guess jeans. Maybe that was the other difference between her and Rachel, Jessica

36

decided: Rachel still talked about her dad as if he added something to her life. Jessica wasn't similarly deluded.

"Two years? You really think it's going to be two years?" Laura propped herself up on a slender elbow. "I'll die of boredom if it takes two years."

"I want your USC sweatshirt before you go," Lisa said. "Your mom doesn't even have to wash it."

"I'm serious," Laura said, as if someone was calling her bluff. "There is nothing to do in this stupid town. We don't have celebrities or sports teams or video arcades or bowling alleys or ..." Laura was rapidly losing steam. "... or malls or ..."

"Tigard has a bowling alley," Layla said, "and 300 Taco Bells. Wanna move to Tigard?"

"God, no." Laura sat up. She was wearing her favorite black Juicy two-piece, which Layla was sure she'd swiped from her sister. The ridges of her spine formed a delicate Jurassic arc as she leaned forward, arms around her knees. "But we're stranded in a cow town."

"Stranded? Who's stranded?" Lisa asked. "At least you have a sister who'll drive you to the mall."

"Molly's turned psycho," Laura said. "I can't even talk to her."

There was a pause, a sigh, a small breeze lifting off the water. "That sucks," Emily said. Older sisters were pure gold. Everyone knew that. They were the local Nordstrom outlet. The cheat sheet. Older sisters did the babysitting and most of the dishes. They knew which Lake Oswego cops you could talk to after the sun went down at Westlake Park. They were your unofficial guardians, making sure no one gave you grief after you crossed over to the high school on Bridge Day.

Emily *was* the older sister, and it really ticked her off.

"You just got back from two weeks at Black Butte," Rachel pointed out as she lazily rubbed oil onto her bare left shoulder, "and you're already bored?"

Laura shook her head. "This place is dead. That's why we wet our pants when we see a black guy on a water ski. Why would anyone want to live here?"

There was an odd silence as the sun slipped inside the envelope of a high cloud. "Well," Emily said, "there's that kick-ass Fourth of July."

Suddenly, they were all sitting up and laughing, remembering that glorious night on the dock. The city's Fourth of July fireworks show was such a big deal that the cops set up barricades on the roads leading down to the lake. You needed a written invitation from one of the house parties to drive your car onto South Shore or Lakefront, so they'd met Rachel and her dad at the Methodist church and walked. Carter – that was Rachel's dad – hadn't exactly gone overboard with the refreshments – six different bags of Doritos and a dozen Diet Pepsis – but he left the girls alone. At dusk, they could see the Tiki lights, barbecue pits and sparklers from 50 different backyard parties. They could feel Kelly Clarkston and Sheryl Crow rising out of Bose speakers in second-floor windows, and see "A Night at the Museum" babysitting the toddlers in a basement theater on the other side of the lake. They could hear the anticipation in a hundred different conversations, the pop of champagne corks, the unhinging of the lawn chairs in the growing pockets of darkness.

Then the fireworks began.

In the summer before eighth grade, there wasn't much future in letting your guard down. It wasn't cool to get excited, exposing yourself to those who were unnerved by enthusiasm. But the light show over Oswego Lake got a pass. From the muffled opening *thupt*, when the first rocket catapulted out of its tube aboard the Lake Corporation barge, the fireworks were a hoot, a solid hour of waves and ripples, crosettes and kamuros, dahlias and crackling palms. Each time you thought the show was over, the barge empty, the armada turning toward home, another dozen spiders lit up the night sky. The fireworks were so close, you felt as if you were inside an I-Max theater. As if you'd been given a present you didn't deserve. As if there might be something special about LO after all.

"Anyone want to go in?" Jessica peered at the water with undisguised disdain.

"Gross!" Layla said. "I'd rather wade into a tub of Herbal Essence."

"Split pea soup," Lisa said.

The water wasn't as bad as all that, especially if you were tubing at lake center where the aerators worked overtime to stuff fresh oxygen down the water's throat. But Oswego Lake had a serious algae problem, thanks to the phosphorous leaking off the fertilized lawns that skirted the lake. As the summer wore on, the water color turned from muddy blue to lagoon green as the algae feasted on the sunlight and the phosphorous, gaining strength in the shallows. When Emily passed her swimming test in third grade, she felt the algae grabbing for her legs as she kicked the final 50 meters.

"Are you almost done?" Layla asked, nodding at Emily's book. First period Language Arts was one of three classes they would share in the fall.

"Halfway," Emily said, as she closed the book and tucked it under her towel.

"Is it hard?"

"Not really. Allie read it when she was seven."

Layla emptied a bottle of Arrowhead on her shoulders and let the water slide down her back. Watching her, Rachel stretched like a cat and slowly drew her legs beneath her. "I'm heading up for water," she said. "Anyone want anything?"

"Any Wheat Thins left?" Laura asked.

"Are you serious? We have 15 cases in the garage." Like most of the single fathers in LO, Rachel's dad shopped at Costco to buy in bulk and meet bored women.

Layla pulled the elastic band from her hair and began collecting the loose strands into a new bundle. "Can you get Allie to write the paper for you?" she asked Emily.

Emily glanced up, checking for mockery, and found, instead, a gentle blend of wry consolation. "Not this fall," she said. "Not when she's studying for her SATs."

Layla laughed. Emily shook her head. "God," she said, "I wish I was the cliché."

She was, instead, Emily Yu, the only Chinese-American on Eldenberry Lane who'd ever limped home with a "B" on her report card. Three, all told: two in social studies and a third in PE when Mr. Avakian complained she'd missed too many classes to earn the "A." Well, isn't that perfect, Emily thought, given that she'd only missed the rat-ball games because she was rewriting English papers and staying atop her Chem labs. Her parents – college valedictorians at Berkeley and Cal Tech with flawless transcripts and terrifying expectations – didn't understand this. They were forever staring at her report card with shock, anger and the growing suspicion that someone at Good Sam brought them the wrong Chinese kid. Allie didn't help. Allie was talented and gifted. Just starting sixth grade, Allie had already cruised through eighth-grade math. She had perfect grades, perfect skin, a perfect body for those petite sizes and, worst of all, a flawless social life. She was always giggling with one buddy or another on her cell, and she already had a dozen eighth-grade "friends" on Facebook. Emily couldn't believe her parents allowed the little twerp to take the Facebook plunge, but Allie's precociousness and Allie's brains guaranteed her a free ride and a free pass when it came to doing stuff around the house. Emily was the chore whore. Emily was in charge of the laundry – talk about your Asian clichés – and making sure her mother never came home from the law firm to face a soiled laundry basket.

Emily loved her sister. That wasn't it. Allie knew she was blessed, and she didn't rub Emily's face in it. She was noticeably frustrated when she didn't make classic soccer as a fifth grader, that she didn't have Emily's speed and anticipation. Allie envied those skills. Her parents didn't. They were so focused on success and freshly pressed laundry that they didn't notice how good she was at the game. Cal Tech didn't have a women's soccer team, so it counted for nothing. She was their problem child, their A-minus. It made Emily want to scream, but the one time she tried, panicking in the shower, her mother flung open the bathroom door and ordered her to quit the karaoke.

Emily felt that dull, sour ache in the pit of her stomach. Hunger? Anxiety? She couldn't differentiate between them anymore. She checked her watch. Her mother would arrive in 45 minutes for the drive across town to Chinese School. She felt oddly conflicted. She hated the Chinese, but she enjoyed sitting in the back of class and drawing in the margins of her workbook. Only last week, Danny Chin complimented her art. Even when he wore sunglasses, his face was perfect. She'd die if he knew how often she stared at those ungodly cheekbones.

Lisa and Laura were suddenly squealing at dock's edge. Rachel had returned, juggling water bottles, a copy of *Cosmo* and the Wheat Thins as a tiny white fluff ball in her right hand began to twist and squirm.

Posh! Leslie had brought Posh down to the dock. "Omigod, Rachel, can I hold her?" Layla begged, scrambling to her feet. *"Kitty, kitty, kitty."* Posh paused just long enough to dismiss her as the village idiot, then reached up and inserted the claws of one tiny paw into the left cup of Rachel's bikini top.

"Here, take her," Rachel said, gently tugging at the kitten until its claws detached from her suit. "Don't let her near the water. She can't swim." As she set the kitten down, Posh arched her back, oiling the hinges as she shook off her nap. She was a total muff, pure white Angora and six weeks old, and not quite sure what to make of Layla, who had dropped to her knees and elbows. "She is *soooo* cute," Layla said again, extending a tentative hand. Posh sniffed at the lubed fingers, then winced as Layla scooped her up and, rolling over, brought Posh into her lap.

Rachel dropped the Wheat Thins at Laura's hip and twisted the top off an Arrowhead. "Any messages?" Lisa asked.

"Everyone 'cept Emil. Laura has six, and she was buzzing when I left."

They'd dumped their phones in the wicker basket atop the dryer in Rachel's mudroom. It was terrifying to be disconnected from the endless stream of news bulletins, but that was a necessary accommodation for the tanning sessions. Oil and water and Blackberries didn't mix. Tanning oil was death on cellular screens. And Lisa and Rachel both had dropped their phones into the lake earlier in the summer, leaving both without human contact for the three weeks it took their parents to get over their disciplinary jihad.

"Mom must be bored," Laura said, smoothing the creases on her towel. That, of course, was the silver lining in their radio silence: they were liberated from the incessant check-in calls. Rather than admit they left their phones at the house, they blamed the lousy reception so common at the water's edge.

"It's probably Mattie, wondering about tonight," Rachel said. "Laura, gimme three crackers."

Laura dutifully passed the Wheat Thins. There weren't many options about this or any other summer night. Westlake Park was the common gathering spot once Junior Baseball cleared out and – at exactly 10:10 p.m., by Parks & Rec fiat – the park lights shut off. Sophomores ruled the park – everyone older had a driver's license and total freedom -- and staked out the parking lot just behind the fire station. That forced the freshmen onto the basketball court and the rising eighth graders to gather around the playground equipment. Only the sophomore guys actually marked their territory, after a beer or two, by pissing on the perimeter, but the boundaries were fairly inflexible, unless you had an older sibling and an all-area pass.

"Anyone want to see a movie?" Emily asked. Westlake was off limits for the Yu clan, even Princess Allie.   Emily's mom was convinced it was the neighborhood needle exchange.

Lisa's eyes narrowed to a malicious squint, as if she was trying to decide where to send Emily for shock treatment. "Are you kidding? Ian and Danny and K-Smut will be at Westlake." Lisa did not have similar boundary issues. Since her mother had disappeared, neither did she have unannounced strip searches of her room, which is why she kept a bottle of Stoli in the bottom drawer of her vanity.   K-Smut – Kenny

Smuthers – had drained enough vodka the week after school let out that he barfed all over the back seat of his mom's Mercedes SUV.

"What are ya doing with that kitten?" Laura asked Layla. Posh had her eyes closed and her motor running as Layla's fingers worked the tender ridge just above her tail.

"Making her happy," Layla said.

"Where'd you learn to do that?" Leslie asked. "You don't even have a cat."

"My dad," Layla said, "and Frank, the neighbor's cat. He comes by every day. Mom won't let him in the house, so Dad feeds him sliced turkey on the back deck."

"And I thought my life was boring and pathetic," Laura said.

"When'd you hear from the guys?" Jessica asked Lisa, who was fiddling with her iPod headset.

Lisa waited a half beat too long, then answered the real question Jessica was asking. "Ian," she said. "They're going to Players after dinner, then coming over."

Jessica watched as Lisa found the right Jay-Z rap, corkscrewed the speaker plugs into each ear, then dropped back on her towel. She didn't believe her but was of no mind to say so, not out here in front of everyone. Lisa was sensitive to Jessica's thing for K-Smut, just not sensitive enough to discourage his thing for Lisa.

Jessica stared for a heartbreaking minute at Lisa's flawless tan and killer bod, trying not to hate her or her cup size. In the unfair order of things, Lisa, Rachel and Laura had a pronounced head start in the boob department, and there was no disputing the advantage this gave them. Boobs were magnetic. Jessica had seen guys crawl the length of the cafeteria for an unobstructed view of Rachel's. If Lisa made the mistake of going out for popcorn during a basketball game, Danny or K-Smut invariably dribbled the ball off their foot. Jessica could layer on the makeup, bind her dirty blond hair into killer braids, and steal a few splashes of the Ysatis her mother no longer had much use for, and those nerf balls wouldn't blink. They only had eyes for the bumps in the road.

It was hardest when they hung out together. In the dark at Westlake, Jessica trusted she could hold her own in the caustic repartee or the mad dashes across the baseball fields. Catch K-Smut alone in her garage and they just might end up against the freezer door, his A-Frame burger breath in her ear and his hands clawing at her belt or her bra, as if he'd know what to do if he ever got one of them off. But when the sun was overhead and nothing lost in the shadows, Jessica didn't stand a chance. Rachel had those endless legs, Emily that incandescent black hair, and Lisa and Laura the makings, padded or not, of a long, sweet life with hooters. In their company, only Layla was equally *average*, Jessica thought, and yet Layla was armed with a combativeness guys found irresistible. When they were still in grade school, Layla scared the boys with her rat-ball intensity, but once the guys caught up with her athleticism, it was Layla's ticket into all their stupid games. Jessica? She wasn't on the comp list, what with her split ends, her mediocre tan, her pass-me-down clothes and a chest, as her mother once said, that was flatter than eastern Nebraska. "Which may be a blessing," she added, "if they're forced to love you for something they can never get their hands on."

"Did Ian and Natalie really hookup last Saturday?" Rachel asked. She wasn't using the phrase in its technical, Kate-and-Leonardo-steaming-up-the-back-of-the-Renault sense, but everyone understood that.

"In Natalie's dreams, maybe," said Laura, who fantasized about Ian on a regular basis. Everyone understood that, too.

"Brandon said he saw them walking toward the dugout," Rachel persisted.

"First or third?" Layla asked. Ever since the story went around that Ellie Stone let an entire American Legion team see the rose tattoo on her butt in the first-base dugout, it was understood that the visitors' bunker was reserved for the more serious sex play.

Rachel shrugged. "It's not like he followed them."

"Which wouldn't surprise me," Emily said. "Brandon is gross."

"What's that supposed to …"

"C'mon, Rachel, he has the foulest mouth I've ever heard. And the day school got out, I watched him 'accidentally' bump into five different girls in B Hall."

The hallways at Lake Oswego Junior High were notoriously congested, particularly when the locker doors were open and the band geeks in bloom, but everyone could relate to the ignominy of getting frisked by some guy late for class.

"My God, Emily, you didn't just mention school, did you?" Lisa said, sitting up again, earplugs in hand.

"Eight more days," Rachel said. "Careful, sweetheart ..." This last was directed at Posh, who had wearied of Layla and was stalking a crane fly by the boathouse.

"I can't wait," Laura said. "This place is so dead. I need a vacation."

"I need a vacation from soccer," Rachel said, nibbling on a Wheat Thin and idly flipping through *Cosmo*. Lisa and Layla grunted in affirmation; Emily and Jessica stayed quiet. While Lisa, Layla and Rachel played both soccer and basketball, Emily and Jessica were content with soccer. Laura, who played neither, looked like she'd bitten into a bad slab of rockfish. "Why are you playing soccer?" she asked. "It's 95 degrees."

"We're always playing soccer," Lisa said.

"I thought you just got back from regionals. Don't you get a break?"

"Sure," Emily said. "January."

"That's bullshit. Every sport has a season, why doesn't soccer?"

Emily formed a cross with her two forefingers to fend Laura off. "You coming out for basketball this year?" Layla asked Laura, who had twisted her head dramatically, trying to read the story blurbs on Rachel's *Cosmo*.

"'Dirty Sexy Sex'?" she asked.

"Whipped cream, exercise balls and BJs in the shower," Rachel said.

"In the shower?" Lisa cooed. "What's dirty about that?" Emily had a sudden vision of decorating Danny's cheekbones with Reddi-wip. A chill rippled down her spine.

"I haven't decided," Laura said. A graceful 5-foot-6 forward, her quick hands had won her a starting position on the junior high's seventh-grade team but she'd never tried out for the traveling squad. "That's why I keep trying to talk to Molly."

"She played?" Jessica asked.

"Once. She quit."

"You should try out," Layla said. "You can take Chelsea's place."

"What happened to Chelsea?" Rachel said, and Layla winced. She'd promised her dad to keep her mouth shut. She gave Rachel the conspiratorial, tell-ya-later shrug.

In the shadows of the boathouse, Posh lunged for the crane fly, trapping it between her paws and her chin. When she raised her head to inspect her prize, it spiraled upward like a whirligig, skirting past the spider's web beneath the roofline before disappearing around the boathouse and out of sight.

The Nautique made another pass, the SC song girl wobbling on two skis inside the wake. Small waves lapped against the dock. A hummingbird feasted on the sugar-water feeder hanging from the pear tree, then vanished. The sun was still pouring it on, so bright Emily found it hard to stay focused on the print unless the words fell inside the shadow her head dropped on the page. They could all feel the afternoon slipping away.

"What's for dinner?" Layla asked Lisa.

Lisa chewed on that for a moment, as she plucked a small peeling of skin off her shoulder. "I don't know. Potstickers. Kung pao chicken?" Lisa ordered take-out from Shanghai Kitchen at least twice a week; she never grew tired of the food or the shyness of the kid who delivered it. "Why? You inviting me over?"

"Dinner at Layla's? I'm there," Rachel said.

"Good luck. We're probably doing take-out, too," Layla said. "Mom hardly ever cooks after work."

"If I have another Trader Joe teriyaki stir-fry, I'll hurl," Rachel said. "I've gained six pounds this summer."

"You know what I hate?" Jessica said. "Greasy Costco chickens. Gag me."

"Raw chicken. Worst smell ever," Lisa said.

"You're forgetting the Port-o-Potties at Canby," Emily said.

"Barkley passing gas," Laura said. Barkley was the Koertje's aging Springer Spaniel.

"K-Smut passing gas," Lisa countered, and everyone laughed except Jessica.

"Molly once told me nothing's as scary as the dance after a home football game," Laura said. "The football players never shower. They sweat like dogs for two hours, then go right to their lockers and pull out the Dockers."

"Wow," Rachel said. "Another reason to get excited about high school."

"Why don't the coaches hose 'em down?" Layla asked.

"With Tag Body Spray, maybe," Rachel said.

"Why does Mr. Buchanan like to shop at Tigard?" Layla asked.

Lisa stepped in and stole the punch line. "Because boys' pants are always half off."

"Tramp."

"Thief"

"Poser."

"Hypocrite."

"Drama queen."

"Drag queen."

The sun in her eyes, the heat in her pores, Layla opened her mouth once more, then surrendered the last word. That's what you did for your best friend. You watched her back. You shared her locker. You told her when the guy laying on the full-court press gave you the creeps. You opened your closet. You weathered her sarcasm. You trusted her instincts, except on the nights when she went all drama on you and started quoting Good Charlotte.

Friendship had a strange tempo and Layla didn't know if she had the rhythm down yet. When she was in grade school, she hung out all the time with Hannah and Gwen, two girls who rode the bus and invited her over every weekend for a sleepover. In that last year at Uplands Elementary, Layla figured she slept with Gwen in her four-poster bed on 20 different Saturday nights, overdosing on fruit snacks and Adam Sandler movies. She could still see that bedroom, saturated in yellow and gold, Amy Grant and the Backstreet Boys on the walls and those tiny stars that glowed in the dark spotting the ceiling, but she could barely remember a conversation. All those nights singing along with Billy Madison beneath the down comforters had vanished when life began to pick up speed. Her father still drove Gwen and her to school but, trapped together in the Durango, they found it hard to look at one another, as if they were embarrassed they once shared so much.

Layla didn't get it, and she tried not to think about the things she didn't understand. Had she taken a wrong turn onto the set of one of those Disney Channel shows, like Lizzie McGuire, where they were best friends in sixth grade and mortal enemies in junior high? One moment you were talking about boys and bathing suits and those family vacations you were sure would end in your parents' divorce. The next, you were talking down to one another, harboring some mysterious grudge, stabbing her with a sarcastic comment in the hall – "Oh, I love your hair!" You were trying to remember the secrets you shared that might come back to haunt you. You were promising yourself you'd never allow yourself to be so careless and vulnerable again. You couldn't afford transparency in junior high. Especially when everything sucked. When Lisa's mom left, Layla kept waiting for Lisa to roll over one night on the couch and talk about it, but she knew she wouldn't, and there were times she wondered if Lisa found comfort in the fact that Layla refused to ask questions.

She met Lisa on the fifth-grade traveling team, but they didn't become friends, best friends, until the summer before LOJ. It was awkward at first; their dads were always around, looming, getting in the way, forcing them to sit on the bar stools in the background while they argued about football games or Mick yelled at the television. Lisa's dad was so loud and obnoxious, it took Layla awhile to get over that, too.

Maybe it was the Phoenix trip when they roomed together at the Camelback Marriott and watched "Eyes Wide Shut" on the hotel movie system. Maybe it was the basketball practice when Mick snapped at her for forgetting where to double-team in the full-court trap, and Lisa brushed by her, whispering, "What an ass." Or maybe it was realizing that Lisa was moving through junior high like a snow plow and she was comfortable riding her bumper. Her parents were such overbearing control freaks. Layla was the last girl in North America to get her ears pierced, get unlimited texts on her Verizon plan or – well, except for Emily – get permission to hang out at Westlake after the lights went out. The dweebs were afraid of everything. Afraid Lisa's brother didn't have enough experience driving on snow to take them snowboarding at Meadows. Afraid to let her spend the night somewhere when the parents wouldn't be home until midnight. Afraid of sneaker waves, black ice, R-rated movies, high-school boys, spaghetti straps, kitchen knives, E. coli – "Medium well," her mother droned, "medium well" – killer bees and the dark. Layla felt shrink-wrapped, sanitized, insulated from everything that smacked of danger and risk. She just didn't feel that way when she was with Lisa.

Lisa had her dad trained fairly well. Mick didn't check her laptop history or Facebook photos. He wasn't calling ahead on sleepovers. He wasn't in the way. That must have been Sharon's job. There had been times, Layla knew, when she'd angrily considered how much easier life would be if one of her parents took an extended vacation, so she'd carefully watched Lisa in the beginning, to better understand how truly terrible their absence would be. It turned Lisa quiet at first; then she just started letting go of things, probably because that was easier than forcing herself to care about them again. Not Derek, though. She was dedicated to her brother. She cleaned his room. Put his breakfast dishes in the dishwasher and his empty Mirror Ponds in the recycling bin. Lied like a gypsy to Mick to cover for him. Layla figured she'd counted the remaining bodies in the house and decided she'd best cling to the one she couldn't afford to lose.

Everyone on the deck had their moments of wit, goofiness and passion, but Lisa was a sexton when it came to the uncharted waters of boy-girl relationships. She was fearless, best Layla could tell, as if she was armed with the invisible armor, the decoder ring, the vision of how all this would turn out. Layla sometimes wondered if she'd gotten pointers from Derek. Lisa didn't put on airs. She didn't pretend she had an incalculable advantage in confidence or psychology. She didn't dress like a slut – at least not any more than the rest of them did. But so much of the impossible interplay with the boys – the conversation, the casual flirting, the mercenary politics – came so much easier for her.

Take K-Smut. Jessica had been hot for the brat since sixth grade. She could barely talk when he came within olfactory range during second lunch. She gave him top billing on her Facebook page and never missed his Pop Warner games. K-Smut was flattered by the attention, but he was smitten by Lisa, who found it difficult to suppress a yawn whenever he walked by. Her boredom was genuine; Lisa finished seventh grade with a 4.0 while K-Smut needed tutors to fill out a hall pass. But equally authentic was Lisa's sense that she would only encourage K-Smut with her aloofness. It was a brilliant strategy, if strategy it was. Jessica couldn't complain and K-Smut couldn't get traction, not even when he sucked down the Stoli and blew lunch in the back of the Escalade.

Or was it a Mercedes? Layla really didn't know her top-end SUVs.

Posh came wandering back with a soul-searching meow and, once Layla began scratching her back, took to kneading a warm corner of the burnt orange towel, her eyes slowly closing. The afternoon heat had scared off the breeze and stolen their energy. Rachel was out cold, the Tar Hell blue t-shirt over her eyes, Jessica humming a tune only she could hear. The quiet was so hypnotic that no one sensed the intruder on the wooden walkway angling down from the house until she barked, "Laura!"

Startled, Layla whirled to the sound of the voice as Posh popped out of her lap. A girl she'd never seen before glared at them from the walkway, flush with anger. You might have thought they'd stolen something. "I called you four times," the girl snapped. "If you're not in the driveway in two minutes, you can walk home."

She headed up the ramp. Lisa rubbed the sweat from her forehead. "Jesus," she said. "That your sister?"

"I told you," Laura said, staring after her. "Bitch."

It was 90 degrees, yet Molly was in sweatshirt and jeans, her hair bound in a frazzled ponytail. She didn't look back before disappearing around the azaleas.

"She used to walk us down to Baskin Robbins," Layla said. "She didn't even say hello. What …"

"She's not normal," Laura said, gathering her things. "She won't talk to anyone. She locks her door. I don't even knock anymore. My parents are always whispering in the kitchen. She's the reason my mom won't keep pills in the house." Laura shook her head. "I'll call you," she said, to no one in particular. Then she charged up the ramp, as if taking Molly's deadline seriously.

Emily closed *Bridge to Terabithia* and rose to her knees. She was struggling to slide the book into her backpack without bending the corners when Layla said, "Don't go."

"What?"

"Don't leave."

"My mother will be here in three minutes."

"Call in sick. Fake an injury."

Jessica lifted her head off her towel. "What are you talking about, Layla?"

"Summer," Layla sighed.

High above them, thin clouds were forming. The dying wake of a long-gone ski boat tagged the dock with a gentle slap. On the other side of the lake, someone had set their Bose speakers in a bedroom widow and fired up, "It's a Beautiful Day."

"Summer?" Emily said, ever so quietly.

"Summer," Layla said once again. "And if you leave, it's all going to start slipping away."

She closed her eyes. Rachel was working the Wheat Thins in the tiniest of nibbles, hoping to spike her appetite before her dad – too lazy or too loaded to cook – dragged her out to Manzana. Emily went back to stuffing her backpack, loading up for the trip to Chinese School, staring at the box of crackers and wondering if a quick handful would help her through the night or screw everything up. Gain a little ground on Allie or lose it. Give Danny a reason to glance up from her drawings or another reason to look away. She closed her eyes and tried to focus. It was a piece of cardboard. A slab of plastic with no nutritional value. It meant nothing to her. Dead weight. Dead weight. When she opened her eyes again, Emily was light-headed but resolute. She would sit quietly through her mother's squalls and the hour of Chinese. And when she closed the door to her bedroom, she would dream of Danny and Terabithia and another summer day just like this one, light on the clouds but heavy with friends.

H e sat in the parking lot, his left arm out the window, relaxed, listening to the radio. Tom Leykis was telling some gutless wonder to dump the wench who resented his trips to a Long Beach strip club. "Grow some balls!" Leykis roared. "Aren't you sick and tired of peeing sitting down?"

Taze Elliott loved Leykis, especially when the loudmouth was ridiculing fat girls or sticking it to single women with kids. He wished the Professor had been active back in the day, whispering in his ear.

The heat was thick and dry, too heavy for a breeze. Elliott was parked in the shade of a giant oak, well back from the entrance to Hoop Heaven, waiting for the girls to roll in. Read the body language. Gauge the energy. Check to see whether Mom or Dad was driving and how anxious their daughter was to exit the Lexus.

Why do you have a girlfriend, anyway? Leykis was asking. *You're 21. You shouldn't be tied down to one whining bitch. You only have one mission and that's to 'F' as many girls as possible.*

Dad behind the wheel was a bad sign. Dads got in the way. Moms were easier to manipulate. They'd grown up as cheerleaders or flag girls, standing on the sidelines, tits against the glass, voyeurs to the athletic experience. They'd rarely been pushed, never had their bell rung, never been subject, as Bobby Knight used to say, to the motivational power of ass meets bench. Dads were different. They'd played the game or still anguished over why they hadn't. They had experience to fall back on. Moving them out of the way so he had room to maneuver was a pain in the ass.

Little brothers helped. Younger brothers were money. When a girl had a kid brother, Dad eventually forgot about her. He was too busy standing in the mud at Pop Warner, molding the brat into the team's star quarterback. He was reliving his childhood. With only so much time, he'd invest it all in the stud who watched SportsCenter.

Guilty? Why should you feel guilty? The gold-diggers are using you. To them, you're a wallet, a free drink, a meal ticket ... to a restaurant you can't afford. You're the handy-dandy ATM 'til someone better comes along ... and while they're waiting for that someone, they make your life miserable. Don't give 'em the chance.

Elliott took a pull on the Mountain Dew. The Wilsons' Audi glided up and Anita hopped out of the front seat. She'd started at small forward for the Black Tornado but Taze didn't like her game. She was soft. No killer instinct on D. Too good-natured. Good nature didn't get you jack.

Jenna arrived, then Chloe Ward and Cici Bishop. Cici was edging up on 6 feet and about as mobile as a bicycle rack. She'd be lucky if she played a minute in high school, though that wasn't what Taze told her father. "Great drop step," Elliott kept telling him. "Tough on the boards." Total bullshit.

His head was drooping, surrendering to the heat, when Debra Giuliani came marching across the lot, dragging the twins. Sierra and Sarita had skills, not to mention their mother's relentlessness, but Elliott wasn't convinced they'd ever make it as the Tornado's starting backcourt. Sierra was a decent 2, a tough but frail defender, Sarita a slender point guard with a sweet stroke. Neither had enough muscle on the bone and, judging from their mother's bod, neither would find it in their high-school locker. Owing to those two-hour morning workouts at 24-Hour Fitness, Debra had the same amount of body fat as his Chevy van and a more impressive grill. Drove the other moms nuts.

Taze felt the sweat leaking from the back of his neck. A girl he didn't recognize was hustling to catch up to the twins. He squinted through the haze of light and shadow. He'd seen her before, moving across the lane in some nickel-and-dime tournament, back in January. Her father was trailing her by 20 yards. Taze grabbed the clipboard from the passenger seat and climbed out of the van.

Hoop Heaven had an aimless foyer, a climbing wall (with a "Temporarily Closed" sign jammed, permanently, at its base), a couple soda machines, two glass trophy cases, two skanky restrooms and four full-size basketball courts running parallel to one another. Six of the girls were sprawled on the court closest to the door, stretching in their black t-shirts and sweats. Debra Giuliani was standing beneath the hoop, her dark, Tuscan hair held back by the pair of sunglasses, clearly exasperated. She reminded him of Marisa Tomei. Sometimes he wanted to smack her. Taze handed her the clipboard. "What have I missed?" he asked.

"Thalia had to pick up Shelby and Lisa. She'll be 10 minutes late. Caitlin is still … I don't know where Caitlin is. She's not answering her cell. I'll hand out the schedule for the Hudson's Bay tournament at the end of practice." The sunglasses were drooping and Debra pushed them past her temples. "Oh. You remember Chelsea, don't you?"

Like he kept a flipping card catalogue on every 14-year-old project in his head. "Keep after Caitlin, will ya?" He rotated his eyes right. "Yeah. Tualatin, right?"

"Lake Oswego," Debra said. "Jack?" She waved him over. "Chelsea's dad."

Taze turned his back to the approaching lumberjack. "You got the check?"

"Two hundred. Five weeks."

"Mr. Elliott? Jack Lider," the big man said, closing fast, leading with his right hand. "Played at Franklin, didn't you?"

Taze shook his head. "Your daughter looking to play serious basketball?"

"Chelsea," Lider said. "She starts eighth grade at LOJ next week."

"What makes you think she's good enough?" The guy had six inches on him, but no poker face. Thought he was parked on pocket kings. "She's a natural," Lider said. "You'll see."

"Saw her last winter. Wasn't impressed. Can't go left. Doesn't play D. Who's been coaching her?"

"Alex ... Blessing. And Mick Hilton."

"Mike Dunleavy wannabes. Why'd you wait this long to bring her over?"

Lider had a scowl growing. "She's in the Laker program. Varsity coach expects everyone to play on the LO traveling teams."

"'If she's any good, she don't need the Laker program. Coach tell you that?"

"I played for Lake Oswego," Lider said. "I expect she will, too."

"Times have changed. Back then, college recruiters had nowhere to go but the high-school gym. If they didn't see you there, didn't see you at all. Now, they have options. You know how many graduates of *my* program playing D-1 right now?" Taze didn't wait for an answer. "Four. Cindy Stevens at Oregon, Sarah Innocenti at Faith Christian, and Cheryl and Jessie down at Stockton. They all played for me." Granted, Cheryl

Keston hung around for all of three days before he got that restraining-order look that said she was wise to his act. "They didn't need LO. I gave them the stage. Took 'em to Slam 'N' Jam and End of the Trail. Nothing but college coaches at those games, waiting for the Black Tornado to come through the door."

"I've heard you do a good job with fundamentals," Lider said. "Mind if I hang out and watch for awhile?"

"Damn right I mind. What do you do for a living?"

"I sell cars."

"On commission?"

"I own the dealership."

Damn. And Debra had only rung this guy up for five weeks? "BMW?"

"Volvo."

"You want me hanging around when you're closing the deal?"

"Why not? You might learn something."

The guy didn't blink; Taze gave him that. "I don't need the distraction. Come back in two hours."

Lider stood there, searching for something else to say. Taze turned and waded through the girls still scattered across the floor, leaning on their hamstrings. "Two minutes," he barked. Lider took a step or two toward his daughter, then felt the sting of the electric fence. "Chelsea," he called out. She turned, obediently. "I'll be back at 5." The girl gave her father a quick wave and he turned sheepishly toward the door.

Waiting for Thalia, his assistant, to arrive, Elliott started the eight girls on a relaxed lay-up drill. He stood glowering on the baseline, whistle in the corner of his mouth, gauging how comfortably the girls attacked the basket, how painlessly their legs found a rhythm. At their age, he'd already spent a thousand afternoons on the Oakland courts. Learning on the fly, he'd purged his bad habits without the benefit of coaches or clinics, puzzling out what worked seven nights a week. Most of these girls were clueless. They were soccer players. Rarely found the flow of the game 'cause they'd never been lost in it. They thought basketball was a game of one-on-one with their lumpy old man.

He stressed fundamentals. Repetition. He didn't have much choice. A lot of coaches taught a system, an over-analyzed collection of plays designed to benefit the coach's daughter. They ran the girls ragged, if only to keep them too tired to complain about the stupefying dullness of the offense. Taze preferred the Coach K approach: in-your-face, man-to-man defense. Kick-butt attitude. A fear that if they ever let up, someone would take the ball or take their place. Elliott couldn't always inspire his girls to take that fierce pride in their own fate, so he required they take pride in the Black Tornado. In their black jerseys and black sweats and black high-tops.

He charged $40 a week, plus expenses: a share of the van rentals, the tournament entry fees, the hotel rooms. If a parent wanted in for a week, a month or a season, he didn't care. Debra maintained the books and the website, an online scrapbook of results, clippings and player profiles. Taze had to hand it to her: a mercenary heart beat beneath that smug, Stepford exterior. She was his ticket into the upper-middle class enclaves where parents would peel off $2,000 for a year at Hoop Heaven without batting an eye. Debra would introduce him to Mom and Dad on the sidelines of some dingy gym and Taze would close the deal. He had a knack for cheap, green-eyed sincerity. He had 40 kids currently playing under the Black Tornado label: a 7th grade team, an 8th grade team and a national AAU team that Thalia ferried up and down the West Coast. Taze preferred the younger girls.

He'd seen his share of talent. Talent no longer impressed him. Fact is, he doted on the mediocre players. Their bitter fathers were his best customers. Something had gone wrong at the junior high and they were inconsolable. They were still trapped in that video-taped moment when their seven-year-old daughter made a steal, gliding in for a sweet lay-up on an 8-foot hoop, and the future opened up, a future of high-school crowds and recruiting trips and Erin Andrews interviews. They couldn't let that vision go. They were morally obligated to coach that third-grade team, if only to protect their golden child. And when their coaching careers were done and no one else would give their daughter a free pass, they came looking for Taze with open wallets, scrapbooks in hand. "She has a gift. I don't know how a coach could miss that." Hell, they'd swallow anything. They were desperate to believe their daughters still had a chance to morph into

Cheryl Miller, and one day hand good ol' dad the state championship trophy.

He loved mediocre players.

When Thalia arrived with Shelby and Lisa, Taze sent them into a 3-on-2 drill. Early on, Chelsea twice pulled up on the wing and banked in 12-footers. After the second, he blew his whistle. "Proud of that shot?" he asked. Chelsea flashed a quick smile, then glanced nervously at the other girls, none of whom were giving much away.

"Well?" Elliott said. She nodded, cautiously. "Just so you understand. That shot ain't your first option. We run 3-on-2, you attack the basket. Know what that means?"

Chelsea stared at him. "Attack the basket," he repeated. "Anyone want to tell her what I'm talking about?"

"You go to the hole," Sarita said.

"And if someone gets in your way?"

"Knock 'em over," Cici said.

"Damn right. And if you get that offensive foul, don't sweat it, 'cause the next time you roll down the lane like Charles Barkley, they'll dive out of your way."

He stepped back. Next time through the rotation, Sierra and Cici were on defense, Chelsea back on the right wing. Sarita didn't disappoint: She dropped off a bounce pass Chelsea picked up in stride. Cici moved to her left, to the edge of the paint, so she could take the charge on the bony ridge of her shoulder. Following orders, desperate to please, anxious to leave that glowing first impression, Chelsea came roaring in

... but at the last moment, with a sleight of hand that caught both Taze and Cici flat-footed, she swerved right and flipped the ball between Cici's hip and Sierra's ear. Anita, flying in from the left, caught the ball in stride and banked an easy two off the glass

"Wow!" Anita said, circling beneath the basket. "Nice pass, babe." Chelsea accepted her high five without a word and trotted back to mid-court without a glance at Taze, who was chewing on his whistle. Where did that move come from?

"What are you all looking at?" he finally barked. "Keep it going, now. Keep it moving. Thalia? Run 'em." Elliott stepped back to watch, to recalculate. That girl just play him for a fool? Did she really have that kind of attitude?

He wasn't in the mood. Not today. Some afternoons he showed up feeling like John Wooden, determined to add a few more blocks to the pyramid of their success. Other days, he didn't give a damn. Worse, he resented their youth, their resilience, the chain of events that exiled him at Hoop Heaven instead of allowing him to prowl the coaching box at Jesuit or the University of Oregon.

He watched for another 10 minutes. Time and again, his eyes were drawn to Chelsea. She had stage presence. She knew when to push, when to ease back. Her jump shot wasn't as good as she thought. She didn't, or couldn't, go left. Defense bored her. But she had game. He'd need to break her down, of course, but that wouldn't pose too many problems. Never did.

Thalia was guiding them through inbounds plays when Elliott blew his whistle, offered them three minutes around the water bottles, and waved Chelsea over.

"Why you here?" he asked. "You here on your own or is this your dad's idea?"

"Me, mostly."

Taze wasn't convinced. "You done with LO?"

Chelsea glanced up, obviously confused. "I don't ..."

"Damn, girl, it's time you stop playing B team. Now, get back to it. Thalia!" His assistant was slouched at mid-court. "Gotta go. You can handle things, right?"

"Go?" she said, more skeptical than curious. "Ninety minutes early?"

"Stuff to do. I owe you dinner."

"Uh huh, Burger King, right?"

"Where you go ... when you know," Taze said, laughing as he turned on his heel.

When he climbed back into his rig, Leykis was still carrying on.

You're a 9? A 9? An LA 9 or an Oxnard 9?

I don't know. A Santa Monica 9.

How much do you weigh?

One thirty ... 135.

And you're 5-foot-6? Well, you're definitely dragging around an Oxnard ass.

You had to love Leykis' work ethic, Taze thought. The guy never took a day off. Every afternoon, like clockwork, he was on the air, trumpeting "Flash Friday," preaching that women were drawn to the guys who treated 'em like dirt. Taze rolled out of the lot, shoving the van into a break in traffic. The afternoon heat was peaking. The dashboard clock read 4:18 p.m. The clinic closed at 5 o'clock. If they got jammed up on the way downtown, he was screwed.

Luck was with him. Traffic was light enough that Taze was suddenly daydreaming about another drive down 217 a few years back, a sweet young thing behind the wheel. He crossed I-5, then turned left behind the Mormon church, winding his way back to a small retail square that featured a half-dozen of the vanity shops so common to Lake Oswego. He circled the lot twice before he saw Caitlin, sitting in a heap on a bench. When he pulled over, she picked herself up and circled the front of the van to the passenger door without looking at him. Elliott reached to pop the door open with a jab of his right hand. Mother didn't give until the third pop.

"Hey, Cait. Been waiting long?" She stared silently at the glove compartment as he wheeled out of the lot. "Ten minutes," she finally said. "Anyone miss me?"

"I did." Taze surveyed the girl as he sliced past three skateboarding slackers. Eyes puffed up, hair ragged, no makeup. Though it was tough to tell what was going on beneath the stained blue sweatshirt, Taze guessed she'd tacked on 15 pounds since the last time he had her alone. Her nose was running and Taze could see the lines forming, lines that would leave her with the uninspired features of her listless mother. Whatever used to be fresh about her, back when she was 13 and new to the team, had vanished. He could barely remember the girl he'd gotten excited about. What was in her pants hadn't been all that special. What was beneath that belt wasn't coming back to haunt him, that's for sure.

Los Angeles. 1-800-5800-Tom. Jennifer on the Tom Leykis Show, hello.

Hello, Tom. How are you?

Do you care?

You know, Tom, I really don't. I can't believe what I'm hearing today.

Well, you must not have been listening yesterday, Jennifer. I'm nothing if not consistent.

They were swinging through the Terwilliger curves, three miles south of the city, when Taze glanced at Caitlin again. She was biting her lip, a tear inching down her cheek. "You alright, girl?" he asked. Coach Empathy. Father knows best.

"What am I gonna do?" she sniveled. "What am I gonna do?"

"C'mon. Already decided that, didn't we?"

"I have RE tomorrow. My mom'll kill me."

"What the hell is RE?"

"Religious ..." She took a deep breath. "...education."

"Mom will never know." They were passing a triple trailer on the right and the rumble drowned out Caitlin's reply. Taze waited for clean air. "What?"

"So this is better ..."

"Damn right. You get a clean slate."

"And a flat stomach."

Taze shook his head. "Don't be talking like that. Nobody planned this, but, yeah, you got your whole life ahead of you. You don't want kids. This ain't the time. You don't want me, either. I'm old enough ... well, I don't know. You got the papers, right?"

Caitlin opened the hand tucked in her lap, to show him the tight wad. "All right," he said. He turned the radio up.

Tom, there are teenage boys who take you seriously. The damage you're doing ...

Boys, are you listening? Jennifer is all hot and bothered. Are you hot, Jennifer?

I'm stunned, Tom. You can't label single mothers like this. You can't ...

Oh, now I get it. This IS a single mom. One brat or two, dear?

As they approached the city, Taze swung west on 405 toward PGE Park, then exited the highway before the traffic began backing up for the charge up the Fremont Bridge. To his right, construction cranes rose over a dozen different blocks in the Pearl District, clusters of lofts and condos that he'd never be able to afford on what he was making with the Black Tornado. He was making the left onto Glisan, the turn toward the northwest corner of town, when Caitlin sniffled, "You said you loved me."

There it was. He swerved so not to run up the rear bumper of a forest-green Subaru. Her jaw tightened. She was chewing on some attitude. "C'mon, Cait, I never said that."

"I said it." She wiped her nose on the sweatshirt, adding another stain to its sleeve.

"We got caught up, Cait."

"I thought you loved me. Why else would … I only …"

Taze had that sense. An eerie intuition that he was living a split-second ahead of the curve. Peter Parker's "Spidey sense," the ever-present foreboding that the Green Goblin's sled was aimed at his back. On the basketball court, such anticipation was electric, pushing Taze into the passing lane, jumping the crossover. He had that sense, damn it, and that's why his foot was reaching for the brake when Caitlin grabbed the door handle, leading with her right shoulder.

Any other van and she might have completed the dive, but the door, still buckled from the night he'd sideswiped that new Acura, held just long enough for Elliott to snag the elastic band of her sweat pants with three fingers. They hung there for a moment, even as the brakes locked; then the right front wheel bounced off the curb and Caitlin, straining and desperate, tossed her shoulder at the door again. This time it surrendered with a metallic wheeze and Caitlin tumbled onto the sidewalk.

"Shit!" Taze screamed, even as the van completed its arid skid on the I-405 overpass and he rolled out the driver's door, inches from the right front bumper of a Jeep Cherokee that swept past, horn blaring. As Taze stumbled to the back of the van, Caitlin came up off her knees and, lurching forward, grabbed the green metallic fence that rose 10 feet above the sidewalk. "Cait!" he howled as she pulled herself upright. Taze tripped on the sidewalk and went down on the heels of his palms, screaming her name again, just as her body sagged and she collapsed at the base of the fence, sobbing.

"What the hell you doing?" Adrenalin was rippling through him. Forty feet below, an 18-wheeler rushed by in the southbound lanes. Caitlin's eyes were open, her chest heaving, a flap of sweat-pant fabric hanging from her knee.

"What ..." she gasped. "What am I doing? What am I ..."

Taze reached for her shoulder. She cringed, staying his hand. He could feel cars slowing. Twenty feet away, an off-ramp beggar was staring. He had a backpack and a 5-day growth. The loser took two steps toward them before Taze turned and yelled, "Back off, or I'll kick your scrawny ass."

He tried to catch his breath. "You know what we're doing, Cait," he finally said. "We're making things right."

Her body shook again. "We? You're coming in with me?"

"Can't do that," he said, looking over his shoulder, checking the length of 15th Avenue for a squad car. A black man with a white chick on a downtown overpass? Trouble couldn't be far off. He had that sense. "Can't do that," he repeated. "I go in and there are questions, phone calls. For an hour, you're on your own. That's all. I'll be outside the whole time, waiting to drive you home. C'mon now, back in the van."

Caitlin leaned against the fence as a KATU news helicopter passed overhead, accelerating toward the river. "I wanna go home," she said. "I want my mom."

"Mom'll beat the tar out of you, girl. Beat the tar out of me. You know that. It's why we're here. We're through talking, Cait. This has to go away."

He grabbed her elbow. One tug, then another, and she allowed herself to be led to the van. As she slid onto the front seat, Taze slammed the door shut and pounded the lock down with his fist. The punk begging for munchies had retreated to the far side of the street and Taze wondered if he could run the scumbag down without leaving a dent.

Caitlin was curled up in a ball against the door, her feet beneath her, her face buried in her arms. Which, Taze decided, as he roared off the overpass, was just as well, given the bridal boutique on the next corner. He took a deep breath as they passed the Mission Theater and the houses began to sprout bay windows and yawning front porches.

You're a fat chick and you'll always be a fat chick. Yeah, there are enough chubby chasers out there that you may get laid, but you'll know in your cholesterol-soaked heart you're only gettin' it 'cause this loser wants a good story for his frat reunion ...

"Will you turn that off?"

"What?"

"The radio," Caitlin said.

Taze flipped the radio off as he pulled up to the red light at Couch Park. A young mom in white shorts and a jogging bra, pushing a stroller, crossed the street in front of them. An old fart was searching for inspiration on a synagogue reader board.

"Cait, listen to me now," Taze said. There was a sniffle, nothing else. "You remember the Nike tournament? The Emerald City game? The point guard who could shoot the lights out. You remember that?"

There were teenagers in the park, smoking cigarettes by the play structure. A couple brothers on break from the Fred Meyer were sprawled on a bench, laughing loud enough that he could feel their carelessness through the window.

"January, maybe," Taze continued. "Middle of the second half, we're down 12. You remember why?" In the shade of the trees, the breeze coming through his window was soft and easy. "C'mon now, Cait, I know you remember why."

"You were an asshole," she whispered, pulling one hand out of the ball and wiping the hair off her tear-stained cheek.

"Damn right. Two technicals. Seven-point turnaround. Tossed my ass into the parking lot. Had to watch the end of the game through the crack in the door. I know you remember that, Cait, and I know why."

She raised her face off her arms and laid her head back against the seat. Her nose was running, her eyes red, but Taze saw something in the line of her jaw. "What do you remember, Cait?"

"I scored 18."

"Uh-huh. And the last nine."

"Eleven."

"Two free throws at the end?"

She glanced at Taze for the first time that afternoon. "Three-pointer at the buzzer. Like you don't remember."

"I'll tell you what I remember," Taze said. "I lost it. I dropped the damn ball and you picked it up. Best game of your life."

She ran the sweatshirt sleeve across her face. "So what?"

"Don't know. I know I messed up. Got fired up and lost my mind. I told you before, I wouldn't blame you if you wanted to tell your girlfriends, your parents, tell the world. I messed up and I can't make it right. But you can, Cait. You can bail us both out. Keep us a secret, like we always talked about, and ... start fresh. You have the power. You have the ball. You can fix things, not me. I can't go into that clinic. All I can do is wait here 'til you come out."

His mouth was dry, his neck muscles tight. He was in a strange place. Talked out. He was making the left on Lovejoy when she finally spoke. "You have the money, right?"

He opened his mouth, then shut it again. He'd said enough. He had that sense. Taze dug into his right hip pocket for the $50 bills, carefully folded, and handed them to her. At the corner of 25th and Lovejoy, an old coot was parked by the stop sign, his ragged lawn chair no more than 30 feet from the ramp leading to the Surgicenter's front door. As Caitlin reached to unlock the door, Taze said, "Hold on," and eased through the intersection. For all he knew, there were security cameras, what with the bomb threats and the nut cases who camped here every weekend. He pulled to the curb a block up the hill and Caitlin slipped away without a word. He watched in the side mirror as she crossed the street, waiting for doubt or anger to break her stride. It didn't. As she reached the corner, the old protestor's head dropped down onto his chin, surrendering to that afternoon nap.

Taze rubbed the back of his neck. He had an hour to kill. He turned the radio back on, then leaned back and closed his eyes.

... don't you get it? Girls don't put out for the guys who open the door for 'em and spend $100 on dinner and ask permission. They put out for the assholes. They get down on their knees for the assholes. Have I taught you nothing, my son, my son?

Damn, he thought, trying to remember if they'd passed a bar on the drive up Glisan. What he might have done with that kind of fatherly advice.

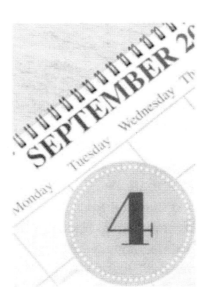

T hey'd missed the bus. Emily couldn't find her Algebra book and Lisa was running her mouth, and suddenly they were standing with their flip-flops on the red curb of the bus lane as the #45 bus rolled down the hill at the far side of the parking lot.

"Emily!" Lisa wailed. "You made us miss the bus!"

Emily opened her mouth to protest, then shut it again. At the bottom of the hill, there was a long light and a busy crosswalk with kids pouring out of both the high school and LOJ. She grabbed Lisa's sleeve: "Let's run."

"Run?" Lisa stammered.

Emily was already picking up speed. She tucked the Carolina blue backpack under her right arm as she darted between a pitch black Escalade and a silver Acura with tinted glass. The screech of brakes didn't slow her down; neither did the concrete steps that completed the slide down to Country Club Road. When she hit bottom, the #45 was fuming in the middle of the intersection, but Lisa was only halfway down the steps, hung up between two skateboarders.

We are so screwed, Emily thought as Lisa finally caught up, howling, "Come back!" at the deaf-mute in the driver's seat. With a final "Aaarrghh," Lisa raised her right arm and flipped the bus the bird, even as a dark blue Land Cruiser pulled up beside them, a guy with a blond halo of hair leering out the passenger window.

"That for me?" he said.

Emily took a cautious step back, Lisa a giant leap forward. "Brent!" she squeaked. "What are you doing here?"

"Cruising," Brent McBride said. "Who's your friend?"

Lisa pulled Emily forward for closer inspection. "Brent, Emily. Emily, Brent." Lisa ducked her head to check out the driver, who had his cell in his fist, mid-text. "Hey, Peter," she said.

"Who ..." Emily stammered, bringing her backpack up below her chin.

"Hey, Emily," Brent said. "Why's Lisa flipping off traffic?"

"Friends of Derek's," Lisa said, her mouth at Emily's ear. "Baseball players." She turned back to the Land Cruiser. "Our bus. It left without us."

Brent turned and said something to Peter Sholien that was lost to Emily and Lisa in the humid swirl of idling buses and passing cars. When he returned to the window, he was Mr. Hospitality. "Hey, we'll give you a ride. Jump in."

Before Emily could begin to explain that sliding into a car with two high-school juniors topped the list of prohibitions that would ground her until she graduated from Stanford, Lisa was opening the back door.

"Thanks!" she said. "C'mon, Emily. I'll skooch over. Emily? Emily!" Lisa made no attempt to conceal the high-pitched desperation in her voice. She wanted Emily to focus: We're in this together. You can't leave me now. I'm already in the car and it's going to be all over school tomorrow that you're scared to death of high-school guys. Emily fell in beside her, trying to regain her balance. She would follow Lisa's lead. She would keep her mouth shut. She would not wet her pants.

Of course, Lisa already had her hand on the back of Peter's seat and was leaning forward as if there was a lot more going on up front than in the back.

"So, where we going? Your house?" Peter said, closing his cell and turning to wave at a Humvee speeding by with its horn blaring. He had dark hair and soulful eyes and a trace of acne. He looked smarter than most high-school jocks.

Lisa shrugged and looked at Emily. "Sure. Have you seen my brother?"

"Not since lunch," Brent said. He was blond and tan and Emily felt the sharp angles of his shoulders through the worn fabric of his Gonzaga t-shirt. As Peter wheeled the car into traffic, Brent pulled down the visor and popped open the mirror.

The back seat of the Land Cruiser housed three Big Mac boxes and a half dozen abandoned fries, a baseball glove, a half-eaten Round Table cinnamon stick and the breathless claustrophobia of possibility. Lisa was nervously smacking her strawberry Bubblicious about three inches from Emily's ear. Semisonic's "Closing Time" was rolling out of the Land Cruiser's CD player, and the breeze was trucking through the windows. Feeling an odd chill creeping along her arms, Emily looked down to discover goose bumps. She was studying the runes when Lisa leaned in and whispered, "Can you believe this?" When Emily glanced up again to see who was listening, she caught Peter's eyes in the visor mirror. He smiled and didn't look away.

She looked past him and out the windshield. They were cresting a hill on the northern edge of Oswego Lake Country Club, and Mt. Hood – 60 miles to the east – lunged out in bold relief. We're in a car with two juniors, she thought, and for some reason she remembered what Lisa said when Rachel was spreading the rumor that her brother was having serious sex with Phoebe Dunham, one of those girls on the dance team whose gorgeous hair dried flat without a straightener: "No way. Juniors don't hook up. Sophomores do. Sophomores are sluts. Juniors move in herds."

Emily had no idea if this was true, but she was more than a little jealous that Lisa had access to this kind of information.

To their right, the golf course, lush and quiet, rolled up to the bluffs overlooking the lake. Brent gazed out at an evergreen-dyed water hazard, then turned to Peter and, barking over the music and wind, asked, "Wanna play Saturday?"

Peter shrugged, his eyes skipping from mirror to mirror. "Or we can do the pool." He glanced back over his right shoulder at Emily with a vacuous look that convinced her he'd forgotten her name. "You guys working on your tans this weekend?"

"Soccer," Emily said, surprised she got the word out. "We have soccer in Medford."

"Medford?" Brent snorted. "Rednecks. If you see anyone in a South Medford baseball cap, ask 'em if they remember that 11-0 pounding in the state playoffs."

Lisa glanced at Emily. Was this a serious request? "We don't belong to the club," she conceded. "We're usually down at Rachel's."

"No shit," Brent said. "Coulda sworn I've seen you by the pool."

Two weeks ago Sunday, Lisa thought. She was wearing the red-and-orange suit that Layla's mom nabbed for her at Nordstrom's. "I go with Rachel sometimes," she said.

"Your dad doesn't golf?"

"Yeah. He golfs a lot," Lisa said, rolling her eyes.

"Where?"

"Pumpkin Ridge."

"Pumpkin?" Brent whistled. "That's right. Derek says he hits it a ton." He was noticeably impressed. Pumpkin Ridge was the elite 36-hole track in North Plains where Tiger Woods won the last of his three fist-pumping U.S. Amateurs. Lisa was not a fan of the place, given that it swallowed her dad and her brother every weekend.

"He's hitting it there right now," Lisa said.

"Living the life," Peter said. They had pulled to a stop at Five Corners and his eyebrows were up. One of the ever-present Lake Oswego cops was idling in the shadows, begging someone to roll through the stop sign.

"So, no one's home?" Brent asked.

In the back seat, Lisa made quiet calculations. Brent had checked her out by the pool, and not because she was Derek's ditzy sister. Brent was asking what was waiting for them back at her house other than the bottle of Stoli in her vanity. This might rate a paragraph or two in her Teen People diary. "You want me to call Derek?" she asked.

Brent shook his head. "No worries. I'll text him later."

Mindful of the cop 50 yards behind them, Peter made a clean stop at 10th, then swung right beneath the sequoias that towered over the tenured homes that dominated this edge of the lake. At its southwestern tip, the '50s ranchers were being bulldozed to make way for $2 million McMansions, but these Tudors and white Colonials had dug in for the long haul.

Picking up confidence and speed, Peter zipped down the quiet streets toward North Shore, 15 mph over the residential speed limit. Emily didn't mind – when Derek drove them home, he drove demon-possessed; he'd already flattened two squirrels and the Entenmeyer's Siamese cat – but she was confused as to how this was going to end. Brent was asking Peter about the Mariners when she turned to Lisa and said, "Wanna come over and do math?"

Lisa shook her head and, reaching inside her shirt, pulled a strap back up onto her shoulder. "No, let's talk later at practice"

"I won't feel like Algebra after practice," Emily said. She'd feel like collapsing on her bed after two more hours of running in circles at Westlake Park.

"Dad wants me to clean the bathrooms before he gets home," Lisa said.

"The bathrooms? Yeah, right." Emily had never seen Lisa drop a nacho-cheese-stained plate in the dishwasher, much less pick up a Wisk brush. That's what the cleaning lady from North Portland was for.

Lisa shrugged. "Can you drop me off first?" she asked, raising her voice above the Gin Blossoms. When Emily met her eyes, Lisa gave her another 'Get with the program' glance. The program? What program? For some reason, Emily realized, Lisa was looking to be alone at the exact time Emily was desperate to be together.

The Gin Blossoms were still following them down when they reached the Hiltons' shrub-enshrined driveway. "I'll call you," Lisa said as she popped open the door. "Don't do Algebra without me."

Algebra would be history in an hour, but Emily kept her mouth shut, even as Brent yanked open his door and hopped out of the car. "Mind if I hang out?" he asked. "Grab a Pepsi, maybe?" Standing in the open door, Lisa pulled the backpack up and over her shoulder. "I don't care," she said, "but we're running low on junk food."

"Doesn't matter. I'm not hungry. I just want the secret guided tour."

"Then, follow me," Lisa said. And just like that, they were walking down the driveway. Lisa never looked back, but Brent did. There was no mistaking the sloppy satisfaction in that smile.

"Climb up front," Peter said, offering Emily the opening between the seats as if he didn't realize she was wearing a denim skirt.

"No," Emily said, "I'm fine."

"C'mon, ride shotgun. You can run the radio."

She didn't care about the radio. She just wanted to make sure she didn't stop breathing. Emily slowly crawled out the back of the Land Cruiser and, through the door Brent had left open, slid into the front seat, setting her backpack at her feet.

"Belted up?" Peter asked. As she nodded, he took a thoughtful look at the shoulder strap as it sliced between her boobs. She thought he was reaching over to grab the strap and make sure it was tight, but he simply tossed his right arm over the top of her seat and backed the Land Cruiser out of the driveway. She sat there, afraid to move, wondering how to ask Peter to drop her off a block from the house so that Allie would have nothing to report to their parents. When Emily remembered to look up again for Lisa and Brent, they were nowhere in sight.

*   *   *

"Shit! You red-ass mother ..."

Thump! Mick brought the head of the 4-wood down hard enough that he would have splintered the shaft but for the same over-watered fairway that caused him to hit the shot fat in the first place. He watched in ill-concealed disgust as the ball dove into the bunker guarding the front of the green.

"You're right," said Butch Rennard, one of Nike Golf's marketing gurus. "Life's a bitch. A 530-yard par-5 and you're in jail, up by the green in two."

"Third one fat today. I'm better than that."

"Must be the Nike woods," Butch said.

"We're down two with three to play," Mick said, sliding back into the cart. "You want these guys to think they can beat us?"

"If it loosens 'em up for the serious bullshit, why not?"

"What is this, freshman psych? They're plenty loose. They've got a lottery pick. Converse has already offered $4 million."

"Maybe Converse needs him more than we do."
Butch cut to the cart path on the left edge of the fairway, swinging behind Steve Sikorsky, a Century City agent,

and Jonah Krevitz, his numbers' guy, both of whom looked tanned and relaxed 248 yards from the center of the green.

"Is that a one-iron? Mick asked, incredulous, squinting at the club in Sikorsky's gloved hand. "No way he gets there with a one-iron."

"Must be more freshman psychology," Butch said. "He's getting to you."

"Bullshit. I've played with him. He doesn't have that shot."

Butch brought the cart to a halt at the crest of a small ridge where they could observe the green and most of the fairway. "What are you now, two over?"

"Four. OB on one."

"You should have taken a mulligan. Sun-Tzu would have taken a mulligan."

Mick laughed. He liked golfing with Butch. He was comic relief when the job was pissing him off or the 4-wood was letting him down. Sikorsky was settling over his ball, a Nike 3 Mick knew had been selected to annoy him. Mick leaned back in the cart. Damn, he thought. Fly it in the hole and let's call it a night. Get an early start back toward Lake Oswego and driving Lisa to soccer practice.

He looked out over the course, the sun hard on his neck. In a small fissure of his self-control, he allowed himself to wonder about Sharon, whose departure from their lives was so irrevocable as to be frightening. One moment, they were following the usual stage directions of a 20-year marriage, delivering their carefully rehearsed lines, honoring the choreography that kept them connected if not particularly close. The next, he was searching her face for the tiniest wrinkle of affection, and not finding one.

Thwack!

Evan at this distance, 80 yards up the fairway, the crispness of Ski's long iron was unmistakable. Mick and Butch watched the ball arch through the September sky, riding the autumnal breeze or the Gulf Stream or some other diabolical force until it dropped like a rock on the edge of the green and then, seemingly, struck one, so inexorable was the hop it took toward the flagstick.

"My man Ski," Butch said, "has been practicing."

Mick kept telling himself it was resignation, not revenge. Sharon had bitched about so many things over the years – his temper, his cheapness, his inability to discipline Derek, his curiosity about old girlfriends – that he wasn't sure when she reached the end of her rope. He left her one morning with the breakfast dishes and that long-suffering look of hers to spend the morning playing golf and the afternoon playing cards, and when he got home at 10:30 p.m. – did he forget to mention the late dinner? – she politely announced her suffering was over. Within 48 hours, she had everything arranged – the division of assets, the allocation of cars, the assurance she would never ask him for another dime – and arranged with the savage efficiency he hadn't seen since their second year in law school. Then she walked out, stopping at the edge of the garage to tell him she'd call when she got settled.

He waited three months. By the time Mick realized this was serious, a clean and uncompromising break, he could find no trace of her. No cell phone slip ups. No credit-card receipts. No trail of crumbs leading back to Lisa or Derek. Now and then, an email arrived for Lisa, invariably laced with regret and remorse and encouragement for the woman who'd been left behind, but devoid of clues as to the location of her Internet café. As far as Mick knew, none of Sharon's friends received similar messages; they looked baffled when he asked. The days simply piled up like a Biblical monument of old rocks, a sign that Mick had been blotted from the face of Sharon's imagination. When her call finally came, Mick was too exhausted, too frustrated, too devoid of any emotion other than astonishment to ask where she was.

Mick's ball was sitting, as they say on the Golf Channel, sunny side up in the bunker, just below a faint trail that traced its descent from the lip of the trap. It wasn't a difficult up and down. The bunker didn't have a shoulder to cry on and he was tossing the ball into the slope and grain of the green, the same combo that would give Ski fits when he tried to lag his downhill eagle putt. He was looking for the perfect landing area when Ski, still flush with success, called out, "You want that stick in or out, Mick?"

His client was 6-foot-8, and leaving Carolina two years early. The kid rebounded like Moses Malone and spent every Sunday morning sharing a pew with his coach, Roy Williams. So, no, Mick didn't blame Ski for his confidence. But this, Mick decided as he stepped down into the sand, was a little obnoxious.

"What the hell," he yelled back, "pull it out."

And even as Ski began his trek across the green, Mick scooped the egg off the grill with a relaxed swing and just the right amount of fluff. The ball dropped 30 inches in front of the flag and – Ski yelped, "Whoa!" and then froze – took a high hop into the cup, laying a sloppy kiss on the flagstick on the way down.

"Or, hell," Mick said, "leave the sucker in."

"Face," Butch said, as he drove to the 17th tee.

"He pushed that putt six inches wide. You planning on contributing anything to this team effort today?"

"Had a birdie on four."

"God, was that today?"

"How many times have we played together?" Butch asked, sliding off the cart seat and jamming his ball into the ball washer.

Mick pulled Big Bertha from his bag and eased the driver out of its Tiger head cover. "I don't know. Forty? Fifty?"

"And how many times have you pulled a shot out of your ass? You do it all the time."

Ain't it the truth, Mick thought. Weird stuff happened. Sixty-foot putts. Inside straights on the river. Vinatieri shanked a field goal when he had the Jets giving three. When the game was on the line, *good* things happened, which may be why what happened with Sharon baffled him. He had no illusions. He hadn't spent enough time at home. He was a cheap bastard, a stoic father, a selfish jerk … but he'd been all those things since Day 1. From the moment they'd met in the third row of Torts, Mick hadn't faked a damn thing. He was motivated, callous and obnoxious. He assumed that was part of his charm. Like most everyone he knew at Nike, he was dedicated to rising early, working late, partying hard, and joining the entourage for trips to Yankee Stadium, Pebble Beach and the Super Bowl whenever Phil Knight called and said, "Wheels up at 3:30 sharp." He wasn't going to mow the grass, chaperone the junior-high dance or – like Alex, that pansy ass – run out every morning to deliver his wife Starbucks and *The New York Times* in bed. But neither was he going to cheat – he never had – or provide the family with less than the best. For 19 years, he'd delivered on the contract they'd signed on their wedding day, only to return home one night and discover Sharon had purged herself of all feeling for him and their marriage.

Ccrrrhhhh! Mick almost came out of his shoes on the tee, lacing his drive down the right side of the fairway with a slight draw. The contact was so pure he barely felt it; the ball came off the club face like a Doberman off its leash.

"You gonna have anything left for dinner?" Butch asked.

"Burgers in the bar?"

"I was thinking Helvetia Tavern."

Mick winced as Ski leaned over and planted his tee between three divots. "Can't. Gotta get Lisa to soccer, remember?"

"You can't get out of it?"

Mick shook his head. Ski put the sweet Sammy Snead on his drive, 260 yards into the first low cut of rough, a perfect angle for his approach shot. After Krevitz thumped his 3-wood straight down the tubes, Butch eased off the brake. "Ever gonna leave Nike, Mick?" he asked.

Mick reached for the bottle of Henry's in the cup holder. "What brings that up?"

"We need to get your mind off that 8-iron."

"I've thought about it. Going off on my own. I know the business better than half the guys I deal with. What's going on in Golf?"

"Tiger. Tiger, Tiger, burning bright."

"Life is good then ..."

"Life is same old," Butch said. "You remember the old days? Curtis and Jake? You went into the weekend never knowing what might happen."

Mick shook his head. "I don't know. Eddie Alvarado called me the other day."

"The columnist?"

"Yeah. Asked me if I'd heard any Tiger rumors."

"What Tiger rumors?"

"Didn't say. He said I'd know."

Butch sighed. "You can't have fun with Tiger anymore. The guy's a building. Drives a Buick. His caddy thinks he's God. Jake didn't have one-tenth of Tiger's talent but he was 10 times as much fun. Maybe 'cause we only took him one-tenth as seriously."

*   *   *

Lisa's mother had sent her a diary for her birthday, a diary and 17 extra-fine point Sharpie pens. "Tell your diary what you can't tell me," she said, and in the last five months, Lisa had written in it twice, first to note, in orange, that "Legally Blonde" was the coolest movie she'd ever seen, then to describe in lime green the night Derek slipped her and Layla a Coors Light. He wasn't trying to get them drunk, he was bribing her so she wouldn't tell Dad that he'd really ripped his pants when they snagged on a chain-link fence as he ducked out of an MIP party at the Greenlicks'. Lime green because Layla wondered aloud, "Maybe it only tastes good with a lime in it", as they dumped the rest of the bottle in the white azalea by the garage door. Lisa stumbled over a lot of things that she didn't know what to do with, but for the life of her, she didn't know why she'd want to lock any of them in a book.

But this ...? She could see herself reaching for the Navy blue. She could feel the words settling into place on the beige-lined pages with the scarlet hearts in the corners.

I don't believe what happened today.

They were barely inside the house when Layla called on the cell.

"Hey."

"Hi."

"Home yet?"

"No. Yes. Call you later."

She didn't know what to say because she didn't know what to make of this. She was suddenly and uncomfortably conscious of the fit of her clothes, the bend of her legs, all the utterly stupid things she'd said ever since the Land Cruiser pulled up at the junior high. Lisa knew what she wanted: She wanted to wipe the clumsiness from her face and just enjoy the ride, thrilled that every moment and passing car might bring her face-to-face with someone else awed that she was being chauffeured home by a junior guy, even if he was one of Derek's friends. But she couldn't get comfortable. She couldn't shake the sense that she wasn't ready for this, she wasn't …

"Malice?" Brent said, standing in the front hall. "What's Malice?"

"My soccer team," Lisa said. Why was she wearing this stupid sweatshirt? Why had she decided to save the teal Abercrombie zip-up jacket for the weekend? And why had he glanced at her chest a half dozen times before he figured out the word stenciled across it? Junior jocks didn't know how to read?

"Any good?" Brent asked.

"We won state last year."

"You the keeper?"

Why, Lisa wondered, do I look chunky? "Inside mid. Do you play?"

"Rec. Back when I was your … well, in junior high. *I* was the keeper. I was the reason we usually lost 8-3."

"Why'd you quit?"

"I sucked. I was lucky."

"Lucky?"

"Yeah," Brent had finally stopped looking around like he thought someone was poised to lunge out of the closet. "I got out early. Everyone who didn't suck eventually quit, too. They were sick of it. They'd played forever. Aren't you sick of it?"

"No. I mean, yeah, practice sometimes, like in February. But, no ..."

"You sure no one's home?"

Should she lie? Should she tell him Layla was coming over? That Derek was curled up with the X-Box in the basement? "Yep."

"Got any Cokes in the fridge?"

"Let's go find out," she said. As she dropped her books on the granite counter, Lisa took in the utter disarray and bit down on her embarrassment. Derek had not only left a half-eaten bowl of Cinnamon Toast Crunch by the sink but he'd abandoned a half gallon of milk on the counter. The Round Table box – last night's dinner – and three days of mail were piled near the toaster. Two thick, black flies, sent aloft when she dropped the books, completed their slow circles and touched down on a wedge of bagel and cream cheese by the sink.

"I'm sorry," Lisa said. "I'm sorry this is such a mess."

Brent shrugged. "What's that smell?"

Damn it, Mom. Why? Why did you give up? Why did you leave? Whatever Dad did, how could you quit on me? How could you leave me behind? How could you ruin every Christmas for the rest of my life?

You couldn't suck it up for just a little longer? You couldn't leave me with something more than a diary?

"Probably the milk." Lisa opened the refrigerator door. A quart of mustard, five bottles of Hefeweizen, orange juice, and a three-day-old chicken from Costco. Her dad loved Costco. "Diet Pepsi OK?"

"I guess. No Dr Pepper?"

Lisa shook her head. Mom was the Pepperhead. Maybe that's why Dad wouldn't buy the stuff anymore. She handed Brent a Diet Pepsi. The milk had turned in the Indian summer heat and the stench was gaining on her. Brent was studying the Malice script again. Lisa thought about crossing her arms across her chest. *What's Malice?* She was pretty sure she wouldn't stem his curiosity by handing him a dictionary. She also knew this: She had to get out of the kitchen. "Wanna watch television?" she asked.

"Sure. For a while. We've got fall ball practice in a half hour."

Lisa nodded. Practice? Of course. "We have the big screen in the living room," she said. "Or the regular TV in my room."

"Those big screens give me a headache," Brent said, taking a draw on his Diet Pepsi. "Let's try your room."

Lisa nodded. That made the most sense to her, too.

* * *

Standing in the 18th fairway, Mick had two choices. He had an easy 9-iron to the green, 130 yards to the flag on the back edge and a fluffy lie. If he put any kind of swing on the sucker, he could spin the ball back to the pin and roll in the 8-foot putt that would give him $750 off the top of Ski's wad. On the other hand, Mick also knew he could put the same perfect swing on the ball, ease off on the spin and send the ball trickling off the back of the green and rolling all the way to Bogey Town. If Ski got up and down from 30 feet, he'd win the match one-up, take Nike's money and start drinking early enough that he'd be off his game for tomorrow's power play involving his client.

Plan B, Mick realized, made the most sense. Plan B, however, wasn't his style.

From the way Ski was sprawled in that golf cart, he didn't have a care in the world. He hadn't really lost the last holes to a sand save and a 40-foot birdie putt. The fool had his feet up, a Heineken dangling from his right hand, and a smug grin dripping off his chin. Block it out, Mick told himself, settling his feet, centering his focus, feeling the contact at the edge of his consciousness even before he began his backswing.

Woooo ... ick!

It was perfect. Dead-solid, Dan-Jenkins perfect. Mick had hit enough of 'em to know. He didn't bother to follow the flight of the ball; instead, he ambled to the back of the cart, his 9-iron hitting the bag about the time his ball touched down on the hour-glass shaped green. The next thing he heard was Butch laughing.

"Birdie range?" Mick asked.

Butch patted the cart seat. "That'll do, pig. That'll do."

Mick hopped in and Butch set off down the fairway. "Pissing my man Ski off like this? A bit self-defeating, isn't it?"

"Maybe. We'll deal with it later."

When they reached the green, Mick's ball was lounging five feet below the pin and Ski was standing off the back edge, taking lazy practice chips in the light rough. He had a circumspect grin on his face. "So, you've played this track before?"

"Every weekend," Mick said. "It's a little tighter when the wind kicks up."

"How often do you get your butt kicked?" Ski asked, moving over his ball.

"Whenever Phil or Mark Parker is in the foursome."

Ski laughed, just like he was supposed to. He seemed oddly relaxed for a guy who had to hole this sucker to prevent Mick and Butch from winning 1-up. And he never changed expression as he flipped the ball eight feet onto the green and watched it slowly pick its way through the bumps and grinds until it rattled the stick.

Krevitz loosed a rebel yell. "Damn," Butch said. "Hellacious chip, Ski."

Sikorsky shrugged as he sauntered across the grass. "Nothing to lose, I guess," he said. "Think you could hook me up out here with Phil and Parker?"

"If everything goes right tomorrow," Mick said, "Phil'll caddy for you."

"Putt's good," Ski said, nodding toward Mick's ball, and ending the match all-square. "You got time for a beer and burger?"

"I don't ..." Mick stopped. He didn't. Lisa was waiting for the ride to Westlake. But something had changed. His internal barometer was quivering. Something was in the air, and it wasn't the warm breeze or the smell of dry grass. It was a hot iron, waiting to be struck. "Yeah." Mick was nodding. "Gimme a minute." As Butch climbed into the cart, Mick dialed Lisa's cell. She picked up immediately. "Where are you?" she asked.

"Still on the course. Can you get another ride to practice?"

"You're not coming?"

"I don't know," Mick said, sheepish at how easily the lie rolled off his forked tongue. "I'll probably be late. Really late. You can get to Westlake, right? You want me to call Alex?"

Lisa was silent. "Look," Mick said, "it's business. It's import..."

The line went flat. The cell phone felt like a brick in his hand.

*   *   *

Lisa rolled off her bed. Business. She approached her vanity, the one her mother brought home from one of those trips to Grandma's in Medford, and took her reflection apart, piece by piece. The eyebrows bothered her. The cheekbones worked. Another gift from Mom.

Are you livin' the dream, Mom, wherever you are? I'm happy for you, I really am.

Her cell phone rippled. Layla. "Can your dad come pick me up?" she asked after flipping the phone open.

"Emily's giving me a ride. What's wrong?"

"Golf," Lisa said with that end-of-discussion grunt. Emily. She'd forgotten all about Emily.

"Why didn't you call me back?"

"I don't know. Let's talk at practice." She clicked off before Layla could protest and stared at the cell for a moment, then dialed Emily.

She answered on the fourth ring. "Hey."

"Hey." There was a strange and unexpected pause. "Well ..." Lisa said.

"Well, what?"

"What happened?"

"When?"

"On the way home."

"Nothing."

"Nothing?"

"Why, what happened to you?"

Lisa laughed. She couldn't help it. "Brent ..."

"Brent what?"

She wanted to hold it in, but she couldn't help that, either. "How do you define second base?"

"Second base?"

"Yeah."

"You let him … ?" Emily's voice dropped to a whisper.

"I don't know. On the outside. I think he was scared."

"Weren't you?"

"Not really. He's a lousy kisser. He tasted like a corn dog."

Emily was laughing. "Can your mom come get me for practice after you pick up Emily?" Lisa asked.

"Sure. I guess."

"OK. Text you later. Don't be late." And Lisa hung up.

Emily didn't. Not right away. She sat without moving for almost two minutes, then rolled over to the edge of her bed, replaying the drive home with Peter, wondering what she'd done wrong. He asked her if she'd ever had Ms. Devereaux. He'd talked about his family's place in Sun Valley. He'd only looked at her once or twice, and he never said a word about baseball.

Emily stood up and walked over to the mirror on her closet door. She could hear her mother and Allie moving around in the kitchen as she stared at her reflection, wondering what it was that Peter didn't like.

Maybe if she lost a little weight …

He was driving past the high school when he saw the lights, and the lights drew him in. He pulled into the right-hand lane without slowing down, without asking himself which of the varsity teams was out on the turf, without giving Olivia and dinner a second thought. The driver's window was open. He saw the lights. He felt summer fading and lost the will to go anywhere else.

He'd spent the afternoon sorting through a fresh supply of marble; then he closed up the shop and swung by the remnant yard to check on his mentor. Alex had hired on with Tomas Keller Stonecutter in the summer of 2001 and bought him out two years later. There were no negotiations. Keller was done. Worn out on disappointment. He'd dreamed of refitting the city in black marble, and the Alaskans, the Mormons and the

Italians – in roughly that order – left him high and dry. When Alex made the offer, Keller slept on it for one rainy night, then signed the papers. His marriage with stone hadn't ended, he said one morning, but the affair with bookkeeping had.

Stone was in Keller's blood. His father had joined Cold Spring Granite at the age of 17, eventually moving to San Francisco to help rebuild a city that was still recovering from the 1906 earthquake and fire. At that turn of the century, the stone saws were placed where the glaciers had already done most of the heavy lifting – in Cold Spring, Minnesota, say, or Rutland, Vermont. The saws were so slow, the slabs so heavy, that cities were defined by their indigenous stone. Brownstone reigned in New York, pink granite in Austin, cream travertine in Rome and Sierra white granite in San Francisco because that stone was in the neighborhood. A 4' x 4' x 8' block of pink granite weighed between five and nine tons, so the cost of hauling stone was prohibitive. Architects and contractors made do with what they could winch out of the local quarry.

That changed when the Italians developed the diamond-tipped gang saw. Not only was the cutting time on a slab reduced to a matter of hours, but you could roll out ¾-inch slices of stone that were as mobile as they were affordable. As sheets of granite – Juparana, Blanco Romano and Labareda – and marble became available, the stone fabricators suddenly had options beyond vanities, fireplace surrounds and the occasional coffee table. By the mid-90s, kitchen counters were the rage, and Keller hired Alex to attract a larger piece of the business.

Keller didn't care for kitchen counters. In the spring of '94, he was fishing in southern Alaska when he beached on Marble Island, 300 miles south of Juneau and due east of Tsongas National Forest. There were black-legged kittiwake, sea lions and a marble quarry Vermont Marble abandoned when the Depression and the war shut the industry down – in North America, at least – for good. The quarry workers left behind a pile of stones 40' high, 40' wide and three miles long, all tucked under four inches of moss. The rights to the leftovers passed to a former Weyerhaeuser exec, who offered Keller an unlimited supply of black marble in exchange for the rough cuts and finish work for the bars and bathroom counters at his Cascade mountain retreat.

As luck would have it, Keller had two fishing buddies who were happier harvesting stone than halibut. One owned a World War II landing craft that ran aground on the northern tip of Prince of Wales Island. He spent four months patching the hull and overhauling the twin Chrysler motors, then ferried Keller back up to Marble. They needed 16 hours to winch the first massive block off the beach. The first of many.

As President Clinton had virtually shut down the Tsongas at that point, a lot of equipment and sullen loggers were sitting idle in Ketchikan. Keller figured he could cut the stone in Alaska and sell it out of his shop in Portland's burgeoning stone industry. He had a healthy business going when the chief construction buyer for the Church of Latter Day Saints walked into his shop. The church was commencing work on 60 tabernacles around the world, he told Keller. While he preferred to use raw local materials, he was utterly taken with the quality of the Alaskan jade. He made two return trips to Portland before sending along his sincere regrets. The local architects, it turned out, preferred the pilgrimage to Italy to scope out the Carrara marble.

Keller spent another summer in Alaska, spiriting out sheets of marble that he stored on a small gravel lot in Portland's central eastside, a dusty bunker hemmed in by warehouses, abandoned wooden pallets and razor wire. Once or twice each month, Alex would drive past the remnant yard to check on him. There was no point in calling first – Keller didn't have a cell phone – and as he turned the final corner, he realized this trip had been for naught. The chain-link gate was locked, the old Ford pickup nowhere in sight. Alex turned toward home … and got as far as the high school.

As Alex drove up the hill, he checked the field. Girls' varsity. Home whites, the visitors in the dull maroon that muttered Milwaukie. A quick glance at the scoreboard: 2-0, 21 minutes left in the half. He parked in a space reserved for staff. He was rushing. He didn't want to hear the sudden crowd burst that meant he'd missed another goal.

The stands were almost empty, two dozen parents bunched beneath the radio broadcast booth. Closer to the field, small pockets of students sat near the railing. Now and then, a bare-chested runner charged past on the track, accelerating into a sprint each time he passed the grandstand.

Alex dropped on to a bleacher bench and felt the weight of everything leave him. The night was clear and warm, and the game didn't matter. He could watch the back-and-forth without wincing each time his daughter and the ball crossed paths. He could listen to the game, waiting for the miracle that allowed the Mustangs to clear the ball. The Laker varsity was relentless, bombarding the Milwaukie goalie with shots and corner kicks. When the gawky keeper or her indefatigable sweeper managed to loft the ball toward safety, LO's defense knocked it down and flipped it back into the shark tank. The Lakers' forwards were big and quick, dominating play at the 18-yard mark. There were nine minutes left in the half when one of their shots rocketed off the bar and dropped at the feet of a wing at the far post. She was so open she could have popped it into the net in any number of ways; she chose her right knee.

The parents rose with polite applause, then returned to the banter about restaurant openings and freshman year at Northwestern. Alex recognized their utter carelessness, a calm that didn't ring the field at the club soccer level. They weren't sweating the score or their daughter's playing time. They weren't berating the refs or anguishing over the details of their daughters' lives that they could not control. They were beyond that. Their daughters would never replace Christine Sinclair at the University of Portland, but they were varsity athletes. They played host to pasta feeds twice a week. They wore jerseys on game days. Their lockers were festooned with word balloons that squealed, "Rock Gladstone, Rachel!" After 10 years of petty rivalries and parental obsessions, the girls could relax and enjoy the game they'd never mastered. Camaraderie superseded competition. The game was pulling the girls together, not tearing them apart, and their parents could lean back and congratulate themselves. Their daughters belonged. Their daughters would have more to remember than Honors English and cheerleading outfits.

At halftime, Alex wandered onto the track, walking slowly toward the net Milwaukie would defend in the second half. The two coaches had their teams gathered at their feet. The sophomores were attentive, the seniors bored. High on the hill above the west end of the field, the Shepherds had turned on the Christmas lights that hung from their roof and back deck and spelled out "LO." Three first graders were dancing in the red gravel of the long-jump pit. It was, Alex thought, a perfect night, the heat of the day slipping away, the breeze filling the gaps. When the halftime clock dropped to 1:00, Alex called Olivia. "What are you doing?"

"Kendall Jackson," Olivia said. "My first refill."

"I thought you'd be exercising."

"The bumblebees are working up a sweat, not me. You're interrupting."

"And Layla isn't?"

"Layla is at Lisa's. What are you bringing home for dinner?"

"Chinese? Steak sandwiches? What are you in the mood for?"

"Kendall and I want you to decide."

"The second half of the LO girls' soccer game is just starting."

"Perfect. You need the extra time."

He closed the cell phone. He wasn't hungry and Olivia was in good hands. At midfield, the Milwaukie forwards, their backs to him, waited for the referee's signal. At his whistle, the smaller of the two forwards took the one-touch pass and sent the ball to her wing deep down the right sideline. It was this motion, 10 girls moving in unison, filling gaps, searching for seams, flowing to empty space, that had finally hooked Alex on the game. Because he never played soccer growing up, he harbored the usual biases for years, discouraged by the lack of scoring, the utter monotony when a team dropped everyone back to guard a 1-0 lead, the spectacle of a Brazilian forward writhing on the pitch, hoping to convince the Peruvian referee that the Mexican's slide tackle had just ended his career. Girls' high school soccer changed that. When Layla was 9, already a whirlwind of aggressiveness, Alex began carting her to LO games mid-week and the Pilots' game on Sunday afternoons. While she pranced to the snack shop, he focused on the field, baffled by the choreography, the random suddenness with which a series of seemingly disconnected passes crystallized into a lightning strike from the top of the box.

He wasn't sure, even now, that he understood the game, a game that was much more about drama than justice. Maybe, as Franklin Foer once wrote, soccer explained the world. Just not his world. All too often he found himself using basketball to explain the game's philosophy. Play the passing lanes. Give and go. But the game and the girls who played it captivated him as the sports he understood no longer did. There were no pro paychecks down the road, no guarantee the best team would triumph over the refs or the turf or the errant offside calls. The high-school field was the Promised Land. This was where the story ended happily or where it didn't.

Alex set up behind the Milwaukie net, far enough back that he wouldn't intrude on the keeper's peripheral vision. She was standing at the right post, warily watching as the Lakers reversed the field. When the Lakers' center mid sent a perfect lead pass down the sideline, the keeper readied herself for the cross, only to watch the ball sail over the box, and settle low on the forehead of the same center mid who'd raced the ball into scoring position.

Give and go. The header sailed five feet over the crossbar, eventually settling in the red cinder crescent behind the end zone, 40 feet beyond the net. The keeper ignored it, grabbing the spare ball from the side of the net and setting it, with the same care she would show a glass egg, at the top of the goal box. Her kick, a low line drive, unexpectedly skipped through the midfield and sent the game stumbling the other way.

No one made a move for the ball in the cinder bed. The keeper was preoccupied, the linesmen above that sort of thing. Something about it upset his sense of order. Alex set off across the cinders, collecting the ball, then rolling it to the side of the net. The keeper never glanced back. The game glided on.

For the next half hour, he collected long balls and deflections. He watched the clock wind down, the sky darken, the Laker second-team slice through Milwaukie's defense and the keeper try to keep her balance on the artificial turf. He made sure the extra ball was always waiting for her, sparing her the loneliness of that long walk across the cinders. She kept her dignity. She never so much as nodded his way.

By the time the game ended, he was thinking steak sandwiches. He saw the teenage girl in the old letterman's jacket cutting across the track toward him, but he wasn't focused on her until, 15 feet away, she glanced up and pushed the dirty blonde hair off her face. "Hey, coach," she said.

Damn. "Molly?" He remembered that shrug, the quick smile, the clear blue eyes turned to him in a fourth-quarter time-out. Alex took a step toward her, his right arm poised to wrap around her shoulders, but Molly Koertje flinched, jamming her hands deeper into those jacket pockets.

He let it go. "How've you been?"

"Okay, I guess. They paying you by the hour or the ball?"

"Just trying to make myself useful." Alex was surprised at the clarity of his memories of her on the basketball court. "What are you now, a sophomore ...?"

"Junior. At Lincoln."

"Lincoln? When did you ...?"

"Last spring." She'd grown four inches since the last time he'd seen her but he wasn't sure she'd gained a pound. Her jeans hung loosely on her hips.

"Lincoln," Alex repeated, half to himself. "Your parents move?" Scott and Lisa, if he remembered right. Two of the quieter sentinels in the stands when Molly played for him in eighth grade. Never yelled at the ref or balked when he needed a host for the post-season party. They even called when Molly quit to play for a select team the summer after they won the Three Rivers League title.

"No, just me."

He remembered the last time he'd seen her. He'd passed her in the crowd exiting a Saturday matinee at Tigard Cinemas, and called her name. She'd stared right past him. "Still playing ball?" A stupid question, he knew.

For the first time, she met his eyes. Those high cheek bones. That Keira Knightly nose. She shook her head.

"Molly! You're kidding, right?"

That quick smile. "Your cell phone is ringing," she said.

So it was. Cooking in his hip pocket. The opening piano solo on the live version of "Tenth Avenue Freeze-out." Alex dug the battered Nokia out of his jeans. Olivia. "Hey."

"Kendall and I are thinking steak sandwiches," she said.

"Great minds think alike. Potato salad or beans?"

"Don't even think about them beans."

"See you in 20."

Molly had turned toward the stands, as if checking for her ride. "You quit basketball?" Alex didn't mask his disappointment. "What happened?"

"I don't know. I got tired."

"Tired? You?" Alex laughed. "I don't think so. When I didn't see you playing for LO, I figured you'd gone WNBA. *That* I could believe. But Molly Koertje? Tired of basketball? Never happened."

"You must be still coaching."

"Yeah. Layla's playing."

"Layla? How old is she now?"

"Eighth grade," Alex said. "Out of control. Queen of the junior high."

"I remember her sitting in my lap, calling me a butthead. That is so weird. Well, tell her I said hey." Molly was backing away when she paused, then came slowly back to give him a quick, tentative hug. "I'm sorry," she said, her voice damp with regret.

"For what?" Alex said. Another flutter of the shoulders and she was gone, heading for the ramp to the parking lot. He watched her legs move across the turf. He didn't know what to do with this age, with the ripples that remained after they made the leap to high school. The speed with which these girls erased you from the team photo was amazing. One moment, they were singing in the back seat of your van, begging you to take them by 7-Eleven for Slurpees; the next, they couldn't spare you a nod. Were they embarrassed they were once so dependent upon you? Annoyed they once asked for your advice?

Molly Koertje had disappeared, and Alex felt her loneliness as he walked to the car.

* * * *

When he turned into the driveway, he found Layla in his headlights, shooting free throws. Showing off, she hit four in a row before knocking one off the back of the rim.

"Did you eat?" he asked.

"At Lisa's. Chicken tenders."

"Where's your brother?"

Layla shrugged. Her I'm-better-off-without-him shrug.

"You don't have homework?"

"LAS." Language Arts. "Wanna play one-on-one."

He wanted his steak sandwich, but dinner could wait. It might be the last time she ever asked. "Five minutes."

"I'm taking it out in three."

He fumbled away the game when, trailing 10-9, she poked the ball away, drifted into the corner at the low end of the driveway and banked in the game-winner. He rebounded free throws for another five minutes before they called it a night. Olivia was just getting started on her sandwich when he came through the kitchen door, but he caught up soon enough, tossing out questions on Graham, picking through the remains of her day lobbying the movers and shakers, checking to see if a new property had been listed on the lake.

Olivia had long dreamed of retiring to one of the North Shore bungalows, and whenever Alex worked a kitchen on Summit, she spent the evening curled up with the MLS listings and their bank statements, trying to reconcile the two.

He had dropped down to the den to finish his Henry's with LeBron and the Celtics on TNT when Layla reappeared and asked if he had time to help with her LAS.

Alex swallowed the sigh. "What do you need? Vocabulary sentences?"

"Well, if that's the way you're going to be, never mind."

Alex shook his head. Not only was he on 24-hour call with homework, he had to pretend it was a privilege. "I'm not that tired. Whaddya got?"

"I need to write a movie review."

"Well …" He was trying to think of something easy. Was she old enough to watch "The Professional?"

"Dad. I've picked the movie."

Initiative! Initiative was good. "Which one?"

"*Mean Girls.*"

"*Mean Girls?*"

"Yep."

"She'll let you review *Mean Girls?*"

"Yeah. Emily and Lisa are reviewing it, too." Layla was staring at him as if she wasn't sure how he'd learned to breathe on his own.

"I've never seen *Mean Girls.*"

"I have. A bunch of times."

"Have you ever read a movie review?"

"In class. Mrs. Storm said you can't just tell what happens. A review is more than that."

"More than that."

"Yeah, like why's it's better or worse than other movies and whether there's a social com … ?"

"Commentary. Is there social commentary in *Mean Girls*?"

"Well, yeah."

"What is social commentary, by the way?"

Alex could hear the gears turning. He drained the beer.

"Like when someone comments on … society?"

"Close. Usually the way it works is that something happens in the movie that represents what happens to all of us at one time or another."

Lauren brightened. "You mean like when Regina gets hit by the bus?"

"Regina gets hit by a bus?"

"Almost."

"How am I supposed to help you if I've never seen it?"

Layla dug a DVD case out of her backpack. "Can you watch it tonight?"

"When's the review due?"

"Friday."

"Layla! I don't know if I have time …"

She picked up her backpack, gave him the whatever, and left.

LeBron was going to the hole, tossing a bank shot high off the backboard. He had design work to do, shipping orders to check. He stared at the DVD case.

And when he came to bed two hours later, he laughing. "The Daily Show'?" Olivia said, looking up from Richard Russo's *Empire Falls*.

"*Mean Girls*," Alex said, stripping off his shirt. She didn't resume the conversation until he eased himself into bed. "You're watching *Mean Girl*s."

"Layla needs help with her movie review. It's pretty funny."

"In a God-I-miss junior-high kind of way, I'm sure."

"There's a scene where Janis Ian gives Lindsay Lohan a diagram of the ..."

"Janis Ian? *The* Janis Ian?"

"Who's Janis Ian?"

"'Society's Child'? 'But that day will have to wait for awhile, baby I'm only society's child ...'"

"I'm supposed to recognize that song?"

"Back in the day."

"Well in the here and now, Janis Ian is a character in the movie. And she's ..."

"Who wrote this?"

"Tina Fey."

"Saturday Night Live Tina Fey?"

"No, the reigning MVP in women's roller derby."

"They still have women's ... oh. OK. You want to finish your story."

"As you wish. She gives Lindsay, the new girl in town, a diagram of the high school cafeteria, showing the seating chart for all the cliques. And she runs down the list. You've got the Asian Nerds, the Unfriendly

Black Hotties, the Burn-Outs, the Girls Who Eat Their Feelings, the Sexually Active Band Geeks, the Plastics …"

"The Sexually Active Band Geeks? And Layla has seen this how many times?"

"I'm thinking 10."

Olivia sighed and returned to her book.

"What?" Alex said.

Olivia swiveled off her left elbow and onto her back, wiggling to get comfortable. "She's too young for this and you're too old for this."

"You think? You're welcome to cut in."

"And interrupt this father-daughter bonding? I wouldn't think of it. I'm the principal and you're the playground. Tomorrow, I'll ask Graham if he needs help with the binge drinking."

Olivia readjusted one of the down pillows trapped between her shoulder and the headboard, and returned to Richard Russo. Alex was reaching for Alice Hoffman when her head popped up again. "We were the Presbyterians with the Push-Up Bras."

"We were the Hyper-Sensitive Student Body Officers."

"Drove the guys in youth group crazy."

"Drove the principal nuts."

"They only pretended to pray with their eyes closed."

"Given a choice, he used to say, he'd prefer to deal with the neo-Nazis."

"And you wonder why Layla has issues."

* * *

Queen of the junior high? Molly Koertje remembered the feeling. Floating down the hall like Anne Hathaway. Watching the guys shove each other as they lined up to ask her to dance. The eight straight free throws she hit in the fourth quarter of the league championship game and that hug her dad laid on her afterwards.

The room was dark save for the glow of the computer screen. Rolling the mouse beneath her fingers, she cut and pasted the AP story onto her Facebook page:

Frankfort, Ky. – An 11-year-old boy was killed at a local gun expo Saturday when the Uzi sub-machine gun he was firing kicked back on a practice range, discharging a bullet into his head.

The boy, whose name was not released, "was shooting the automatic machine gun down range," according to the police report, "when the recoil forced the weapon backward and the muzzle beneath his chin." Although county medical officials were on hand within minutes, the boy was pronounced dead at the scene.

The Uzi was originally designed for use by the Israeli military. The machine gun shoot at the Bluegrass Sportsman's Club, a private nonprofit that features nine firing ranges, was conducted under the supervision

of the Mason County Sheriff's Deputy .38-
Caliber All-Stars.

Too bad there wasn't a video, Molly thought. She scrolled down the page, to see if anyone had commented on the story about the clown who'd been crushed by a Waste Management truck as he exited his bachelor party. Nothing. She used to draw all sorts of feedback on these vignettes. Molly checked her friend tally. Only thirty-three left. Two more had disappeared since the weekend.

Molly Koertje? Tired of basketball? Never happened.

She couldn't remember the last time she'd seen either of her coaches from 8th grade. She'd written one of them a note that fall, after she'd been thrown out of practice for the third time. She told him how much fun she used to have and how different it was now, always fighting to stay on coach's good side, never knowing how ugly he'd get if her man scored on a back-door move. She remembered thanking him but ... god, did she ever even mail it? Probably not. So many things fell through the cracks back then.

Like Nate Delise. They were hanging out that fall. Nothing serious, but she was wearing his jersey to the football games. That's probably what got Coach going, asking her at a tournament in Seattle if she was screwing the guy. "You giving it up?" That's exactly what he said, riding up with her in the hotel elevator. "That's all the punk's looking for," he said. "All he cares about, getting some." Like what else could matter, right? Like Nate Delise couldn't possibly be sweet on the way she played the piano or the help she gave him with Algebra.

It was strange Coach would talk to her about sex, but no one else was, and he talked about it to a lot of people. Carrie was still playing for Black Tornado that fall and she swore Thalia was one of Coach's old girlfriends and he was trying to piss her off with all the sex-ed counseling.

There was a single notification at the top of her Facebook page, and Molly clicked on it. Heather Blain was asking her to join the Gay, Lesbian, Bi- and Transgendered Teens of Lake Oswego. Who the hell was Heather Blain?

She should have quit. Carrie did. "He's messing with our heads," Carrie said, and she was gone after Christmas, back to Silverton or Albany. Molly couldn't do that, and not just because her father kept saying Coach was teaching her how to play the game and deal with pressure. Molly was determined to prove she was good enough to play for him, better than the girls who were his favorites, better than the girls who'd gone D-1, better than the girls who left practice crying, better than the girls who only made headlines in the dugout at Westlake. She wanted to believe she was special. She wanted to be noticed, no matter what she had to do to get his attention.

She never gave up anything to Nate Delise, as it turned out; he was clumsy, a sophomore in high school. He didn't have a car, didn't have a line, didn't have Coach's experience. God, but he kept her off balance. One day, he'd tell her she was the only reason he looked forward to practice, the next he'd throw her ass out for not hustling back after a turnover. He was a jerk when he was pissed. That's why they ran their asses off for him. Anything to keep him happy. Anything to keep a smile on his face.

Mom was usually there after practice to pick her up, but there was one night, Laura's parent-teacher's night at Uplands, maybe, when they told her to catch a ride home with Carrie. That was the night Coach made her shoot 50 extra free throws and by the time she was done, no one else was around. "I'll drop you off," he said. "Might as well, it's on my way home."

He was pimping around in his Mercedes back then and halfway to Washington Square, he pulled over to the side of Scholls Ferry Road and asked if she wanted to drive. Are you kidding? She was 14. She felt like a big shot when she rode in the front seat, and he was asking her if she wanted to drive his 320E? She was shaking behind the wheel. She was so excited she barely noticed when he reached over and fixed the seatbelt between her breasts, like he was going out of his way to make sure she was comfortable. She was so excited she almost hit a telephone pole pulling out of the parking lot while he was sliding some Motown crap into the CD player, but the next 10 minutes were the best 10 minutes of her freshman year. She was so scared and he was so cool about it, giving her driving tips with his arm on the back of her seat, telling her she was too close to the center line, not losing it when she hit the brakes too hard coming up on the traffic lights. When she pulled onto 217 and pushed the speedometer, at his urging, up to 60, it was an out-of-body experience. She was so jazzed, so pumped, so desperate to get home and call up Jennifer or Alison to tell them what had happened that it might have been 10 or 20 seconds before she realized Coach had his hand on her boob.

Was this really happening or was she dreaming all of this? Were they really going 60 mph down the freeway while he was, like, groping her? Molly couldn't even focus. She was totally freaked out – no on had ever touched her there before – but once she realized what was happening, she couldn't separate the part of her that was screaming down the road at 100 decibels and the part of her trapped in the cup of his hand. And to make it even worse, or even better, depending on which seat you were in, she'd never seen such a smile on his face. For a reason she didn't understand, what he was doing on his side of the car had him as excited as she was on her side of the car. His head was back and his eyes were closed and he was singing along with the Temptations, but he looked so relaxed. Like he was cruising into a wet dream. Like the Black Tornado had scored the first 12 points in overtime. By the time they reached I-5, his hand was moving around on her boob almost as if he was looking for something he couldn't find. It hurt that night when she stared at those inconsequential bumps through the thin veil of her nightgown, stunned by the flush on her cheeks and the certainty that fear and embarrassment had sworn her to secrecy. It still hurt three days later when halfway through practice, Coach got so angry he told her to run 50 laps around the court while they scrimmaged and she ended up throwing up into the water fountain. He benched her that weekend, only letting her up during garbage time, acting as if she could do nothing right, which made her all the more desperate to make an impression on him. The next time Mom couldn't be there after practice, she purposely stayed behind, and she was still working on her jump shot when Coach came back inside the gym and asked her where the hell her ride was.

"I don't know," she said. "Can you ..." He was shaking his head, acting like she had some nerve and she wasn't sure what gave her the guts to ask, walking through the darkness of the parking lot, if he was gonna let her drive again.

"Yeah," he said, shaking his head like he wasn't sure she was worth the bother. "But lose the sports bra."

And she did. She stripped it off in the back seat of the Mercedes while he cued up the Temptations, afraid to look up and meet his eyes in the rear-view mirror.

Anything to keep a smile on his face.

The tropical fish were back on Molly's computer screen, floating without a care in the world. She followed the black swallowtail until her eyes teared up. The colored gravel was still sitting at the bottom of the empty fish bowl on her bookshelf. When her last fish died, she left him in the murky water for two weeks before Mom finally came in to change her sheets and nearly passed out from the smell.

Alison had changed her profile. Molly clicked on the photograph, which looked like a group hug at a

Duck game. Alison was in a relationship. Alison had graffiti all over her wall, and a photo gallery in which her left hand was choking the hell out of Jose Cuervo. Alison still had a soft spot for tequila.

They'd started drinking that summer before freshman year. It was no big deal, just pushing the edge of the envelope, Anne Hathaway betting on the roll of the dice in "Havoc." One of the baseball players always had a bottle at Westlake, and they passed it around in the outfield grass as the LO squad car cruised by. She never brought the stuff to school in a water bottle or spiked her Coke Slurpee in the bathroom at 7-Eleven, but she didn't hesitate to lie about the sleepover at Alison's house when Ryan Fowler, the skinny second baseman, had his party on the lake. Of course, she and Alison snuck out. She and Alison did everything together. They were manacled at the wrist and ankle, which made it all the more strange that Alison slipped out a window when the police arrived and Molly ran into the arms of the cop with the mustache by Ryan's boathouse.

She couldn't prove Coach called the cops about the party – the Lake Oswego police had a sixth sense about those blowouts and an MIP setting on their radar guns – but Coach wanted her to think he did. Better yet, he wanted her parents to think he did, if only to suggest he knew the girls like no one else and was looking out for them. Molly was grounded for two months after the MIP. She was under virtual house arrest, save for basketball. Basketball, her parents decided was part of the solution, not part of the problem. Basketball was discipline. Basketball was progress and self-esteem. Basketball was short-term sacrifice for long-term gain.

Basketball was Coach putting her hand on the front of his sweats and asking her if she dreamed about him the way he dreamed about her.

Coach was always so good at that, singling her out, cutting her off from every other lifeline. "No one wants you to succeed like I do," he used to say. "Nobody else understands how damn cool you are." The coaches at the high school only cared about their program and their summer camps. Her friends wanted to drag her down because they couldn't deal with her talent. Her teachers were too lazy to give her their individual attention. And her parents weren't willing to push her hard enough to guarantee she fulfilled her potential. They were good for that $200 each month but in the crusade to get her that scholarship at Santa Clara, they were dead weight. He alone had the magic. He alone knew the combination. He alone.

There were guns in the basement. Dad had a safe. And one of these days he was going to forget to lock it when he went out to the range in Sherwood.

She stared at Alison's picture. She changed her profile photo three times a week. Sometimes she was at the beach, sometimes the lake, a pumpkin patch on Sauvie Island or a dance at the high school, but she was always surrounded by a bodyguard of friends, their arms around her waist, smug belonging on her face. Molly barely remembered when her arm, her waist, her clunky eighth-grade butt was inside Alison's picture frame, but it was hard not to take each photo as a slap in the face, an acidic reminder of all the ways Alison had moved on and the many ways she'd been replaced.

It had been a year since Molly last heard from her. Molly had posted a link to a school shooting in West Virginia and Alison's was the only comment. "Stop it," she said. "You're better than this." Which proved just how out of touch they were.

W hen Alex reached the high school, 30 minutes before the launch of the 7th-8th grade basketball traveling team tryouts, six parents were waiting in the lobby or communing with a cigarette outside the gym doors. Ray Tripp, Jill's dad, was sitting on the curb, taking the end of summer much too personally. Jody's mom, Lisbeth, was leaning against the trophy case, flipping through *Vanity Fair*, and Melanie Harvey, Rachel's mom, was wrapped up in the Style section of the *Times*. Three parents Alex didn't recognize were thick against the gym doors, trying to peek around the sheets of paper Jerry Mulberry had taped over the windows to keep such parents at bay.

Mulberry, the Lakers' varsity coach, was running the 5th and 6th grade kids through their paces.

On the second and final night of tryouts, the groups would switch, the older kids running the gauntlet first. Alex and Mick might be allowed in the gym to watch the selection process ... and they might not, as they had daughters trying out for the team. Mulberry ran the show. In the traveling basketball program, everyone served at Mulberry's pleasure. The girls were being groomed for varsity basketball. In another year, the best of the bunch would be playing for Mulberry, or trying to attract his attention from the cheap seats on the JV bench. Like most coaches with tenure, Mulberry had invested considerable time in the feeder program. He'd also coached varsity for 22 years, winning a state title in the early '90s before Oregon City began its daunting run. He'd earned the right to set the schedule, bully the volunteer coaches, call the shots.

Alex settled behind the table in the gym lobby and set out the track-meet numbers and safety pins, even as Jill and Jody stumbled out the restroom door. They approached the table together and grabbed two numbers and a handful of pins. After checking their names off the list, Alex looked up to find Ray Tripp at his elbow, angling for a better look at the roster. "How many coming out?" he asked.

"Eighth graders?" Alex said. "Nineteen. Hopefully enough for a B team."

Ray hadn't shaved. Ray hadn't bathed, either, not this morning anyway. He was wearing three days of stubble and two nights of pesto. Alex wondered what he could possibly say to nudge him back out onto the curb.

"Any transfers?" Ray, Alex knew, was tangled in the math, counting the obstacles between Jill and the starting assignment that would lead, midway through her sophomore year, to that initial home visit with Pat Summit at Tennessee.

"I doubt it," Alex said. "They don't like us on the other side of the lake. You hanging around for the parents' meeting?" Ray stuck his hands in the pocket of his Oregon State windbreaker and walked off without reply.

By the time Mulberry let the 5th and 6th graders out, Alex had checked everyone off his list except Chelsea Lider. "I guess the rumors are true," he said when Mick wandered in, fashionably late. "Chelsea's playing for Black Tornado."

"Is she taking her dad with her?" Mick said. "Chelsea *and* Jack Lider for a relaxing year on the bench? I'd make *that* trade."

"You up for the meet-the-parents deal?"

"You must have the speech memorized. I'll see you inside."

"Mulberry's gonna let us sit in?"

Mick nodded. "I'll take care of Jerry."

When the girls disappeared into the gym, Alex led the parents outside. October was Oregon's surreal month; it held the summer heat like a barbecue pit in the dunes.

"Thanks for hanging around. I'll try to make this quick," Alex said. The veterans of previous campaigns looked oddly relaxed. Several other dads stood uncomfortably on the sidewalk, measuring him with distrust, wondering who died and made him coach. "I know most of you, and the others I'll …"

Alex stopped. He knew this guy. "Hey, Scott! Who are you- "

"Laura," Scott Koertje said. "Last of the Koertjes. Fresh from Our Lady of the Lake." Our Lady of the Lake was the largest Catholic parish in town. Ray Tripp was shaking his head, royally ticked he'd forgotten to scout the Catholic League.

"Good to see you again, Scott. Good to see all of you. Mick and I are back for our fourth year coaching A team. Eighteen girls have signed up, so there may be rosters changes, but our approach hasn't changed. We'll put a lot more emphasis on man-to-man this year, but most of you know how much Mick and I love the 1-3-1. We'll give every girl a minimum of eight minutes of playing time. We've signed … Scott?"

A tentative hand. "Eight minutes? How long are the games?"

"Eight-minute quarters. Thirty-two minutes, total."

"Playing time's not equal?"

"Hasn't been since 6th grade. We're hoping to keep nine players on the A-team," Alex continued. "Coach Mulberry may ask us to keep 10. We hope the girls who don't make A team play B, but we don't have a coach yet. Once we get the lineups, someone will step up, probably one of the dads. Maybe one of you."

Two dads in the back were nodding, as if to say, "In your dreams." Alex let it go. "A team will play five or six tournaments this year," he said, "including

Westview, Oregon City and Seaside. We go to the beach in December and, yes, we're back at the Surf & Sand. In league, Oregon City has returned. They had so much fun kicking our butts over the summer they can't wait for the regular season. Between the 14-game league schedule, playoffs and tournaments, I'm guessing the year costs $500."

"What about uniforms?" asked Melanie, Rachel's mom. She was married to the StairMaster. When Mick lobbied to put Rachel on the team as a spastic 5th grader, he had no idea she'd grow six inches in the summer of her 12th year; he just loved the idea of having a trophy mom behind the Laker bench.

"Jerry has last year's 8th grade uniforms for us, so we don't have to shell out for new ones. Shoes may be another issue. Varsity has switched from adidas to Nike. We may have to go along. Any other questions?"

"What happened to the Liders?" Ray asked. He had the gaunt look of nicotine withdrawal.

"I don't know. Maybe they're away for the weekend. We only require that you come to one of the tryouts."

Steve Kincaid raised a hand. "How many games altogether? And when's the league tournament?"

"Most of the tournaments have a four-game guarantee," Alex said, "so that's 18-20 tournament games. Fourteen league games. The league tournament is the first weekend in March. That makes about 40, but we'll be done by spring break.:

"How'd the team do last year?" Kincaid asked. "Sorry. I wasn't around."

"Beat Wilsonville in the finals."

"So when do we find out who made the team?" Melanie asked.

"We're back tomorrow night," Alex said. "Coaches will talk afterwards, then send the postcards out. Everyone filled one out, right? That doesn't mean your daughters won't hear something before that postcard arrives. Word does travel."

Scott Koertje stepped closer to the front of the scrum. "You said the team is going to Seaside? For the weekend?"

"Leave Friday, back Sunday," Alex said.

"Why Seaside? There aren't enough tournaments around here?"

Alex had no idea where Scott was going with this. They'd gone to Seaside while Molly was on the team. "The clam chowder is great and the competition sucks. Heck, parents even go bowling together one night."

"Parents go along?"

"You couldn't pay me enough to baby-sit these girls, Scott."

Scott laughed, looking oddly relieved.

"We should be done at 6:30," Alex said. "See you then." He was halfway through the gym door when Ray grabbed his elbow and said, "Can we talk?"

The man was frighteningly earnest. There was enough sweat on his forehead to baste a large pizza. "C'mon, Ray," Alex said. "Call me later."

"Two minutes." He looked so hang-dog Alex wanted to slap him. He made no attempt to disguise his impatience. "Alright, Ray, what?"

Ray had his eyes fixed on the concrete walk. "Jill's been practicing," he said. "Every night. I'll go over there and Noah tells me she's out on the driveway in the dark, shootin' and shootin' some more. I don't know if she's doing homework but ..."

"Hey, Ray, c'mon. You don't have to sell Jill to me."

"You're damn right I do. I know how this is gonna go. How long you been coaching my daughter? Three years? You even see her anymore? Or is it all decided?"

Alex opened his mouth, then shut it again, his jaw tightening. He didn't remember his last face-to-face with Jill. She didn't like him – no, she didn't *trust* him – and she didn't pretend otherwise.

"You see the kid who bikes down to Noah's every Saturday and brings me back a chocolate-chip bagel? You see the kid who sits at the end of her brother's bed and reads him to sleep, knowing he's afraid of the dark? What about the girl who is constantly humiliated 'cause she can't meet her mother's expectations? You see anyone in that crowd, Alex, or just the same old bench-warmer?"

Over Ray's shoulder, Alex saw Margaret standing at the door of her Miata, looking on with undisguised dismay, terrified her ex was torpedoing her daughter's hoop season before the opening tip.

"She's only 13, Coach. Things are just getting started for her. You don't think she hasn't figured it out? That you've given up on her?"

"I haven't given up …"

Ray held up a weary hand. "Maybe you have, maybe you haven't. I'm pissin' you off, and that doesn't get me anymore. I know Jill has an attitude. Gets it from her mom. I know she doesn't play defense like your girl does. I'm not saying she should be starting. I just don't want her thinking, every time one of her coaches yanks her off the court, that she's a disappointment. I don't want her believing 'fore she gets to high school that there are girls who are going to be successful and there are girls who aren't, and she's locked out. Not just in basketball, but in everything else. I want her to know that if she works hard, she can change things. She can practice every night in the dark and someone might notice other than her little brother. Is that asking too much?"

Margaret was striding purposefully toward them. As if he could feel the barometer dropping, Ray shook his head, then headed across the parking lot in the other direction.

Alex had to pound on the gym door three times before one of the Laker seniors trotted over to open it. The girls were running a sloppy five-person weave. Standing at mid-court with a whistle in his mouth, Mulberry gave Alex a curt nod as he sat down next to Mick in a row of plastic chairs. "What'd I miss?" he asked.

"And here I was, congratulating you on having the good sense to head home," Mick said. "It's ugly out there."

A slender blonde took a pass from Lisa at the elbow and, after two long strides and a deft dribble, laid the ball gently off the glass with the left hand, generally a misguided weapon in 8th-grade girls' basketball.

"Who's the southpaw?" Alex asked.

"Koertje's kid. The good news. Nice hands. Great wheels."

Alex watched quietly as the girls sliced up and down the court. The next time Jill received the ball at the end of the break, she fumbled it off her knee. Instead of galloping after it, she dropped her head and disappeared into the crowd beneath the basket.

"What about Jill?"

"What about her? Same old same old."

* * *

They hit Chili's on Kruse Way for dinner. They grabbed a booth in the bar, where the three TVs were turned to the Colts-Bengals game on ESPN. Lisa and Layla demanded an Awesome Blossom and peeled strips of onion from the bulb as Alex and Mick split three Hefeweizens. The girls were loose and talkative. Peyton Manning had just pump-faked the safety and hit Marvin Harrison for a 45-yard TD when Layla announced, "I don't like Jerry."

"You don't?" Alex said, reaching for a tortilla chip. "I hope you told him that."

"Yeah, right," Lisa said.

"I'm serious. If you think he's washed up, let him know so he'll clean out his locker and get out of the way before you try out for varsity."

"I'm not trying out for basketball," Layla said. "I want to play soccer."

"All the better. When you tell Jerry he sucks, he'll know he's getting an objective, unbiased opinion."

"What are you guys hearing from Chelsea?" Mick asked. "You ever see her?"

"She's in Spanish with me," Lisa said. "I hate her. She aces every test."

"Well, sit next to her," Mick said. "Has Black Tornado had tryouts?"

"We don't talk about basketball that much."

"Since when?"

"Chelsea says her dad never shuts up about it."

"I'm so jealous," Layla said. "I wish I could get my dad to talk about basketball."

Alex was looking for the check when Rachel came through the door with her grandparents. After a flurry of whispers, Lisa and Layla asked for quarters and 10 minutes in the game room.

"Five," Mick said. As Lisa exited, quarters in hand, he turned to Alex: "See anything you like tonight?"

Alex drained his glass. Joseph Addai picked up eight years off tackle. "Laura Koertje reminds me of her sister. Smooth and quick. She might be able to play the middle if Chelsea bails. I liked Mattie; she's been working on her post moves. Jody doesn't look like she touched a ball all summer. Like our daughters, in other words."

"We're thin. Mulberry says he'd rather go with eight or nine. Give the keepers more playing time."

"What'd he say about Chelsea?"

"Chelsea? Nothin'. He ... whoa ..." Mick was suddenly focused on the door of the bar. "Eddie! Eddie! How ya doing?"

"Hey, Mick," Eddie Alvarado said, keeping his hands in his pockets. The newspaper columnist was at least 6-foot-3, runner thin and ashen blond. His eyes were working the room.

"Mick, this is a good friend, Alex Blessing." Alvarado held out his hand and Alex took it. "You want to join us?"

"I'm meeting someone," Alvarado said, "but I don't see them." He grabbed a chair. He looked like he'd lost a few fights since he'd updated his mug shot. "Another Nike guy?" he asked Alex.

"Granite and marble work," he said.

Alvarado leaned forward. "No shit. Kitchen counters?"

"You can't afford him," Mick said.

"I'm remodeling," Alvarado said. "Don't like anything I've seen. Can I call you?"

"Sure," Alex said, digging a card out of his wallet and handing it across the table.

Alvarado snared a passing waitress and asked for an IPA. "How do you guys know each other?"

"We coach a girls' traveling team," Mick said. "Which reminds me: You ever hear of a guy named Taze Elliott?"

"Tell me that's not a Portland cop," Alvarado said.

"No, an AAU coach. Coaches a select team."

"I don't waste much time in sports."

"Hold on," Mick said, as much to Alex as Alvarado. "This gets interesting. I'm playing poker out at Pumpkin Ridge with an agent named Steve Sikorsky. Lives in the Bay Area. Gets around. And he starts telling me about Elliott. Sikorsky went to high school with him in Oakland. They played on a state-championship team. Ski sat on the bench. Taze ran the point."

"How many beers before you guys started comparing high-school stats?" Alvarado asked.

"He knew I was coaching. He has grade-school kids. He wanted to know what sort of background checks they ran on me."

"Background checks?" Alex said. "Why?"

"Taze Elliott."

A Colts fan two booths away cursed as the Bengals' Chad Johnson took a Carson Palmer' pass in full stride and pranced into the end zone.

"Junior year, he scores 38 in the state finals," Mick continued. "Two months later, he's nailed for statutory rape."

Alex stared at Mick. "Rape?"

"That's what Ski remembers."

"Arrested? Or convicted?" Alvarado asked.

"Ski was pretty sure Elliott ended up in a juvie lock-up somewhere. He never came back to school. A lot of stories were floating around. Black kids had their version, white kids had theirs. I guess the school pulled in blacks from the inner city and white kids from the hills east of Oakland. Elliott was bigger than the racial divide. Star of the team. Tark recruitied him. Screwed around a lot. Nobody complained until he got a 14-year-old pregnant. A 14-year-old whose father had a law office in North Beach."

"And frat brothers at the DA's office," Alvarado said.

"It was a big deal, 25 years ago. Ski doesn't know how much ever got in the papers but everyone at school knew the story. That's why Ski was surprised a couple years back when he heard Elliott was coaching. What kind of background checks are you guys running up here, he asked me. How can a story like that disappear?"

The waitress set the IPA down in front of Alvarado. He didn't pick it up. "This guy was, what, sixteen? Probably tried as a juvenile if the case even went to court. Or maybe he pled to some third-degree sex assault BS so the girl didn't have to testify. A lot of stuff from your teenage years is expunged. For which you and I should be thankful."

"They did background checks on us," Alex said. "I remember filling one out."

"Three Rivers League took our social-security numbers and drivers license," Mick said. "I don't know what they ever did with them. Black Tornado is a different deal. Elliott put the team together. They play by his rules."

"Wait a minute," Alvarado said. "A black guy has a team called Black Tornado?"

"We've coached against him," Alex said. "Subtle isn't his style."

Alvarado was suddenly on his feet. "My interview just showed up," he said, collecting the beer. "I'll call you, Alex, about the kitchen." He nodded at Mick, and was gone.

"Taze Elliott, huh?" Alex said. "The 14-year-old have the baby?"

"Ski said there were different versions of that story, too."

"I'm not sure what makes Elliott the bad guy. Half the LO football team is screwing 14-year-olds. They'll be scouting ours this time next year. That's what high-school jocks do."

"Ski said there was other stuff going on. He blames Elliott for screwing up his senior prom."

"Ski still *remembers* his senior prom?"

"His date was some girl named Stacy. After the prom, they went into the highlands at the north end of the Golden Gate to drink Boone's Farm, mess around and watch the sun come up. Ski said he had Stacy semi-naked on his USC Trojan blanket when she came unglued."

"What does that have to do with Taze?"

"Took Ski an hour to figure that out. Stacy was going out with Elliott before he got arrested. They were out one night in Elliott's Barracuda when Taze grabbed her by the back of the neck and forced her to go down on him. When she fought back, he slapped her twice in the face and booted her out of the car. Middle of nowhere. She told Ski she still has nightmares about the guy."

"How'd Ski find out Elliott was coaching again?"

"Taze tracked him down."

"What?"

"Hustling. Looking for an agent. He told Ski he was working with a high-school junior who would make people forget Cheryl Miller. Elliott asked Ski if any WNBA teams would be interested in the first high-school girl to jump to the pros. All he wanted, Elliott said, was 40 percent of the agent fee when she signed her first contract."

"Ski go for this?"

"There's no money in WNBA contracts."

Lisa and Layla came around the corner of the bar, their pony-tailed heads together, their voices low. They were losing their grip on the tans they'd picked up over the summer on the lake. They could have been twins.

"We're still waiting for the check," Mick said.

"Wait by the front door," Alex said. "We'll be there in two minutes." The girls, strangely enough, complied without complaint.

Mick slid out of the booth and crossed the bar. While he paid for the beers, Alex sucked on the red-and-white mint from the maitre d' stand.

"So, do we call Jack Lider?" he asked when Mick returned.

"With what? Ski's senior prom?"

"If my daughter was playing for a convicted rapist, I'd want to know."

"Jack might be a suspicious about the motives behind that call."

"Maybe," Alex said as the blond hostess with the official Chili's headset begged them to come again soon. "Maybe I'll make an anonymous call."

"There's a pay phone down at the 7-Eleven."

*   *   *

Since she walked through the door at 6:10 p.m., Chelsea had read 45 pages of "To Kill a Mockingbird," and polished off her math. She might have been finished the rough draft of her history project if not for the parade of texts and the sweet, lush scent of the gnocchi and gorgonzola Mom was nursing on the stove. Nursemaid was the best Mom could do in the kitchen; the gnocchi was from Trader Joe's – or Trader Giotto's, as it said on the amber-and-yellow package – and it signaled that family dinner wasn't in the cards. Her father liked his pasta fresh, his sauce red, the wine glass full.

Her hair was wet. Loosed from the usual bands, it hung thick and black on her shoulders. Jimmy Donovan sat next to her in the cafeteria three days ago and suggested she had the best hair in school. Jimmy was a 5-foot-1 geek who barely came up to her chin and she guessed he was testing her resistance to a Halloween dance invite, but she appreciated the compliment. It was a relief when a guy wasn't focused on her butt.

She was typing the obligatory "LOL" when she heard the front door open, then rumble shut. For a moment, she thought her father was home and the gnocchi in serious jeopardy, but the clumsy rhythm of the entrance was unique to Nick. Chelsea wandered into the family room, trying not to look too obvious, too curious about this intimate stranger. He was standing inside the refrigerator door, reviewing his options, a Snapple Lemonade in the fist parked atop the door.

"Save a little of that cold for the rest of us," Mom said. "And don't eat anything. Dinner's on the table in five."

Nick shrugged, as if dinner was far more than he'd planned on, then squeezed onto a stool at the kitchen island. He was painfully thin; his coat hung from his shoulders like a cheap suit on a broken wire hanger. His hair fell dark and greasy over his collar. It was longer each time Chelsea saw him.

As he opened the Snapple, he acknowledged her with a lazy nod. "Hey," she said, opening the cabinet door next to the microwave and pulling out three plates. The lace plate mats and cloth napkins were already on the table.

Mom pushed a wooden spoon through the mulch of pasta and chips of frozen cheese. "Your pants are filthy," she said, like a weatherman reporting a mud slide. "Where've you been?"

"Stopped by Alex Blessing's place after work."

"What for?"

"Checking it out," Nick said. Folding a cloth napkin, Chelsea wondered just how old you had to be to signal "piss off" to your parents without ever opening your mouth. Nick was 17 and a senior. He had enough credits that he only went to the high school half days; then he drove his '91 Mercedes downtown and worked weird hours at a Guitar Center on the east side. Although Chelsea knew the store closed at six, Nick was rarely home before she turned out her light. He wasn't avoiding her, she knew. He was avoiding their father.

"Well, don't sit down on anything else before you get a shower," Mom said. "You want anything to drink with dinner?"

Nick raised his Snapple in a mock toast, then moved slowly to the dining room table, theatrically laying a copy of *The Oregonian* sports section atop the seat of his chair. No one said another word until everyone was parked in front of the gnocchi. "You wanna say grace?" Mom asked Chelsea, right on cue. It was a question that never came up when Dad was at the table.

Thank you, O Lord, for these thy gifts, which we are about to receive through the bounty of Jesus Christ, the Lord.

Chelsea picked at her food. Nick had more of an appetite. Mom watched him eat with a combination of pity and gratitude. His bowl was clean before he looked up again. "How's basketball?" he asked.

"Harder than before," she said, staring at the hollows of his cheeks, choosing her words carefully.

"Get used to it."

An odd shudder of confidence emboldened her. "You want to shoot later?"

Nick drained the lemonade. "It's 40 degrees out there, Chelse. You filming a Nike commercial?"

"I need to practice."

He stared at her for a moment, as if remembering an old friend, then pushed back from the table and carried his plate to the sink. He left the kitchen without a word.

She read another 40 pages of Harper Lee, then slid into a pair of sweatpants and her traveling team sweatshirt. The basketball was where she'd left it, in the wicker basket outside the front door, and she carried it out into the amber tents beneath the streetlights. Nick's Mercedes was parked by the curb, all dull paint and unattended dents. She ran her fingers along the hood, savoring its flaws. Like her brother, she loved that it wasn't a Volvo.

The sky was clear, the moon almost full, the outdoor hoops 211 steps away, illuminated by the half-hearted security lights below the eaves of the elementary school. She swung right into her routine. She couldn't hear her father's voice but it still provided the cushions and bumper guards for her movements. *Keep that elbow straight. Aim for the back of the rim, not the front. Never take a shot in practice you wouldn't take in a game.* She started with a small arc, five feet from the hoop, banking short jumpers off the fiberglass backboard, moving left to right, baseline to baseline, then reversing course. After two round trips, she took a step back and repeated the drill, alternating set shots and jump shots, bank shots and swishes. It wasn't cold enough to see her breath, but Chelsea could feel the night air in her lungs. Focus, by now, came naturally. Squaring up. Ball on her fingertips. Air under the ball. She was a creature of so many habits.

When she extended the arc to 17 feet, and she began to tire, she missed now and then. *Three seconds left*, she told herself, *down by one*. She shanked an 18-footer, then banked one in at the buzzer. She was chasing the rebound when she felt the shadow at the edge of the court, watching her, almost invisible against the arborvitae.

"Let me guess," Nick said. "Back of the rim."

She giggled. She couldn't help herself. She was that glad to see him. "Wanna play P-R-I-C-K?" she asked.

He laughed. An inside joke. He held out hands and she hit them mid-chest with a bounce pass. Nick spun the ball in his fingers and, seemingly without aiming, lofted a 22-footer from the left elbow.

It fell three feet short. "Been awhile," Nick said. As she chased down the ball, he headed for the backboard. "You shoot. I'll rebound."

Chelsea banked in a 14-footer. "Rebound? What rebound?"

"That used to be my line." He wasn't smiling.

"I remember." She shot again – *back of the rim* – and swished it from 16. "I remember everything."

"Everything?"

"You. And basketball."

The light was lousy. Shadows were everywhere. "No kidding," Nick said, his voice flat. "My brilliant career."

"Well, you're the best I ever saw," Chelsea drawled, in her best Wilford Brimley. She strained for a read of his face. She couldn't tell if he was smiling or not, so she cut to her right with the ball and pushed off for a jumper, mimicking, as best she could, her brother's weird overhead shooting form.

Another air ball. Nick just let the ball bounce toward the stairs that dropped to the wood-chip playground and the tether-ball poles.

She'd grown up around Volvos and basketball because that's what the family was all about. Volvos were their father's business; basketball was everything else. When Chelsea was still in elementary school, he'd pull into the driveway, tell Mom to toss dinner in the warming oven, then drag Nick to the outdoor court at Westlake Park. If you wanted a piece of the guy, or to feel part of the family, you went along. You ran down rebounds. Eavesdropped on his hoop seminars. Tried not to get in the way.

For three years straight – ending the winter Nick was in 8th grade and Chelsea still stuck in 4th – every weekend was a basketball tournament. Dad was the coach, Nick was the star and Chelsea sat with Mom behind the bench. Dad was a lava dome on the sidelines, always on the edge of eruption, but Nick was the show. Nick was so good that Chelsea fell in love with the game watching him. He wasn't exceptionally quick, or exceptional in any other way, but he played with a radiant confidence that overwhelmed both opponents and the flaws in his game. Nick had the unique ability to instantly forget the turnover, the bad pass, the ill-advised shot, to walk away from his mistakes. Their father was a relentless kibitzer on the sidelines, but he was smart enough to keep his mouth shut whenever Nick screwed up because Nick was already focused on what he needed to do to erase the mistake and regain momentum.

This being Lake Oswego, two Trail Blazer offspring were on the team, one of them duty-bound to end up 6-foot-8, but both played in Nick's shadow on the way to high school. Their genes were no match for his instincts, his leadership, his delight at having the ball in his hands. What's more – and Chelsea only figured this out later, when she'd played enough to understand the difference between naturals and synthetics – his instinct was not to lord his leadership over anyone. His confidence was contagious. The team lost a total of two league games in three years.

He didn't make varsity as a freshman. Nick and his father argued about that for most of the season. The high-school team was carrying seven seniors, two of them point guards, and the coach decided Nick was better off playing 32 minutes a night on JV. Nick accepted that; his father didn't. He complained to the principal, then sulked high in the stands, sullen and bitter, before boycotting the games altogether. He derided Nick for accepting the second-rate status that came with a 5:45 p.m. starting time.

"Derrick and DaRon only leave the bench during garbage time," Nick argued. "I'm averaging 27 a game."

"Your coach is never there to see it," his father shot back. "He's in the locker room with the prime-timers."

At season's end, the coach told Nick he would suit up for the state playoffs. The day before the second-round game against Barlow, as the first-string worked on its half-court trap, Nick spun out of a double-team at mid-court and tore his ACL. The injury was so severe that doctors at St. Vincent spent 11 hours putting the knee back together. That didn't stop Jack Lider from asking the lead surgeon if summer basketball was out of the question. Nick wore his cast until the middle of May and didn't start jogging until August. He was in no hurry to put the new knee to the test, and the longer he stalled, the more frustrated his father became. Their arguments were the main course at family dinner until Nick stopped coming home for dinner. At the end of try-outs, Nick was the starting point guard, once again, on JV. Two nights later, he came home from practice as Mom was serving lemon meringue pie and announced he'd quit the team.

Jack Lider dropped his fork. "You what?"

"I quit."

"You can't quit."

"Yeah, that's what Fitzgerald said. I changed his mind."

"How's that?"

"I told him I'd kiss his wife's ass before I'd ever play basketball for him again."

Chelsea had seen Mrs. Fitzgerald work that ass into the seat of her Ford Windstar in Starbucks. Nick, she concluded, had lost his mind or his taste for basketball. Jack Lider decided it was the former. He grounded Nick for a month. When their mother told him he couldn't punish Nick for quitting a sports team, Jack didn't come home for several nights. Before the arguing was done, Jack announced that Nick – unlike every other Lider for three generations – would not rise on his16[th] birthday and discover a new Volvo in the driveway.

"I thought you were rebounding for me," Chelsea said, trotting after the ball.

"Rebound? What rebound?"

She rehearsed the question as she retrieved the ball from beneath the deluxe Jungle Gym. "So, how's your car?" she asked as she climbed back up onto the court.

"My car? Running on empty. Wanna trade your allowance for another lap around the parking lot?"

Chelsea shook her head. She'd decapitated a 7-foot sapling the last time Nick let her drive the Mercedes. Besides, she was saving her allowance for a laptop.

"Mom said you switched teams," Nick said. "Dad sucker-punch your coach?"

Chelsea picked up the ball at the foul line. "Dad said Alex and Mick aren't serious enough."

"About what?"

Chelsea couldn't remember the last time a conversation with Nick had moved this far. She didn't know if he was really interested or just looking for another reason to rip their father. "Basketball," she said. Wasn't that obvious?

"Who you playing for now?"

"Black Tornado."

"Who's coaching?"

"Taze Elliott."

"What kind of a name is Taze?"

Chelsea stopped dribbling the ball. "I don't know."

"Is *he* serious enough?"

"I guess."

"Black guy?"

"African-American," Chelsea corrected him.

"Whatever." Nick put the hood of his sweatshirt up. "Damn, it's cold. Didn't he used to coach DaRon? Big neck? Mean-looking? I remember seeing him at games, sucking up to the Blazer dads."

Chelsea dribbled beneath the basket and reversed the ball in. The cold was quietly kneading the feeling from her hands. "His neck isn't *that* big."

"He like your game?"

"He doesn't know my name."

"Are you starting?"

"Are you *trying* to sound like Dad?"

The dark hole in Nick's sweatshirt turned toward her, then slowly swayed from side to side. "Sorry," he said, with a trace of sarcasm. "I'll go back to not giving a shit."

"You haven't come to one of my games in two years."

"Bull. I saw you play last spring."

"West Linn. Seventh grade. You got there at halftime." That dark hole turned toward her again. "I went to every one of your games," Chelsea continued. "Every one."

"Congratulations," Nick said. "You have better memories than I do."

He watched silently as Chelsea hit three in a row from the baseline, then added, "A better jump shot, too."

"Maybe that's 'cause I practice," Chelsea said. "Do you miss that?"

"What?"

"Practice."

He shook his head. "Not really. Or the baggage that comes with it."

"I don't know if Dad would ever talk to me except for basketball," Chelsea said.

Nick pulled his hands from the sweatshirt pockets, and gestured for the ball. This time his shot caught rim. "He hasn't wasted more than a sentence on me since I quit. Which makes sense. Hoop was all we ever talked about anyway."

The headlights of a passing car strafed the court. The siren of a police car, a mile out on the interstate, swelled and faded. Chelsea had the ball in her hands, but she didn't know what to do with it, so she stood quietly, staring at her brother as his breath leaked out in small pockets of fog.

"I'm done," Nick said. "You coming with me?"

Chelsea shook her head. "I need to practice."

"Back of the rim, Chelse, back of the rim."

When he disappeared through the hedge, Chelsea stood still for a moment, inexplicably depressed by the loneliness of the court. She thought about running after him and walking her brother home, but, instead, she slowly turned back to the basket. She squared up, set the ball on her fingertips, tucked in her elbow and tried to forget about everything but the weave of the net. She was a creature of so many habits.

The downstairs mobile rang at 11:47 p.m. Olivia was already asleep, Alex keeping an eye on Stephen Colbert. The call had answering machine written all over it, but the hour was so far beyond the pale that Alex set off looking for wherever Layla had abandoned the phone two hours earlier. "This better be good," he said when he found it wedged between the toaster and an open sleeve of cinnamon-raisin bagels.

"Alex? Casey Waiwaiole. What the heck is going on?"

"That's my line."

"I'm serious. What's the deal with the merger?"

"What merger?"

"Southside, Westside and Lake Oswego. Pooling players to form a super club."

"When?"

"Damn soon. I'm the chum bucket in the food chain."

Waiwaiole – an old gym rat from the noon pick-up games at Lewis & Clark – coached the Dynamo, the U-14 soccer team on Portland's eastside. They played on a lumpy field at Gresham High. Layla's team, Malice, had beaten them 2-0 on Saturday.

"What the hell is a super club?"

"A real-estate buddy does business in Wilsonville. He tells me three soccer clubs have an option to buy 10 acres of farmland on the freeway south of town so they can build a giant soccer complex. You haven't heard any of this?"

"Nope."

"Then why the hell am I calling you?"

"I think we've covered that," Alex said. "I'm still stuck on 'super club.'"

"It ain't complicated. How many games Malice win at regionals?"

Alex sighed. With the mercury at 102, the Malice was smoked 9-0 by a group of pony-tailed assassins from California, then shut out in an embarrassing 1-0 loss to Montana. "None. Everyone was in a great mood on the drive home."

"How many goals did your daughter's team score?"

"I'm hanging up."

"Don't take it personal, man. Lake Oswego was outclassed. The Oregon champ always is, going up against all-star squads from Arizona and California, teams that draw from thousands of U-14 girls. How do you compete with that?"

"You're asking me?"

"You form a super club. Pool resources. Assemble a group of all-stars. Just like they do in Arizona and California."

"On 10 acres of pasture south of Wilsonville."

"You need your own soccer complex, or the local school district might boot you off the field to make room for rec. Empire building, amigo."

"Wait a minute. You said three clubs, right?"

"Southside, Westside and LO."

"Which means you're blending three A teams into one … and giving only one-third as many girls the chance to play A."

"Cold, ain't it?"

"What's the point? Those are the state's three best teams at U-14. Combine them and you knock two-thirds of those girls down to the next level. Doesn't make sense."

"It's not about sense, it's about dollars and prestige. You ever talk to these yahoos, Alex?"

Colin Welch, the head of the Lake Oswego Soccer Club, was Layla's coach. He was a British expatriate, a liter of ego in a pint-sized jar. "As little as possible."

"Well, it's all about them. Their resume. Their reputation. They all want to punch the ticket that takes them from a flea-bag operation in LO to that U.S. national team in California."

"Do me a favor, will you?"

"I'm listening"

"Stay in touch with me on what's happening in Wilsonville. I'll go down to the soccer club tomorrow and ask them what's going on."

"Don't mention my name."

"I'll play stupid."

"Born for the role."

*   *   *

No matter when they pulled up in front of Gwen's house, 15 minutes early or running desperately late, Gwen needed three minutes to slip out the door. Peggy Sue, Gwen's mom, was anal as all get out, Layla remembered from sleep-over days, and Layla could see her at the foot of the stairs, clipboard in hand, running down the checklist: "Homework? Backpack? Lunch? Cell phone? Tampons?" All the while, Layla and her dad sat in the Durango with the motor running, listening to ESPN Radio. She'd never admit it to her dad, but she found the sports riffs a lot more relaxing than the creepy junior-high obsession with sex on the Morning Zoo.

About the time Layla reached for the cell phone, the Parkers' door popped open and Gwen came gliding down the sidewalk, backpack on her shoulder, Tootsie Roll pop in her mouth. "Hola!" she would always say as she settled into the back seat. "Good morning, Mr. Blessing."

"Hey, Gwen," her dad would reply, checking to make sure Peggy wasn't standing at the front door with whatever Gwen left on the kitchen counter, then making one dumb-ass stab at conversation. "How are your parents?" Or, "How's baseball going for your brother?" It was just as well. Other than a question about Spanish or choir, she didn't have much to say to Gwen, either. They were inseparable in sixth grade but that was two earth-shaking Apple inventions ago. There was no reason to carpool to school, other than the usual guardrails of junior-high life: Their parents were stuck in the '60s, convinced nothing ever changed. They sure weren't gonna ride the bus with the loners and losers. Even strange company was preferable to showing up at school alone.

"... already had four games rained out," Gwen was saying, completing the update on Max Parker's uneventful career at second base. Layla waited to make sure the conversation didn't take a wild swing toward the batting cage, then asked, "Are we late?"

This wasn't a difficult question, but her father had something on his mind. She could always tell. "The big hand is still on the nine," he said, but she felt the Durango pick up speed. Speed was good. Speed meant extra time. Extra time meant options.

There were two doors into LOJ, which was laid out like a high-back chair. The main entrance brought you into a sprawling lobby, the kingdom of the Goths, and direct access to the cafeteria, the main office and the gauntlet of B hall. The door was always open at 6:30 a.m. so the cafeteria chefs could get an early start on torching the grilled-cheese sandwiches. The door at the bottom of A hall, on the other hand, didn't open until 7:55 a.m., five minutes before morning announcements, no matter how much Alberta was in the air. That door led straight to band camp. Everyone with a cello case had a locker on A hall, reducing traffic to a crawl. No one but band geeks and clueless seventh graders used the back door. No one in her right mind braved the front door alone.

Now and then, everyone's timing was so out of whack that Gwen and Layla took the plunge together, but more often they tumbled out of the Durango with hurried goodbyes and latched on to their disparate friends without so much as a nod at one another. It was their silent concession that the world had changed. The need to survive superseded their previous vows to double-date at senior prom.

Jackie and Samantha were waiting for Gwen; Lisa had the life preserver out for Layla. She'd gone with the Guess jeans and sweatshirt ensemble, which screamed   I-showered-the-night-before-so-I-could-sleep-in, but she was wearing the cool Charlotte Russo sandals and her favorite hoop earrings. Morning updates were unnecessary; they'd exchanged a volley of texts before they jumped into their separate limos and were forced to hide their phones from the chauffeurs.

"Should we wait for Rachel?" Lisa asked, her backpack still at her feet. Rachel was an automatic late slip. "Thirty seconds," Layla said, waiting for a flash of the Harveys' Subaru. Lisa waited five, then maroon backpack to her shoulder and said, "C'est la vie."

When they stepped into the lobby, the clock over read 7:54 and the Goths had cleared out. The Goths were a small frat at LOJ, a spectacular starting line-up but precious little bench. They camped in the darkest corner of the lobby at 7:30 a.m., repairing the chips in their black fingernail polish. They were the gentlest cluster at LOJ. They didn't care what people thought. They didn't have a smile for your face and the bird for your back, nor engage in the leering mockery that was B hall morning ritual.

Unless you were an untouchable – Chelsea Lider or K-Smut popular – you caught it from all sides. You heard the derision when the guys scoped your bod, and in the sideway glances in the bathroom mirrors. You felt the judgment of God every time two or more gossip girls gathered together. And you saw it coming as you worked your way up the hall, dodging convoys and science projects.

In seventh grade – was that only a year ago? – they were lost sheep, eyes on the floor, books in front of their chests. As eight graders, each clique planted its flag at one locker or another and camped there each morning. The volume of sneering depended on the proximity of teachers and talent shows, the week's athletic competitions, the melodrama of the day. It must be like this in a prison yard, Layla decided: You invited the shank if you tried to ignore it. Each morning you had to remind the local gangstas you wouldn't be bullied.

"What time you get to sleep?"

"Two. Maybe. I hate Spanish. Then K-Smut called," Lisa said, frowning at a fresh update on her Razor.

"Hey, Em … aren't you going to LA? Em? What's the … K-Smut called? What did he want?"

"I dunno. Never said."

"Hold on … hey, what kind of cookies today for break? Thank you!"

"It's always chocolate chip. Stop eating that junk, Layla."

"We're out of cereal and the lunch cookies suck."

"You want my banana?"

"You *have* been talking to K-Smut."

"It's not my fault if … Shit! … Can you believe
.."

"That should be illegal."

"It *is* illegal. Hawkins is death on spaghetti straps, even without the black bra. He'll send her home."

"Hey, Suzanne! Not before she draws a crowd."

The Goths weren't the only cluster in uniform. Each clique had its unique fashion sense. On a Saturday at Washington Square, each group camped out at its favorite store. Abercrombie. Nordstrom. Victoria's Secret. Dressing alike was another line of defense, sucking you into the heart of the clan. If you followed the Alpha Female's lead, she couldn't ridicule your outfit.

"C'mon, we gotta run. Gonna be late."

"Hi, Jill! Jesus … were they laughing at us?"

"She is so two-faced. I bet …"

"She knocked me into my locker last week. With her shoulder! On purpose!"

"You got a great left foot, Layla, use it."

"She'd never see it coming."

"Excuse me ... hey! Knock it off!"

"Baby Huey."

"Oprah!"

"Same diff. Hey, Mr. Buchanan!"

"He's so weird. I can't believe you like him."

Lisa gave her flip of the hair. All teachers played favorites. They were murder on some kids and let others break all the rules. Mrs. Laidlaw hated girls. Mr. Chen was toughest on the Asian kids. Mr. Buchanan had never been quite the same, Lisa realized, after she wore the ridiculously short jean skirt that showcased her Cabo legs. It was weird to realize Mr. Buchanan might be thinking the same stuff as those creeps at 7-Eleven who froze in front of the beer case when you walked by, then followed you into the parking lot, but Lisa didn't see the harm in showing up early to class now and then. Especially when Mr. Buchanan was telling her what merited special attention when she was studying for Thursday's pop quiz. Or turning a blind eye to her texting in class. Who else let her get away with that?

"Hey, Les? Les ....?"

"That was cold."

"She's weird like that. She'll sit with you at lunch and ten minutes later, she looks right through you."

"Hey, there's Marissa ... have you see 'Guys and Dolls,' yet?"

"No, we were ..."

"She is tremendous. Her voice … hey, Marissa! … Thanks … you were *so* good!"

They were the most popular kids at LOJ, the drama kids. They didn't put on airs. They were surprisingly humble about the gifts they dragged onto the stage, and so flattered when you popped up on opening night. You might think they'd found some secret place beneath the lights where they could express themselves without ridicule or catcalls, and they carried that same self-awareness back down into the pit.

"Careful … Kelsey Depp and Charlie G dead ahead."

"Oh, please … at eight in the morning?"

"If he wants a piece of gum, just ask her for one."

"Maybe they're flossing."

Their lockers were crouched at the end of B hall, a T-intersection with C hall that led to the gym or got you moving toward the library. Lisa opened the door with three flicks of the wrist, then stepped back so Layla could grab her essentials from the landfill at the bottom of the chute: Trail Mix, gum, half-eaten Halloween candy, half-empty Snapples, the occasional textbook. She was backing out when the 30-second horn sounded and the energy level in the hall switched from shapeless chaos to Def-Con 3.

"What'd your dad make for lunch?" Lisa said.

"Bagel. Sun chips."

"Save me half."

Like she even had to ask. The volume of the morning tide was more pronounced than usual, and despite how far they had yet to go to reach first period, neither Lisa nor Layla wanted to surrender to it. Leaving one another meant tackling the day and the bathroom stalls solo, wondering who to trust, second-guessing your hair, going cellular silent, pretending to care about Manifest Destiny, and questioning whether anyone else could penetrate your various disguises to wrap their arms around the embraceable you.

Leaving one another was what the daily grind was all about.

Layla grabbed for Lisa's hand and caught the sleeve of her sweater, even as Rachel burst out of the pin-wheeling mob scene in B hall with her eyes lit up and her hair on fire. "Omigod! Omigod! Omigod!" she squealed, aglow with the secret that had brought her flying up the hall. "Come quick. Come …"

"Britney in the lobby?" Lisa asked.

"Emily. On the floor. I think she fainted," Rachel said. Then they were running.

*   *   *

Alex didn't bother to call and make an appointment. No one ever answered the phone at the club office and Colin Welch didn't return calls. Welch was only there when he needed you. Alex once thought he might be good company over Guinness and darts at the local Hog's Head, but that was a faulty first impression. The Brit was too bloated with self importance to let someone sneak up behind him with a steel-tipped Harrow.

Colin Welch had assumed control of the soccer club in a coup that rippled with chutzpah and deceit. He hailed from one of those other slate-grey dead-ends in northern England; he always described it as Grady Allison's hometown and that was enough, given the cache Allison's name still had in Portland. Allison was the star mid for the Portland Timbers, back when the Timbers truly mattered, and 15 years later, after Allison emerged from the breeding shed, Welch coached his son. The kid didn't need much coaching before winning three state titles at Jesuit and an NCAA championship team at Indiana, but Welch relentlessly promoted his role in the lad's development and began hiring himself out as personal trainer. Nick Bollettieri without the tennis academy, in other words. For $25 an hour, Welch promised you Renaldo. Within 18 months, he was mentoring four members of Lake Oswego's elite U-12 boys' team, so it wasn't long before their parents realized they could save hundreds by hiring Welch to help coach the classic team. It took him less than a year to depose Geoff Patrick, the head coach whose easy-going demeanor was his downfall, and a few more weeks to gain control of the club.

Like most of Lake Oswego, the soccer club took itself far too seriously. Welch set that attitude in stone. The Classic program had a 32-page rule book that laid out Welch's philosophy on uniforms, travel gear, sideline deportment, and chalice ownership: State-champion cups were the property of the club, not the team that spent a muddy year in the trenches. Instead of restricting weekend games to Saturday, Welch turned

Sunday into soccer's high holy day. Parents who complained that 8 a.m. Sunday games interfered with church were reminded that winning soccer was quality family time. So were the incessant trips to Seattle and Medford for weekend tournaments. As a result, annual dues went up 50 percent, and Welch repeatedly told the coaches and team managers to pull the player card of any kid who wasn't paid in full.

You didn't wait for guys like this to call you back. You waited in the parking lot, outside Starbucks. Alex had been waiting for a half hour before Welch crossed the parking lot with his mocha and USA Today, then slipped through the door behind him.

LOSC headquarters logged in at 1,500 square feet, not counting the trophy case with the Malice's state-championship cup. It felt like a Goodwill sorting dock, the floor and a dozen buffet tables littered with jerseys, sweatshirts and equipment bags. Welch had his head in a box as Alex negotiated the maze, and emerged with a start. He was small and ferret-like, his hair trimmed down to its Northampton nubs.

"Scared the shite out of me, mate," Welch said, his eyes shifting toward the door. "My memory must be slipping. You and me have a date?"

"I saw you at Starbucks. Thought I'd check in. How the boys doing?"

Welch was still coaching the club's U-12 boys team. A physical crew, with plenty of speed. "Still making me proud. Two shutouts last week."

"I saw the last 20 minutes against Southside. You up four or five at the end?"

169

"Why, Alex, I didn't know you were a fan. Don't know that I remember. Comes a point where you don't worry much about the score."

"With that group, I imagine that point usually arrives before halftime."

"They play hard," Welch said, setting his mocha down on the desk and picking up a stack of file folders.

"Sub any out in the second half? Or were you shooting for double figures?"

Welch glanced up, taking stock. "Drag a pout in with you this morning?"

"You see them in practice, Colin, I don't. For all I know, only the starters play hard and the other six coast."

"As I tell their parents, mate, the boys came to me late. I had nothing to do with whoever gave them speed or aggression. All of that was decided before the first tryout." Welch turned back to his files.

"At 11 years old?"

"Now, there's an attitude, Alex. You remember what you were doing at 11? Watching 'The Jetsons'? I was on the pitch, working my ass off. Football's all I cared about. Some lads are built that way, some aren't, but they made their decision before I came along. We got a rec team for you love-of-the-game types. Don't bring that attitude in here, not this early. It doesn't do the boys much good. They're in or they're out. They can compete or they can't. Best if they figure it out now."

"Better for whom?" Alex said. "The kid who may not get his act together until he's 13? Or the coaches who don't have the patience to wait?"

"I got that covered," he said, dismissively. "They're paying me to run the club. You stand on the sidelines with the other dads for free. Be thankful."

"I believe *I'm* paying you. And as a dues-paying member of the club, I'd like to know if the board has already put money down on that pasture in Wilsonville"

Welch straightened up, confused. "Come again?"

"Ten acres. The merger with Southside and Westside. The super-club scheme." Alex paused. "Has the board voted yet, or you doing all this behind the scenes?"

Welch closed his eyes. "That conversation is beyond your pay grade, mate."

The room felt cramped and claustrophobic. "My pay grade? You're the only guy in the room making a living off this gig. You combine three soccer clubs and only one kid in three plays A. I'm guessing that conversation will get two thirds of the families involved fired up."

"Only if they don't think their child makes the cut. Who concedes that?"

"I can think of quite a ..."

"You're a bloody fool. You think it's an accident I'm running this club? You think the locals don't recognize me for the jerk I am? That's what they *pay* me for! They don't want a second-place trophy. They don't want to stand in the rain when Malice or the

Tsunami lose to Gresham, and they're tired of watching our best teams get clocked by Montana. You're damn right they want a super club. They want to compete. Competing is what made them the money that got 'em here. It'll never enter their heads that their kid might not make the team. It only enters yours because you're a realist … and you don't think your gal can cut it."

"Kiss my ass."

Welch laughed, a spontaneous riff. "That one hurt, did it? Pissed you off. It's about time. That's what we feed off, that anger, the possibility that a kid from Westview might get that free ride to Stanford, not the blond sweetheart we tuck in at night." Moving to the door, Welch reached out and flicked off the lights. "That prospect is a worse fright than a few squirts not playing A ball. Am I locking you in or out?"

Alex followed him outside. "I'm calling the board."

"Wish you would," Welch said. "Save me some time."

Taze Elliott loved 14 year-olds. He was a week shy of 13, lean and raw, when he got his first taste of that lush age, in the back of Guilford Tyler's blood-red Rambler. She was fat and drunk on Thunderbird, but she didn't complain as he clumsily fought his way inside her and she swore, even as Guilford shattered a wine bottle against the base of the streetlight, that he was better than the fools who had her first.

When Taze was running with those clowns, poon was never a problem. When you averaged 31 points in the Oakland Athletic League, young and eager were waiting for you in the parking lot, and the white chicks were the quickest to wrap their ankles around your back. The night the Trib named Elliott 1st team all-city as a sophomore, he celebrated with a wild ride

aboard the Homecoming queen. If memory served –
and, increasingly, it had to – he racked up her envious
19-year-old sister two nights later.

The year in juvie derailed a lot of Elliott's plans,
but little of his attitude. He spent 11 months at a
minimum-security work farm outside Stockton and 20
years with a hard-on for Tark – who'd recruited him
hard – and his disappearing act. After he followed his
mother to Portland and enrolled at Grant, he had to start
fresh, but the Oregon girls were easy enough. For years,
that was a constant. Even when Elliott felt himself
slowing down, he was convinced the Fuller's waitress
or the Korean trim at the Acropolis got damp just
thinking about him.

He was in his mid-30s when the 115-pound
secretary in the black dress and stiletto heels looked
through him for the first time, dismissing him like the
first pick in the third round of the NBA draft. For a year
or two, he could not wrap his head around the fact that
he was no longer in his well-hung prime. Whether he
was in the clubs downtown or with the crew at Irving
Park, his natural aggression convinced him he still had
a shot. But once his stubble began to gray, every rock
star dancing by in a jogging bra was a reminder that he
didn't have game. They didn't care what he could do
with Luther Vandross humming in the background.
They only cared about the Gold Card and the Willamette
Athletic Club membership, the upper middle-class
benefits he did not have.

He was living with – and off –a floral shop
operator at the time, coaching an AAU team while

lobbying for a job at Portland State. On a rainy Saturday morning, as he stood on the sidelines during warm-ups and studied the White House Black Market sorority in the stands, two things became clear. He hated 44-year-olds. Back in the day, they were the high-society cheerleaders who would jerk him off during a Saturday afternoon matinee of "Kramer vs. Kramer," the Barbie doll grinding on the hood of the Trans Am after he dumped 35 points on St. Ignatius. A quarter century later, they thought he was out of their league.

Their teen-age daughters, on the other hand, thought he was God.

These 14-and-15-year-olds regarded Taze with the same wide-eyed intensity he once found so addictive. They made eye contact, at least until he put the hammer down. They shut up when he preached. They struggled to please. And they were so damn thankful when he paid attention to them that their gratitude bubbled forth in a myriad of ways. Loyalty. Adulation. Subservience. Obedience. Awe. All the essentials.

Taze, curiously, didn't rush to exploit that eagerness. They were teenagers. Clumsy wasn't the half of it. They were dumber than an outboard motor. More often than not, they were losing interest in basketball, and they were increasingly distracted by the stuff filling the void.

Elliott never had to worry about that. Nobody messed with him in high school. Not when he averaged 31 points a game and Delroy Jackson, one of his Oakland homies, came off the bench with 19. A Glock

19. People gravitated toward him or gave him a wide berth. Empathy, like algebra teachers, never got in his way. Neither did college prep courses, summer camps, sleepovers, dance-team auditions or the harping interference of parasitic soccer coaches.

Taze Elliott had a righteous hard-on for soccer coaches. He'd take his van up onto the sidewalk after a damn soccer coach.

He had no sense of the daily BS these kids had to deal with until, desperate for the paycheck, he signed on to coach that west-side all-star squad. Given how focused he'd been on the skills that were his ticket out of East Oakland, he was appalled by how difficult it was to force the girls to concentrate. In the first two weeks, he banned cell phones, pagers, iPods, backpacks and schoolbooks. That he still struggled for their undivided attention was one reason he was now coaching 8th and 9th graders, though obviously not the only one.

Lindsay Carroll was a semi-decent small forward on that team who could swing up to the 2. Her flexibility usually brought her off the bench in the first quarter, but she was too short to cover the athletic forwards and too chunky to beat the shooting guards to their favorite spot on the wing.

As was the case with half the girls he coached – and most of the girls he would eventually fondle – Lindsay's parents were divorced and her father increasingly aloof, the heart of her many issues. She fretted over her weight, obsessed about the upcoming weekend with her dad, worried about her friends, and was certain there was something terribly wrong because other girls sustained the illusion they had less to worry about than she did. Her anxiety was palpable and annoying. Ordinarily, Taze would have cut the girl loose, but her father paid for a year up front. As a last resort, Taze pulled Lindsay aside after practice one night and asked what was bothering her. She was guarded at first, unable to believe an adult had an interest in anything she had to say, but at some point the weight of her tears trumped the her skepticism, and she cut loose on the incomparable burdens facing a rich white chick with an MIP, a sex-obsessed boyfriend, a shrinking circle of friends, three teachers who couldn't deal with how busy she was, and a basketball coach who barely looked at her.

Lindsay Carroll wasn't hard to figure out. She needed someone to talk to who considered her issues more important than their time. Taze assumed that's what parents were for, but at the Carroll home, like so many others, Dad was MIA and Mom was berating the kid for the makeup she left on the bathroom counter. Taze had no inclination to step into the breach, to pretend he was sympathetic to these soap operas, and he was warming up to tell her so when Lindsay unexpectedly closed the distance between them and gave him a quick, tentative hug.

Taze didn't move. Taze wasn't into hugs. Sensing his discomfort and fearing his wrath, Lindsay released him almost immediately and ran off. Taze stood there, confused and annoyed. He understood the heavy hand, the clenched fist, the jab designed to chop someone off at the emotional knees. He'd been well schooled in the utility of fear and ridicule in a relationship, the necessity of putting people on notice and off balance with a sharp elbow. But the girl had hugged his ass. What was he supposed to do with that?

An off-hand comment from Thalia eventually supplied the key. Taze was cursing the difficulty of motivating 14-year-olds after a long practice when Thalia said, "Might help if you remember what you're coaching. With boys, you're coaching pride. Girls, you're coaching emotion."

Elliott wrestled with that for a day or two before he grasped the genius of it. Pride is precisely what supplied his motivation growing up, the bloodless compulsion to prove he commanded respect on the blacktop, if nowhere else. When he backed a man down, it didn't much matter if the home had passed him the roach or the quart of malt liquor under the Nimitz Freeway; Taze had to re-establish his superiority. That same ego drove the brothers on the playground and the white shadows like Larry Bird in French Lick. Guys found their security in the damage they could do, even to their own crew.

Girls were a different game. Teenage girls arrived with emotional baggage and found *their* security in the emotional connections they made with other girls on the floor. Elliott could always tell when two of his players were ensnared in a cat fight over the neighborhood Romeo. They couldn't park the spat at the gym door. Girls were just as competitive and motivated as their older brothers, and Taze's experience with all-stars like Sarah Innocenti suggested they were equally resilient at playing with pain. Physical pain. Emotional duress was something else.

Coach emotion? Taze Elliott was a seasoned manipulator, and emotion was far easier to jerk around than pride. So it was that when Lindsay Carroll needed someone to talk to, Taze Elliott was endlessly attentive, even if he steered the conversation toward the guy she was dating and which of her teammates were putting out and where.

When Lindsay Carroll needed to vent about her mother, Taze Elliott found a variety of ways to tell her that she couldn't expect the woman, bitter and jealous as she was, to understand her, all the more reason she should come to him with her questions and her need for unconditional love.

And when Lindsay Carroll needed a hug – at least when they were alone – Taze Elliott was open arms and full body contact and "you're-one-special-lady," or whatever else served to distract her while her boobs were hard against his chest. When they weren't alone, Elliott was brutal, savaging the girl's mistakes, ignoring her small victories, celebrating teammates at her expense. It kept the girl off balance and insecure, forcing her to work that much harder to gain his approval. And in some small way, Taze realized, she seemed to expect the unfairness of it as the price she paid for those secret hugs, those long conversations in the dark about which of her buddies were still virgins and the stupidity of giving it up to a clumsy amateur. The first time Taze pushed Lindsay's head into his lap and held it there, well, that was the price she had to pay, too, to maintain her unique hold on his affection and his attention.

In due time, Lindsay came down with a rebound on a teammate's foot and collapsed with a severe sprain; after two weeks on the bench, she quit altogether. Twice when he was drunk the following summer, Elliott sent her clumsy e-mails, neither of which she answered, but it was some time before she relinquished her hold on his imagination. A little time, and fresh opportunity.

*   *   *

Chelsea Lider understood mind games. At 14, she had a graduate degree in mind games, thanks to her father. She knew that's what this cold, plastic seat on the bench was all about. Mind games.

She'd been practicing with Black Tornado for three months. There was no longer a lot of mystery about where she fit in the team, and it wasn't on the bench. Chloe Ward was the squad's best player. Chelsea had seen the Oregon City coach at several tournaments and she wasn't surprised. Chloe was scary good. She could rebound, she could run and when she came off screens in the paint, you couldn't stop her from scoring.

Sarita was a classic point guard, quick, intense and unselfish. Chelsea also deferred to Shelby. But that was it. Cici was a cow and Anita had nothing but a 3-point set shot from the top of the key. Lisa and Sierra, Sarita's sister, couldn't create their own shots and Caitlin, everyone said, wasn't coming back. Kris and

Melissa? Please. Chelsea was easily one of the four best players on the team. Thalia thought so, too. Yet here she was, sitting on the bench as the starters skipped to mid-court for the opening tap.

Mind games. Maybe Coach Elliott was trying to piss off her dad. Across the court, her father was chewing that unlit cigar, and muttering to Mom, who was knitting another Christmas afghan. Coach enjoyed sticking it to her father, and he was almost as good at it as Nick. He first barred him from practice, then banned him from games for two weeks when Dad got T'd up in Medford for yelling at the refs. Now that he was back, her father had no outlet for his anger. Chelsea wasn't looking forward to the ride home.

She camped at the end of the bench. Watching the game was impossible closer to the scorer's table. Coach roamed the sidelines like the Doberman that lived in the shed behind Jack Lider Wilsonville Volvo and patrolled the lot at night. He couldn't sit still, at least not until the lead hit 20. On the last Saturday of the month, playing Eugene in the semis at Tualatin, Chelsea guessed Coach would chill by halftime.

She understood she was the newcomer. Normally, she wouldn't care about starting. But Lisa and Layla and their dads were sitting in the bleachers. She guessed they wouldn't stay long. Lake Oswego had lost by two in the first semifinal. The Lakers were down 12 when Coach took the Black Tornado into hallway, so they must have gone to the three-quarter court trap in the fourth quarter.

Buttering her English muffin at breakfast, while Dad was out back yelling at the yard crew, Mom asked Chelsea if she missed playing for LO. She didn't know. She missed the silly games Alex and Mick used to play at the end of practice, when everyone ran lines after missed free throws and everyone knew the running was over when Chelsea stepped to the line. She missed the trips to Baskin & Robbins when Layla's dad played Journey or Kelly Clarkson and they all sang along. She even missed the freedom she had inside that 1-3-1, where she easily averaged six steals a game. But she understood her dad's reasoning that Black Tornado was a ticket to that college scholarship. Her father was also right when he argued that if she could deal with Coach's anger and Coach's intensity and Coach's menopausal mood swings, she could deal with anyone down the road.

Dad, of course, hadn't heard Coach slap Cici with the "C" word. Thalia hadn't, either. When Thalia was in the gym, Coach didn't cuss as much.

He was standing, suddenly, in front of her, scowling. "You be ready, now," he said, slapping her on the knee, then returning to the scorer's table. She guessed he was more nervous than she was. Which was hard to figure. They were playing Sheldon, the whitest, clunkiest team Chelsea had ever seen.

They had the usual play set up off the opening tip. As the ball went up, Anita took off. Chloe tapped the ball to Sarita, who barely glanced at Anita before launching the two-hand chest pass that hit her in mid-stride at the free-throw lane. One step, two points. The ball never touched the floor.

"That's what I'm talkin' about!" Coach barked with that quick fist clench. Right away, the Black Tornado starters picked up everyone man-to-man, full court. No double teams, just one-on-one pressure with one eye on the passing lane.

Mind games. Coach loved mind games.

Four minutes into the game, it was 14-2 and Coach still had them hassling Sheldon full-court. Chelsea wasn't surprised when Sheldon's 3 twice snuck behind Anita for lay-ups. Anita was always the first to start wheezing.

Chelsea didn't get the deal with Anita. She liked her well enough. She was hilarious in the locker room. Had a great Jay-Z ring tone and shared Chelsea's passion for Avril Lavigne. But she sucked at basketball. She could shoot when she was fresh, but that was it … and Coach still started her at the 3. That galled Chelsea today, what with Lisa and Layla laughing like idiots because they had the rest of the weekend off, and knowing they might just show up at school Monday telling everyone Chelsea rode the bench. She was chewing on that when, with 14 seconds left in the quarter, Coach sent her in for Anita. Sarita was shooting free throws, and Chelsea felt ridiculously self-conscious at the scorers' table. Her father was shaking his head. Lisa was strolling back into the gym, a box of Mike & Ikes in her hand. She shut her eyes for a moment as Sarita swished the first free throw and the ref called her in. Focus, she told herself. Focus.

Chelsea waited at mid-court for Sarita to knock down the second free throw, then latched on to Sheldon's small forward. Down by 16, Sheldon was under orders to play for the last shot, but Sierra forced their point guard to pick up her dribble and Chelsea intercepted the cross-court lob on the dead run. She needed three dribbles to lay the ball off the glass. The ball was barely on the floor when Chelsea spun and sprinted in the opposite direction. She was crossing mid-court when the ball sailed over her shoulder and into the hands of the lazy-ass Sheldon 3, who hoisted up a wild shot that banked in at the buzzer.

Chelsea took one glance at the scoreboard as she flopped down on the bench, then turned her attention to Coach. That 22-7 looked better than he did. There were no celebratory hand slaps and no conversation; Coach never had to ask for quiet. He handed his clipboard to Thalia and positioned himself in front of Chelsea, hands on his knees and his nose three inches from hers.

"Under 10 seconds. We have the ball. What's Rule One?"

He smelled like coffee and barbecue sauce. She could see a thatch of hair in his right nostril. The last time her father had gotten this close, he'd boxed her ear because she'd left an empty Diet Pepsi can sitting in the mouth of the newspaper box. Chelsea stared at him. She knew the answer. She also knew she'd had a breakaway.

"Hold for the last shot," she said.

Coach straightened. "Good answer. Melissa!" he barked. "In for Miss Know-It-All here." He reached for the clipboard. "We're still at F-5" – their code for full-court man pressure – "and running Arizona."

Chelsea didn't move as Melissa, Shelby and the three starters ran onto the court. She sunk her teeth into her lower lip. Mind games, she told herself. She could hear her father's subsonic grousing at the far end of the gym, but she could not bring herself to look at him. When Sheldon put the ball in play, she risked a furtive glance at Layla and Lisa, but they were gone. Alex, Layla's dad, was standing alone in the doorway, staring back at her and in the moment before Chelsea frantically looked away, he gave her a quick thumbs up.

She pulled a towel from the Black Tornado travel bag closest to her chair. She could hear Nick's voice somewhere in the distance: "Never let the assholes see you cry."

At halftime, Coach took the team and its 28-point lead into the hallway. The battleship-gray lockers were festooned with love notes from the cheerleaders to the football team. Debra Giuliani was pulling water bottles out of her travel bag and passing them around. Coach stood several feet apart for a moment, listening to Thalia, then smacked the clipboard with his free hand.

"Not bad," he said. "Tigard coach dragged his china dolls out after the first quarter. Realized the Black Tornado was R-rated. That's for damn sure. We're serial killers. Suicide bombers. We gonna turn it up, not down, you all understand? We're going F-4. Pick your man up at half-court and don't let her breathe. I want pressure. You get tired, give me the fist, but I want full-bore. Starters back out. Now, warm up."

Chelsea struggled to her feet, and jammed the water bottle, unopened, into the trash can. She was one of the four best players on the team and she'd played 14 seconds. Coach never looked at her once.

She scored 24 in the second half. With Coach leaning back on his throne like Jabba the Hutt, Thalia motioned her in with three minutes to go in the third quarter. She never raised that fist. She had four steals, two for breakaways. Seven of nine from the field, including five threes. During the perfunctory hand slaps after the game, the Sheldon coach ignored Coach's hand and grabbed hers. He had a hawk nose and dark circles under his eyes. "You ever get tired of sitting on his bench, you can play for me," he said. "You're the best player here."

Coach didn't waste time in the post-game wrap-up. Debra gave them the game time – 2 p.m Sunday – and Thalia reminded them to get to bed early. They were dispersing for the reunions with parents when Coach called Chelsea back. He was trying so hard to sound casual. "What that coach say to you?" he asked.

Chelsea stared back at him. "'Good game.' The usual."

"That all?"

Whatever, she thought: "He said I should be starting."

Coach hooted. "Shi ... ittt," he said. "And what'd you tell him?"

"I told him you're the Coach."

His eyes narrowed, predictably. Her father did that now and then when the thought occurred to him that he might have underestimated the opposition.

"That I am," Coach said. He was chewing on something. "You got time this week?" he finally asked. "After school, maybe. Need to fix that shot. You hit a bunch today ... but you got the elbow flapping all over the place. Go talk to your old man and see if he can bring you by Wednesday in one of them Jack Lider Wilsonville Volvos."

Chelsea nodded. That could be arranged. Then she turned, looped the travel bag strap over her shoulder and trudged back into the gym, where her father was warming up for the pointless drive-time lecture. Didn't look back at Coach even once.

Mind games. She knew the drill.

*   *   *

To hear Qui Zhao tell it – and this was the first Thursday in three years Emily Yu hadn't been forced to do just that – Chinese calligraphy was slowly losing its character. Each time a confession, observation or prayer was rendered in the simplified script mandated on the mainland by Mao, another pebble dropped from the Great Wall and another tortoise shell crumbled beneath the march of time. Locked in that prison cell, a hundred years before the star of Bethlehem, the cleric Cheng Miao had transcribed Chinese culture with li shu, and that culture lost a bit of dignity each time someone cheated history and reduced Cheng Miao's characters to the Communist shorthand.

When her parents carried on about all that was lost and all they'd left behind, in Canton and the Bay Area, Emily retreated to her soundproof room. She cut her honored teacher slack. He was so resolute in keeping them tethered to a China that was growing smaller in their consciousness, and so elegant with the brush or felt-tip pen in hand. If the li shu and kai shu characters felt thick and clumsy at the end of her fingers, they came to life beneath his.

Emily checked the clock on the nightstand – 5:20 in the afternoon – then rearranged the pillows and pulled the blanket over the IV-tube snaking from her left wrist. Qui Zhao must have realized by now that she wouldn't dash in late, and she could imagine the gravity of his disappointment. He took his students' discipline as seriously as their devotion to calligraphy, and Emily knew he'd assume the worst: She'd succumbed to coarse temptation. She'd turned one more degree from East to West. She'd reduced one more elegant Chinese character to a stick figure.

The door opened and Dr. Dave swept in. Dr. Dave was creeping up on 35 and, Emily thought, a 24-Hour Fitness billboard. He'd introduced himself that first afternoon at St. Vincent, after her heart rate stabilized and they began pumping brown sugar into her veins, insisting she call him by his first name, not the Polish concoction on his name tag. As self-conscious as Emily felt in these stupid pajamas, she could picture herself marrying Dave when his trophy wife began taking him for granted.

"And how is Emily today?" Dr. Dave said, delivering the line with a verbal wink.

"Emily wants her cell phone."

"And why is that?" Dr. Dave was wearing a dark blue cardigan sweater instead of the official physician's uniform.

"Because you're holding me prisoner, and I'm allowed a phone call."

He stared for a moment, not unkindly. He didn't look quite as edible today as he had yesterday, but those blue eyes were incredible. "We're trying out a new routine."

"I liked the old routine."

"You came in weighing 93 pounds, Emily. When the EMTs reached the junior high, your heartbeat was under 70. The old routine hasn't been good to you."

"There's nothing wrong with me."

Dr. Dave nodded. "I think you're right. Nothing permanent. I understand you play classic soccer. And your team won the state cup last year."

The IV-tube was suddenly itching in a way Emily hadn't noticed before. "No way my mom told you that."

"I bumped into two of your teammates down the hall."

"Who?"

"Lisa and …"

"Layla?" Emily yelped, and the doctor nodded. "Can I see them?"

"Sure. When we're done. And we're almost done." He set a clipboard down on the edge of the bed. "What position do you play?"

He didn't want to swap state playoff stories, did he? "Sweeper."

"You the fastest player on the squad?"

"Yeah, sorta. Me … or Jessica."

"Ever black out on the field?"

"What?"

"Gone down on one knee from dizziness? Either in a game or at practice?"

He was awfully cute. He had Brad Pitt's nose and great skin and in the 100, he might give her a run. But there was no way she would open a vein and bleed all over Dr. Dave, no matter how warm and fuzzy his smile. No way she was going to open the diary and explain what the li shu characters meant, and what they kept hidden behind their shuttered windows.

"No."

"Are you being honest with me, Emily?"

He sounded sincere enough. If wishing made things true, he sounded as if he cared about what she was thinking and not just because she was making him late or deflating his expectations. But Emily knew her parents were on the other side of that door, their faces warped by disappointment, their ears tuned for anything they might use against her. If she let the secrets out, she might never get them back.

"Why would I lie to you?"

"I have a theory about that," Dr. Dave said. "When I was in college, before I decided to become a doctor, I took a writing class in which the professor said something I've never forgotten. Every writing assignment, he told us, is a trick."

"A trick."

"A trick to find out who we are. A temptation to reveal something about ourselves."

Emily didn't know what to say, so she stared at the Brad Pitt nose.

"That's what he said. And gimmicks and sneak attacks and tricks are necessary because revealing who we are is dangerous. Holding onto our story comes naturally. Letting go, or trusting it to someone else, is hard. They might laugh. They might throw it away. They might ridicule things that are important to us. So, we play it safe, and keep our mouths shut. When English professors fire questions at us, we duck. And when doctors ask if we've ever gotten dizzy on the soccer field, we just say, 'No.'"

She liked his voice. It reminded her of the low drone coming out of the Panasonic on the kitchen counter when her father listened to McNeil-Lehrer.

"I never pulled the covers over my head," she said.

"No, you didn't," Dr. Dave conceded.

"Did you play?"

He waited for a beat or two. "A long time ago."

"Sweeper?"

"Center-mid. I wasn't fast enough for sweeper."

"Can I talk to Lisa and Layla now?"

"Sure. I'll send them in."

"Are you coming back tomorrow?"

"Only if I can slip past your mom."

"And I'll still be here tomorrow?"

"You'll be here for awhile, Emily. We'll talk more in the morning." Dr. Dave picked up his clipboard and left, leaving the door open behind him. Emily heard the heart monitor pick up speed as she waited for her parents to swing into view, but the next thing she knew, Lisa and Layla were peeking cautiously around the door jamb. Lisa let go first, bounding onto the bed. "Hey, drama queen, what gives?" she said, giving Emily a quick squeeze. "And what," she added, eying the IV, "is that all about?"

"They're shooting Peach Snapple straight into my veins," Emily said. "How'd you get down here?"

"My dad," Layla said, still in her schoolhouse skirt. She was sizing up the EKG.

"Did he come up with you?"

"He's in the parking garage. He's weird today. He's pissed at Colin."

"Where's your phone?" Lisa said. "I sent you a million texts."

"They took it away."

"Why?"

"They don't think I'm miserable enough."

"Are you OK?" Lisa asked.

"I'm fine." Like what else was she supposed to say? These a-holes think I have an eating disorder? I'm locked in a room with no WiFi or cell service? I'm sharing a bathroom with an old lady who falls asleep on the toilet? My mother just spent $220 on groceries at

Costco and my father wants me to transfer to Catlin Gabel?

"Do they know why you fainted?" Layla said.

"I skipped breakfast. Can we talk about something else?"

"Who's on the other side of the curtain?" Lisa whispered, her eyes suddenly aglow with the possibility that an Owen Wilson look-alike was sharing her room, needing only the tender, loving embrace of an over-anxious eighth grader to hasten his recovery.

"Flora Wilson. And you don't have to whisper. She's deaf," Emily said. "You should hear it when her family shows up. They talk about her like she's not even there."

"What's wrong with her?" Layla asked.

"She's old." But the echo of that last thought was still circling overhead. Emily remembered her parents' last conversation as they watched her eat lunch. Tracking the flight of the spoon. Staring into a future they had not reckoned on.

Lisa reached inside her backpack. "We came bearing gifts," she said, extracting a small, oblong package wrapped in silver paper with a red bow.

"Guys!" Emily took the package in her hands, dragging the IV-tubing out from beneath the blanket. She examined the crisp corners of the wrapping job and laughed. "No way you guys wrapped this," she said, poking gingerly at the symmetrical coils of ribbon.

"My mom," Layla acknowledged. "Open it."

"I don't ..."

"C'mon, open it!" Lisa barked.

It was so tightly bound, so self-contained, that Emily really wanted to set it carefully down next to the bed, but she dutifully tugged at the ribbon until the bow came apart and the gift wrap began to unwind in her hands. Even before Emily pulled back the thin blanket of tissue, she realized how familiar the 6 x 12 package felt, but she was still surprised Lisa and Layla had found her favorite sketchbook, the one with the archival, 93-lb heavyweight drawing paper.

"You came in weighing 93 pounds, Emily. When the EMTs got to the junior high, your heartbeat was under 70."

"Wow," she said, half to herself. "I can't believe this. How did you ..."

"Art Media. Downtown," Layla said. "Allie told us that's where you like to go."

Allie? Emily didn't move. She knew what would happen if she looked down. The disbelief gathering at the corners of her eyes would spill out onto the sketchbook. Fortunately, Flora Wilson chose that moment to roll over in the middle of her nap and snort, which set everyone to laughing. She tried to catch her breath by saying, "I can't wait to grab my pens," which sent Lisa diving headfirst into her purse again, emerging with another oblong package the girls hadn't found time to wrap: a Pentel brush pen.

The sheet of paper – Wang Xi Zhi wrote in the 4th Century – *is a battleground; the brush: the lances and swords; the ink: the mind, the commander-in-chief; ability and dexterity: the deputies; the composition: the strategy. By grasping the brush the outcome of the battle is decided; the strokes and lines are the commanders' orders; the curves and returns are the mortal blows.*

"We thought," Lisa said, "you might need something to stay busy while you're here. And since you can't have sleepovers …"

"Qui Zhao will be so excited," Emily said.

"Qui who?" Layla said.

"My teacher at Chinese school. And Lisa, my friend Flora is already sleeping over, thank you very much."

They were still laughing when Layla said, "We have one more thing for you," and retreated into the hall. She returned with a sheet of poster board that had been transformed by a battalion of felt-trip pens into a get-well card. Leslie in burgundy. Jessica in Carolina blue. Lisa in forest green. Danny, below the "M" in "We Miss You," in jet black, with three Chinese characters:

Bu, dou, fei: To divine. To fight. To fly.

Once again, Emily knew better than to move her head, and her eyes were still locked on these desperate prayers – "Come back soon!" and "We can't humiliate Mr. Ballister without you" – when Lisa and Layla wrapped their arms around her and held her until the blimpo nurse with the red hair frumped in to announce visiting hours were over for everyone but immediate family.

"I love you guys," Emily said as the huddle broke.

"I'll ask my dad if he can bring us back tomorrow," Layla said, reaching for the Malice windbreaker she'd dropped at the foot of the bed.

"Where's your dad?" Emily asked Lisa.

"Miami. Sucking on sunshine that belongs to me."

The nurse popped out from behind the curtain and her reunion with Flora. "C'mon girls. Your friend needs her rest."

They exchanged smiles and sighs and secret waves. But on the way out, still tightening the windbreaker around her waist, Layla leaned close to that kettle of red hair and said, "We *are* immediate family."

The next two hours were a mess. Dinner was a slab of chicken and breadcrumbs and Mom glaring at the tray until she ate every bite. Dessert was Big Red following her into the bathroom to make sure Emily didn't chuck the cutlet into the bowl. "This is ridiculous," Emily said, unable to pee, the IV-stand looming over her. "I'm not bulimic."

Elise – that's what Big Red's name-tag said – shook her head. "The doctors can't help you, dear, until you're ready."

"I know. It's a trick."

Her parents left at 7:15 to go pick up Allie, who was in dress rehearsals for the role of "Dorothy" in the fall play, "The Wizard of Oz." Emily watched "Seinfeld" for 20 minutes but the TV was off when Elise came in with a 12-ounce fruit frappe loaded with protein and vitamins. "Promise me you'll drink *all* of this," she said, "and I'll remove the IV and leave you alone until lights out."

"You mean you trust me?"

"Not really, so why don't you surprise me?"

She drank the frappe in small sips, enjoying the feel of the cold glass in her hands. The last four ounces weren't easy but she kept raising the glass to her mouth until there was nothing left, listening to the night traffic in the hospital hall. The slow wobble of a wheelchair. The rubber-soled urgency of a nurse on her rounds. The slow shuffle of immediate family, heading for the exit doors.

Sometime after nine, she lifted the 6 x 12 sketchbook from the night table and took up the Pentel brush pen. Because the light was over her right shoulder, she couldn't see the completed figure until she pulled her hands away:

Not bad … but she could feel Danny and Qui Zhao shaking their heads, convinced she could do better with the lance and the sword and her mortal blows. She bent over the figure again, pressing down a little harder on the pen to give this immortal character more weight and depth.

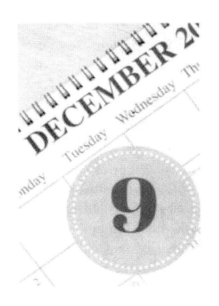

What r u packin?
Shorts jns duke sw gap top
Mine?
U said I cld keepit
Bsuit?
In dec?
Isn't their a pool?
Kids n fat ladies
Where r guys?
Shilo
How we gtn out?
?????

By the time Rachel followed her gear into the Durango, it was 4:30 p.m. and Alex had given up on beating the rush-hour traffic to the Sunset Highway. They had room for one more – Alex had suggested Jill – but Layla slapped that idea aside. Anyone outside her intimate cluster would upset the delicate, iPod-laced chemistry of the 80-minute drive to Seaside.

"Cluster" nailed it. The concept was a gift from an old Young Life guy named Chap Clark, writing about the social networks of teenagers. Back in the day, Clark argued, kids had one or two devout friends and a sizable fraternity of acquaintances, but he'd observed something substantially different moving through the high schools and teenage traumas familiar to his children. Kids now moved in "clusters," Clark argued, groups of eight to 10 friends that formed in middle school and solidified – through countless sleepovers and summer vacations – in the transition to high school. Members of the cluster were not only intensely loyal to that select group of friends but also to the rules and decorum of the pride. While it wasn't altogether clear how those rules were established, they set tone and tempo, overwhelming parental influence and moral independence. If the girls in the cluster drank, Clark argued, your daughter would end up with a beer at Westlake Park. If the guys found status in soliciting oral sex from the sirens of the freshmen class, your son would get an early initiation into friendships with benefits. The rules of the cluster were sacred, the advice of parents and Young Life leaders expendable.

As he merged onto the Sunset, Alex stole a glance at Layla, bent over the math homework that was illuminated by the makeup light in her windshield visor.

She sensed his interest and rotated her head toward his with exaggerated theater. "What?"

"Nothing. Just checking. How much homework do you have this weekend?"

"Math. Language Arts. But just my outline."

"*To Kill a Mockingbird*?"

"Yeah. Are we staying at the same dump in Seaside?"

"We've camped out there for three years. When did it become a 'dump'?"

"Mom said there was mold in the shower."

"That's why she's staying home. You and I are made of sterner stuff."

"I like the Shiloh," Rachel popped up from the back.

Alex eased in front of an old Chevy pickup. "I'm not a big fan of the Shiloh."

Layla looked at him in disbelief. "It's more expensive, isn't it?"

As a matter of fact it was. Alex received the dowdy hotel manager discount at the Surf and Sand, which he'd secured when he brought their fifth graders over the Coast Range during a torrential downpour. When Alex did a convincing impression of a clueless suburban dad, he was offered eight rooms for the price of six. When he called back a year later, Teri Sue Stine sounded so delighted the team was coming back that Alex asked if the same rate was available. "Of course, honey," she said. "That discount's good until the end of time."

"Yeah," he agreed, "it's cheaper. Which means I have that much more money for the Christmas shopping."

Lisa snorted from the back seat. Layla rolled her eyes. Rachel whispered something to Lisa that never rose above Shaun Colvin on KINK, then popped her iPod earplugs back in and closed her eyes. Alex studied her face in the rear-view mirror as brake lights flared in front of him. Rachel had grown two inches in the last year, and shed the soft fleshiness so familiar to junior high. If she ordered a Hammerhead at the Fulton Pub, she wouldn't be carded, and he'd seen the ratty collection of boys who showed up for their first league game, a 15-point win over West Linn.

A year earlier, he and Olivia had agreed – much to Layla's dismay – to chaperone the Halloween dance at LOJ, duties that didn't extend far beyond guarding the exits. All the escape routes off the dance floor were locked an hour after the doors first opened, just as the kids realized the dance, like most forms of self-expression, was a potential disaster, and began searching for a way out.

"Pretend you don't know me, OK?" Layla said before disappearing into the shadows. Which was just as well. Watching kids struggle with their dance steps, in the lobby, by the Coke machine, in the cafeteria was painful enough without watching the fox trot of someone you loved. The kids were trapped between horseplay and hormones, sneakers and 3-inch platform heels. They emerged at different speeds from the sanctuary of a hooded sweatshirt, but the girls were far more aggressive on the dance floor, flinging themselves at one another like Sumo wrestlers or spinning across the floor like ice-skaters. When the girls realized the baseball-capped wallflowers couldn't match their energy, they partnered with their best friends, losing their self-consciousness and, eventually, their awkwardness, as they skipped through the darkness.

Something happened between seventh and eighth grade. The boys took a half step back, the girls a giant leap forward, both socially and physiologically. Even as the girls grew into their bodies, the boys grew terrified of same, intimidated by the increasingly visible evidence that they were losing the sack race through puberty. As Layla and her friends came to terms, in dramatic fashion, with the value of presentation, the guys retreated into video games and fantasy leagues. At least, the eighth-grade guys did. Whenever Graham's friends bumped into Layla's in the kitchen, Graham's crew couldn't pretend not to stare.

By the time they reached the North Plains, Alex had the Durango at 65 and an eye out for motorcycle cops. Layla still had the math book open, but her head had slumped against the window. *Pretend you don't know me, OK?* Alex reached up and turned off the visor light, then quieted Five for Fighting on KINK until you could barely hear them over the rumble of the radials.

*   *   *

The girls woke on the approach to Camp 18, a reliquary of old locomotives and tractors that boasted the best menu between the coast and the Coast Range. The road to the beach was a lonely chill in winter, especially at night. The clear cuts were shrouded in darkness, the highway awash in sunken grades. You'd round a corner and lose all confidence the road was designed to keep you out of the path of the next logging truck.

They reached the coast highway at 6:15 p.m. Before they turned west toward the Seaside dunes on G Street, they passed two restaurants, shuttered and dank, that had closed since hosting victory parties in previous years. When Alex greeted Teri Sue, he asked if business or the latest cold front was responsible for her goose bumps.

"Must be the draft, honey," she said. "We haven't flashed "No Vacancy' since Labor Day."

"Well, then, you gotta love youth basketball," Alex said, digging for the MasterCard. Layla, Lisa and Rachel were standing outside, shivering in their impatience to storm the hotel pool.

"Six rooms this year?" Alex rolled down the roster. Jill. Mattie and Rachel. Natalie and Katie. Laura. Lisa. And Layla. Jody's moms were due in first thing in the morning, well before the Lakers' opening game. "Six tonight. Seven Saturday."

"More the merrier. I'm putting the squad on the third floor." She was flipping through the stack of registration cards. "I think the Koertjes are already here. And the Dawkins. You want anything special, give ol' Teri Sue a call."

"Thanks. Are the first two floors full?"

"Nope. But this might be Tsunami Weekend."

When Alex reached the car, Layla fleeced him of the key to room 303 and led the charge up the wooden staircase, leaving Alex to unpack. He was on his third trip up the steps, loaded down with backpacks and car trash, when the girls came roaring out of the bathroom, suited up for the indoor pool.

He stretched out on the bed for a minute with SportsCenter, and he was out like a light until Layla pounded on the door, screaming about hunger pangs and hypothermia. Steam was rising off the girls as they vanished into the bathroom for the hot showers and hair dryers. Alex was already an afterthought. Just past 7:30 p.m., Layla finally hurdled the rumbled bed closest to the window and asked if they could hit the arcade.

"What about dinner?"

"We're not hungry. Can we rent a movie?"

"There's a Blockbuster up by the Safeway," Lisa reminded him.

"A movie?" Alex said. "Like what?"

"'Love Actually'?" Layla tendered cautiously.

"'Love Actually?' Isn't that R-rated?"

"PG-13," Rachel sniffed, pulling a sweatshirt over Layla's sweat-gray Georgetown t-shirt, "but don't worry: It doesn't have any sex."

*   *   *

"I thought you told Alex there wasn't any sex," Lisa said as the screen split into the movie's closing montage at Heathrow.

"Well, not real sex," Rachel said, gingerly stretching her legs so not to wake Natalie, who'd fallen asleep with her head in Rachel's lap and was gently snoring through her braces. "Just fake porno."

Rachel's cell burst into a grating 50 cent riff, ending Natalie's nap. "Mustang Ranch," Rachel said, low and sultry. "What's your pleasure?" The comeback clearly didn't impress her. "Guys are beyond stupid," she finally said. "It's a *brothel*, Ian." A short, distressed pause. "A whore house!" She screwed up her face in mock concentration as Ian fought to catch up. "Whoa! Nice thing to say about the place where I was conceived."

Lisa howled. Rachel waved her hand, quieting the room. "When'd you get in?" Laura and Layla were clinging to Rachel, trying to hear Ian's end of the conversation.

"You want to what?" Rachel said. "When?" She listened intently, then buried the phone against her hip. "He wants to know if we can come out."

Gasps all around. Natalie and the remote rolled off the bed together, squealing. Laura had her hand to her mouth in the scruffy easy chair by the window. "They want us to *go out*?" she said.

Rachel nodded silently, trying to focus. "Call you back in two minutes," she said.

"Where are they?" Layla asked.

"Down at the Shiloh."

"Who's there?" Lisa asked.

"Ian. Brandon. Danny. I heard K-Smut kung-fuing in the background."

"What are we gonna do?" Natalie asked, even as Rachel's phone rang again. Rachel didn't waste time with introductions. "I said two minutes," she snapped. "What? I don't …"

She glanced feverishly around the room. "What's our room number?" she asked.

Natalie and Lisa were giggling. "Don't give 'em our room …" Laura began, even as Layla barked out, "303."

"303," Rachel said into the phone. Her eyes widened as the connection broke. "They're coming down," she announced.

Before Natalie could unleash another howl, Lisa slapped a hand over her mouth.

"What do you mean," Layla said, "they're coming down?"

Rachel shimmied off the bed, reached behind the polyester drapes for the drawstring, then jerked them open with several vicious tugs. In the haze beyond their own reflection, they could see the boardwalk, catnapping beneath a lonely row of streetlamps, and a plume of fogs rolling off the ocean, a deep shadow in the distance. "I'm thinking boardwalk," Rachel said. "Easy escape routes to the beach."

"It's dark out there …" Laura piped up, backing into the bathroom alcove.

"No shit, Sherlock," Lisa said.

"… which means they can SEE in our window."

Laura, Layla realized, was ahead of the curve. Everyone was in their post-pool, DVD-and-popcorn sleepover gear, loud T-shirts and loose sweats. Rachel looked more refined in her UC-Santa Barbara sweatshirt but Rachel was already stripping off the sweatshirt in a dash for her overnight bag.

"How far is the Shiloh?" Lisa asked.

"Three blocks," Layla said. "Were they in their room or on the boardwalk?"

"Sounded to me like they were running," said Rachel, who'd taken up position beside Laura in front of the bathroom mirror. Just to be safe, Layla switched off the lamps by the bed and the window. As she pulled the curtains shut, she checked the boardwalk's northbound lanes. A guy in raincoat and floppy hat was shuffling along with a cockier spaniel, but she saw nothing beyond him but those pockets of fog.

"Where's your dad?" Lisa asked Layla.

"Drinking a beer with my dad," Laura said, gliding over to the door and setting the chain. "I can't believe ..."

The room phone went off like a small grenade. Lisa and Layla both jumped. Natalie ripped off another squawk. "Strip City," Rachel purred, then winced noticeably as she extended the phone to Layla. "Your dad."

Perfect, Layla thought. "What's up?"

"What's going on?" her father asked. "And who was that?"

"Rachel being Rachel"

"What's all the yelling?"

"Natalie was showing us the routine dance team used to win state," Layla said, no longer surprised at how easily the lies rolled off her tongue.

"It's 11:40. I'll be back in 10, so start thinking about shutting down for the night."

Layla didn't buy the 10-minute scenario. "We'll be quiet. Love you!" She replaced the phone in its cradle, turned to her chastened audience: "My dad says ... Shuuuush!"

Lisa burst out laughing. "Gee, I wonder what *my* dad would have said."

Layla motored to the window, pulled back one of the drapes and laid her cheek against the glass. She could hear waves breaking, and see the fog gliding toward the headlights on the coast highway. The cocker spaniel had disappeared and the boardwalk looked like Sunday morning, a hideout for slugs and gulls and broken sand dollars and ...

Something moved. A shimmer under the pale dome of light 100 yards down the boardwalk. Not a shadow, but a shape. Two shapes. Four shapes, darting beneath the light. Layla clenched the drapes shut in her right fist. "They're coming!"

In the scramble for cover, Laura killed the bathroom light, Rachel clipped the corner of the TV and Lisa stumbled over the travel bag Layla had left in the middle of the floor. They were still laughing when they reached the window, pushing past Layla so they could see for themselves. The boys, she realized, were trying to stay cool but they were clueless as to the location of Room 303. That uncertainty kept them bunched together as they approached the hotel and searched its façade.

"Is that K-Smut by the ... No, that's Danny ... Natalie, quit ... They must be freezin' ... That's my foot, Rachel! ... Close the drapes, close the drapes ..."

"Chill," Layla said, pulling the drawstring and creating a four-foot viewing area. "They can't see us. It's darker in here than it is out there."

"Better keep your mouth shut, Natalie," Lisa said, "or you'll give us away."

"Are you sure ...?" Rachel whispered.

"Look at 'em," Layla said. The boys had paused at the corner of the building. Danny and Ian were pointing toward another third-floor window. "Unless you're up against the window, they can't see you. We could flash 'em and they'd never know."

The silence lasted all of five seconds. "You thinking what I'm thinking?" Rachel said.

"We can't! We can't! We can't!" The needle, clearly, was stuck in Natalie's braces.

"No one has to know," Rachel said. "Our secret. The greatest secret of all time."

"I dunno ..." Layla said. The boys were bunched by the scrub pine, scanning the gallery of windows. K-Smut began doing jumping jacks, waving his hands over his head.

"Geez," Laura said, "how horny are those guys?"

"Mr. Buchanan calls that a constant, not a variable," Natalie said.

"So, who's with me?" Rachel said, floating at the edge of the shadows and the damp light creeping into the room from the boardwalk. She was stripping off the Georgetown t-shirt. The darkness in the room was thick and seductive.

"Alright," Laura said, "I'm there," and she casually pulled the sweatshirt over her head, leaving nothing behind but her trademark scarlet bra. They all stared for a moment, surprised that someone had finally taken that leap off the 3-meter board, long enough for Laura to raise her arms and wrap them around her chest. Then Rachel howled, "I love it," and pulled off her T-shirt, revealing the same bikini top she'd taken into the pool.

Danny and Ian were leading the scouting party back down the boardwalk. Natalie moaned from the pile of extra blankets, "We're dead. We're all dead."

"C'mon, they're right there." Laura's voice was a fierce whisper. She wrapped her sweatshirt around the lower half of her face like Bonnie following Clyde into the bank, and glided toward the window. "Put 'em up against the glass!"

Layla followed Laura and Rachel to the window, using her Reggie Bush jersey as a shield. The heating unit was chugging away, and Rachel climbed atop it and began pounding on the window. As Layla stepped up to the window, covering her face with the jersey, the boys froze. Ian was pointing, which really wasn't necessary. At 11:52 p.m., there weren't many burlesque shows available on the third floor of the Surf & Sand.

For a moment, and only a moment, the drama was exhilarating. They had flown a long way from those "Peter Pan" productions in the Uplands cafeteria, but there was a similar sense of grandeur. The curtains were pulled back, the spotlight on. They had a captive audience and the stage to themselves, to show off, to masquerade with anonymous abandon, beyond the reach of second thought or repercussion. For a glorious moment, the performance art was magical, indeed.

Then Lisa turned on the lights.

In the ragged second before Rachel's scream rattled the window pane, Layla got a peek at how ridiculous they looked, the lights bouncing off the glass and tossing their reflection back into the room. They were sleepover tarts, drunk on birthday cake and Diet Sprite. Then that reflection splintered, as dramatically as if someone had side-armed a rock through the window. Laura dropped to the floor and Rachel dove for the bed. Layla scuttled into the bathroom. The harmony of their panic and Lisa's laughter was so raucous there was no telling how long it took someone to hear – like the echo of the drums when Pippin knocks the skeleton into the well at Balin's Tomb – the pounding on the door.

"Shit!" Rachel barked. "How'd they get up here so fast?"

"It's my dad," Layla stammered.

"Or hotel security," Laura insisted. She cracked open the door. In the anxious silence, everyone heard Jody say, "Dude! Where's your shirt?"

Laura swung the door open. Jody was standing in her trademark backwards baseball cap, travel bag at her feet. "Sorry I'm late," she said, staring at the scarlet bra, "but you might want to cover up. Mom's girlfriend's in the parking lot."

"Is K-Smut laughing or choking to death?" Rachel asked. At which point Layla heard her father on the motel steps. "Hey, Lisbeth, let me carry that."

Everyone was covered by the time Alex reached the door. He wasn't happy when he saw the room, Layla could tell, but he didn't say anything, simply crossing to the windows and closing the curtains. If he saw the boys racing off, he gave no sign, and he was asleep by 11:40 p.m. Layla spent 10 minutes listening to the uneven rumble of his snoring, then slipped out of bed and padded across the carpet to the crack in the curtains.

Once again, the boardwalk was empty but she stood silently, watching the fog drift past the streetlights. She wondered what Ian, Danny and K-Smut had seen. She wondered if Lisa was going to regret all the sex that was creeping into her text messages with Brent McBride and whether Emily was getting better or worse. While her father slept, she wrapped the curtain around her shoulders and wondered what was coming next.

* * *

The Lakers' opener against Astoria wasn't scheduled in Seaside High's main gym but on one of the midget courts upstairs. Alex pegged the temperature at 55 degrees; the seven LO parents were huddled together for warmth on the bottom row of the bleachers.

The Fishermen were a perfect opening act, bristling with enthusiasm, hurting for talent. In Lake Oswego, parents could handle the traveling fees and Club Sport memberships, but there wasn't the same disposal income at the coast. Astoria had two players, max, who could play for LO, so Alex wasn't sweating the final score or Mick's absence.

Rachel stole the opening tip, Lisa broke in the right direction and Laura fed her for the easy lay-up. No one else scored over the next five minutes. The Fishermen couldn't penetrate the 1-3-1, and the Lakers weren't doing much better with Astoria's zone, packed in the lane. Chelsea would have picked the zone apart, shooting over it from the wings and feeding cutters from the high post, but Chelsea was 75 miles away.

With two minutes left in the quarter, Astoria scored off the break and Alex called for time. His initial call never rose above the celebration of the Astoria cheering section, so he barked it out twice more before one of the officials took the hint. Alex recognized most of the refs on the circuit, even on trips to the coast, but these guys – a top-heavy gym teacher and a Steve Buscemi look-alike – were strangers. As Mr. Woodcock gave him the time-out, he said, "Calm down, coach. No need to yell."

"You didn't hear me the first two times."

"Heard you just fine, coach," the ref said, reaching for a water bottle.

Rachel and Lisa were slumped in their chair, Jody climbing into her white warm-up sweatshirt. "What does frostbite look like?" Laura asked, examining her fingers.

"I'm sorry," Alex said. "When school budgets get tight, they skimp on the heat. After the game, we'll find a fireplace."

"We have one in our room," Jody said.

In your room? Damn, Alex thought, Teri Sue was holding out on him. He buried his hands in his sweatshirt. "Dad …" Layla said. "Didn't you call time?"

Alex nodded, slowly. "We're tied with Astoria. And it's 2-to-2." With that, he returned to his chair. The girls looked at one another without saying anything, straightening their hair, adjusting their jerseys. Lisa was the first to speak. "Consolation round?" she said. Grins all around. And no one was shivering when they walked back onto the court.

At the start of the second quarter, Alex subbed in Jill and Katie, determined to ignore the traveling violations and the refs' refusal to whistle the moving screens. It happened now and then, usually on Saturday mornings when the refs wanted the afternoon off. It was girls' basketball, after all. Blocking fouls didn't count. Whatever. Alex knew it didn't matter, except that Astoria had a 5-foot-10 linebacker bolted in the paint. With three minutes left in the half, she'd scored three times on offensive rebounds, twice bowling over Mattie in the process. LO was leading 15-12 when She-Hulk set up in the low post, both Reeboks firmly planted in the lane, and called for the ball.

One Mississippi, two Mississippi, three … When he reached five, Alex stood up and yelled, "Three seconds!"

Steve Buscemi, parked under the basket, promptly blew his whistle. Alex was turning away when the ref pointed at him and said, "That's a technical."

"A technical?" he said, as the ref approached the scorer's table. "For what?"

Buscemi gave him a look. "Trying to influence game calls from the bench."

"That's a first. And I've been playing and coaching this game for 20 years."

Mr. Woodcock was directing Astoria's point guard to the foul line. His partner took two steps toward Alex and pointed to the bench. "Sit down," he said, "and let the girls play. You have anything to say, you tell your team captain and have her talk to me."

Alex nodded. He could work with that. "Layla!" he called out, "tell the ref that 54 hasn't left the lane since breakfast."

Layla took a half step forward, then stopped. Buscemi turned back toward Alex, inserting his whistle in his mouth. His mustache was quivering. "One more word, coach, and you're gone."

Alex opened his mouth, then shut it again as Astoria's point guard air-balled her second free throw. This was an unfamiliar calculus for a Saturday morning at the beach. He could feel the eyes of the Astoria parents on him as he reviewed his options. Layla was suddenly at his elbow. "You got a technical?" she asked, with begrudging admiration. "Because you yelled, 'Three seconds'?"

Alex nodded. The ref was rolling up behind Layla. "C'mon, 4," he barked, reading the number off Layla's uniform. "Back on the court."

"Relax," Alex said.

The word was barely out of his mouth before the whistle cut through the frigid air. "Have it your way," Buscemi said. "You're done. Hit the road."

"You're throwing me out for saying three words?"

"You didn't even swear," Margaret observed helpfully at the scorer's table.

"You're through, coach," the ref said. "Get moving."

"You're a joke," Alex said.

The ref leaned over the scorers' table and the two Seaside sophomores tending the official book. "I need the tournament director up here. Now!" The second ref suddenly appeared, stepping between Alex and his partner as if the latter needed a bodyguard. "Are you watching this?" Alex asked.

"You need to leave, coach," the ref said, as if he'd just realized the gym didn't have metal detectors and Alex might be packing. At the scorers' table, the blond sophomore said, "I think he's down at the Safeway, buying poppy-seed muffins."

"I'm getting thrown out for saying 'Three seconds' and 'Relax'?" Alex asked.

"'Got nothing to do with me, coach," the ref said. "But you need to leave right now or your team's gonna forfeit."

At times like these, your high-def, in-house projector began spinning the fantasy reels. You three-fingered a basketball at the dork. You keyed his car.

You challenged him to a game to eleven and spent 10 minutes dunking on his ass. You …

"We don't have a coach?" Laura said. The girls were bunched around him.

"What'd you do?" Layla asked, something caught in her throat.

"I got tossed," Alex said. "Laura, tell your dad we need him on the bench."

"My dad," Lisa said, "is gonna be so jealous."

Rachel had the back of her right hand across her forehead in a superb Scarlett O'Hara: "We'll never play in this town again."

"Stay calm," Alex said, needing them to focus. "Win by …"

Buscemi was back. "If you're not off the floor in 10 seconds, I'm calling the game."

You stuffed the whistle down his throat. You told him to kiss your ass. You …

You beat a retreat. The nervous silence in the gym was broken only by the solemn thump of the ball as Astoria lined up for another free throw. Alex could feel the eyes of the crowd. He passed Lizbeth, who stared at him with a large bag of popcorn in her hands, then asked, "Halftime already?" Only when he reached the door did he feel Layla behind him.

"Are you OK?" she asked, her hand gripping his arm, as maternal as he'd ever heard her.

"I'll be waiting outside," he said. "Score 30." He pushed through the door, took a deep breath. It was warmer in the stairwell than the gym. In the lobby at the base of the stairs, the woman guarding the cash box and the admission tickets glanced over her shoulder, smiled, then returned to her gothic romance. The snack shack lights were on but no one was home.

Alex needed someone to talk to, if only to release his frustration. He stopped at the cash box. "Excuse me," he said, "but who's running the tournament this year?"

... convinced the governor of Oregon to marshal the National Guard. You arranged for Vincent Vega and Jules Winnfield to pay a little visit to Steve Buscemi's double-wide in Warrenton ...

"Jerry Walker," the woman said, adjusting her reading glasses. "Do you ..."

"I need ..." Alex stopped. An elderly couple, each 60 pounds overweight, came bustling through the door, Grandpa trying to dig the wallet out of his back pocket.

"Directions to the best coffee shop in Seaside," Alex said.

"Morning Star Café," the cashier said. "Right on 101, down about D Street."

As Alex stepped outside, a line of geese passed overhead, painting the windshields in the parking lot.

*   *   *

They spent an hour that night at the pizza end of Gearhart Pizza-Bowl before walking down the hall to the bowling alley. This being Saturday night, they could only secure a single lane, so Alex and Mick rounded up the pink 10-pound balls for the girls and ordered a pitcher of Mirror Pond. Alex scanned the *Daily Astorian* while Mick ducked into the can. A junior-high gym teacher in Clatsop County had been suspended after three high-school seniors accused him of fondling them in his office after seventh-grade volleyball practice. The details were purposely vague.

The Mirror Pond arrived before Mick did. Alex set the paper down, even as a flurry of screams rolled up from Lane 1. Rachel was dancing like an "American Idol" contestant on her way to New York, collecting high fives and appreciative glances from the alcoholics in the adjacent lane. Mick settled in at the other end of the table, and took a deep pull on the Mirror Pond. Boston's "More Than a Feeling" was rocking the alley. Dale Earnhardt Jr. was enshrined on the nearest wall, above the cases of Budweiser that didn't fit behind the bar. Mick re-examined his glass, then asked, "Since when do the Gearhart bowling alleys serve microbrews?"

"The march of progress," Alex said.

"When did you make it back to the gym?"

"In plenty of time. The tournament director met me at the door."

"Just the one-game suspension?"

Alex nodded. "My Seaside red card."

Margaret and the Koertjes were standing by the bowling check-in desk with Sherri, Mattie's' mom. Mick waved them over. "So, where'd you end up?"

"The Bellevue-Seaside game. Bellevue was up 32-6 at the half."

"Bellevue's that good?"

"Seaside's that bad." He hoisted his beer glass. "I drink to forget."

As the Koertjes pulled up chairs, Sherri Dawkins collapsed between Alex and Mick. Sherri was a big girl – the source of Mattie's power on the boards – and she wasn't ashamed of her size. A partner in a downtown law firm that specialized in divorce, she generated raw and entertaining cynicism. Alex often wondered what it would be like to live with her. Sherri's husband, Ricardo, was never around to ask.

"Missed you this afternoon," Sherri said, reaching for the pitcher. "You follow that lard ass home?"

"Does my answer fall under attorney-client privilege?"

"Hell, no."

"Sounds like the girls got along fine without me."

Sherri nodded, confirming that he exaggerated his importance in their lives. She leaned past Alex as another celebration broke out on Lane 1. "Jesus. They have no dimmer switch. They're either full on or full off."

"I can't keep up," Alex admitted.

"Part of your charm. You're a chronic under-achiever."

Not a trace of a smile. "Sherri, you say the sweetest things."

"You've met Mercedes, right?" Sherri's older daughter. "When she was playing classic, the coach was this Iraqi midget named Khalid. All-world back in

Baghdad, but he never fit in here. Got fired at Intel, I think, and decided the soccer club was the only place he could draw a paycheck. Wound way too tight. When Mercedes was a sophomore, the team had a tournament in San Diego. Three days, four games, half an afternoon to enjoy 75-degree San Diego in mid-November. So, I finesse a field trip to Sea World. Bought the tickets, arranged transportation, the works. Then the team loses 3-2 that morning – on PKs, for God's sake – and Khalid cancels the Sea World get-away. Rents a bus to take everyone to the Olympic training center so the girls can finally confront the sacrifices they need to make to play for the U.S. Olympic team."

"The Olympic team."

"Uh-huh. That was Mercedes back then: We couldn't get through dinner without her stripping down to the black sports bra, just to prove her dedication."

"What'd you see at the Olympic training center?"

"I didn't see anything. Me and Mercedes had a date with Shamu. Told Khalid that if he gave her any grief I'd INS his ass. Must have been a damn fine motivational speech because half the team joined us on the bus."

Sherri drained her beer. "And that," she said, "is part of your charm. I've never had to give you that speech. Mick is a dick, but you keep things in perspective."

"Technicals, aside."

"Natch. Now, be a dear and get the team moms another pitcher of Miller Lite."

"You mean Mirror Pond?"

"You mean I look like a girl who gives a damn on a Saturday night?"

He weaved through the cramped tables, angling for the taps. He was still trying to get the bartender's attention when Scott Koertje arrived, sawbuck in hand. "Let me get this one," he said. "You've had a bad day."

"Thanks." Alex looked back at Sherri, who was howling in Mick's ear. "Maybe we should each get a pitcher."

Three bands of pins exploded in rapid succession. Alex watched Laura shimmy back from an 8-10 split. "Your daughter having fun?"

Scott nodded. "I think so. Are we friends talking or coach and dad talking?"

"What happens in Gearhart, stays in Gearhart."

The barkeep arrived and Koertje handed him the $20. "She's fine," he said, lifting his voice over Rick Springfield's guitar. "I don't know if she takes it as seriously as the other girls."

"Probably not. But it doesn't matter, not yet," Alex said. "It's weird watching her on the court. How much did she play with Molly when they were …"

He stopped. Growing up? They weren't finished growing up.

"All the time. For a while, at least. Why?"

"Echoes. Those cuts to the basket. Molly was always one of my favorites. You know that. And I keep thinking I see stuff she passed on to her sister."

"They're nothing alike."

"Nothing?"

The pitchers arrived. So did the change. Scott didn't reach for either of them.

"I saw her a couple months ago," Alex said. "Molly, I mean. End of summer. She was at the high school, watching a soccer game. Told me she's going to Lincoln."

"Just barely. She's not fitting in. At Thanksgiving, she was thinking about transferring again. We're worried. About a lot of things."

"I can't believe she quit playing basketball. When did she burn out?"

"I don't know. She went to play for that traveling squad the summer before high school. Missed her friends, I think, but things were fine. And then ... I don't know. She just didn't want to do it anymore. When I'd try to talk to her about it, she shut me down. Shut us all out."

"At the first team meeting. You were asking about Seaside. Like, why were we going out of town?"

Koertje waved him off. "No big deal. Least it wasn't once you said parents could come along for the ride. That was verboten on Molly's AAU team."

"Why"

Scott shrugged. "Sherri's calling for the beer," he said. He picked up one of the pitchers, Alex grabbing up the second. When they reached the table, the tumblers in Alex's memory vault finally aligned. "That AAU team," he said, "the summer before high school. You remember Molly's coach?"

"Sure. Taze Elliott. A real piece of work."

Alex was up early. As he slipped out of the shower and quietly dressed, the mound that was Layla never moved beneath the Gordian knot of sheets and blankets.

The streets were wet and empty, the seat of the Durango stiff and cold. On the six-block drive to the Coast Highway, he passed a brocade of Christmas lights and a chimney communing with a wood stove, but most of Seaside was passing on 8 a.m. mass. There were three cars in the Morning Star lot, and one old-timer sitting in the corner. When he shuffled out the door, Alex snared the newspaper he left behind. He worked his way through the high-school hoop scores, the obituaries of the women who'd married Marines after the war, the rationale for the latest utility-rate hike. It was Sunday morning. The girls were sleeping in.

On the way back to the Surf & Sand, he stopped by Safeway for donuts, filling two pink boxes with Maple bars and apple fritters. When he reached the motel, the door to 303 was cracked and five girls on the two double beds, watching a movie with the sound turned low. They murmured good mornings and not much else. When he set the donuts down, no one moved. Layla took a sip of his lukewarm coffee, then disappeared beneath the blankets. Alex felt as if he was intruding, so he settled into the corner chair, the paper in his lap, even if he suddenly lacked the strength to open it.

The girls were watching "Love Actually" again. Joni Mitchell was singing, Emma Thompson shivering beside her bed. In the quiet, Alex couldn't be sure who was awake and who still sleeping. He was pretty sure that was Rachel's head atop his bunched-up pillow and Laura curled inside the comforter at the foot of the bed, but the last set of remains was a mystery.

He couldn't believe how lucky he was. For all he knew, Mick and the parents in the rooms down the hall were feeling much the same, luxuriating in a hot shower or the stillness of the morning. He was happy here, grateful that his room was the theater balcony, the staging area, a place where the girls didn't care how they looked or how old he felt. You spent so much time as a parent on 24-hour call, resolving dilemmas, rescuing spiders, the tutor or chauffer of last resort, and then you were suddenly unnecessary. His son made that clear in dozens of ways. With these girls, he didn't know how much time he had left.

He was reading the Op-Ed pages when Mattie arrived in an Oregon sweatshirt and freshly washed hair. She stared at the slumber party. "Hey, Laura, you awake?"

Laura lifted her head off the pillow in weary protest. "This can't be good."

"Will you braid my hair?" Mattie asked.

Laura opened her mouth, then shut it again, and rolled into a seated position. "French?" she said.

Mattie nodded, opening her right hand to reveal a half dozen hair braids in black and blue. Laura pulled a brush off the nightstand and crawled to the end of the bed, gesturing for Mattie to lean back between her legs. Rachel shimmied aside without complaint, and Laura went to work, running her fingers through Mattie's hair to clear the tangles, then applied the brush. She didn't hurry; the rhythm of the brush was hypnotic. By the time she reached for a three-inch section of hair just behind Mattie's forehead, Lisa was watching from the other bed.

"Can you do mine next?" she asked. Raindrops were striking the window pane. And for the longest time, there wasn't a sound other than the crinkling of a newspaper, the soft soundtrack of the movie, and the journey of Laura's hands through Mattie's dirty blond hair.

January. Mother-f'ing January. From one dark end to the other, the month deserved to be locked in a garage with a deuce and a quarter with the motor running. January in Oregon was a vicious rain that turned to ice whenever the wind kicked up in the Columbia Gorge. An endless stream of broken umbrellas, wet dogs, clogged drains, and malevolent clouds. A month-long enema.

Taze Elliott opened his eyes at 7:20 a.m. with the usual erection and Carrie complaining she had better things to do. "This'll only take a minute," he promised, rolling her onto her back. He told himself these were moans of pleasure when he spent 90 seconds later, not that he gave a good goddam. His mind was elsewhere, on that afternoon he was entertaining Caitlin with some serious sexual healing when her two roommates returned early from "The Lion King" and began pounding on the cheap hotel room door. He didn't know if it was the sound of their adolescent whining or Caitlin's frantic gyrations beneath him, desperate to escape and curl up in some hiding place, but Taze came like a freight train, so gloriously that he was contemplating another happy ending when Cait finally got her head out from under the weight of his right hand and convinced him her roommates would be back, armed with a key from the front desk. He couldn't count the times he'd replayed the scene over the years.

With no sense of gratitude, Carrie shoved him away, and disappeared into the bathroom. Taze stayed in bed, trying to remember the last time the sun had been waiting when he left the house. Why did he settle for this BS when there were coaching jobs and deluded parents in Santa Barbara and Scottsdale

He showered at 9:30 a.m., then dressed – slate-gray Nike sweats and a Hoya T-shirt – and wandered into the kitchen, looking for breakfast. There was Carrie's grazing garbage – granola, yogurt, bran flakes and dried fruit – and not much else. He slapped the kitchen counter with his open palm, loud enough for the love birds in the living room to lunge for one another. Carrie's lovebirds, Gus and Lorena. This was Carrie's house, Carrie's fridge, Carrie's four-poster bed, and Carrie's stack of bills on the side table in the hall. He never reached for his money clip. He owned the van in the driveway, the barbells in the basement, and the Hustlers in the garage, nothing he couldn't collect in a

New York minute at the first sign of pressure or obligation.

They'd met two years ago at Lakeridge High School. He was late leaving the gym after another Black Tornado blowout; she'd arrived early with the floral decorations for the drama club's production of "Dark of the Moon." Seeing that she was white and mangy blond and closing in on 40, he was surprised when she met his gaze as they passed in the parking lot, then turned back around when he said, "Hey there, sugar."

"Sweet and Lo," she said, with a laugh. "Sweet and Lo."

Elliott had an instinct for weakness, a feel for the badly stitched wound. The combination served him well as a coach, and brought him back that night after the final curtain. He was behind the wheel, the window open, a fifth of Jim Beam in a paper bag on the passenger seat when she floated past with a small bouquet of roses. "Just how sweet, sugar?" he asked. "Just how low?" Twelve minutes later, she was blowing him in a church parking lot, the roses crushed between her knees and the worn upholstery of the passenger seat. He needed several weeks to piece together her story – gardening diva, divorced, nine-year-old kid living with the ex – but he picked up on her flaws straight away: neediness, recklessness, her masochistic tendency to collapse toward the source of her pain. Taze didn't waste any time testing her tolerance for abuse. She was unfazed by cruelty and invective. The resignation in her eyes when his will overwhelmed hers reminded him of Unique, his kid sister, in the last year he lived at home, after his mother got the liver cancer and his father began foraging to get what was coming to him.

They never talked about his moving in. After two months or so, Taze walked out of his Barbur Boulevard apartment, forfeiting the damage deposit, and began unloading 12-packs of Michelob in Carrie's fridge. They both knew the rules. He didn't have any. He'd bring in the paper and spring for the occasional bottle of vino from Trader Joe's. Carrie brought home the paycheck. He'd give her "The Daily Show" and keep the toilet seat down, but he didn't take out the garbage or take no for an answer in bed.

Taze left the house just before noon and stopped by McDonalds for the Pulp Fiction special, wolfing the quarter-pounder down as he listened to Jim Rome and the white trash. He had just dropped his trash out the window when his cell phone busted out with Sly Stone. Taze took his time. Too often the cell was bad news, someone trying to track him down or even the score. Elliott had a dozen numbers blocked and he never picked up if he didn't recognize the caller. He recognized this one.

"Hey, Sarah."

"Hey, Coach," Sarah Innocenti said. "Whacha doing?"

"Usual. Watching old game films. Just saw you throw down 28 against Prairie."

"Prairie? Eight steals, right?"

"Eleven. Dumb ass at the scorer's table."

"Coach, you say the sweetest things. You catch last night's box score?"

"Couldn't find it in The Oregonian." Taze racked his brain. "Northern Arizona?"

"UC-Santa Barbara."

"And?"

Sarah laughed, a good sign. "Nothing for the highlight reel. Four points and two assists in garbage time."

Innocenti was one of Elliott's Oregon City kids, the starting point guard on two of the Pioneer state championship teams. Taze first saw her play as a sixth grader in Canby when she was smaller than anyone on the court by a third, and quicker by a half. Her father serviced the prop planes at the Aurora airport and couldn't afford the private lessons Elliott recommended, but Taze recognized a resume builder when he saw one stealing every ball that came within reach. He brought Sarah on board in seventh grade.

"Garbage time? No such thing. Left the game better than you found it, right?"

"Always."

"How's the knee?"

That cursed right knee. By the time she entered Oregon City as a freshman – Taze helped her family relocate to the 1200-square foot house on South End Road – Sarah was one of the top three point guards in the state. As a sophomore, she averaged a double-double in steals and assists on the Pioneer team that won all three games at the Chiles Center by 20 points or more, and Elliott fielded a dozen calls from mechanics in McMinnville and Medford who also had a diamond in the rough. They kept Taze in Johnny Walker Black and paid for the used Mercedes before Sarah collapsed in summer league on a slippery court in Corvallis with a torn ACL. Elliott rushed her back to Emmanuel for the surgery that kept her on crutches for the first half of her junior year. She came back strong as a senior, winning the MVP trophy and that second state title, but by then the D-1 coaches had moved on, recognizing that Sarah had lost the magical step that separates the best Pac-10 players and the girls who end up at Faith Christian.

"The knee?" Sarah said. "Still talking to me at night."

"Oh, yeah? And what's it saying?"

"Can we sleep in? Just this once?"

"Pain bothering you?"

"What pain?"

"That's my girl."

She'd never hurt for attitude. Most girls never came back from that moment when the knee snapped, but the knee wasn't the only thing that aged in the year she spent on crutches and painkillers. Both her desperation and her determination were tempered upon her return. Panic had given way to patience, the reticence that kept you whole when a greased court tore your ticket to the big time in half.

"You gonna tell me about the assists?" Taze asked.

"They weren't much. One on the break, another on a back-door cut. Nothing that brought Sadie Hawkins out of her seat."

Sadie Hawkland, Faith Christian's coach, was a frontrunner, slavishly devoted to her starters. "Last time I saw a seat like that," Taze said, "it was attached to Bighouse Gaines."

Sarah giggled. "Bighouse who?"

"Gaines. Eight hundred damn wins at Winston-Salem. Coached ..."

"Earl the Pearl. Forgive me, father, for my occasional memory lapse."

"What'd you have for breakfast?"

"Nothing ... yet."

"Then hustle that skinny white ass of yours down to Elmer's for the French toast and bacon."

"Yes, sir."

"That's what I like to hear. Playing this weekend?"

"Fullerton Saturday night."

"Call me after."

"No. 1 on my speed dial. Thanks, coach." And Sarah cut the connection.

Elliott fired up the van, cutting off Jim Rome's interview with Steve Elkington and sending the wipers streaking across his windshield. Damn rain would not let up.

*   *   *

The wipers were still pounding, the sky still dark, when Taze reached Westview High, 50 minutes before the Tornado's second game – in three nights – in the Westview Winter Classic. He was glad to see

Thalia's Camry parked by the gym doors, considerably less excited about the Volvo C70. Chelsea Lider and the Giuliani girls were sitting on the front row of the bleachers in their jet black sweats. Alone of the three, Chelsea was working on her dribbling, moving the ball back and forth under the bridge of her legs. Debra and Jack Lider were standing by the scorer's table, and they glanced over, checking to see if Taze was approachable. He wasn't. He'd called Carrie to make sure she had the prime rib ready when he got home, and the bitch ignored the cell.

Several members of the Heartbreakers, the second best select team in the Northwest, were goofing at the far end of the court. Elliott's girls were equally ready but they wouldn't move until the entire team was assembled. Anything else looked bush. Beginning with warm-ups, Taze wanted the Tornado to leave the impression it was fully loaded, exquisitely focused, perfectly in synch. They'd need that edge against the Heartbreakers, 17-1 and riding a nine-game winning streak. Taze had watched three of the nine wins, sitting across from the team bench, large popcorn in hand, memorizing their pressure points. They didn't have many. Good outside shooting, a tremendous small forward – currently swishing free throws at the stripe – aggressive man-to-man D. They had the edge in talent. They just lacked a quality coach.

At 6:30, Elliott instructed Thalia, "Take 'em out," and the girls rolled onto the floor, bearing the attitude you'd expect from a team that hadn't lost in more than a year. Taze remained in the lobby. He wanted their opponents looking over their shoulder, wondering when the legend would step from the shadows. The Heartbreakers were beyond this jive, he guessed, but he wouldn't break the routine. With four minutes left in warm-ups, he sauntered to the bench. He made a point of nodding at the refs as if he was glad to see them, ignoring the Heartbreakers' wannabe coach.

*   *   *

"Tornado up or down?"

"Down, I think. They're the home team."

"First time all year."

"Heartbreakers beat Oregon City over Christmas by 12."

"Which one is … never mind."

"She went right by Chelsea."

"You see Jack?"

"Mid-court. Halfway up. Surprisingly calm. What's wrong with Layla?"

"Her stomach hurts."

"Stress?"

"Nerves. Then she doesn't eat, which doesn't help."

"Damn."

"No kidding. Dribbled right around them."

"Think we can trap her?"

"No. But I'm a Blazer fan. The optimism has been bled out of me."

"Who do we have so far?"

"Everyone but Lauren. Damn. Two in a row. Point guard penetrates, then kicks it out."

"NBA threes."

"Thank you, Stewart Scott. Jack is giving us the shit-eatin' grin."

"He says one word and I'll congratulate him for enlisting Chelsea with a rapist."

"We don't know that. All we know …"

"… is parents never ask questions. You believe her hands?"

"Girls try to dribble against that and they're dead."

"I asked around at Nike. Rumors are out on Taze. And we can run press break."

"Chelsea *knows* press break."

"Mattie can throw it over the top."

"Yeah. Once."

"Damn. Weren't they down four when we came in?"

"Yep. Twelve-point turn-around."

"In what? Two minutes?"

"Taze is quiet."

"What does he have to get upset about?

"You sure you want the girls watching this?"

"I know. NC-17. Is that Burt and Flossie? By the door."

"We'll be fine."

"Geez. Why didn't Chelsea shoot that way for us?"

"She did … 'til you decided she was the Big Fundamental in the low post."

"I did, didn't I? Why the heck did you listen to me?"

"Hero worship."

*   *   *

He was feeling magnanimous after the game, generous enough that he might have told Flip Armour, the Heartbreakers' coach, he had one hell of a team if the punk had followed his girls through the congratulations line. Taze used his absence to fawn over Vanessa Leonard, who'd scored 19 against the Tornado D, but she had that glazed-eye reaction of a kid who'd heard too much praise over the years.

His players were waiting by the bench. "Championship game is 4 o'clock tomorrow," he said. "I want you in bed by eleven, computers and cell phones off. Eat a decent breakfast, a light lunch and be here by 3:15. And don't listen to a damn thing your parents say on the way home. Buckle your seat belt, nod as much as you want but don't listen to a single dumb-ass word. Got that?"

Nods all around. The girls dispersed, save for the Giuliani twins, who hung back, awaiting further instructions. "What?" he said. "You looking for the limo?"

"Nope," Sierra said. "Cici's mom. What time you coming over?

"Fifteen years old and I'm already on the clock," Taze said. "Thought you were going to a movie."

"Fourteen," Sarita corrected him. "We are. 'Spider-Man 2.'"

"Lay off the popcorn."

Sierra glanced over her shoulder to make sure no one else was within earshot. "White Russians?" she whispered.

"Get outta here," Elliott scowled, and the twins scampered off, laughing. As Taze collected the practice balls, the two other semi-finalists came onto the court with the usual tin-eared enthusiasm. Taze didn't look up. He'd checked the bracket. Nothing but B teams in the other draw. This had been the title game. Tomorrow they'd win by 30.

He was thinking about dinner – New York strip at the Acropolis? – as he marched outside and into the rain. Taze was soaked before he got the duffel bag into the van and his ass behind the wheel. Friggin' January. He cranked up the van and reviewed his options. If memory served, Tigard was playing at Jesuit. He could pick up ribs at Busters, then curl up in a corner of the Crusaders' gym, maintaining stage presence as he sucked pork and sweet sauce off the bones.

*   *   *

It wasn't much of a game, Jesuit leading from beginning to end. The Crusaders' coach, Jenni LaPorte, didn't have stand-out players, but she got the most out of the leftovers. They ran the offense – back screens and dumping the ball into the post until shooters shook free – and got into people's faces on D.

Taze recognized the point guard, whom he hadn't seen since she transferred in from Milwaukie at the start of this, her sophomore year. Meleta Sanchez. Her old man, Hector, was a Caron Butler-style small forward, the best player ever to come out of Milwaukie. Taze had talked to Hector when Meleta was 10, but Sanchez was adamant. "She's a Milwaukie girl. Her friends are here. Why would she wander off with you?"

"I got a half-dozen girls playing D-1 who'll answer that."

"I have a 10-year-old who's happy in Milwaukie."

"Mustang varsity team didn't win a game in Three Rivers last year."

"And they'll never win again if the best players hightail it for Oregon City. When the girl's got me, what she need with you?"

The *famiglia* Sanchez toughed it out for a year, a year in which Meleta averaged 14 points and Milwaukie finished 2-23. Oregon City already had a boatload of girls, Taze guessed, so Hector enrolled his daughter at Jesuit. Meleta had a nice set of hands and a gift for pushing the ball up against the press, but she couldn't resurrect an entire athletic program on her own.

After the game, Taze lumbered onto the court. He couldn't find Hector or Angelina, his wife, and he was ready to bail when Meleta emerged from the locker room, black hair pulled back and pinned above her head. Taze set off across the floor. He was halfway home when LaPorte broke away from several parents and stepped into his path. "May I help you?" she said.

He was focused on Meleta, not the question, when LaPorte slid right and cut him off. Surprised, he pulled up short. Thanks to her heels, they were eye-to-eye. He didn't know what to say. "I'm Taze Elliott."

"I know who you are," LaPorte said. "Can I help you?" She was gorgeous. Maxim cover quality.

"It's good. Just checking in with Meleta." Once again, Taze stepped around the coach and once again LaPorte cut him off.

"I don't think so," she said. "You're bothering a player in my gym. I want you to leave."

"Bothering? What the hell you mean, 'botherin'?' I'm talking about Meleta Sanchez. I'm a friend of the family."

Jenni LaPorte didn't blink. She had an Anne Tyler jacket on over a dark blue blouse and a blush high on her cheeks. "You're not a friend of the Jesuit family," she said. "And if you don't leave now, I'll call security."

Taze took a step back, then paused. Several parents had stopped talking and swung their focus in his direction. "Ain't right," he finally managed. "I'm a family friend. Me and Hector ..."

"I know who you are," LaPorte said. "I know ..." – she was drawing the words out now – "who ... you ... are. And if you ever approach one of my players ..." She left the threat hanging there, and Taze understood this was personal. How or why he didn't know, but this was deeply personal.

"Ain't right," he said again, covering his retreat. "Ain't right." He didn't look back as he cut past the concession stands and trophy cases. There was an umbrella leaning against one of the metal chairs at the ticket table and he grabbed it without hesitation as he stepped outside.

The rain was falling at a 45-degree angle. As he hydroplaned back into Lake Oswego, listening to Miles Davis, his mood darkened. "The Jesuit family," he muttered more than once.

The Giulianis lived in a neo-contemporary monstrosity on the high shoulder of Mountain Park. The key was in the lock box to the right of the front door. When the door swung open and the Brinks' warning alarm sounded, the damn cocker spaniel, Yosemite, cut loose in the basement. Taze silenced the alarm and dropped his overnight bag in the kitchen, then began turning on lights as he moved through the house. The spaniel's yapping intensified until Taze popped the lock on the pen door. Yosemite came bounding out, took a whiff of Elliott's shoes, then bounded off, in hot pursuit of someone who cared he was hungry. Taze could hear his toenails clattering across the hardwood floors as the dog cascaded into the kitchen, and he took a quick detour up the stairs. The kitchen was spotless. Debra had left the Black Butte phone number by the fridge. They hiked over the pass every six weeks or so, spending the weekend cross-country skiing or baking by the Glaze Meadow pool. Healing their wounds. Pouring cold water on Debra's obsessions. Pretending the sex was all it used to be.

He was in the family room 20 minutes later when Yosemite went off like a firecracker and, moments later, he heard Sierra and Sarita at the front door. They were flushed and animated, shoving past Elliott as he waved to Cici's mom at the top of the driveway. They were perched on the bar stools when he returned to the kitchen, their coats and purses on the floor, Yosemite begging to climb up into Sierra's lap. "How was the movie?" he asked.

"Sucked," Sarita said.

"No, it didn't," Sierra said. "I liked it better than the first one."

"Shush," Sarita said. "You start without us?"

Taze looked at the girl. She had that sheepish grin that suggested she wasn't oblivious to the innuendo. "Start what?" he said.

"The White Russians," Sarita said.

"Just got here. Haven't even checked the fridge."

Sarita hopped off the bar stool while Sierra reached down and pulled the dog into her lap. Opening the refrigerator, Sarita pulled the pint of Half & Half off the door and set it on the counter. "Two rounds, easy," she said.

Elliott gave her the dirtball glare. The oven clock read 10:43. "You two get ready for bed. Eleven o'clock is lights out." The girls dashed out of the kitchen squealing, Yosemite clattering after them. Taze could hear them laughing as they slammed dresser drawers and fumbled around in the upstairs bathroom. He was pouring the Kahlua over ice when they reclaimed their bar stools. Sierra, always the more modest of the two, had a bathrobe on over her flowered flannel nightgown, though she hadn't bothered to fasten it in the front. Sarita was wearing a pair of basketball shorts and a sleeveless UCLA Bruins' T-shirt.

"Well, I think she's cute," Sierra was saying. "I love 'Bring It On.'"

Taze set the Kahlua down, examining the label for pencil marks or other indications Debra was monitoring alcohol consumption. "Bring it what?" he asked.

"'Bring It On,'" Sarita said, swiveling on the bar stool. She was still wearing the yellow flowered bra. "White cheerleaders vs. the black cheerleaders. You haven't seen it?"

Taze poured a shot of Stoli into one of the glasses. "You'll never guess who wins," Sierra said.

"How come we don't get that?" Sarita asked as Taze returned the Stoli to the freezer.

"Because you like the Kahlua, not the alcohol," Taze said. "Vodka adds to the buzz, not the taste." He opened the Half & Half. "The sisters," he said, glancing at Sierra.

Sierra's mouth popped open. "How'd you know?"

"Damn thing's a movie. Pure fantasy to make you skinny Lake Oswego chicks feel better about yourselves."

"Yeah, right," Sarita said. "Where'd you disappear to after the game?"

"Jesuit-Tigard."

"So, who won? White girls or the black girls?"

Elliott laughed. You always knew when girls this age were talking to their parents. They were much more tuned to satire and subtlety. They could talk about something other than Facebook and "American Idol." He handed over the White Russians. Sierra crossed her long, slender legs and, leaning back against the counter, took a gentle sip. Sarita tossed half of hers down in a salacious gulp, then licked her lips.

"Stop showing off," Taze said. "Lights out in five minutes."

"Can we have a sleepover tomorrow?" Sierra asked.

Elliott flexed his shoulders. "Depends," he said. "On what?"

"You winning by 20. Who you got in mind?"

The girls looked at one another. "Chelsea, maybe," Sierra said. "Or Chloe." She was spinning back and forth on her chair. One glance was enough. She had stripped off her bra before donning the nightgown.

He capped the Kahlua. Chloe? "I'll think about it," he said.

Sierra pumped her fist. Sarita drained her glass. "What's Carrie doing tonight?" she asked.

Elliott picked his glass off the counter with a scowl. "None of your business. Put those glasses in the dishwasher 'fore you go upstairs." Then he walked back into the family room, drink in hand, muttering to himself as he settled onto the leather coach.

"Like I'm the damn nanny," he said, as the girls and the spaniel retreated quietly up the stairs.

                        *   *   *

He was back at Westview, Giulianis in tow, at 3
p.m. The rest of the team was waiting. Chloe Ward had
shown up eight minutes late for a game the weekend
after Thanksgiving, and Taze not only suspended her for
a week, but forced her to run ten suicides after practice.
The message took. They were on the clock. He didn't
give a damn about rush-hour traffic. They couldn't
afford the distraction.

Thalia had a copy of *Ebony* in her lap. The
Heartbreakers were up 28 in the consolation game.
Taze felt was an edginess in the girls, an undercurrent,
as if they'd buried something and didn't want him
looking for it. "What?" he finally asked. "Am I missing
something?'

Anita and Sarita glanced at one another. When
Chelsea dropped her head, Sierra stepped up: "We're
playing Lake Oswego."

"Yeah? So what?"

Sierra glanced at her teammate. "Chelsea's old
team."

"Well, you know what that means," he said.
"We kick ass for old time's sake."

Several girls nodded. Not Chelsea. She had her
scuffed-up, grease-stained leather ball in her lap. "How
long you play with them?" Taze asked.

"Starting in 5th grade."

"Still playing that junior-high 1-3-1?"

Chelsea's eyes opened a little wider. "How'd you know?"

Because you file stuff away. "You nervous?" he said, trying to keep a straight face. "You want to come off the bench?"

Chelsea went pale. "N-n-no," she stammered. "I want to score 50."

It turned out this way, now and then. You didn't need to push or roll out the stirring pre-game speech. You only needed to slide over so and allow the petty details of their young lives to work their magic.

Taze forced himself to watch the Lakers warm up and saw nothing that concerned him. A decent shooting guard who couldn't handle the ball. Clumsy forwards. Fat redhead in the post. That damn pajama party was inevitable.

The Tornado went up 10-0, straight off the opening tip. Chelsea stepped out and hit two threes on the wing, Sarita and Sierra each scored off steals on the press, and one of the LO coaches – he reminded Taze of someone he used to see hanging out at Nike – was off the bench, stompin' his foot, calling time.

"Eyes here," Elliott told the girls. "Don't be looking at those losers. They're making plans, changing formations, wanting to believe they got a fighting chance. They don't. Climb all over them. Foot on the throat. Don't let 'em breathe."

They hadn't broken a sweat, but they were into it. Taze sat down, telling himself to listen to his own advice, to stop checking out Chloe and focus on the matter at hand, especially when the Lakers came stumbling out and scored the game's next 14 points.

Some of it was luck. Girl banked in a three. Refs didn't call a walk. And when the Tornado pressed, an LO forward chucked the ball 50 feet for a breakaway. But the coaches also made adjustments. They junked the 1-3-1 and put their best defender on Chelsea; she had three or four inches on the guard, but the girl overplayed her right hand and stripped her twice.

Elliott saw no reason to call time-out. He set Chelsea down to let her catch her breath, brought in Shelley and Anita for the twins, and ordered Anita to pound the ball into Cici. Basketball was a game of cycles, of seasons, Elliott knew, and spring was generally in the air when these pissant traveling teams went to their bench. Eleven seconds into the second quarter, Cici scored on a back-door lay-up and Taze signaled Anita to spring the half-court trap. The Lakers' backup point guard walked right into the double team, and Shelley picked off the cross-court pass for the game-tying lay-up.

"You remember their press break?" Taze asked Chelsea, plotting several moves ahead. "Get back in there ... and bring the pressure."

It was an entertaining eight minutes. Chelsea was everywhere, stepping into the passing lanes, greasing the offense, annoying the Lakers with the daunting vision of who they used to be. Even when the starters came back onto the floor, LO couldn't regain the goofy exuberance that energized them in the first quarter.

It was 29-21 at the half, and 40-27 midway through the third quarter. Some coaches had the good sense to sit down and shut up when the issue was decided. Not these clowns. They were clueless, adjusting to a defense or a trap even as Elliott was pulling out of it. And after setting their best players up to fail, they ripped into them for arriving on that flight deck with the mission accomplished. Taze knew the type. He'd scored over them all through high school because their sense-of-where-you-are bullshit was no match for what he brought onto the court.

Early in the 4th quarter, Taze turned his attention from the girls – 48-31, and pulling away – and watched the annoyance of losing, of failure, work its way on these guys. Barking like sullen dogs. Cold shouldering the girls when they trudged off the court. He played Chelsea to the end. She scored 21. They won by 24. On the drive home, the twins crammed into the front seat and crawled into his lap to yell out the window in the drive-thru lane at McDonald's. Then they got on Sarita's cell phone and convinced Chelsea and Chloe to come over at 8 o'clock, which gave them plenty of time to stop by Blockbusters on the way home.

Once Chelsea and Chloe arrived, the girls left him alone. They had a computer, the dog, and a flat screen in their bedroom. Taze helped himself to bourbon and caught SportsCenter, then dozed on the couch. Now and then, there was a burst of laughter from the upstairs' bedroom, a stampede into the bathroom and the shudder of water rolling through the pipes in the walls, but everything was quiet when his eyes popped open just before midnight. Yosemite was at the end of the couch, sniffing his feet. Taze turned and found Chloe standing by the doorway into the kitchen.

He hadn't heard her come down. She was wearing a Washington State University hoodie and her practice shorts, and she looked both surprised and dismayed to see him.

"Sorry, Coach," she said, one hand flitting nervously to her heart. "I thought you were sleeping. In the basement."

The Giulianis' guest bedroom was downstairs, though more often than not when Taze stayed the night, he passed out, snoring, on the couch. He waved his hand. "Heading that way," he said. "Need something?"

"A drink," Chloe said.

"All sorts of stuff in the fridge," Taze said, rising to his feet and stretching. Chloe disappeared through the doorway. Her hair was bunched into a ponytail. She was wearing one limp white sock. Taze heard the cupboard door open and close, the rattle of ice in a glass. Yosemite had settled onto a worn blanket by the fireplace.

The light went out in the kitchen. Chloe was in the doorway, apple juice in hand. She opened her mouth, then closed it again, as if she had no idea what else to say.

Emotion. With girls you coached emotion. "You looked good tonight," Taze said. Her eyes narrowed, as if she was waiting for the crack of the whip at the end of a good-news-bad-news routine. "I didn't see your mom."

Celeste Ward. Fitness freak. Perma-tan. Spent two hours every morning on the Elliptical, then bitched at Chloe for sprinkling brown sugar on her oatmeal. "She had a date," Chloe said. Her voice was flat, but Taze heard something in the dim light.

"That been going on long?"

She rolled her eyes. "Lately? Yeah."

"Bother your dad?"

"Maybe. He doesn't call very often."

He hadn't been to a game this year, the self-absorbed shit-head. "He still in Bend?" She nodded. "How often you call him?"

"Not like I used to." Chloe took a sip of the apple juice. She was uncomfortable, trapped between his questions and the impulse to hurry back upstairs.

"Sit down. Just for a minute." Her coach talking now. Taze pointed toward the chair at the end of the couch. She approached it hesitantly, setting the glass on the table beneath the reading lamp, putting as little of herself into the chair as possible. "You have an older sister?" Taze asked, knowing full well she didn't. Chloe shook her head.

"I never knew who to talk to, either, growing up," Taze said. "Dad cut and ran when I was 11. Mother, sick as she was, would slap me upside the head when I reminded her of the fool."

"You grew up in Portland?"

"Oakland. Dad was driving a bus when they met. I used to ride BART all day looking for him."

"To talk to him?"

"Talk to him, kick his ass, I don't know. Never had to decide."

"What's BART?"

"Transit system, buses, trains, in the Bay," Taze said, looking at his glass and wondering how long it had been empty. "Older I got, easier it was for me to understand why he didn't hang around."

"Not me," Chloe said. She was shrinking into the chair. Yosemite shivered in his sleep. Taze couldn't remember hearing anyone moving upstairs since Chloe sat down.

"He ever explain? Your dad?"

"He wasn't ... He didn't talk much at all. Not at the end. He was always mad ... or at work. When I wasn't perfect, he'd get upset. I remember ..." She stopped, arrested by the past, a memory stuck in her throat. "He could be nice when he wanted to be, but he stopped wanting to be."

"And you're thinking that's your fault."

"No, not ... I know it wasn't me. He got worn out by Mom." She was staring outside into the rain. "Tell me about it."

Taze milked the silence for a moment. Silence was a sly ally, a time-honored friend. "You tired now?" he finally said.

Chloe looked at him directly for the first time, as if she was surprised he wasn't already bored by the conversation. "Not really," she said.

"You want a White Russian?"

"What's a White Russian?"

Taze heard a creak in the distance, a tree branch slapping at the gutter, the house settling in on a windy night. "Sweet and smooth," he said. "A drink for girls who don't drink much. All chocolate and caramel. Twins love 'em."

"What's in it?"

"Kahlua. Half & Half. Oh, and a little vodka. Vodka is the crowning touch."

Subject: Appeal
Date: 2/11/2006 8:35:12 AM Pacific Standard Time
From: Jacknjill@yahoo.com
To: fuzzywombat@qwest.com; soccerQT621@aol.com;
oopsimapresbyterian@yahoo.com; gapeach@gmail.com;
bktbaby07@comcast.net; starbrite@gmail.com;
jessicawannab@comcast.net; andrea7575@yahoo.com;
yufamily@intel.com; tlpreston@nike.com; layladida@aol.com;
sobsisters7@gmail.com; mickhilton@nike.com;
meshaworld11@aol.com

More of that Malice Mayhem!

Great game, girls! And get those heads up! Coach Colin has
appealed our PK loss at Westside to OYSA. The two OT periods
were only 10 minutes long, instead of 15 minutes, contrary to
OYSA rules. So our first loss of the season isn't in the books yet!
We'll let you know as soon as we get the news, but Coach Colin is
VERY optimistic!

ATTENTION, parents: Fees are now past due for the Winter Wonderland tournament in Phoenix, Feb. 26-28. Checks are $1,150 and should be made out to LOSC, which includes two nights lodging at the J.W. Marriott Desert Ridge Resort & Spa, Saturday & Sunday breakfast buffets, bus transportation to the fields and tournament entry fee. ALL families are required to make payment, even if your daughter does not make the trip, per LOSC rules, and families are on their own to make airline and car rental reservations. Jack reports there is free complimentary parking at the 316-acre resort! Coach Colin also asks parents to please remind the girls they may not bring laptops or cell phones on the trip.

More of that Malice Mayhem!

*   *   *

T he day Emily Yu returned to LOJ was, strangely enough, the morning Esmeralda Hernandez disappeared. Emily had been dreading her first morning back, unnerved by the flush of her cheeks and the melodrama she was convinced would be waiting for her in the lobby, but even she was surprised when she and her Mom pulled up in the Lexus and three LO squad cars were lined up in the "No Parking" strip.

"Let me guess," Emily said to her mother. "My bodyguards."

As Layla, Lisa, Rachel, Emily and Jessica huddled in the lobby, several theories were advanced as to Esmeralda's undoing. Lisa reported that Mr. Hemingway told his 7th grade Bio class that the girl pulled a knife to settle an argument, while Ray-Ray Bowden insisted she was the vanguard of a gang from Colombia that was taking over meth distribution in

Clackamas County. From whom, exactly, Ray-Ray didn't say.

The Latina? Esmeralda? Was that her name? Jessica alone remembered sharing a class with the girl with the long, black hair, a first-semester U.S. History class in which Esmeralda – or was it Escondido? – sat by the heater and never opened her mouth. "She understand English?" Rachel asked. "Yeah," Jessica said. "She just didn't like it." Other than that, they could barely place her on the Google map of junior high, no matter how closely they zoomed in or moved the mouse around. That her locker was only eight down from Layla's – who was in the library, handing Danny a note from Lisa when the fight started – was just plain weird. That the Lake Oswego police found nine ounces of weed in the subsequent search of Esmeralda's backpack, well, that was off the charts.

That someone would bring tree to school wasn't surprising. Drugs were as common in the massive organism's daily life cycle as skateboards, even if the practitioners were less demonstrative. Emily Sohlstein and Laura Koertje snuck over to Waluga Park every Monday at lunch and scored speed from a couple high-school guys, returning red-faced and obnoxious for their afternoon classes. On sunny days, joints were passed around in the woodland behind the high school, and Ray-Ray's brother, J.J., it was generally understood, knew where to find the major meth supplier in Milwaukie. That someone would bury nine ounces of marijuana in her backpack, then drag it into the school was, however, beyond the pale. "Who do you think it was for?" Layla asked, scrambling to recall the strangers who'd loitered near the lockers in recent weeks.

"My money's on Mr. Mauney," Rachel announced. Mauney was the skinny dweeb who taught Earth Sciences and told stupid stories about his college days at the University of Hawaii. "He's always here late, sitting at his desk with the door closed."

"That *is* suspicious," Lisa agreed. "I always thought he was looking at porn, but you're probably right: He's dealing dope."

"Maybe she wanted to slip it in the Thursday brownies," Jessica said. Brownies were the weekly Thursday staple in the cafeteria, chocolate wedges you couldn't hack down without a pint of milk.

"I'm there for that," Emily said.

Rachel gave her a sideways glance as if to say, "You're eating brownies, now?" and Emily could hardly blame her. She'd missed seven weeks of school, not counting winter break, and she knew re-entry would have its share of bumps. Dr. Dave had given her the free pass right after Christmas, but her parents' weirdness only intensified as they'd rolled into January. Emily was allowed back to Chinese School, of course, and onto the soccer team a week later. If the tutor who came four times a week, reeking of Chipotle, hadn't snared the teaching job in McMinnville, Emily might still be sequestered in the downstairs dungeon, choking down 2,500 calories a day, but her parents were more unnerved by the prospect of another B than the imagined horrors of LOJ. At least until Mom saw the squad cars.

On Friday, the LO police returned to LOJ with Elvis, the drug-sniffing German Shepherd, the most exciting thing to happen since Sammy Post had the mini-seizure and struck his head on the bleachers behind the softball diamond. Sammy's mishap wouldn't have been a big deal except it happened on the last day of fall term, when the teachers tried to deliver a subtle lesson about disguise and self-image by dressing up like total loons. Actually, loons were out this year and super-heroes were in – Mr. Buchanan as the Batman, Mr. Chen as Captain America, Mrs. Laidlaw as Catwoman and Mr. Hastings the Green Somethingorother – which would have been funny enough if Sammy hadn't taken the header off the bleachers. The fire trucks arrived within six minutes and hustled out to find Sammy surrounded by the Justice League of America and most of the Avengers.

"Looks like we've got competition," one EMT said, surveying the first alerts.

"Yep," his partner said, "and we're over-matched."

Elvis spent an hour padding the halls while the student body sat in the gym and listened to Mr. Hawkings lecture on the scourge of drugs. He got everyone laughing with the tag line, "Just say ... Whoa!" but it was distracting, the group of them bunched together at the foul line, wondering who would be stupid enough to pack in Esmeralda's wake. Damn if it didn't occur to everyone at once: "K-Smut!" And everyone laughed. Except Emily. Sitting on the gym floor, arms around her knobby knees, Emily Yu realized she wasn't laughing about much. She felt strangely adrift from these friends, from the familiar, from everything she wanted to be true. She was tired. Her Language Arts teacher was speaking a language she didn't understand. K-Smut was ignoring her last text. And three times a week, she was back at soccer on the turf field at the high school, running ragged through the rain until the cold iced her joints.

Her legs ached. Colin Welch had welcomed the team back to practice on February 1 with the announcement that their "flame out" at regionals and their lackluster fall – in which they'd won 10 of their 12 games, the two losses coming with Emily on the sidelines – owed to a lack of conditioning. "If we're gonna run with the big dogs in Hawaii this summer," Welch said, "we better start running now."

It was a familiar threat, the last resort of meathead coaches who knew no other way to impose order, but Emily and her precious legs were ill prepared for the unrelenting drills that followed. They ran laps, suicides, stripes – 10-and-back, 20-and-back, 30-and-back, and out to midfield – three times without a break. They ran until the heat inside the sauna of their sweats was so intense that several girls braved the last half hour of practice without them in the rain, which explained why Mesha and Amanda missed the drug scare – and the last three days of school – with borderline pneumonia.

What she wouldn't give, Emily thought, for a 103-degree temperature. This preoccupation with running didn't jive with her sense of the game. From her perch in the middle of the defense, she recognized the value and the danger of speed, but great soccer was more about angles and anticipation. She didn't have Jessica's speed at her back, but she didn't need it when her instincts gave her a half-second head start out of the blocks. When you had that jump on the flight of the ball or the angle of attack, you had your opponent beaten before she changed gears and reached the speeds you couldn't find.

When she was still playing rec, Emily had never been fooled into thinking Alex and Mick knew much about soccer. Layla's dad, in particular, kept framing strategy in terms of basketball – give-and-gos, weak-side help – because he thought that would make the game easier to understand. But after watching her for a week, they moved her from forward to stopper, Alex telling her, "I want the smartest player on the field on the back line, instead of standing around on the front one."

That first week, Emily was aghast, doubting herself, suspecting his motives – "His daughter plays forward?" Allie scoffed. "How convenient" – but then the pieces fell into place and she realized that everything she understood about the game came into play at her new position. She could employ the aggravating defensive tactics that used to frustrate her, and anticipate the counter attacks spawned by frustration and boredom. And when, encouraged to press forward, she scored the tying and winning goals in a game against FC Portland, she was stunned to realize Alex and Mick hadn't relegated her to the margins but moved her that much closer to the heart of things. Not so much to fulfill *their* needs but her own.

Emily had played soccer for five years. She couldn't count the times she'd been encouraged to sacrifice, or lectured on the need to surrender what mattered to her for the sake of what seemed so deathly important to someone else. She didn't know what to make of adults who understood what was best for her before she did. And she was under no similar illusions about Colin Welch. The guy was a control freak, and plain vicious, as evidenced by the way he treated Layla and Melissa.

Melissa was a size 10 forward with a .45 caliber left foot; twice in practice, she'd bent a corner kick into the far upper pocket of the net, both times on a wet field. But she'd also been twice late to practice and Colin had twice ridiculed her for it. Emily understood the sacred nature of practice, but Melissa lived in Hood River, 60 miles east of Portland in the Columbia Gorge. Three times a week, Melissa sprinted from her locker to her dad's pick-up truck and conjugated Spanish verbs and square roots by the dashboard lights on the drive down I-84. That was an hour's drive on the quietest Sunday morning; when the clouds were spitting freezing rain and the semis chaining up, it might be twice that, meaning the pick-up pulled into the parking lot when Colin already had the whistle in his mouth. Emily didn't know which was worse, watching Melissa run laps while the team stretched, or seeing her father slouched in his truck, white knuckles on the steering wheel, the Skol-laced steam on the windshield.

She didn't get it. OK, so there wasn't a decent classic program in Hood River. Who decided soccer was so important that three times a week Melissa and her dad drove 60 miles … just to practice? It was, after all, another 90-minute drive back to Hood River in the dark, which meant Melissa and her father spent three hours each day on the road just so Colin Welch could run Melissa into the ground and ridicule her big bones.

Layla had it even worse. With Layla, it was more personal. Whether it was her exhaustion or her body fat, Colin's jibes bounced off Melissa; they buried their heads in Layla's skin like wood ticks and drew blood, and no one dared step forward with a match to ease her pain. Honing in on her sensitivity to criticism and her fondness for "Star Wars," he called her "Princess Layla," He stopped practice twice an hour to rip her fundamentals. In the light scrimmages before the marathon runs at the end of practice, he dumped her on the "B" team, replacing her at forward among the starters with Melissa.

Twice, Emily heard Layla tell Lisa, with tears, that she wanted to quit.

*   *   *

Subject: Regionals
Date: 2/13/2006 19:13:55 PM Pacific Standard Time
From: Jacknjill@yahoo.com
To: fuzzywombat@qwest.com; soccerQT621@aol.com; oopsimapresbyterian@yahoo.com; gapeach@gmail.com; bktbaby07@comcast.net; starbrite@gmail.com; jessicawannab@comcast.net; andrea7575@yahoo.com; yufamily@intel.com; tlpreston@nike.com; layladida@aol.com;

sobsisters7@gmail.com; mickhilton@nike.com;
meshaworld11@aol.com

More of that Malice Mayhem!!

It's not too early parents to start making plans for the Western
Regionals, which are scheduled this year for July 24-28 on the
island of Hawaii. As defending state champs, the Malice are the
clear favorite to win State Cup in June and represent Oregon in the
regional competition at the Mona Kila soccer center in Honolulu.
We've reserved blocks of rooms for 5-night stays at two 4-star
hotels, the Outrigger Waikiki on the Beach and the Outrigger Reef
on the Beach. The girls will stay three to a room at the Outrigger
Waikiki, where Coach Colin promises to keep them focused on
soccer, and Jack and I will enforce the nightly curfews. Family
members will be booked at the Outrigger Reef. You are welcome
to make your hotel reservations independently but Coach Colin
wants to fly the Havoc flag at one unique Hawaiian venue.

Players and their parents will gather each night for dinner at the
Outrigger Waikiki's evening luau – all expenses paid for by LOSC!
– but parents and family members are on their own for breakfast
and lunch.
We'll provide additional details in the coming weeks! For now,
Coach Colin considers it critically important that the girls focus on
the task at hand – winning the Western Regional!

A hui hou kakou, more of that Malice Mayhem!

* * *

Colin Welch was drinking more than usual.
He'd swing by the Moon and Sixpence in the
Hollywood district and knock down a bitter or two,
catch a few cigs, toss a few darts. On the afternoons he
carried the smoke and Guinness onto the practice field,

Jill Johnston, the team manger, turned her nose up something fierce.

Things were tenuous; he didn't have time for stress. Ever since Blessing had surprised him with the questions about Wilsonville, he'd tried to low-key it. He didn't need a palace revolt. That's why he'd gone soft when Emily and her parents came crawling back with their anorexic sob story. Still, he was drinking more, and staring at the calendar, keeping a wary eye open for something he might have missed. Welch wasn't prone to self-doubt, but Winston Westbrook had pushed him to the edge of his comfort zone.

Oregon United Soccer was Ray Lynch's idea. Welch hadn't been around long enough to know how badly outclassed Oregon was in the regional playoffs, much less give a shit, when Lynch began grousing about it after a Timbers' game. "Whole system sucks," he said. Oregon sent clubs to the regionals, Lynch explained: California sent gonzo all-star teams that steamrolled the Oregon state champs.

"So, change the rules," Welch offered. "Sneak a few selects onto your bench. It ain't cheatin' if everyone's doing it, right?"

"Doesn't work that way," Lynch said. "Clubs that think they have an advantage going in – and yours is one of 'em – don't want to give it up. Most parents would rather lose 7-0 at the regional than sit home with their daughter."

Welch shook his head. The place was full of arse bandits, whining like little girls. He took a pull on his lager. The beer was the dump's only saving grace.

"You a sportsman, mate?" he finally asked. "You follow darts? Cricket?"

"What are you talking about?"

"Auto racing is the whizz for me. Stirling Moss, John Surtees, Mark Donohue. Names mean anything to you, Ray?"

Lynch was chewing on a pretzel. A waitress swung by the table, chest out, tray high, asking him if he was ready for another beer, and Lynch shook his head. "Never won Indy, did they?"

"Donohue did, back in the '70s. An Ivy Leaguer with a bite. Wrote a book called 'The Unfair Advantage.' His philosophy, on and off the circuit."

"'The Unfair Advantage'?"

"You do what you have to do. Play by the rules if you must, but never stop looking for whatever gives you an edge. You quit lookin', Ray?"

"Been married 21 years, Jack. Tends to put blinders on your outlook."

"Pissed the selects from California and Arizona kick your ass? Stop wanking and do something about it."

"Don't know what. Our best players are scattered all over the map. Not much you can do to bring 'em together unless you ..."

The brainstorm blew out most of Lynch's circuits, including the volume control. Welch stared at him with detached amusement. Inspiration, he'd decided long ago, was at a premium; perspiration, vastly overrated. "Unless you what, Ray? The suspense is killin' me."

"Combine clubs. Merge the best elevens, and collect the best player cards."

Over Lynch's right shoulder, a ringer at the dart board floated three straight tips into the triple-20. "Ain't exactly rocket science, is it, Ray?" Welch said. "You have any arcane rules that might stand in the way?"

"Egos, maybe."

"So, let's give the bastards an offer they can't refuse."

Finessing the mechanics of that arrangement, Welch eventually realized, came more naturally to him than to Lynch. He convinced the titular heads of the Southside and Westside clubs that if they doubled the annual fees, he could guarantee them a $15,000 raise and another $5,000 in free gear. He made sure the plum coaching assignments – and the Hawaiian vacations – were divided equally among the hot shots who surrendered their autonomy. He hired the Hispanic wunderkind from Woodburn, weakening that burgeoning program and raising the club's profile in the Latino community. And he sought out Winston Westbrook to investigate the creation of a soccer facility that would put FC Portland to shame.

Welch didn't know the man, but his name was always in the papers. A hot-shot developer. A wise-ass, if they were quoting him correctly. He called a half dozen times before Westbrook finally rang him back, and Welch asked him if he wanted to partner with him on the biggest deal in the history of Oregon youth soccer.

In 10 minutes, Westbrook convinced him he was thinking far too small.

* * *

Subject: Superstars
Date: 2/17/2006 7:18:58 AM Pacific Standard Time
From: Jacknjill@yahoo.com
To: fuzzywombat@qwest.com; soccerQT621@aol.com; oopsimapresbyterian@yahoo.com; gapeach@gmail.com; bktbaby07@comcast.net; starbrite@gmail.com; jessicawannab@comcast.net; andrea7575@yahoo.com; yufamily@intel.com; tlpreston@nike.com; layladida@aol.com; sobsisters7@gmail.com; mickhilton@nike.com; meshaworld11@aol.com

More of that Malice Mayhem!

Many of you no doubt have heard the news that the Southside, Westside and Lake Oswego soccer clubs plan to merge next season to form the largest soccer club in the Pacific Northwest. As several critics of the plan are fueling the rumor mill, Coach Colin wants to set the record straight.

Once negotiations between the clubs are finalized, and the Oregon United Soccer Club is formalized as a non-profit, LOSC will disband and the club's records and resources will move to the new league headquarters in Wilsonville. The site of the proposed OUSC complex is on a 14-acre property adjacent to the freeway, just south of the Wilsonville Volvo showroom.

While nothing will be finalized until the new OUSC board is approved by a vote of membership, the facility will feature eight turf fields, a club house and locker room complex, a gymnasium and weight room, and a 15,000-square feet administrative headquarters. Interim OUSC president Billy Harbaugh announced last week that the club has already secured an option on the property with a purchase price of $2.4 million.

Coach Colin reports that the preliminary club budget anticipates annual dues of $1,500 from OUSC members in the first three years of operation. While this is 66 percent higher than the current LOSC dues, the revenue is necessary to pay down the debt. The benefits of owning its facility are numerous. Admission, parking and snack-shack revenue will accrue to the club. Area soccer families will no longer be victimized by city schedulers who consider Pop Warner and spring lacrosse more important than the local soccer club.

Bringing these three clubs under one banner will finally allow Oregon to compete on a level playing field with the all-star teams from California, Colorado and Arizona. It's about time.

We'll continue to pass along updates to current and prospective members as the need arises.

More of that Malice Mayhem!

*   *   *

The last thing Jack Lider needed at his mahogany dinner table was stress. He wanted calm with his steak and potatoes. He wanted his dinner break to be a port in the coming storm, just as it had been when he was growing up in Chicago.

He remembered one memorable sermon from the years when he and Annika still attended the Covenant Church: When couples were having marital problems, the pastor said, he asked them to describe the dinner hour when they were growing up. Was it a special event or a dash to Kentucky Fried Chicken? Were there assigned seats? Was the television on or off? All of that mattered, the pastor came to understand over the years. It shaped the expectations husband and wife brought into a marriage, and it helped to explain the anguish they felt when the arrangement didn't meet their expectations.

In the Lincoln Park of the mid '60s, the Lider dinner table was a smorgasbord of salmon profiteroles, arctic char, grilled asparagus, mustard herring, lingonberry bars and intense conversation – on the mayor, the Cubs, and the Jews – when the cousins poured in from North Park and Andersonville. When Jack and Annika's parents arrived for Sunday dinner, the dining room had the same fragrant, lush and leaden feel, but that mood was harder to maintain when it was just the four of them gathered over the Ekelund tablecloth. Jack found the hollow clatter of forks and knives against the dinner plates unnerving. Annika would occasionally ask about school or unfinished chores, and Nick stayed mum unless he was in a mood to pick a fight. Chelsea, thank God, had yet to disappear inside that shell. Chelsea was still making use of the athletic ability he'd pumped into the gene pool. Chelsea …

"You have practice today?" Jack asked.

Chelsea's fork cut a gentle swath through Annika's mashed potatoes. "Yeah, but we didn't practice much."

"Why not?" Jack said, attacking the lamb kabobs.

"Coach wasn't there."

"So, who ran practice?"

"Thalia. It was shooting drills, mostly."

"Where was Coach Elliott?"

Chelsea kept her eyes on her plate. "Nobody asked."

"Nobody asked?" Jack reached for his wine glass. When he was writing Elliott a check for $200 each month, he expected the guy to put in the hours. "How often is the guy skipping out?"

"He's usually there," Chelsea said, leaning back. "It's not like it matters."

"He's your *coach*."

"I know. And he sits on the bench while we do all the work."

Jack opened his mouth, then closed it. At the other end of the table, Nick chuckled. "That silence," he said to Chelsea, as if they were alone at the table, "is the old man realizing he's been had."

"Can I get anyone fresh gravy?" Annika chimed in. Annika was convinced Jack's migraines were rooted in moments like this, when the muscles in his lower jaw tightened and he continued the grinding process that was reducing his molars to enamel dust.

"I've been had?" he asked.

Nick looked at his father for the first time in a month. He was an extraordinarily handsome kid, Jack realized. The daily workouts at Club Sport had left the kid with a lean cut. "Earth to Capt. Volvo," Nick said. "Taze Elliott is a scam artist."

Jack had a temper, an attitude and a chip on his shoulder. All three were crucial to his ability to sell more cars than anyone in the Metro area except the carny barkers at Toyota. But he was also sensitive to the suggestion that someone knew something he didn't.

His son, for no discernible reason, had emerged from his sullen silence, wreathed in smug certainty. "What are you talking about?"

Nick met his eyes for a moment, then broke contact. "Nothin'."

"No, no, no, don't go running off. You ever met Chelsea's coach?"

"Nope." Nick picked up his butter knife and tried to stand it upright on the shaky foundation of his dinner napkin.

"Ever dropped by one of her games to watch him coach?"

"Nope."

"So you're just shooting your mouth off, then, right? "

"Whatever you say, dad."

Jack could taste the enamel. This was how it started. It was as if Nick had a dim memory of once subscribing to his father's advice, and resented the hell out of it. Jack didn't get it. He'd devoted himself to the kid. Why was he now the enemy? He loosened his tie. Sipped the Pinot Gris. Tried again. "A scam artist? What does that mean?"

Nick took a breath. "That's the word on the street."

"We must live on different streets. What are you hearing on yours?"

"People say stuff."

"And what do they say?"

"He's full of shit."

"Nick! Not at the table!" Annika yelped.

Jack held up a meaty hand. "Go on." Chelsea was watching Nick, not her father, waiting for him to say something. He didn't. Jack twirled the stem of the wine glass between his fingers. "What I hear," he said, "is he's the best AAU coach in the state."

"You know how stupid that sounds? I hear the best 'AAU coach' is coaching sixth-graders in Gresham. He just doesn't have a marketing degree. He can't exploit the dads who want to buy their kid the hoop career they never had."

Jack winced. He'd told Nick that story a few times, the story of how he was the last kid cut from his varsity team at Lincoln Park, how he came home in tears, how he gathered himself and swore to the bathroom mirror he would never again be caught unprepared or unmotivated. He was surprised Nick remembered all that.

"Jack, don't you think ..." Annika began in that whiny let's-not-spoil-the-tiramisu-I-made-for-dessert voice.

"Maybe I was hoping *you'd* help your sister," Jack said. "But you walked away from the game."

"Still pisses you off, doesn't it?"

"Wasn't that the point?"

Nick met his sister's eyes. "You ever ask her, dad?"

"Ask her what?"

"What she wanted. What she needed. I mean, after I failed you so miserably, that would have made sense, right, to make sure she kept playing?"

"I don't justify myself to you."

Nick stared at his father for a few seconds, and Jack had the sense his son was taking the measure of everything in the room: the distance between them, their relative size, the one-on-one games they used to play, the water under the bridge.

"Ditto," he said, sweeping his plate and his water glass off the table.

"Get back here!" Jack yelled after him. "We're not finished with this."

Nick turned by the French doors into the kitchen, but he was looking at Chelsea, not his father. "Help her?" he said. "I know less about motivating people than you do. Thank God she doesn't need either of us."

As Nick dropped his dishes into the sink and disappeared, Jack turned to his daughter. "Is there a problem I don't know about on your team?"

"I don't ..."

"Are you unhappy? Aren't you learning more than you ever did playing with Alex and Mick? Aren't you ..."

"Dad, it's OK. It's just Nick being ... Nick."

While Chelsea and her mother cleared the table, Jack retreated to the den to watch "The Shield." Only Annika was in a mood to talk. Her mother knew better than to ask direct questions; instead, she circled Chelsea nervously, asking about classes and outfits and the friends who no longer came by the house. Chelsea had long ago mastered that all-is-right-with-the-world tone, and before she'd scrubbed the lamb-kabob serving dish clean, she'd rocked her mother back to sleep.

When Chelsea slipped upstairs, Nick's door was closed and Coldplay leaking through the cracks. She sat at her Ikea desk and updated her Facebook status – "Chelsea is FREAKING OUT" – but she couldn't get comfortable. Kicking the Nikes into her closet, Chelsea stepped into the hallway, barefoot. The only light in the hall was floating up from the veiled reading lights in the living room; the family photographs – Vail and Whistler, the Christmas in New York when the Towers were still standing – were drenched in shadow. She told herself she was headed for the bathroom, but at the last moment, she reached for the knob on Nick's door.

She didn't know what to expect, his shoulder, his voice ("Get the hell out of here!"), his annoyance, his indifference. She found him on his bed, curled up against the headboard with a copy of *Maxim*, the old Dell computer churning out the iTunes on his desk. Given the angle of his body, she guessed he was expecting Mom, armed with homilies and Haagen Dazs, desperate to restore the peace.

"What's wrong?" he said.

"Nothing," Chelsea said, focusing on the Yellow Card poster above his head.

"Bullshit. If nothing was wrong, you'd be watching the Blazers and the Knicks. What have I done wrong now?"

"They're playing the Hornets. Can I ask you something?"

"I'm not doing my homework," Nick said, sinking lower into the valley of his unmade bed. "I sure as hell ain't doing yours."

"It's not about homework. I ... I don't know what to do."

"About what?"

She wished there was a place to sit. Her knees were sore, as if she'd run another heavy-duty set of lines. Her throat was a dull ache. And she really didn't understand what the big deal was with Coldplay anyway. "My ... coach," she finally said.

"Your what?"

"Coach Elliott."

"I already voted. He's an asshole."

Chelsea turned to leave, but before she took a step toward the door, she heard the flutter of pages and felt the thump against her back. When she looked down, the *Maxim* cover girl was flashing that coquettish smile.

"You've come this far," Nick said. "Don't chicken out now."

"We had a sleepover at the Giulianis. Two weeks ago. Coach was there."

"You invited him to your sleepover?"

"Their parents were in Sun River. He was house-sitting."

"Mom and Dad know that?"

Chelsea shook her head. Nick seemed oddly impressed. "It was late," she finally said. "I was thirsty, so I went downstairs. And I saw them. By the fireplace."

"Saw who?"

"Coach and Chloe. They were kissing and he had his hands under her T-shirt."

"Chloe his girlfriend?"

"Chloe on my team."

Nick shimmied to the edge of the bed and, reaching over to his desk, pulled the plug on Coldplay. "An eighth grader?"

She nodded.

"And he's messing with her?" She nodded again.

Nick leaned back again his headboard. "Wow," he said, shaking his head.

"Wow."

* * *

Subject: Appeal
Date: 2/19/2006 5:55:12 AM Pacific Standard Time
From: Jacknjill@yahoo.com
To: fuzzywombat@qwest.com; soccerQT621@aol.com; oopsimapresbyterian@yahoo.com; gapeach@gmail.com; bktbaby07@comcast.net; starbrite@gmail.com; jessicawannab@comcast.net; andrea7575@yahoo.com; yufamily@intel.com; tlpreston@nike.com; layladida@aol.com; sobsisters7@gmail.com; mickhilton@nike.com; meshaworld11@aol.com

Unbelievably, girls, the OYSA has rejected the team's appeal of our PK loss to Westside earlier this month. Coach Colin made the case that the two OT periods were 10 minutes long, instead of 15, an officials' error that seriously impacted the team's ability to rally and force a shootout. The referee responded in writing, saying there was an approaching thunderstorm and he shortened the overtime periods out of concern for the girls' safety. Coach Colin has reserved the right to pursue the matter before the OYSA board of governors.

More of that Malice Mayhem!

" **b** ut Melinda is the key. Stay in front of her. Slow her down on the break. Overplay her left hand. And don't go for steals off the dribble. Refs call the reach, whether you touch her or not. Let her make that first pass, then don't let her get the ball back. They want the ball in her hands, and when they make that desperate pass back to her, step in and make the steal. You got that?"

Sitting in the passenger seat, Layla nodded. The headlights of a passing car flickered across her face and she could feel her father looking at her. "When," Layla asked, peering up through the windshield into the overcast, "is it going to be light again?"

"What?"

"Light. Will it ever be light out again?"

Alex was playing his weird music on KINK and his face was twisted, as if he'd just had his feelings hurt. "I don't know … six weeks, maybe? Why?"

Layla didn't try to hide her disappointment. This guy got 1400 on his SATs? "*Why?* Because the dark sucks. Why do we live here?"

"The sun also sets in southern California."

"At three in the afternoon? We're the Mole People. Have you and Mom decided about San Diego?"

Sea World was Layla's newest Spring Break obsession. Rumor had it you could swim with the dolphins. "Layla …" Alex began, then hit the brakes as traffic slowed behind a Tri-Met bus. "We have a game in …"

"Mick's taking Lisa to Cabo. Why can't we go to Cabo?"

"Listen to you. Do you know how spoiled you sound?"

On a scale of 1-to-10, Emily being a one and Lisa, that smug little Cabo queen, a 10? "Lisa's been to Cabo twice. She comes back looking like an over-ripe banana."

"I'm sorry, but one of us, at least, has his mind on something else."

"One is enough," Layla said. "Are we late again?"

Alex didn't answer. In his head, Layla knew, he was already at the game, anyway, wondering about switching to man and putting Layla on the Wildcats' point guard, Melinda Nolan; obsessing on Lisa's hobbled ankle; or wondering if Jill and Jody would have their heads up their ass. Why he couldn't relax, Layla didn't know. Jill and Jody always had their heads up their ...

"Dad!" Layla yelped, even as Alex hit the brakes, the Durango shimmying to a stop 18 inches behind the rear bumper of a Mini Cooper with its turn signal on. Layla glared at him: "Will you pay attention?"

They drove in awkward silence up South End Road. "Did you eat anything before we left home?" Alex finally asked.

"An orange. Some grapes. There was nothing in the refrigerator."

"We'll stop on the way home," Alex said. He'd ask Mick and Lisa to join them. They'd plot strategy against Oregon City in the championship game while Olivia and the girls drained their chocolate shakes.

"Is Mom coming, too?"

"Yeah, she'll be there."

"Why didn't we all go together?"

"Well ..." Alex swung left into the ground-down neighborhood that skirted Gardiner Middle School. "She knew we'd want to talk about the game."

"Are we done talking?"

Alex took a deep breath. Gardiner was two blocks away. "I'm sorry. I'm nervous. You get to run around out there. I sit on the bench and obsess."

"Wanna trade?"

"You don't mean that. This will be fun. One last crack at Oregon City ..."

"They beat us by 25."

"Twenty-two. But first things first. You need to take Melinda out of the game."

Layla just stared out the window as they circled for a parking space. She couldn't believe she had to spend the whole stupid weekend playing basketball. "I'm tired of the dark," she said.

"Relax," Alex said, squeezing in next to a battered RV. "You feeling OK?"

"My stomach hurts," Layla said.

*   *   *

Given that the Lakers were back at Gardiner, where they'd been crushed twice by Oregon City, Alex was fairly upbeat. They weren't playing the Pioneers. Lake Oswego had finished second in league play with a 13-3 record, one game ahead of Wilsonville. For the playoffs, the top four teams were seeded, LO playing Wilsonville and Oregon City facing Sherwood, a rematch of the last game of the regular season. Sherwood had won by three, a score no one took seriously. Jeff Reisler only played his starters for a quarter and, wary of scouts, kept his reserves jammed in a docile 2-3 zone.

"You couldn't go with the sunglasses and a trench coat?" Alex asked Mick.

"It was Sherwood," Mick said. "I was the only guy in the gym who wasn't chucking F-bombs at the ref."

Wilsonville presented a few problems – particularly in their quicksilver point guard – but LO had beaten them twice in the regular season and in the championship game of the Canby tournament. Alex was awash in expectancy. In the looming weekend, there were college financial aid applications, garage overhauls, Canadian thistle, and fences to mend with Olivia. But there were also two games, virtual spiritual retreats from the ordinary.

Wilsonville was warming up. They had a hockey center in the middle and forwards who loved to shoot the 3. They were nothing special beyond Melinda, the coach's daughter and a force of nature on the break.

Margaret was curled like a ferret at the scorer's table, the official book open, her Sharpies neatly aligned. Ray Tripp was alone at the top of the bleacher in that ratty windbreaker, and it was in the reflexive need to avoid eye contact that Alex took the half step toward the Koertjes. He was halfway into his, "Hey, how you guys doing?" before he realized the woman sitting next to Scott wasn't his wife, Lisa, but his daughter. Molly gave him a forced smile and one of those self-conscious waves that begged him not to come any closer. She was wearing jeans, a loose sweater and sandals.

Mick had his clipboard on his hip, staring at the dumpy couple crossing the court: Burt and Flossie, fresh from the Country Kitchen buffet.

"Evenin', coach!" Burt said. "Send out the captain at the three-minute mark."

"Hell, Burt," Alex said, "you just want to go over those extensive rules changes with me?"

Burt was fighting his way out of his black windbreaker. "Rules haven't changed, coach," he said as Flossie tried to un-snag a sleeve. "And I think you know how I feel about profanity."

Fuckin' A. And it almost slipped out.

*   *   *

She was at the end of the rebound line, fresh off her third missed lay-up in a row, when she realized Melinda was staring at her. Layla came to a full stop, wondering what this was about, which was when the Melinda gave her a nod, and Layla remembered the Saturday they'd bumped into one another at the mall. Layla and her mom were heading into Abercrombie's, Melinda exiting with three of her buds, and their eyes met in that awkward way they do when you know you've seen someone before and you can't wrap your arms around where. Layla was inside the store when she caught Melinda looking back over her shoulder, similarly confused or annoyed, her friends already cruising toward Nordstrom without her.

She was raising her hand to acknowledge that bond when Melinda swiveled toward the basket and was gone. Against her will, Layla followed her as she cut across the lane and spun a reverse lay-up in off the glass. She had split ends. She was skinner than Emily. She did everything with her left hand.

Laura offered her a hand and Layla slapped it without enthusiasm. The ball felt heavy. Dad was acting like lay-ups were sacraments. She was getting her period and she still couldn't believe Leslie and Jessica were going to "Return of the King" tonight without her. Like they couldn't wait another day and give her something to look forward to this weekend.

The end of basketball season? She definitely was looking forward to that. Between basketball and soccer, there wasn't time to breathe, much less study, text, party or catch up on her so-called life. She'd stayed up until 1 a.m. Thursday, mucking around Jacksonian America and copying Emily's math homework. She was two chapters behind in Bio, she hadn't cracked "The Scarlett Letter," and they had soccer practice tomorrow at seven in the morning. She should quit soccer.

Lisa arrived at her elbow, fresh off a blown lay-up. "Can you believe the ass on 25?" she said, nodding toward the Wilsonville end. "Are those bike helmets in her shorts?"

Layla snorted. "Weber grills."

"Monster truck tires," Lisa said, tugging on the rim of her sports bra. "I hate 2."

"2?" Layla said. 2 was the point guard, Melinda.

"She's so stuck-up. All attitude and elbows."

Layla pondered that as she grabbed a rebound, fed Rachel in the corner, then trotted back to the mid-court stripe. "Look at her," Lisa said, back at her side. "She thinks she's better than everybody else."

Which made Melinda a fairly good judge of talent, Layla thought. "What's with your dad?" Lisa continued.

"He's obsessing. You should have heard him on the drive over. He wouldn't shut up. How's your dad?"

Lisa glanced at Mick, who was sprawled on the bench, chatting with Margaret. "OK. He's thinking about his 7:00 tee-off time tomorrow at Pumpkin Ridge."

"It's winter."

"He's obsessing, too."

*   *   *

They started Lisa, Layla, Rachel and two wild cards, Laura and Jill. "You're a sentimental fool," Layla heard Mick tell her father and he didn't argue. What there was to be sentimental about concerning Laura and Jill, she had no idea. Laura didn't play defense and Jill was a train wreck with liquid nitro in the tanker cars. They'd been playing basketball together for three years and Layla could no longer remember when Jill had been the least bit normal.

Laura was acting major-league weird, tripping over the fact her sister was in the stands. Layla could relate – if Graham came through that gym door, her coronary arteries would explode – but she wasn't in the mood for drama. Lisa had obviously shared her thoughts on Felicia Fat-ass with Rachel because Rachel was laughing too hard to jump for the opening tap. The ball went straight to Melinda in the backcourt, who dribbled across the 10-second line expecting to see the 1-3-1 and, instead, found Layla waiting for her. She didn't look disappointed. There was a flicker of recognition, as if someone had slipped her the answers in Algebra. Then she flipped the ball to the wing and cut to the basket.

A lot of the every-day grief was stuff you'd never seen or heard before: the unexpected insult, a vicious twist in math, that unsigned note in your locker. But you learned from your mistakes. You knew better than to run the gauntlet of football players sitting outside Jamba Juice. You slowed down on the wild bike ride down Kerr Parkway. And if you had half a brain, you remembered being embarrassed on a back screen.

Melinda was almost by her before Layla felt the low bridge looming. In the days when Chelsea had her back, Chelsea would have called out the screen and switched, but this was Laura on the floor and Laura didn't realize the game had started. As there wasn't much doubt where Melinda was going, Layla tried to slide past the screen but before she cleared the monster truck tires, Melinda had a freebie at the hoop.

Lisa took the ball out. "I hate 2," she said. Layla turned to find one and the same waiting for her at the front of Wilsonville's full-court press.

Dribble through the minefield or pass the baton? Laura deserved that undressing, but Layla knew someone had to take charge here, and the loudmouths on the sidelines considered her Option One. Feeling pressure coming from her right, she spun left out of the double team. In the instant she broke free and looked for the open teammate downstream, Layla heard the whistle blow and found herself staring down at Melinda, sprawled on the court in front of her. As Mrs. Doubtfire signaled the charge, Layla continued to stare, wondering how the girl had beaten her to the spot.

Not a good start. It happened, frequently in this gym. It didn't mean anything. Layla knew she should tell Laura to call out the screens, but she wasn't in the mood to talk to Laura. She could go one of two ways, she told herself, as Wilsonville inbounded the ball: Get in Melinda's face and risk another potential embarrassment, or back off and dare her to crank up a long jumper before she was sufficiently warmed up to …

Damn. Was that a three-pointer? And here she was again, back in her face, daring her to take the press on by herself.

Why not? Layla faked the kamikaze dash right and squeezed between Melinda and two other Wildcat defenders, breaking free at mid-court in a 3-on-1 break. Normally, Layla would have cut straight to the hoop but she couldn't afford another offensive foul, so she lurched left, then flipped the ball over her head to Jill. She had a four-lane to the basket, but she did the weird jump-stop thing and uncorked a flat-footed jumper.

It banked in off the glass. "Nice shot," Layla said. And better timing. A 7-0 Wilsonville lead and molten lava would be flowing at Coach's Corner.

They traded baskets, Layla picking off a cross-court pass and feeding Lisa on the breakaway, before Melinda lobbed in another three. Predictably, this brought Mick to his feet, yelping for a timeout. "Girls," he said, once they'd gathered 'round him, "did someone not get the memo? 'Friday. Five o'clock. League semifinals'?"

Lisa's head was glued to the floor. Layla knew the feeling. "Let's keep it simple," Mick said. "Relax on offense. Bear down on defense. Press break: Rachel, you take the ball out. And start taking this personally, OK?" They slapped hands and mumbled, "LO!" Layla was turning back toward the court when her dad grabbed her elbow. "What did I tell you," he began, "on the ..."

Layla jerked free and left him stammering. She checked the scoreboard: 10-4. The first quarter wasn't even half over. When would *their* dads get the memo that the time-out and kindergarten lecture embarrassed them more than being down six?

Wilsonville was back in a weird match-up zone, with Wildcats running at the ball handler, screaming like spayed cats, Melinda waiting to pounce on a stupid mistake. There was no shortage of them, and Wilsonville pushed its lead to 15-4 before Jill drained an I-may-never-start-again three and the Lakers found their groove. Rachel hit four straight free throws, Wilsonville made several turnovers and Laura scored at the buzzer to make it 15-12.

When Mattie, Jody and Natalie subbed in at the start of the second quarter, Layla took her bottled water to the end of the bench and hid under a towel. Her dad made his first decent call of the night and kept his distance, giving Layla time to check the bleachers and see if Danny and K-Smut had followed through on their threat to show up with the camcorder. There was no sign of them. The ache in her knees was louder than the background music in the gym. Melinda was still on the floor and Layla tracked her movements from inside the flaps of the towel. Dad often said you could learn as much on the bench about your opponent's game, spying on their secrets, their habits, their weaknesses. Sure you could. Did she cheat on her bio tests? Did she wake up in the dark to the sound of her parents fighting? Were her teachers forever asking her about basketball, as if that were the only thing about her that mattered? Did she see Tyra Banks or Kate Moss when she looked in the mirror? Did she wonder, at the edge of sleep, if she'd ever swim with the dolphins?

With three minutes left in the half, Mick told her to sub in for Jody. Layla knew what this was all about: This was Dad's I-can't-talk-to-her-you-deal-with-the-brat portion of the program. Kneeling in front of Margaret and the scorer's table, she glanced at the scoreboard for the first time in the second quarter and was surprised to see that the Lakers had a 5-point lead. "How'd we get ahead?" she asked Lisa when she joined her at the top of the key.

Lisa wiped the sweat from her fake-bake, Cabo-ready forehead and hooked a loose strand of hair behind her ear. "We're taking it personally," she deadpanned. "Who has 2, you or me?"

"All mine," Layla said. "All mine."

* * *

Mick kept it curt and sweet. "You have to finish," he said. "You know that. This is our 35th game, our fourth against these clowns. They scored the last eight because you let up. They finished. You didn't. And they have their confidence back."

They were leaning against the bleachers, catching their breath between pulls on the water bottles. Mick had three-fifths of their attention, max, a lot less from Lisa and Layla, who'd both seen Burt put his hand on Flossie's butt when the refs headed for the refreshment stand. "You see that?" Lisa asked.

"He cupped her ass," Layla said. "I was so hoping I was hallucinating."

"I'm gonna hurl."

"Well, hurl on Laura," Layla said, "'cause we need Mattie in for press break." She sought out her mother in the bleachers and found her sitting with Rachel's mom, wrapped up in some animated conversation on their daughters' shortcomings. Olivia, Layla noticed, was doing most of the talking.

When Mick quit his half-time shtick, Layla retrieved the last basketball on the bench. Her dad was sitting with his legs crossed, watching her in that baleful way that betrayed his neediness and made her want to scream. She fought the urge to run and hide. "Are you gonna talk to me?" she asked.

She could see the pulse in that artery along his throat, the blood rushing in to help him get the words out. "You have two fouls." She nodded. The charge and a silly reach that put Melinda on the foul line. "One more, and it changes everything."

Perfect, Layla thought. Another thing to obsess about. "Don't worry about it," her father continued. "Just play basketball."

Yeah, Layla thought, what were the odds of that? She dribbled toward the foul line, where Rachel was lining up one last freebie, and just shy of the three-point circle rolled the ball up into her right hand, straightened the elbow and let fly. Nothing but net.

*   *   *

First time down the court, Wilsonville had fallen back into a 2-3 zone, so Layla pulled up at the top of the key and lofted another three. The ball felt strangely light on her fingers, the basket much closer than usual. The net barely moved.

Confidence ebbed, confidence flowed. She picked off a pass on the wing, sold Melinda on the reckless drive to the hoop – one of her specialties – and pulled up for another three that rattled through. She could hear buzzing in the distance. Suitably unnerved, Melinda rushed a three-pointer of her own, and LO crisply worked the ball in to Rachel, who missed the lay-up. Mattie, however, controlled the rebound and fed Layla, still floating in a zone out past the three-point circle. She wasn't even aware of taking aim before she released the ball, but she heard the Wilsonville coach say, "That's in," before the shot reached the top of its arc.

He nailed it. Lisa high-five, Wilsonville time-out, Alex and Mick lit up like the Christmas ships.

Standing at her father's elbow, half-listening to him recite the obvious, Layla took one more wistful look around the gym. Still no camcorder. Danny & K-Smut. Always in the way. Never there when you need them.

"Be ready, now," Dad was saying. "We just shot them out of that 2-3." *We? What do you mean, 'we,' kemo-sabe?* "They'll go man and bring back the press, so let's switch to the 1-3-1. Rachel and Mattie, hit the boards. Lisa, pressure Melinda's left hand out front, and Laura, be ready for the double-teams."

The strength of the 1-3-1 is the pressure you apply out front, guiding the opposing point guard into traps on the wings. The zone clogs up the lane but with diligent ball movement, or a skip pass or two, jump shooters invariably break open on the baseline. Twenty seconds after inbounding the ball, Felicia Fat-Ass swiveled at the high point and found a waifish teammate wide open. The high-arching jumper cut LO's lead to four.

As Lisa brought the ball up, Melinda was dogging Layla, denying her the ball, her quickness such that she slipped casually around the screens. She twice ran the baseline in her eagerness to get open. On the third dash for cash, she waited until she felt Melinda on her hip, then spun 180-degrees in a sweet little back-door cut. Mattie had the ball and Mattie was paying attention, so the bounce pass arrived on schedule, just as Melinda yelped, "Help!" Felicia did her best to get her fat ass across the lane but Layla had plenty of time to flip the ball in off the glass before Felicia, hands high in the air, hit her chest first. Bumped off her feet, she was sitting on the baseline when she heard the whistle, and she was so proud of the move that she snuck a peek at Dad and Mick. Oddly enough, they were paying her no attention. They were, instead, screaming at Flossie, who was signaling a charge and waving off the basket.

Layla rose slowly to her feet as Flossie lofted four fingers at the scorer's table. Felicia was clapping her hands, as were most of the Wilsonville parents, jumping up and down as if they'd scored floor passes at a Springsteen show. Layla heard Mick's clipboard hit the floor and her dad stomp his feet like he did when he couldn't get the lawn mower to start, but she ignored that, catching Flossie at the foul line.

"That foul was on me?" she asked in sincere disbelief.

"Player control," Flossie said, looking over her shoulder, searching for the ball.

"She ran into me. I didn't do anything."

Flossie turned toward her with the puzzled who-is-this-that's talking-to-me glower that Edward Longshanks made famous in "Braveheart." She had three chins and makeup caked in the grooved wrinkles beneath her eyes. "She had position. You committed the charge."

"She ran into me," Layla repeated, still convinced truth was the best defense.

Flossie's glare softened, as if she'd just realized she was dealing with a total moron. "If you're going to play this game," she said, all exasperated and maternal, "learn the rules. You can't put your shoulder down and run her over on the way to the basket." She paused, the basketball wedged under her arm, and glanced at the bench. "If your dads aren't going to teach you that," she continued, "I guess the job falls to me."

When adults were wrong, Layla figured out long ago, they couldn't shut up. Whenever Mom freaked over the mess in her room or the weight of the cell phone bill, she always appeared at Layla's bedroom door 20 minutes later, unable to keep her mouth shut. It was as if the apology got jammed in that air duct that fed oxygen to the brain and she had to keep flapping her gums to unclog the pipe. Usually, it was all Layla could do not to jam a pillow over her head or run screaming into the bathroom.

Mick, clearly, wasn't keen on that kind of discipline and self-control because Burt had just T'd him up. The hollering behind the Wilsonville bench only intensified as Melinda followed Burt to the foul line. She looked strangely bored as she set her feet and drained both technicals. The LO lead was down to two, and Wilsonville had the ball.

Layla wanted it back. Something about all this didn't feel right. They couldn't lose this game. They couldn't come this far and fall apart, could they? How stupid would that be? They were playing Oregon City for the championship. That's the way the season was supposed to end, her and Dad in the car, driving home on Saturday night, stopping at Burgerville to complain about the refs and her dumb fouls and the unfairness that left Oregon City with twice as many clutch players as anyone else.

Melinda was bringing the ball down, and Layla, floating on the right wing, knew she was taking the next shot. Her dad had called out the play for her. She'd curl off a screen and they'd try too hard to get the ball back to her before they made a mistake. All Layla had to do was look tired or a little timid, hang back out of sight, wait until …

She broke almost *too* early. She made her move before Wilsonville's off-guard even glanced back toward Melinda, and got there so soon that she had to reach back for the ball to make the interception. She was at half court before anyone seemed to know she'd made the steal and for once she didn't miss the lay-up.

Up four. Layla latched onto Melinda as soon as they inbounded the ball. She knew what to do. Overplay the left. Force her to go right because whenever she went right, she pushed the ball out in front of her instead of protecting it on her hip, giving Layla just enough ...

She stole the ball on the fifth dribble, reaching in as soon as Melinda tried to change direction, picking it so cleanly that Melinda simply reached out and grabbed her before the steal became a breakaway.

With two minutes left in the quarter, they weren't shooting free throws yet. Layla found herself fidgeting, still anxious, waiting for Mattie to inbounds the ball at mid-court. All they had was a little breathing room, if that. Melinda was fronting her, denying her the ball, so she curled into the backcourt, hoping to give someone else room to take the inbounds. At the very moment she broke off the cut, Mattie tossed the overhead …

Over … her … head.

Against anyone else, Layla would have won the race to the ball. But Melinda was used to the mistakes her defense caused, and a superb soccer defender besides, and she got the jump. She was half a step ahead of Layla when she reeled it in, just shy of the foul line, and Layla should have let her go. The memory of that last steal fresh in her mind, she instead made a stab for the ball as Melinda went up. She wasn't sure which surprised her more, that she poked it cleanly away or that Flossie, painfully out of position, whistled her for the foul.

Layla stood for a moment at the edge of the lane, hands on her hips, sweat running down the slope of her neck. She didn't want to come out. She could play with Melinda. She could protect the lead. She could keep them a half step ahead of disaster. The calm made her light-headed and that didn't change when the horn sounded and Jill came trotting out to replace her.

"You can't take me out," she said when she reached the bench.

"You have four fouls," Mick said. "I can't leave you in."

She didn't even glance at her father as she walked to the end of the bench, but she knew he was staring. She didn't need that. She didn't need his disappointment looming over her, but there it was, the whole pathetic package. He was shaking his head. It was no time to get defensive, but Layla didn't know where else to go. "I never touched her."

With a hefty sigh, her father crouched in front of her, so close she could see the tufts of hair in the well of his ears. Further down the bench, Rachel was staring at them. Jill was chucking up an air ball. Burt and Flossie were huffing and puffing like they needed oxygen. Layla finally locked eyes with her dad, searching for a strand of support, a life vest of encouragement, and found, instead …

"You can't do that," he announced, sounding positively Levitical. "When you already have three fouls, you can't reach like that. You can't take the chance …"

"I never touched her," Layla repeated, angrier now. She felt trapped against the back of the chair. Was there somewhere else she could sit? The stands? The Durango?

"The refs don't care. They see your hand go out and …"

"So, they suck, and that's my fault?"

Her dad came out of his crouch, rising over her. Past his right hip, Felicia Fat-ass was driving to the hoop as Rachel and Mattie watched in flat-footed amazement. The Wilsonville boosters burst into song. "No," her father said, "but our best chance to win is now pouting on the bench. And you put her there."

She wanted to slap him. Worse than that, she wanted to curl her fingers into a fist and pop him on the nose. Knock him on his ass. Whack him so hard the blow put tears in his eyes, just so he wouldn't see the tears forming in hers.

"Go away," Layla said. "Go *away*. Just leave me alone." And he did. He walked to the end of the bench and sat. At the end of the quarter, when Mick tried to convince them Wilsonville's five-point lead didn't mean anything, he ignored her. When he sat down again, Layla sneaked a glance across the court at her mom, who – happy to catch her eye – went palms up as if she didn't understand what was going on. Like Layla had anything to tell her.

With 4:20 left in the game, and Wilsonville's lead at seven, Mick came down and told Layla to sub for Laura. She was kneeling in front of Margaret when Melinda, who'd caught a 90-second breather, dropped her towel and glided up to the table. Wilsonville was working the ball around the zone, milking the clock and savoring the lead, and for 30 seconds they knelt there, three feet from one another, searching for different things, rooting for different teams. When Rachel finally fouled Felicia on an errant jumper and Burt lumbered over to report the foul, Layla started onto the court, anxious to be free of her cage, desperate to unwind, only to hear:

"Layla."

She stopped, and looked back at the sound of her name. Melinda was still kneeling there, her right arm on the scorer's table. "She's shooting," she said.

She's shooting? Who's shooting? I'm not going in for the shooter, Layla thought, and then it came to her, as the girls began to fill the lanes and Felicia knelt at the foul line to tie her shoe: Two free throws. You didn't sub in under after the first shot.

Melinda knew her name.

"Oh, yeah. Thanks," she said. Melinda turned back to her bench, looking for instructions. The bands binding her ponytail were Laker blue.

Felicia missed the free throw. Flossie waved them onto the court. Layla glanced at the clock. Still down seven. Lisa was giving her the we-could-use-a-little-help-out-here grimace, and Layla was surprised at how calm she felt, how loose, how anxious to take the ball and get moving. Somewhere in the distance Layla heard her father yelling, but she wasn't listening to him anymore.

Felicia was tired; she missed again, and Rachel almost fumbled the rebound out of bounds. Layla arrived and snatched the ball away, then pivoted to find Wilsonville dropping back into a 2-3. That made sense. Time was running out. They had the lead.

The 2-3 was different than the 1-3-1. It shut down the baseline and left open that sweet spot at the foul line for the off-guard sneaking in from the weak side or one of the forwards curling off a screen. They worked the ball around for 30 seconds before Mattie popped into the open and Lisa flipped a pass just beyond Melinda's fingertips. Mattie turned, head-faked two Wilsonville defenders into the air, and scored on the six-footer.

They were in a man, trying not to panic as the seconds began to disappear. You wanted their nerves to fray before yours did, and what was the likelihood of that when they were five points up and you were five points down? Time and again, Layla tried to deny Melinda the ball even as she applied the kind of double-teaming pressure that would force a bad pass. She was running in circles, imitating windmills, losing her mind.

Yet this was eighth-grade basketball, not Connecticut-Tennessee, and weird bounces were the rule not the exception. With just under 40 seconds left, Melinda decided she couldn't pass up a wide-open 10-footer and pocked it off the back of the rim. Mattie took the rebound and catapulted an outlet that hit Lisa in stride crossing mid-court, and she sailed in for the lay-up. Instead of following her to the basket, Layla followed Melinda as she flared out for the inbounds, and got one hand on the ball, one being enough to knock it off Melinda's knee and out of bounds.

They were down three with 17 seconds left, and Mick called time out. He had the clipboard out. His black Sharpie was sketching lanes and three-point circles and arrows. A back-door here, a double-screen there, a quick foul if they couldn't get the steal. Each of the girls was staring intently at the board, desperate to find their place. Dad finally put his hand on Mick's elbow. "Do you all get that," he asked the girls, "or should we call another time out and go over it again?"

Lisa was staring at the clipboard, Rachel and Mattie at the floor. Wilsonville was breaking its huddle and Flossie was marching up to shatter theirs. Layla finally stepped into the middle of the circle. "Just like 'Hoosiers,' Dad," she said. "I'll make it."

She fed Rachel the inbound pass, then got it back on the wing, Melinda on her hip. When Lisa rolled to the top of the key, Layla flipped her the ball, then spun into the lane, running the baseline, hoping to lose Melinda in the thicket of elbows and twigs. She had a step of breathing room when Lisa got her the ball deep in the corner. She gained the rest she needed when she took a quick step toward mid-court, then spun back to the baseline. She heard Melinda yell her name again as she pulled up just outside the three-point line and launched the ball toward the top corner of the rectangle etched in the backboard glass.

Everyone started yelling when the ball banked off the glass and through the net to tie the score. Everyone except Melinda.

To speak French, her mom once said, you must think in French. If you think in English and force your brain to translate each word on its way to your mouth, it ruins everything. That must be it, Layla told herself later. The best players never slowed their feet and hands by asking their head for permission. They moved without doubt or regret. They spoke basketball without thinking about it.

Layla watched the shot go in, just the way she remembered from "Hoosiers," Jimmy going straight up over an outstretched hand. Melinda didn't. As soon as Layla let go of the ball, Melinda was moving toward the basket, a half-step ahead of all the things that might happen next. If she hadn't grabbed the ball from the bottom of the net, if she hadn't tossed it in to Felicia so quickly, maybe her dad would have called time out, too, to draw circles on a board. When Melinda got the ball back on the wing, the jet pack on. Layla could only chase.

She didn't know how much time was left. There wasn't time to check. While Melinda, was still picking up speed, Layla thought she might have the angle on her. At the top of the key, Melinda sensed her approach. Someone on the sidelines was yelling, "Shoot," and for a moment, she thought Melinda might pull up for the jumper, just to be safe. But, no, that would mean caution. That would require doubt and thinking too much. Melinda was going to the hole with the half step, the open lane, the clean air. All Layla could hope for was to somehow knock the ball away. One more dribble, she knew, and Melinda would bring the ball across her body and go up with the left hand. They were together suddenly, side by side in the lane, Melinda straining, Layla reaching, the backboard looming. One moment Melinda had the ball in the cradle of her arms; the next, it was loose, bobbled, rattling around and fumbled out of bounds.

And Flossie was blowing her whistle. Traveling? LO ball? End of regulation?

No. Layla's foul.

She guessed later that it must have been fairly loud in the gym, but for a few seconds, the most important ones, all she felt was the quiet. The stillness of the coaches. The silence of her teammates. The zeroes on the clock. The emptiness in her stomach as Melinda walked impassively to the free-throw line. Three bounces and the ball went up, bouncing off the side of the rim, the backboard and in, sparking the wild celebration in the stands, during which Layla regained her hearing. Melinda's teammates abandoned their slots in the lane and joined the sprawling team hug in front of their bench. The last shot didn't matter but Melinda shot it anyway, three quick bounces and a soft one-hander that snapped the chords in a final salute.

Layla was numb. She went through the motions, lining up to slap hands, stuffing the water bottles into her carry bag, gathering at the bench while Mick and her dad took a heroic stab at praising their comeback, but she was numb. They all were. The moms were huddled together like relatives at the airport, waiting to hear if the men they loved had survived the crash. Laura was crying on the bench, and Lisa was sprawled next to her. Dad and Mick were standing next to one another, the air leaking out of their tires, unable to summon the energy to leave the court. "Did you foul her?" he asked when she'd brushed past him earlier. He didn't know, he didn't understand, he didn't care what this meant to her, and she couldn't bring herself to even look at his ashen face.

She slipped the strap of the travel bag over her shoulder and headed for the parking lot, dodging Mom on the way out the door. In the lobby outside the gym, a small contingent of Wilsonville parents grew quiet as she passed, one of them saying, "Good game." She nodded and kept walking, out into the dark, trying to remember where they'd hidden the Durango. She dropped her bag by the rear tire and sat on the bumper, leaning back against the lift gate and searching the gray wash overhead for the trace of a star. She didn't know how long she sat there before she heard the crunch of a footstep on the gravel. Expecting, and dreading, her father, she opened her eyes to find Melinda, instead.

"Hey," Melinda said, hands in her warm-up pockets. She was wearing flip-flops. Her hair was loose atop her shoulders.

"Hi," Layla said, sheepishly dusting the dust and bumper grit from her butt. She had no idea what this was all about. She was shivering again.

"You never touched me," Melinda said.

"What?"

"I lost the ball. You never touched me."

Layla started at her, searching for a hint of gloating, and found the tiny sparkle of an earring, freshly reinserted into Melinda's left earlobe. She wondered where she'd gotten her ears pierced. She wondered why Mom kept saying she wasn't old enough yet.

"It wouldn't be like Flossie to get the last one right," she finally said. Melinda laughed, and reset the strap of the travel bag. Layla glanced at the doorway into the gym. There was still no sign of parents.

"How'd you know my name?" she asked.

"Your name? My dad," Melinda said. "He said I had to stop you for us to have a chance."

"He did?"

Melinda nodded. "Didn't tell me to guard the three, though."

Layla didn't want to think about the game. "Yeah, well …" she said, then stopped. "Maybe your dad can give me a ride home."

A half-smile. Recognition. "We could switch cars," Melinda said.

"You, too?"

"All the way home. I can't get him to stop."

The lights of a turning car flashed over them and the dumpster. "Me neither," Layla said. "At least, not until the season ends."

The gym door opened. The Wilsonville coach poked his head out, searching the parking lot. He didn't see Melinda and she didn't say anything, so pretty soon he went back inside and the door closed behind him.

Melinda took a deep breath. "Gotta go," she said.

Layla pulled her sweatshirt tight. "Good luck against Oregon City."

Melinda nodded, took several steps toward the gym door, then turned back.

"You know what?" she said. "When I have a daughter someday, I want to be the parent who says, 'You did great,' after every game. Like my mom. She doesn't know any better, so she just says, 'You did good.'

"That's all. 'You did good.'"

E ddie Alvarado lived two blocks from Alpenrose Dairy and rode his battered Tech to work. The last serious push was the roller-coaster ride past Wilson High, then up Terwilliger, where the view of the river and Mt. Hood opened up so dramatically that he stopped thinking about his knees and the rib still bruised by the bumper of a Range Rover that cut him off one morning. Terwilliger got him inspired. Terwilliger got him thinking. On a warm and drizzly March morning, Terwilliger helped Eddie Alvarado figure out the sleight of hand Colin Welch was working on the old Wilsonville Highway.

Alvarado was a dinosaur, one of those rare birds still cranking for a newspaper because he loved the work. He was under no illusions about how dramatically the industry was coming undone, as the news cycle shrank from 24 hours to 24 seconds. The morning paper was no longer an essential read. Eddie pulled in several offers each year from law firms that needed his investigative skills, but he never seriously considered the offers. He'd never gotten over the rush, in his early years as a sportswriter, of spending the night covering an NBA game, then waking the next morning to find everyone in town hooked intravenously to their coffee and his commentary. Even as times changed – ESPN making the morning sports section irrelevant, Alvarado moving to *The Oregonian's* I-team – he still found joy in chasing the lying, cheating, conniving scumbags who thought they could get away with it because no one was paying attention: No one was pulling the 1099s, reading the quarterly reports, doing the math.

That presumption was understandable. The bureaucrats were overmatched. The IRS spent its resources nickel and diming the middle class, not plugging the loopholes that benefited the top tenth of one percent. Every year, the Legislature passed more laws that made piracy legal. Fewer government agencies had the budget to bring the thieves to justice, so when an Eliot Ness remained, outraged and uncompromised, in the U.S. attorney's office, he considered Alvarado a lifeline, not the competition. He could cross lines they couldn't, given a nudge in the right direction. He could proceed on theories and perceptions, not the rarified oxygen of an air-tight case. He could ask the unnerving questions – many supplied by the frustrated AG or auditor – that would induce panic in the miscreant. Some of Alvarado's best tips, in other words, came from the very watchdogs he chastised for falling asleep at the switch.

Early on, Alvarado realized shamelessness was an incredible advantage if you wanted to succeed. He didn't hit his stride as an investigative reporter until he learned to suspend his disbelief at the audacity with which the scam artists screwed those who trusted them the most. The schemes were rarely orchestrated; more often than not, the opportunity that presented itself weighed more than the anxiety over getting caught. He didn't know how else to explain the duplicity of what was transpiring with the Wilsonville soccer center.

Alvarado would never have stumbled upon the deal if he didn't have a hard-on for Winston Westbrook and a soft spot for granite counters. Westbrook was one of the city's pre-eminent downtown developers, impeccably connected, routinely feted, the darling of the editorial board. Alvarado considered him a self-aggrandizing asshole with an outrageous gift for convincing Joe Six-Pack to keep him stocked in Vin Santo. Westbrook routinely used urban-renewal dollars, low-income housing programs, and transit initiatives to secure public funding for his private real-estate projects. Twice, he'd taken fallow pieces of land in the inner city and leveraged so much public assistance that he never put a dime of his own money in play. Granted, one of those projects was an urban showcase, a former east-side rail yard now sporting 900 condos and townhouses, 60 retail units, six acres of green space and streetcar connections out the yin-yang, but its success only heightened Alvarado's suspicions of how Westbrook played the system.

Over the last three years, Alvarado had written half a dozen pieces connecting the dots between Westbrook's campaign contributions, disgruntled investors, broken promises and undue influence with the Portland Development Commission, slowly building the case that the developer was a powder keg who would one day detonate and take tax-increment financing and the city's bond rating down with him. Westbrook enjoyed the attention. He returned Alvarado's calls, invited him out for oysters on the half shell, and outlined future projects, all the while entertaining the reporter with an exaggerated Southern charm designed to convince Alvarado he had nothing to hide … or mock his inability to find it. Alvarado took meticulous notes, and paid for his own shooters.

Alvarado's unique place in the newsroom was enhanced by the fact that he was intent on jamming stories into the morning paper, rather than finding excuses to keep it out. Unlike the reporters who thrived on six-month projects and leisurely lunches at Higgins, Alvarado had a compulsion to generate copy, which generally – the news hole was shrinking along with ad sales – suited the interests of the editors. Thus, he had free rein to identify the bad guys and drag them inexorably toward justice.

Winston Westbrook had his heels dug in, but Alvarado was a patient guy and he kept pulling records, checking signatures, and scoping projects. That's how he stumbled onto those 14 acres of converted farmland in Wilsonville. Alvarado stared at the deed for weeks, putting it aside, then picking it up again, before he finally called Alex Blessing, who'd dropped a $20,000 granite counter into his remodeled kitchen.

"Hey, Eddie," Alex said. "Glad you called. Counter holding up?"

"Like 21-year-old Scotch," Alvarado said. "Why are you glad I called?"

"That conversation we had about Taze Elliott? I might have an update for you."

"An update."

"Yeah. A kid in the neighborhood comes by the shop every once now and then. He was telling me an unbelievable story about Elliott and an eighth-grade girl."

"Eighth grade? Jesus ... Let's talk over the weekend. I have something else here. Wasn't your daughter playing for an elite soccer team back when I remodeled?"

"She still is. Lake Oswego Soccer Club."

"You in tight with them?"

"Not even close. Management and I disagree on a few things."

"Like Oregon United Soccer?"

Eddie loved that dead silence on the phone. "What's going on, Eddie?"

"Bear with me. Oregon United Soccer is a new soccer club in town?"

"*The* new soccer club in town."

"And it's competing with Lake Oswego?"

"It's cannibalizing Lake Oswego. The three best teams in the Metro area outside FC Portland are merging."

"Merging? Like the Yankees merging with the Red Sox?"

"More like Portland's Triple A team merging with Salt Lake City's and Spokane's so they can *match up* with the Yankees down the road."

"You're not playing the Yankees."

"We're playing elite teams from California. They're the '27 Yankees."

"Why are they parking the new club in Wilsonville?"

"The nation builders found 10 or 12 acres of available land off I-5."

"Actually, I think it's off the old Wilsonville Highway," Alvarado said. "You know what the plan is?"

"Not really. I can get you a number if you need to talk to someone who does."

"I think I called the right guy. Winston Westbrook: What's his connection to Oregon Soccer whatever?"

"Oregon United. I didn't think Westbrook is connected to Oregon United."

"Any chance he's sponsoring the thing?"

"I doubt it. Oregon United is set up as a non-profit. They have people lining up to write $800 checks. They don't need a sponsor."

"Eight hundred bucks? What the hell do you get for eight hundred bucks?"

"A traveling bag. A sweatshirt. You pay another $1,400 to send your kid to Phoenix in February."

"Club have an auditor?"

"Why would the club need an auditor?"

"To file tax returns? Guard against embezzlement. There's a raft of that shit going on."

"I know: LO Little League got stung for $40,000 a couple years back. Parents are still gun shy. That's why the Oregon United concept was a hard sell."

"For who?"

"Just about everybody. The land alone is $2.4 million."

"$2.8 million."

" ... and they're jacking up the annual due to $1,500. Even LO families are gagging. They're pondering return on investment."

"What are you talking about?"

"I'm speaking metaphorically, not financially."

"Metaphorically."

"Are they getting their money's worth, given the odds against their son or daughter turning that obsession with soccer into a college scholarship? I'm not talking about a financial stake in the new complex."

"I sure hope not. There won't be a financial stake in the new complex."

"I know. Not for these families, at least, but Oregon United will own the property and the ..."

"No, it won't. Oregon United is just renting the place."

"I'm not tracking, Eddie."

"I can tell. This elite club of yours isn't *buying* those 14 acres on the Wilsonville Highway. They're leasing the property back from Winston Westbrook."

"I don't think so, Eddie. I've seen the emails, and ..."

"I've seen the contract. The cosigners on that $2.8 million note are Oregon United and Winston Westbrook. But after 24 months – and every 24 months after that – the developer retains an option to buy out Oregon United's interest for $10,000."

"What would Westbrook ..."

" ... want with eight soccer fields in a cow pasture? He probably doesn't know, which explains the 24 months. But he owns three or four chunks of land down there, right up against the urban growth boundary. Back in '92, as a matter of fact, he had an option to buy this very piece of land."

"Is he building on any of it? What's he waiting for?"

"Westbrook can only keep so many plates spinning at once. He's invested a lot of time and energy in the Railyard over the last few years. Condo sales are slumping. Credit is tight. I wouldn't be surprised if he's waiting to see what impact the complex has on property values. There's not a lot of land left inside the UGB. If the housing market sucks, he backs off, bides his time. But if war breaks out in the Middle East, the price of gas shoots up, and all the soccer moms suddenly want to live around the corner from Soccer Central, he has a gold mine. He can throw in a pool, user fees. With a zoning change, he can subdivide and bend it like Beckham, converting it into a nifty gated community."

"What's in it for the soccer club?"

"That's what I'm trying to figure out, Alex. And that's why I'm calling you. Alex ...? You still there?"

* * *

Alex gave Eddie Alvarado a few quotes and a few names, and the story – "Developer Uses Soccer Complex as Marketing Gimmick" – was stripped across the top of the Sunday business section. Westbrook provided the best quotes, alternately complaining he didn't understand why this was a story and moping that he deserved credit for a novel marketing approach. He was curious that anyone thought the soccer club was purchasing anything but access to eight premiere soccer fields. "Club Sport charges $150 a month for a family membership," he said, "and no one thinks those dues buy anything but a towel and 20 minutes on the elliptical."

No one except Ray Lynch and Norah Feuer, the heads of the Westside and Southside Clubs. Although Alvarado buried the quotes after the jump, both were surprised Oregon United Soccer Inc. wouldn't have a controlling interest in the property. "Field space is a precious commodity in Oregon," Feuer said, "and the only reason we'd consider a merger. We were led to believe the soccer complex would serve the needs of children of our community for years to come."

There were no corresponding quotes from officials from the LOSC, and it wasn't hard to read between the lines when the *Lake Oswego Review* followed up with the news that a dozen families were demanding refunds on their down payments. "We knew the fees were excessive," said Millard Lee, Jessica's father, "but we were told we were establishing a legacy that would benefit future generations of soccer families in Lake Oswego. I'm concerned about whether this misunderstanding was intentional."

The most acidic quotes were Mick's. "The level of deceit is stunning," said Hilton, identified as a youth sports coach who worked at Nike's golf division, "and that's coming from a guy who was once trapped between Fuzzy Zoeller and the dinner menu at Augusta. This looks like someone was willing to employ and exploit youth sports to further their business interests."

"'Employ and exploit youth sports'?" Alex said over beers. "You mean, like Nike's summer basketball camps?"

"Hypocrisy in the service of virtue is no vice. I'm prouder of the Fuzzy line."

"No one behind the Berm gave you any grief?"

"Better to ask for forgiveness than permission. The Nike way."

The night the *Review* piece ran, Billy Harbaugh, the soccer club's chairman, dropped by the Blessings unannounced. He was a stock analyst at Piper Jaffrey. He ran marathons. His wife was on the school board. "You have anything to do with the Alvarado piece?" he asked while Olivia put on a fresh pot of coffee.

"Why," Alex asked, "you here to shoot the messenger?"

"He quoted you."

"And he didn't quote you. Which one of us looks worse as a result?"

"Are you enjoying this, Alex? Why, thank you, Olivia." She set the creamer and the Sweet 'n' Lo packets on the coffee table.

"That's hard to say. Your drive-by suggests something happened today that I don't know about."

"Colin Welch is toast. The board met Sunday night."

"He threatening to sue?"

"We made him an offer. I don't know that he ever acquired a taste for Lake Oswego."

"The board gave you a vote of confidence?"

"We agreed that was unnecessary. This caught us all by surprise."

"I called you in October, complaining about the merger."

"As I recall, you had conceptual issues, not economic ones."

"Concerns you didn't share."

A slow but heavy rain began climbing the roof above their heads. "You don't see the connection?" Olivia said.

"What connection is that?"

"Between the man's willingness to use our kids and his plan to manipulate our bank accounts?"

Billy took a sip of coffee. "That's very good," he said, returning the Bosch cup to its saucer. "But I think I'm a better judge of character than that."

"We'd hoped as much," Olivia said with a gentle smile.

Billy's sigh seemed oddly genuine. "Why don't we save that debate for a later day?" he said, loosening his tie. "We need to talk about Malice, and whether you're interested in coaching the team."

"Malice? I want no part of Oregon United," Alex said.

"I'm not talking about Oregon United. The board wants to upgrade the competitive opportunities we provide. But the Oregon United scheme" – he shrugged, conceding the point – "is going back for revisions."

"So, why me?"

"Alex, I'm up to my ass in alligators. And looking for solid ground. Welch fired and replaced five of the club's 12 coaches, four of them since January. I need a new line-up. You're no more special than any of the others."

"That's what Mick tells me," Alex said, as Olivia squeezed his shoulder and left the room.

Another sigh. "I figured Mick for a little more discretion than that," Billy said, "but you two go back. Yes, I approached Mick first. And, yes, he told me he wouldn't consider coaching without you. For a brief moment, you have me where you want me."

"How brief is that?"

"I'll be frank. You and Mick are certified, but just barely, at this level. The girls are better served by coaches who played in college. Adults with kids in the program shouldn't be coaching. But I have more pressing concerns. You and Mick solve a problem for me, but it's not a major one. There's nothing to negotiate. If you're not interested, I'll have someone else in position by next weekend."

Harbaugh rose to his feet. "I think you and Mick have the rare opportunity to coach a group of girls who won the state championship last year and have a decent shot at winning it again. Let me know tomorrow if you want to take advantage of it. I'll say good-bye to Olivia on my way out."

*   *   *

Subject: Transitions
Date: 3/03/2006 2:41:10 AM Pacific Standard Time
From: Jacknjill@yahoo.com
To: fuzzywombat@qwest.com; soccerQT621@aol.com; oopsimapresbyterian@yahoo.com; gapeach@gmail.com; bktbaby07@comcast.net; starbrite@gmail.com; jessicawannab@comcast.net; andrea7575@yahoo.com; yufamily@intel.com; tlpreston@nike.com; layladida@aol.com; sobsisters7@gmail.com; mickhilton@nike.com; meshaworld11@aol.com
More of that Malice Mayhem!

Congratulations once again, girls, on your fantastic showing at Winter Wonderland! Although we only won one game over the weekend, our aggressive play and marked improvement was the talk of Phoenix, and tournament officials have begged – yes, begged! – us to return next year. Circle these dates on your calendars, girls: Feb. 25-27, and start shopping for that new sun dress!

As many of you know, the Malice will continue our march to the state title without Coach Colin Welch., who has decided to pursue other coaching opportunities. It's impossible to detail the impact that Coach Colin had on the Lake Oswego Soccer Club and the teams he coached. Sadly, there isn't time to hold a party in his honor, but Jack and I will be collecting funds to help defray his moving expenses. We wish him a safe and happy landing wherever he ends up.

Even as LOSC begins an extensive search for a new director, Alex Blessing and Mick Hilton will step in and coach the Malice for the remainder of the spring season, leading up to the State Cup finals.

William Harbaugh, head of the LOSC board of directors, asked all team managers to assure parents and athletes alike that while the proposed merger with the Westside and Southside clubs is now on hold, LOSC remains committed to fielding the most competitive and successful soccer program in the Northwest.

The Malice will continue its quest tonight in a 7 p.m. game against the Dynamo at Lakeridge. As always, ladies, be on the field and ready to go one hour before game time. More of that Malice Mayhem!

*　　*　　*

He reached Lakeridge at 6:15 p.m., fifteen minutes late, and none of the girls said anything. Jack and Jill, the team managers, were struggling to erect the Malice tent. No one was missing save Amanda and Mick, who had a late meeting at Nike, so he told the girls to warm up until they heard his whistle. Lisa was surprised to see Alex back off, but his instinct was right. Layla didn't want him looming over the team, and the team didn't need him. The mood in warm-ups was different than on the basketball team. They were more disciplined. She and Jessica set the tone and the timetable, encouraging everything that was precise and eliminating everything that wasn't.

Watching her teammates go through their paces, Lisa was glad they were playing Eastside. Several crucial elements were missing: Amanda's speed, Colin's intensity, Layla's need for revenge. Emily looked so lethargic that Lisa wondered if she was on one of her three-day bulimic benders. And Leslie was still pissed off at Rachel for flirting with Ian during second lunch.

Coaching – and coaches – Lisa believed only brought you so far. Parents were worse. Her earliest memories of the game featured that line of lunatics on the sidelines, screaming like skinny white girls at a Ludacris concert. "Win the ball!" "Run!" "Good kick!" "Open space!" Screaming at them as if they were untrained puppies. Even when her dad threw his clipboard or dropped F-bombs like water balloons, he rarely took himself that seriously. Much better than Layla's dad, Lisa thought, he realized things changed when the girls stepped into their zone. The silence on the field was their reward for all the shit they put up with in practice. The freedom of the game was their reward for being manacled to the sport for 20 hours each week. Once the ball dropped, they were real, and everyone else – parents, coaches, boyfriends, siblings, and teachers – was Patrick Swayze in "Ghost," adrift in another dimension. Or that, at least, was how it was supposed to be. They were at their best when they were released from the gravity of the dumb-ass things that humiliated them on a daily basis. Their parents' disappointment. The disapproval of the bedroom mirror. The dismay of Language Arts' teacher who couldn't get them to open up. The demands of the guys who said most girls didn't think it was all that disgusting.

At the five-minute mark, they dropped, edgy and alert, at Alex's feet. Across the field, parents were lining up blankets, cushions and Starbucks' cups in the bleachers. The stadium lights were on, banking light into the corner pockets of the felt and leaving opaque shadows in the middle of the field.

Alex stood quietly long enough that Layla arched an oh-God-help-me-my dad-is-losing-it eyebrow at Lisa, just as the referee arrived at his elbow. "Coach, let's not waste time," he said. "Lights are off at 10." He was in his mid-20s, with a 1,500-meter body. The girls weren't even pretending not to stare. "Game balls?"

Jill arrived on cue, a No. 5 under each arm, a third at her feet. "Can I ask a small favor?" Alex said. The man's face gave nothing away but he nodded. "State Cup is coming up. A little practice with PKs couldn't hurt. If the match ends in a tie, can we bag overtime and go straight to a shoot-out?"

"You've addressed the other coach?"

"This morning."

The ref nodded again. "Sixty seconds, then my whistle. " He took off like a Targa Porsche.

Alex turned back to the girls. "Sixty seconds. More than enough. You girls look sharp. When did you switch to the 4-4-2?" The girls looked at one another as if they'd been asked to date the French Revolution. "Christmas, maybe," Emily said.

"It's not my favorite," Alex said, as a whistle sounded at midfield, quick and to the point. "We may switch back to the 4-3-3 at the half, but let's stick with what's been working for you. Layla, take Amada's spot up front."

The starters surged out onto the field, while the reserves took refuge beneath the Malice canopy. Jill was dutifully setting out water bottles and quartered oranges, and as the whistle sounded, Alex pulled the small note pad from his hip pocket. "Jill, can you do me a favor? Palisades Market is right down the hill. You'll be back in 10."

*   *   *

"D'Anjou pears? You got D'Anjou pears, Jill?" Jessica said. "What would we be sucking on if we were ahead?"

"I didn't know mangoes were in season," Jennifer said. "Are you sure we can eat these, Mom?"

"Everything in moderation," Alex said.

"Mesha, chuck me a pineapple." Lisa's jersey was stained with tangelo juice.

"You know what I remember?" Emily said, reaching for another slice of over-ripe pear. "Tillamook. Coach Blain would cram us in the maroon monster, like six in the back and four in the front, open the windows and take us to Tillamook for milk shakes.

Cleats on, mud all over us, and it was so funny, everyone thinking we were adorable, asking if we'd won the game. 'Yeah,' we'd say, '11-0, cause Coach loves to run it up.'"

"Hey, coach …" Maggie said, dropping a masticated orange slice into Jill's brown garbage bag. "We gonna talk about the second half?"

Alex checked the clock. "Two-zip is an ugly halftime score."

"They keep pulling that off-sides trap," Lisa said, "and the linesman is a dork."

"He'll have a hard time calling off-sides if you carry the ball in."

"Coach Colin used to scream if I went 20 feet without passing the ball," Lisa said.

"Well, Coach Colin ain't here," Alex said, "so why don't …"

"Yeah, he is," Jessica said. "Over there. In his car."

Alex stood up. "Where?"

Jessica pointed into the shadowed street behind the school. "The Land Rover."

The windshield glass was tinted, so Alex had no idea if anyone was inside the car. "Tell you what," he said. "Let's switch to that 4-3-3 so we have a few more options up front. Any chance you get, Emily, come up, too. Don't worry about them scoring. Maggie will make sure that doesn't happen again."

The girls were climbing to their feet. "D'Anjou pears," Jessica said. "I think I've seen it all."

*   *   *

They were down 2-1 when Mick hopped down the steps with eight minutes to go, then tied the score as he circled the track. Jessica intercepted a crossing pass and lofted a deep, looping pass to midfield that Jennifer read better than the Eastside defender. A sweet touch, and she was suddenly running alone down the right sideline, while the forwards, Layla and Madeleine, attacked the box. Pulled wide to drive Jennifer off the ball, the Eastside sweeper left the middle so wide open that Madeleine had a one-on-one match-up with the keeper from 12 yards out.

"Always the grand entrance," Alex said to Mick.

"One bank of the scoreboard lights is out, right? It's really 12-2."

"No, they've been saving their best for you ... Jennifer, great cross!" he yelled across the field. "And Madeleine, nice finish! Nike still in the black?"

"By a lousy 11 billion. But we're onboard for a breeding program featuring Tiger and Michelle Wie, so the analysts are bullish. Slow start?"

To their left, Jack and Jill had their arms around one another, as if planning a second honeymoon. "They had a header off a corner kick and a freebie when Maggie came out too early," Alex said. "Lisa had our first goal. Free kick. Bent it over the keeper's head."

"I've seen taller keepers," Mick said.

"She was big enough in the first half."

Regulation time ended in that 2-2 tie and the Malice came bounding to the sidelines, loud and loose. "Any mangos left?" Jennifer said.

"Hey, dad," Lisa said, absolutely bubbly, "you missed my goal again."

"You want me to leave during overtime?"

"We're going straight to shoot-out," Alex said. "You remember who we used to send out?" They were standing apart from the girls, trying to get a read on facial expressions and body English.

"Layla and Emily, definitely. Jessica and Lisa. You want to put Mesha out there with the first group?"

"Let's hold Lisa and Layla back," Alex said. "Lead off with Mesha and Maggie. They have the legs."

Malice went first. With the score tied at 4, Eastside had a chance to win the game but their sweeper pulled her head at the last moment and sent her kick off the bar. Rachel, Leslie, Lisa, Jennifer and Layla went out as the second group, and three times in a row, the LO player followed an Eastside goal with a score of her own. With each set of PKs, the small, scattered clusters in the stands grew tighter as parents bunched together, seeking shelter from the potential defeat.

At 7-all, Maggie was too tired to move, which proved fortunate when the Eastside defender buried a shot in her stomach. Layla and Lisa, the last two strikers for LO, looked at one another for a long moment, then Layla struggled to her feet. As Layla set the ball at the 12-yard stripe, Alex could feel his stomach churning. He didn't want her to feel doubt at her throat. He didn't want the seven girls who'd made their shots go walking off arm-in-arm while Layla stayed behind. He didn't want …

Were those LO cheers or Eastside cheers? The far end of the bleachers or …

"Upper right corner," Mick said. "You can open your eyes, Dad."

They met Casey Waiwaiole at midfield. "And here they are," Casey said, "the architects of the palace coup."

"I never thanked you for the heads up back in the fall," Alex said.

Casey waved him off. "No worries. You were in the coaching box tonight, which gave us a seemingly insurmountable edge. Call it even."

The girls were gathered beneath the canopy, packing bags, trading shots, sounding like debutants prepping for the Christmas dance. Alex was startled by how young they looked and how old he felt, surprised by how much he'd missed this. Layla and Lisa were, as usual, joined at the hip, leaving him no room to squeeze between them, so he waited until Layla pulled the travel bag to her shoulder before approaching her. When she looked at him, he remembered how utterly boring his life had been before she came along. "When was the last time you missed a PK?" he asked.

"I've never missed a PK. Mom's taking us to Tillamook. You coming?"

Alex saw Olivia at the far end of the field, talking to several parents. "Sure," he said, "but I need to collect the gear. I'll meet you there."

Layla set off, her teammates fanned out around her. He was retrieving his bag when he heard a car engine turn over. He glanced up to see the Land Rover slide 50 yards before the brake lights flared. Alex half expected to see an upraised finger; instead, the Land Rover idled quietly for a good 10 seconds before the taillights flashed and the Land Rover slowly backed to the edge of the field.

He slowly crossed the grassy slope that separated them. He smelled the acidic smoke before he reached the bumper.

"A sterling comeback," Welch said. "And was that your lass who stroked the winning PK?"

"I'm sorry she disappointed you."

"Disappointed me? Come on, mate. Those are my girls out there."

"I'm surprised you're here."

"And why would I be running off? The town has been good to me. I've got the bank statements to prove it."

"Until Eddie Alvarado killed the golden goose."

A quiet chuckle. A careless pull on the cigarette. Elvis Costello was playing the Land Rover lounge. "I keep thinking you're smarter than that, Alex, and I keep over-estimating you. You don't believe anything you see on Page 3 and you don't believe everything you read in the rest of the rags."

"We must be at the end of the comic book. The villain explains why he did it."

"Candy from a baby. And no shortage of sweet stuff in the cribs down the road."

"That's what Google's for," Alex said. "Every week or so I'll send that pit bull out looking for you, just to see if she picks up your scent. When she does, I'll have a copy of Alvarado's story, ready to go."

"Awfully considerate, mate. You can't buy that kind of PR. Your e-mail might land on a Boy Scout with a similar aversion to success, but the odds are in my favor. Most blokes down the road will more impressed by my dedication to winning."

"You know what I think?"

"Let me guess: the comic-book hero's benediction."

"We draw this line at the most arbitrary time," Alex said, realizing it was a strange night to channel Ray Tripp. "We draw this line when the girls are 11, then tell one group they have potential and the others they're wasting their time. We don't know who'll grow four inches and who's going to gain a full step of speed. Everything is set in stone. The traveling squad gets all the love and we tell the rec girls, 'Better luck with the piano.' We toss them off the field before they have time to warm up."

"Not bad," Welch said. "I'll miss the savage beauty of it."

He flicked the cigarette to the curb. "Honor and dignity don't win in the end, lad," he said, putting the Land Rover into gear. "But I make a living off the fools who think they do."

They came through the door together, Layla fumbling with her purse, Lisa hiding behind her hair. On the sidewalk behind them, a dozen 7th graders were shivering in the gusting darkness, waiting for someone they knew to escort them into the lobby, but Layla and Lisa had arrived together in their designer jeans and layered tops and dancing shoes. Mr. Buchanan and Mr. Hastings were standing just inside the door, Mr. Hastings leaning in to check for the wreath of alcohol, Mr. Buchanan to collect the green beans and artichoke hearts they'd brought for the canned-food drive. Stashed behind those bangs, Lisa ignored the way Mr. Buchanan's eyes rolled over her, searching for a place to land, even as the first six-foot wave of sound rolled out of the cafeteria and washed over them.

"Don't Cha" with Pussycat Dolls and Busta Rhymes, and the bass turned up through the roof.

Don't cha wish your girlfriend was wrong like me?

Don't cha wish your girlfriend was fun like me?
Don't cha? Don't cha?

The lobby was flush with Goths and parent volunteers and Spring Fling posters. Pairs of lightweight girls were darting about as if late for the new episode of "Gray's Anatomy." Lisa and Layla never slowed as they ducked into the cafeteria and under the fractured lights of a disco ball.

Don't cha? Don't cha?

Spring Fling was the last dance of the school year, *their* last dance at LOJ. There were corner tables where the losers gathered to catch their breath, and a buffet table bearing punch bowls filled with red-vine licorice and Gummy Bears. Clinging to the walls, boys on one side of the room, girls on the other, were the seventh-grade midgets, whirlwinds of pantomimed motion. But all the eight graders, all the prospects, all the gossip and the drama were in the mosh pit at the center of the room. Layla grabbed for Lisa's hand, searching for the familiar – a skirt, a pose, a landing zone – but Lisa kept moving, dragging her into the mob.

"Do you see anyone?" Layla screamed in the two-second lull in which Gwen Stefani chased the Pussycat Dolls off the CD player. Either Lisa couldn't hear her or Lisa wasn't listening. She was pushing her way through tangled limbs, trying to find Rachel, Jessica, and Emily before they passed out on the Tag body spray fumes.

All the riches, baby, won't mean anything
All the riches, baby, won't bring what your love can
bring
All the riches baby, won't mean anything ...

They found their crew at the back of the cafeteria, begging Mr. Chen to open the back door in the name of fresh air. He was standing firm, arms crossed. The prohibition against leaving the dance was resolute. The parking lot was Fantasy Island, Jungle Cruise, the Tunnel of Love. The gatekeepers wouldn't budge.

Rachel and Emily looked sharp, just as they had three hours earlier when Olivia drove them down to Mercantile Village to get their nails done. Jessica looked even better in her DKNY jeans and a Navy blue Abercrombie top with ruffled sleeves.

"How long have you had that?" Layla screamed, indignant. They all swapped clothes – those were the house rules – and she'd never seen the top before.

"Christmas?" Jessica's heart wasn't in the conversation. She'd gone over the top with the lip gloss and the burgundy eyeliner, and scraped her brows down to the bone, and Layla felt the tug of envy. Jessica was looking for someone, and unless she darted onto the stage, she had no sure vantage point. They were hemmed in by the Lake Grove glee club, the volleyball divas, and the holy rollers who went to Wyld Life on

Monday nights. She was about to ask if there'd been an official sighting of Ian, Brandon, K-Smut and the rest of the boys when Rachel snared Jessica's wrist, as the pack came into view and the dominant wolf established his authority.

That would be K-Smut, of course. The boys all dressed the same, straight-cut jeans and T-shirts that promoted their favorite grunge band. Ian had three inches on K-Smut and Brandon by 20 pounds, but like the alpha males on the Discovery Channel, K-Smut insisted on being the center of attention, especially with the she-wolves were in heat. He'd shun the guys who challenged his supremacy and sucker punch those who tried to join him at center stage. Sometimes it was a tap on the head, sometimes one of those titty twisters that Layla felt in the pit of her stomach. He once borrowed a Diet Sprite from Lisa and dumped it on Danny's head when he found Danny sitting next to her at lunch. Why K-Smut's friends put up with that, Layla wasn't sure.

Rachel's mouth was suddenly at her ear. "Look at Buck Teeth and Buchanan!"

Mr. Buchanan and Ms. Devereaux, who had the overbite from hell, had climbed atop the stage and were gyrating like the hyperactive goofballs who palmed their Ritalin. Ms. Devereaux was hampered by an ankle-length calico paisley dress while Mr. Buchanan wore Springsteen jeans and a black button-down shirt.

"So, what's it gonna be, Sailors?" Mr. Buchanan shouted into the microphone. "Are you gonna seize the dance floor? Or abandon the stage to *my* generation?" Ms. Devereaux appeared on the verge of a heart attack.

When Kanye West inexplicably shut down, the two teachers shimmered in gut-wrenching silence. Then the DJ cued The Fray:

I never knew
I never knew that everything was falling through

And in their neighborhood, at least, a few of the show-offs – Rachel, Leslie and the girls who'd snuck two fingers of vodka out of the freezer when Mom went looking for the car keys – began to bounce …

"That's it!" Mr. Buchanan bellowed. "Let the dance begin!"

It wasn't dancing, really. Jumping was more like it. Not David Lee Roth jumping, but hopping, feet semi-glued to the floor, shoulders and knees struggling to find the rhythm in plain view of a brain that was screaming into the vacuum:

Everyone knows I'm in
Over my head
Over my head

"Crack monkeys," Emily howled. "Our teachers are crack monkeys!"

The boys were pelting the volleyball divas with the Gummy bears from the snack bar. Layla was feeling totally out of synch when she felt Lisa's hand on her elbow and turned to see the clenched fist, their signal to head to the bathroom whenever they were in the company of strangers. Grateful for something to do other than look fat, lonely and terminally clumsy, Layla grabbed Lisa's hand so they would remain tethered on the slam dance through the gym. At the cafeteria door, a Gummy bear sailed past Layla's ear.

"K-Smut wants attention," Layla laughed.

"He's not getting any tonight," Lisa yelled back. They pushed their way between the haves and the have-nots, the prom queens who used deodorant and the circus clowns who didn't, the smug and the forlorn. They held hands through the gauntlet of Ichiro jerseys and Hollister tops, knee socks and net stockings, flip-flops and platform heels, the girls in lumpy sweaters and the guys who wouldn't turn down a dare. Each group always returned to the same pre-assigned seat on the dance floor, their safe room.

Mr. Buchanan was just inside the door, his forehead dappled with sweat. Layla tried to duck behind the entourage and into the lobby but Mr. Buchanan suddenly had his hand on Lisa's shoulder and his mouth at her ear, and in the dance of light and shadow, Layla realized that once you got past the bald dome, Mr. Buchanan wasn't all that much bigger than K-Smut.

It was 90 degrees in the gym and she was shivering. When Lisa finally gave her teacher the finger wave, they crossed the lobby and rolled down B hall to the girls' room. Lisa gave her a shoulder bump at the door. "You're being so weird," she said.

"You showed the fist," Layla said. "I wouldn't want you to pee your pants."

Lisa went into a stall, Layla to the open spot at the mirror, between a Mariah Carey wannabe, and a trio of Oak Grove airheads. She leaned over the sink to check her makeup and winced. She hated her face. Her face had no highlights, no magic angles, no game. It was all lemon-glazed baby fat and dulce du leche cheeks. The lights over the mirror sucked, and she felt relieved; every now and then, in the radiance of her make-up mirror, Layla saw the beginnings of her mother's face.

The toilet flushed and Lisa came clomping out, re-arranging her strawberry-colored thong. Mariah took one look at the gymnastics routine, and backed out the door, and they both laughed. As Lisa splashed water on her hands, Layla watched her in the mirror, marveling at the way everything came together around her eyes and cheekbones.

Lisa caught her staring. "He's harmless," she said. "He's just needy."

"Teachers aren't allowed to be needy," Layla said. "What time are you going?"

Lisa reached for a paper towel. "He'll be in the parking lot at eight."

"What if you get caught?"

Lisa flexed her shoulders – *Whatever* – and ran a forefinger over that clipped eyebrow. As they turned toward the door, a swirl of color burst through the door, rust and gold and bare shoulders.

"Hey!" Chelsea said. Her eyes were clear, her thick, dark hair splayed out like a dense train behind her. "Are we hiding out or dealing weed?" Esmeralda, rumor had it, had handed out sandwich-bag jolts in this very room before the cops stormed her locker.

"Cooling off," Layla said, instinctively putting a hand out to check the heater, then hopping atop it.

"That's a great dress," Lisa said, her voice steamed with wonder.

"Thanks," Chelsea said, self-consciously smoothing the fabric. The dress looked great on her hips, tight and loose in all the right places, the colors a perfect match for her long neck and dark hair. "My grandmother found it in San Francisco." She turned on the cold water, letting it wash over the inside of her wrists. "I can't believe how hot it is in there. And someone is throwing stuff. Got hit here," she said, brushing her right temple. "I think it was a gummy bear."

Lisa laughed. She couldn't help it. Three seventh-graders arrived like a string of firecrackers. Lisa and Layla scooted back into B Hall and into the rhythm section of the Black Eyed Peas. "What?" Layla said as they passed the display case pitching "Anchor Values."

"Chelse," Lisa said. "Just now. She was looking at *us* in the mirror, not herself."

Baby have some trustin' trustin'
When I come in lustin' lustin

Lisa shook her head. "Who *does* that?"

*   *   *

The wine and cheese – a Santa Margherita Pinot Grigio from Costco and the creamy Tallegio from Whole Foods – were set out before the first guest arrived, along with grapes and the stoned wheat thins. Annika had taken the afternoon off to get the house in shape. Jack could not deal with clutter and disarray. He'd fired two night managers when he'd arrived in the morning to find trash in the service bay. He expected the house to radiate a similar glow when they entertained.

The e-mail had scheduled the meeting for 7:45 p.m., 15 minutes after the start of Spring Fling, but Debra Giuliani rang the doorbell while Jack was dragging chairs into the living room. Her smile was tight, and Jack's gut feeling, as he hung her coat in the hall closet, was that the black boots and the designer jeans were a bit much, the outfit you'd wear to convince the guys at Happy Hour it didn't hurt to ask.

"Great cheese,' she said when he returned from the closet. She was pouring herself a glass of Pinot Grigio. "How many RSVPs?"

Jack ground his teeth. This is why he hired accountants. "I told Annika to expect 15." He cleaned-and-jerked another dining-room chair. The evening's disarray was gaining on him.

By the time the chairs were arranged, Debra and Annika were clucking about the new mall at Bridgeport, and Gazelle, his aging spaniel collie mix was sprawled by the front door. There was a time when the dog could run down every hot rod in the neighborhood, weaving so close that the cowards hit the brakes, but of late Gazelle was deaf, dumb and constipated. Jack forgave her all that; he got along better with the dog than he did with his son, who'd skipped dinner to study with Jessica Edgefield, the limber blond captain of the tennis team.

The Davenports arrived at 7:40 p.m., the Chamberlains two minutes later. Thanks to Spring Fling, no one had the luxury of being fashionably late. The dance ended at 9:30 p.m. and you didn't want to leave the girls standing like tarts in the parking lot. At 7:50 sharp, the doorbell rang again and Gazelle slipped back into the house, along with the Bishops, Don and Shelley Gottlieb – Jack had sold them an S40 the summer before – and Thalia, Elliot's humorless assistant coach. Jack disposed of the coats, cracked open a couple beers, then caught Thalia staring out the picture window in the living room.

"How much longer before Taze shows up?" he asked.

Thalia regarded him like she'd just picked up his description on an Amber Alert. "Taze has no-show written all over him," she said.

"What?"

"Taze is a whole lot better at giving orders than answering questions. You talk to your daughter much?"

Jack stared at the woman. "Relax," Thalia said, her thin arms folded in front of her. "Debra is doing all the talking. It's what she's good at." Thalia turned back to the winter roses. At the other end of the room, Gazelle buried her teeth in what was left of the fur on her hind leg and farted audibly.

"Annika!" Jack wailed as Debra came out of her chair. "Can you put Gazelle in the garage?"

"A few parents may be late," Debra was saying from her stand in front of the piano, "but why don't we get started? Thank you, Jack and Annika for hosting this ..."

She paused just long enough that Raleigh Davenport – Melissa's razor-thin, topspin-loaded father – snapped off a half volley at the net. "Yeah, what is this exactly? Do I get out the checkbook?"

"An informational meeting," Debra said. "To clear the air."

Gazelle included, Jack hoped. For some reason, Shelley Gottlieb had a hand in the air, and Debra, still a mite flustered, flicked out a finger to call on her.

"Where's Coach Elliott?" Shelley asked. She was built like a Hummer. Jack wondered if Don could still remember the last time he wrapped his arms around the grill.

"He had a game tonight in Eugene," Debra said. "But Taze and I have discussed all this and ..."

"Discussed all what?" Davenport asked. He was parked by the stone wheat thins, radiating that my-Subaru-wagon-is-worth-$8,000-in-trade hostility.

"Raleigh, let me finish," Debra said, gathering herself. "Over the last several weeks, the rumor has been going around that Coach Elliott had an improper relationship several years ago with one of his players. I've received two phone calls from parents. Eddie Alvarado is snooping around."

"Eddie Alvarado?" Tom Chamberlain asked. He was 6-foot-1 and the only guy in the room with a *New York Times'* tube at the foot of his driveway.

"Wait a minute," Laurie Bishop said, poised to launch her 130 pounds out of the Klaussner love seat. "What do you mean, 'improper relationship'?"

Debra stood silently. "There was sex," she said. "Or so I understand."

A sharp intake of breath. A drop in the cabin pressure. Then the room erupted. Raleigh Davenport was waving his arms. Laurie Bishop fluttered to her feet. Shelley Gottlieb was leaning back in her chair, her right hand below her triple chin, and Jack felt Annika at his side, her cheeks flushed. Debra let the maelstrom rage for a moment, then raised an arm to calm the room.

"There was sex?" Laurie said. "What kind of sex?"

"Taze and one of his girls?" Shelley yelped.

"Underage? Unprotected? Oral? Group?" Laurie Bishop, Jack realized, also watched the HBO soft-core channel when her spouse dozed off.

"Apparently," Debra said.

"Apparently what?" Annika asked.

"He raped one of ..." Shelley stammered.

Debra's arm went back up like Dick Bavetta's at Boston Garden. "It was not rape," she barked, seemingly outraged by the thought. "It was ... well, a mistake. Taze knows that. But it was a consensual relationship."

"Consensual?" Jack said. "Where do you get consensual? How old was the girl?"

"Almost 18," Debra said.

"So, she was a minor," Raleigh Davenport said. "Which means ..."

"Yes," Debra said. "Technically, she was below the age of consent."

"Technically?" Laurie stammered.

"My bad." Debra looked tired, as if she'd been pulling this barge since an hour before the sun came up. "I'm not making excuses for Taze. He screwed up ... "

"And that's not all he ..."

" ... he got involved with one of his players. But the girl was 17. And the sex was consensual."

Consensual, Jack realized, was so damn polite. When a creep this guy's age screwed a 17-year-old, he did it on the fly. On a locker-room bench. In the back seat of his van. On the top level of the parking garage at Washington Square after a cheap date at the Cheesecake Factory.

"How long ago did this happen?" Shelley asked.

"Several years ago, I believe."

"A Lake Oswego girl?"

Jack didn't know if that was racism or voyeurism reverberating here. Debra shook her head. "No."

"Did her parents press charges?" Annika asked, her face drained of color.

"No. As I understand it, Taze was close to the family and the girls' parents realized there was plenty of blame to go around."

"She asked for it, huh?" Raleigh snapped.

"Plenty of blame?" Shelley Gottlieb said, finally setting her wine down on the granite coffee table. "You mean, like there was plenty to go around when Neil Goldschmidt was screwing his babysitter?"

The room was roiling again. Debra stood, lips pursed. "I don't think the cases are comparable," she finally said. "Several parents were concerned, and I took those concerns to Taze and told him he had to deal with this before we read about it in *The Oregonian*."

Jack felt the roaring in his ears. Chelsea's coach screwed a teen-ager and the story might soon be stripped across the top of the morning paper. He could imagine the questions stampeding through the door at Jack Lider Volvo in Wilsonville.

"Hey, guys ..." Tom Chamberlain was moving toward the Yamaha piano, pulling his sweater vest down over his pot belly and the Sigma Chi belt buckle. "Please. Let's try to sort this out." He ended up at Debra's elbow and she seemed relieved to yield the floor. "We might be getting a little carried away here."

"Carried away, Tom?" Laurie said.

Chamberlain had both hands in the air, ready to ward off the next outburst. "I've heard 'rape' and 'Neil Goldschmidt." And I'm trying to square that with the guy who has coached my daughter for the last two-plus years. Your daughters, too. We've all been there in the stands. Most of us are fairly close to our kids. Any of you seen anything out of sorts? Ever heard your daughter complain something wasn't right?"

Jack was suddenly standing in the din of his own living room, revisiting game tapes, searching the grainy footage for something he'd missed. An arm around the shoulder. A pat on the ass. That fleeting sense of guilt. Chamberlain scanned the room, waiting. "I have my issues with Taze," he said. "He can be tough on the girls. Tougher on us. But has anyone seen anything to suggest this guy is … a threat?"

"Maybe it's not that easy, Tom," Raleigh Davenport said. "What'd I hear you say, Debra? That he was 'very close' to the family? *They* missed it, didn't they?"

"I don't know," Chamberlain conceded. "Maybe they were never around. The girl was 17, right? Hard as it is for me to imagine, maybe they didn't care."

"Well, you better believe I care that Jenna is spending 15 hours a week with a man who had sex with a girl young enough to be his daughter," Shelley said. "How can I ever trust him again in the same room with mine?"

"I've trusted him for three years," Debra said. "Two or three times each winter, Dan and I run over to Black Butte … and Taze watches over the house and the girls."

It was quiet enough in the room that Jack heard the growl ripple through Gazelle as she rolled over in her sleep.

"He … baby-sits your kids?" Laurie said.

"They're not babies, Laurie. They haven't been babies for years. And I'd be surprised if Cici, actually quite a few of your daughters, hasn't attended one of those sleepovers. Some of you are new to Black Tornado, but I've worked with Taze for four years. I trust the man. And nothing we've talked about tonight changes that."

"He had sex with one of his players, Debra," Shelley said.

"Yeah. He did. But he hasn't touched my daughters. He's helped them with homework. Picked them up after school. Been available when they've needed advice you can't expect from your parents. Which is pretty impressive when you realize his father wasn't around when he grew up. I don't have the full story but I think he spent a year in some juvenile boot camp before he turned 20."

"Rough around the edges," Chamberlain said.

Debra gave him a look that suggested she could do without the footnotes. "I don't know why you all decided Black Tornado was the right program for your daughter. I want the best. My girls have gone through a dozen coaches. I recognize the ones who work their butts off and demand my girls do the same. And I've never met a coach who knows more about the game, and motivating teenage girls. I don't know if Sierra or Sarita have a shot at playing in college but if it turns out they have that kind of talent and ambition, Taze will take them to the next level. Does he have his flaws? Did he make a serious mistake with a 17-year-old who might have been desperate for his attention? Yes. Is he a pedophile, cruising the gym for 14-year-olds? No way."

Laurie had a tentative hand in the air. "How long, Debra," she said, "have you been team manager?"

Debra stared into the fireplace, doing the math. "Since the end of Sarah's first year," she said slowly. "Twenty-two, 23 months."

"How many girls have left the team in those two years?"

"What are you suggesting?"

"Indulge me. Who's left Black Tornado in the last two years?"

"Well ... let me think ... "

"Brooke," Annika offered.

"Caitlin," Shelly said.

"Caitlin," Debra agreed. "Marissa. Heather. Molly." She took a sip of the Pellegrino. "Five, maybe six."

"Do we know why?" Laurie asked.

Debra shrugged. "Why they left? They don't always say."

"What do you remember?" Raleigh asked.

"Well ... Heather couldn't play. You all remember that. She was terrible. Marissa's father got laid off at Bonneville, I think, and couldn't handle the team dues. Caitlin and Brooke? I have no idea. Who else ... Molly? Playing time? Soccer? The lead in 'The Wizard of Oz'? What's your point, Laurie?"

"I just wondered if anyone left because ..."

"They were molested by their coach? Don't you think you would have gotten the memo? Do you seriously think you'd be hearing this for the first time now?"

"I don't know what to think," Laurie said.

"You're looking for a pattern, right?" Chamberlain said. "That's what we're all looking for. Was this 'relationship' an aberration … or a warning?"

"I don't understand why the coach isn't here to answer these questions himself," Don Gottlieb said.

"Thalia?" Chamberlain said, turning toward the woman tucked in the shadows at the edge of the living room. "You coach with the man. You see him with the …"

She put her hand up, slender fingers extended. "No, you don't," she said. "Don't even think about putting this on me."

"Putting what …"

"I'm not the designated driver. Or the chaperone. You all don't pay me well enough for that."

"All we're asking …" Chamberlain began again, but Thalia cut hit off.

"I know what you're asking. And you aren't asking me. You want to know about the half-court trap, I'll talk your ear off. You wanna know about SAQ drills, send your girls to me. Been there, done that. But I'm not babysitting those girls, and I sure ain't babysitting Taze. That's not in my job description. It's part of *your* job description. You're the drug and alcohol counselor, not me. You're the sex-education course and the lie detector and the breathalyzer. I'm just a skinny girl with a beat-to-shit PT Cruiser and a mortgage who thought she'd play with Kobe one day."

Thalia scanned the room for the hint of a challenge. Not finding one, she nodded to Annika and said, "Thank you for the hospitality." Then she crossed the wooden floor and left the house, closing the front door quietly behind her. Everyone was still, until Annika swept two plates and a trio of wine glasses off the table and padded into the kitchen.

"I'm glad she didn't take it personally," Raleigh shrugged.

"Probably sleeping with Elliott, too," Shelley Gottlieb said.

"Shelley, please ..." her husband said, shaking his head.

"Maybe," Dillon Bishop said, "she finds it insulting we'd even ask."

"Where do you get that?" his wife said.

"Would she be hanging around if she thought her boss was a threat?"

"I haven't heard anyone suggest Elliott is a threat," Don said. "I think we're all concerned over the fall-out if his ... history, or whatever you want to call it, becomes public."

"I think Raleigh got it half right," Tom Chamberlain said, unrolling the left sleeve of his Geoffrey Beene shirt and buttoning the cuff. "Maybe it is personal ... as in personal responsibility. I don't know what happened between Elliott and this girl. I supposed we could find out if a complaint was filed. I have friends in the DA's office. I could call them. I can call Eddie Alvarado. But while I'm considering that, I think the first thing I better do is talk to my daughter. Maybe not tonight, when she's still jazzed about Spring Fling, but over the weekend. We may never have a better chance to talk to the girls about … well, all of this."

"I don't think that's a good idea," Debra said quietly.

"What do you mean?" Kerry Chamberlain said. "What could possibly …"

"If we rush out of here and jump the girls on the way home from the dance, they'll be talking about it all weekend."

"So, what's the problem?" Laurie asked. "The girls might feel less threatened if they thought curiosity finally got the better of us."

"Maybe," Debra said. "But what about Taze?"

"What about him?" Tom asked.

"You have another coach in mind? If he finds out we're warning the girls he might be dangerous – and he will – you're going to need one."

"Wait a minute …" Don Gottlieb began.

"I know how Taze works," Debra said. "I know the respect he demands from his players, and how important that is in getting the best out of them. We tell the girls their coach might be a predator, and Taze is history. He can't coach under those circumstances. He'll walk."

"Leaving us with what?" Tom Chamberlain said.

"Not my problem. Because I'll walk with him. Taze Elliott is the reason I'm here. Taze has been wonderful with my girls. I've never met a better coach. That's why I invest the time I do in running the website, sending out the emails, making the hotel reservations, taking the team photos …"

"Which gets your daughters a free ride with the program, right?" Jack said.

Debra gave him a long, dark, Italian look. "That's right, Jack. And given the hours I put in, that works out to 75 cents an hour."

"I think I'm with Debra," Dillon Bishop said.

"What?" Laurie said, turning to face him.

Dillon took a half step back, as if he was in no mood for a fight. "We don't know what happened with this 17-year-old. Her parents didn't press charges. Maybe she had issues. Maybe she was looking for attention …"

"I can not believe I'm hearing this," Laurie said.

"Go home and talk about it," Debra said. "I have nothing to decide. I have a lot invested in Black Tornado. Five times as many hours and twice as many daughters. And I'm in, 100 percent. If you're not, fine. But if you plan on hanging around with any less of a commitment, Taze will know it, and there'll be hell to pay."

"Wow," Raleigh said. "When did we go from information session to ultimatum?"

"Can everyone just mellow out?" Tom Chamberlain said.

"I'm damn mellow," Raleigh said. "And I'm tired. C'mon, Connie," he said to his wife, who was – a rough estimate at best, Jack conceded – on her third sipper of wine.

The living room cleared out in less than 10 minutes. Shelley Gottlieb and Laurie Bishop volunteered to help clean up, but Annika shooed them away. Tom Chamberlain tried to corner Jack so he could psychoanalyze Debra – who beat the Davenports out the door -- but Jack suggested they meet Sunday at Starbucks. The last to go was Celeste Ward, who hadn't said a single thing since she entered the house; now, however, she paused in the foyer and laid a hand on Jack's forearm. She was wearing jeans and a white blouse over her heavy breasts. Jack had a vague memory of once finding her attractive, back before her husband, Dex, lost his job at Intel and high-tailed it for central Oregon. "What just happened?" she asked.

A lot of clutter in that question, Jack thought. "I don't know. It sounds like we have one more reason to dislike our daughters' coach."

"I remember when I was that age. I had such a crush on my coach. A bunch of us did. The things we used to say." She shook her head. "How's Chelsea?"

Jack felt nothing but his anxiousness for Celeste to be gone. "So dependable it scares me. And Chloe …?"

"Angry. About so many things. I couldn't even concentrate tonight. It seems awfully early for your daughter to decide you're everything she hates."

"I've been there with Nick," Jack said. "It's brutal. This still about the divorce?"

"I don't know what it's about anymore. Maybe. The divorce changed everything. I'm sure Dex convinced Chloe it was my fault. If you and Annika figure out what we're all supposed to do now, if anything, will you give me a call?"

"Sure, Celeste," Annika said, rolling out of he kitchen with a dish towel in her hands. "I'll call. I promise."

"Thanks." Celeste's hand had never left Jack's arm, and she squeezed it now. "'Night, you guys."

As the door closed, Gazelle came padding around the corner and laid her nose on Jack's knee. "Chelsea or Gazelle, you make the call," he said.

Annika flicked the towel at him. "Enjoy your walk."

He usually did, Jack admitted to himself as Gazelle sprayed the base of the Latimers' mailbox. As the chemistry in the house grew increasingly complex, Jack found the evening walks ever more soothing. As Gazelle skirted marble fountains and light posts, Jack worked his way back through the day, tracing missteps and wrong turns, mulling over whether Annika was in the mood, planning the morning offensive. For appearance's sake, he always dropped a Glad sandwich bag in his pocket on the way out the kitchen door, and invariably dropped it in the high hat of the garbage can by the garage. He'd made several humiliating concessions in his life but no way would he ever walk through the neighborhood toting a sack of shit.

As Jack and the dog cleared the eaves by the garage, the overcast had muted the highlights in the night sky, which smelled of wine cellars and wet mulch. *What just happened?* He was still puzzling that out. Had he heard anything tonight that surprised him? What did it mean that Elliott didn't consider it necessary to address the parents who were paying him $4,000 a month, if only to argue their daughters were safe with him?

Earth to Mr. Volvo: Taze Elliott is a scam artist. Wasn't that what Nick had said? Had he missed something? Had they all missed something? And if they had, why was Debra Giuliani staking her reputation and the safety of her daughters on this asshole?

Sleepwalking down the wet sidewalk, Jack almost lost his balance as the leash snapped tight. He turned back to find the dog with her nose in the Gearys' ivy, burrowing intently beneath the leaves. "Gazelle!" he barked, but she stiffened her legs, straining for enough slack to reach whatever was buried there. Neither the sound of his voice nor his fist on the leash fazed her in the least.

Had he missed something? It happened. One of the showroom guys started hitting on the cashier. A golfing buddy started playing games with his handicap. Your state rep began bleating about a sales tax, forgetting your $2,000 campaign contribution, and you were late catching on. You weren't at the top of your game. The world was trying to get your attention and you were just like this stupid dog. She only heard what she wanted to hear. She only saw what she wanted to see.

*   *   *

Lisa abandoned her by the gummy-bear bowl, which hurt like hell. Layla was under no illusions about going along for the ride – that would defeat the purpose of what Brent McBride had planned for the evening – but she wanted to stick close to Lisa for as long as possible, up to the moment she made her escape. That would defeat the purpose, too, Lisa said. "Maybe you can create a diversion. Tell Jessica that K-Smut is all hers, then get out of the way."

Layla wasn't convinced there was an emergency exit out of the junior high, especially while Spring Fling was on, but they'd never gone looking for one. As far back as she could remember, all the excitement had been inside the building, not on a dark street down by the lake. And even when she knew there was a lot more disappointment than deodorant at the best school dance, Layla couldn't get her arms around the possibility that there was more to look forward to in Brent McBride's campaign to wrap his arms around you.

Nothing Lisa said, in whispered asides, made her the least bit jealous. She was wounded, instead, that Lisa would go off without her. That she would buy the thong and fill the flask and share the top-secret instructions to the fabled escape route from LOJ ... without her. That Lisa was already in the car, wondering where, and with whom, Brent gained such one-armed dexterity with buttons and snaps, only made it hurt a little more.

Something was different with her best friend. It was as if Lisa was already in high school. Eighth graders had a June ceremony in which they matched down the hill to Country Club Road and, together, crossed the street to the high school. "Bridge Day," it was called. Layla still remembered the skywalk of Laker blue-and-white balloons when she was sitting with her mom in traffic while the procession passed, a lumpy cop holding them back as several hundred students marched from one mysterious holding tank to the next. She'd always thought she and Lisa would take that walk together.

One minute she was there, the next she was gone. When the loneliness reached her stomach, Layla waded slowly onto the dance floor,

> *You better shape up,*
> *'Cause I need a man*
> *And my heart is set on you*
> ...

Unbelievable. Someone still had the soundtrack to *Grease*? The cafeteria felt like the sauna at Club Sport, and it was another leaden disappointment when she stepped through a pocket of shadows and came out the other side to find Jessica and K-Smut tangled up in one another's arms, as if the precarious circle of friends was already closing ranks in Lisa's absence, and moving on without her.

*   *   *

Chelsea had just about given up when Ian finally asked her to dance. She'd just about thrown Spring Fling into the wallflower drawer. Three guys had tried

356

to pull her onto the dance floor, drawn no doubt by her dress, but two of them came up to her chin and Ryan Ellington was a gawky seventh-grader whose locker was two down from hers. She was troubled by the slap of disappointment she left on his face, but she didn't want to see that face tonight when, propped up in bed and revived by the fresh air from the bedroom window, the evening flashed before her eyes and she remembered the stupid things she did. So, yes, she was on the edge of giving up, the beautiful dress turned to rags, when Ian came out of nowhere and said, "Dance?"

The question doubled the total number of words he'd said to her in the last two years, but Chelsea nodded before he could change his mind, then followed Ian until he found a small pocket of unoccupied territory. When Ian turned back to her, she gave him the smile that said, "You lead," and he took the hint. It wasn't ballroom, but his knees and elbows, at least, seemed to know what they were doing.

> *But since you been gone*
> *I can breathe for the first time*
> *So I'm movin' on, yeah, yeah*

If the girlfriends were here, they'd be singing along, belting out the lyrics with the desperation that peaked in the last 15 minutes of the dance. For the first hour, everyone was afraid to move, afraid to make a mistake, afraid to end up on the vicious IM grapevine, but the panic turned manic during the bell lap, when Mr. Hastings began hovering around the light switch and everyone realized they had one last chance to end the night better than it began. Twice in the last half hour – first Green Day, then Nelly Furtado – Ian and Chelsea's eyes had met across the crowded room, but it was only that last minute that pushed him across the room. Now that he was within arm's reach, of course, his eyes were on the floor. Or on her legs. She really couldn't tell. He was bouncing around with the sheepish goofiness that convinced Chelsea she could go down in a heap and he wouldn't notice, but she decided to stay upright on the chance he'd grow tired of the tiles or her calves and sneak a glance at her face. Chelsea couldn't see Ian's eyes in the glitter-ball light show but she was fairly sure they were just as calm and just as blue as they were that morning in French when she looked up from her past tenses and felt them on her shoulders, her neck, her face.

How can I put it, you put me on
I even fell for that stupid love song

She could feel the sweat bubbling to the surface; Ian wore a triangular stain at the throat of his SuperSonics t-shirt. Over Ian's shoulder, Staci Wright hung like a crab pot from Jason Trout's neck, her hands locked beneath the curtain of his shoulder-length hair. To her left, Sylvie McCabe was trying to convince Brandon Trivette to swing. Everyone was afraid they'd missed their exit and they were scrambling to catch up on a back road laced with potholes and blind curves. Chelsea was happy just to be dancing. She didn't want to think about the weekend or the ride home. She didn't even care if Ian didn't remember the 5th grade soccer game when he bet a Jolly Rancher she couldn't put it past him into the net and she drilled one into the high right corner off the bridge of his nose.

She snuck a peek at that nose just as Kelly Clarkston shut down and Ian with her. She opened her mouth, trusting something would rise out of the cotton mesh at the back of her throat, but what surged up to meet them instead were the opening notes of Lighthouse and the voice of the DJ, weary but still painfully over the top, announcing, "This is it, Spring Flingers, your last-chance LOJ dance. Your last chance for memories. Your last chance for romance. Why? Because it's late, because your parents are waiting in the parking lot. Because it's you and me and … Lifehouse!"

Chelsea saw the shrug begin at Ian's shoulders, the awkward surrender to dumb luck and this strange turn in the play list, and before it gained momentum, before his eyes glazed over and he said something stupid like, "See ya later," she stepped forward and into him as if all this had been decided a long time ago. His arms came up, almost out of reflex and formed the soft pocket into which she settled, not even looking at him before she laid her head on his shoulder and brought her arms around his waist.

With nothing to do
Nothing to lose
And it's you and me and all of the people …

For a deep breath or two, and as many beats of the heart, he didn't react. Then she squeezed him tighter and he came around. The limp, sweat-soaked rag fell away, replaced by a living, breathing thing who was trying to figure out how to arrange his body, the parts of him that could touch her and the parts of him that could not. An hour earlier, she knew, this process would have been chaperoned by some over-eager parent or ball-hawking Bio teacher, but this late in the game, the hall monitors and sex police had vanished. Because it was late. Because parents were waiting in the parking lot. Because they had some dim memory of how overmatched they'd been in junior high.

She felt his hands on her back, trying to get comfortable, retreating each time they brushed the clasp of her bra. She knew the sweat was rising off her like the mist at Skidmore Fountain, like it always did when the press was on and she was nervous, and Chelsea prayed she didn't smell like the warm-up jersey she left by the toilet when she stepped into the shower. She prayed she wasn't holding Ian hostage, that someone wasn't laughing behind their backs, that her dress wasn't riding up on her hips into a story they'd tell at her high-school graduation party, that the pressure on her thigh was pure imagination, that the dance wouldn't end for another hour or so. She felt strangely comfortable leaning against him, swaying with him, tucked safely away in a cloud where there was something hypnotic about the roaring in her ears. Chelsea closed her eyes to shut it all out: the pain in her bruised toes, the lights at the end of the tunnel, the wonder of what he might be thinking, and her eyes were still closed when Ian pulled back just enough to bring her head off his collarbone and – *what in the world?* -- closed the gap between them by bringing his mouth down on hers.

The corner of her mouth, actually, with a glancing blow across her nose on the way down. But close enough. She was surprised by the kiss, so surprised there wasn't time to contribute much to it. She had no chance to move her lips, to realign the crooked kiss before Ian broke it off and began to backpedal, determined to cut his losses. Chelsea, suddenly, was standing alone on the dance floor, even as the lights popped on, and everyone slid their separate ways, like everything that might be squeezed from the night was already in the glass. She had a moment or two to reach for him, to pull him back, but she was so amazed by the unexpectedness of that kiss, by the clumsiness of it, that she was focused on what she could have done, not what she should be doing. By the time she blinked, the space between them filled with seventh graders. Ian glanced at her one last time, a hitchhiker staring after the pick-up truck that passed him on a lonely country road, then disappeared in the wave of kids moving toward the cafeteria doors.

Chelsea pulled the top of her dress off the damp valley below her neck. Rachel and Laura Koertje walked by, their heads welded together by whispers, and Chelsea fell in behind them, still hearing Lifehouse on her in-house stereo. The cafeteria lights were bouncing off everything she wanted to forget – the tattered corners of posters ripped from the wall, skinny soccer players texting their parents – and nothing she would remember.

At the door, Ms. Devereaux reached out and squeezed her forearm – "You have the prettiest dress" – and Chelsea flicked on the appreciative high beams. The prospect of fresh air pushed her outside where the SUVs were lined up. Kids were dashing between the headlights, and Chelsea walked down to the door of the choir room, just so the night air could pick her up and dust her off. The strip felt like baggage claim at the airport, everyone looking for a spot on the curb. When Chelsea finally found room to breathe, she glanced back and discovered Chloe at her elbow.

"Hey," she said. "Need a ride?"

"No, I'm OK," Chloe said. "Mom's out there somewhere."

"Mine, too. I hope." It would be just her luck, Chelsea thought, if her father cruised up in the Volvo, desperate to talk about weekend basketball on the drive home.

"You have fun?" Chloe asked.

"Yeah, I guess," Chelsea said, trying out her stock, no-risk, go-back-to-your-OPB answer for the trip home. "I'm dizzy," she added, a complete afterthought.

"Heat stroke." They laughed together. Chelsea realized she hadn't talked to Chloe since the sleepover. Chloe was scanning the parking lot, and Chelsea stared at her profile, silhouetted by the passing headlights, wondering if she'd seen what she thought she'd seen, wondering if Chloe was still stamped with an unexpected kiss of her own, if not something even farther beyond the reach of any question she might ask.

Chloe seemed slower at practice. Distracted. Chelsea remembered the summer after 6th grade when her parents had taken her and Nick for a family vacation at North Carolina's Outer Banks. While her cousins had a week at the beach house, they only had three nights because of basketball, and Chelsea spent every waking moment on the beach, collecting shells at low tide. They were set out in glorious array each morning, before the beach walkers were up or her grandmother started the coffee, and Chelsea spent hours looking for the conch shells and scallops without scars. Nothing attracted her as much as the colors. She'd always assumed shells came in one color only, the alabaster that her mother slapped on the trim in the upstairs hall, but these shells were purple and brown, scarlet and funeral gray, tangerine and harvest gold. Her dad couldn't explain the colors – he only let her bring five shells home – but Uncle Morris told her the brightness of the hues spoke to how recently the shell was attached to the crab or clam that vanished in the waves. The shells were full of color when they were home to one of those creatures; only when they were abandoned or discarded did they begin to fade, bleached white by the salt and the sun.

Chelsea remembered those shells now. Chloe was paler, somehow, as if the sun or the rain or the grind was slowly bleeding her energy. Maybe she should say something, she thought as a breeze off the lake pulled the dress from her legs. Maybe it wasn't the coach who had snuck his hands beneath Chloe's nightgown. Maybe it was a diet or the flu or something that just didn't matter. She was still wrestling with that when a gold sedan flashed its lights and the Volvo pulled up next to her, the automatic locks clicking as she reached for the door.

Her mother was behind the wheel. "Hey, mom," Chelsea said, making no attempt to disguise her relief.

"Hey, sweetheart. How was the dance?"

I should have been paying attention. I should have sensed him coming. I should have pulled Ian back or yelled his name or texted him some sign I'll be up all night thinking about him and why he'd decided, at a stupid dance, to come looking for me, and what that was supposed to mean the first time we see one another Monday at school ...

"Fine. Same old."

Her mom had Counting Crows on the radio. Chelsea lowered the passenger seat window to take another sip of the breeze. The line of cars waiting at the light trailed up the hill, and when Mom came face to face with the brake lights, she reached over and turned the volume down. "Your father is out walking the dog," she said. "He's not hiding in the back seat. How was the dance?"

Chelsea sat for a moment, her hands in her lap, mulling the possibilities. Maybe it didn't all have to be guesswork. At the bottom of the hill, the light turned green. Chelsea took a deep breath. "Do you remember ..."

B obby Sorrell had been fumbling with the clasp on her bra for about 20 seconds when Molly decided to call the cops.

She had expected better of Bobby. Smoother, anyway. From the moment Bobby began giving off heat in African-American Studies, Molly would have guessed he was a bra-removing prodigy. For the first six weeks of class, she paid no attention to him, far more intrigued by the rollicking sense of community among the black students in class, from which she was necessarily excluded. But when she finally saw Bobby for the first time, and felt the urgency of his interest, Molly assumed no bra would prove his match.

For the first month of class, Bobby, Molly and Jeff Simich, Lincoln's white fullback, laid low, learning the language, waiting to get their passports stamped.

Molly was more reluctant than the guys to dive into the daily conversation. She was acutely aware that the black students, many of whom she knew in a nodding way, felt uniquely at home in the third-period class and entitled its ownership. The faculty tandem did their best not to make too much of the racial divide, or too little, but the black students were passionate in their attitude that for the first time at Lincoln, they had home-field advantage in the debate on race and society.

Not that they spoke with one voice; the patronizing tendency of the media in appointing spokesmen for the black community was worth a good hour of theater in mid-March. Molly slowly gained a new appreciation of the diversity of Portland's black community in the opening weeks. Portland Public Schools allowed easy transit between its high schools, and Lincoln drew blacks from Alberta, Lents, Eastmoreland, and Mozambique. By remaining quiet, her head barely protruding from the shell, Molly discovered how powerfully these kids were influenced by family, neighborhood, allowance, and church. While Molly was reluctant to believe she could ever understand the "black experience," she was relieved that the most contentious debates broke not on racial lines but on the sharp edges of class, ambition and faith. At least, until Mumia Abu Jamal arrived.

Mr. Snowbridge introduced him. Mr. Snowbridge was white, and Molly knew that when the white guy led the discussion, the black professor, Mr. Millner, was rooting for fireworks.

"All right," Mr. Snowbridge said, unscrewing the cap of his ever-present Dasani, "let's recap: December 1981. Daniel Faulkner, a 25-year-old Philadelphia police officer, pulls over a VW bug driven by one William Cook. Within minutes, he requests the paddy wagon, which is about the time the president of the local Association of Black Journalists, moonlighting as a cab driver, happens by. He sees his brother William being arrested, and comes running across the street, armed with a legally registered .38.

"Seconds later, Officer Faulkner is dead, shot twice – from a distance of 19 and 12 inches – and Mumia Abu-Jamal is sitting on the curb with a gunshot wound to the chest. A wound inflicted by the officer's gun. There's a messy trial, conflicting witness statements and 12,000 pages of testimony, after which the jury needs three hours to find Mumia guilty, then sentence him to death. As his death-row appeals are exhausted, Mumia matures into an outspoken opponent of the justice system and its application of the death penalty, all the while proclaiming his innocence with such eloquence that legal minds and Hollywood celebs – Paul Newman, Maya Angelou and Oliver Stone – rally to his side. So, the question of the morning is, 'Mumia Abu-Jamal: Murdering manipulator or classic frame job?' State your case."

Because Mr. Millner kept urging her to participate more in class, Molly had skimmed the handouts, a heated polemic from the Family and Friends of Mumia Abu-Jamal and a copy of a *Vanity Fair* piece that was more deliberate and persuasive. She vaguely remembered posters on telephone poles on Hawthorne and a rally at Waterfront Park, but she was unprepared when five of her classmates came out of their chairs.

"They framed the brother!" Amir Jackson said.

"Racist cop, racist judge, racist system," Preacher Phillips entoned. "Kendra James before Kendra James."

Amir's reaction was understandable; the senior, already committed to Northwestern, broke everything down in black and white. But Preacher Phillips gave Molly pause. Preacher was an evangelical Christian with a grand sense of humor who'd grown up near Peninsula Park, one of the city's poorer neighborhoods. To hear him pass judgment was unusual; to compare someone to Kendra James – a young black woman shot dead on an I-5 overpass, supposedly for refusing to obey a white cop's command to exit her car – was out of character.

"In the Paris suburbs," Aissiata Huston said, "there is a street that commemorates the political prisoner, Mumia Abu-Jamal."

Aissiata was the most beautiful woman Molly had ever seen. When Molly first realized Bobby Sorrell was giving off heat, what surprised her most was that he wasn't targeting Aissiata. She was the daughter of a Mozambique prince, sent to the United States for a year to round out her education. She was Alessandra Ambrosio thin, her hair a set of extravagant braids that rained down on perfect ebony shoulders.

"That's true," Mr. Snowbridge said. "A dozen foreign cities have declared Mumia an honorary citizen.

Do they all have a better sense of justice than Judge Albert Sabo? Terrence?"

"He started the Philly chapter of the Panthers," Terrence Holland said. Lean and light-skinned, Terrence had transferred from Benson – he'd told Molly in the first week of class, the last time she'd spoken to him – because he wanted to compete with Lincoln's mock trial team, which went to nationals each year. "Dude was expelled from high school for racial activism. He did radio reports on police brutality."

"Mumia wasn't going to get a fair trial, anyway?" asked Mr. Millner, who was perched atop his desk, the only reserved corner in a room filled with love seats, garage-sale loungers, and bar stools.

"White cop gets shot, black man gets shafted," Amir Johnson said.

"In the best of times," Terrence said, "you have to work OT to keep things cool when racial tensions are running high. Philly in the '80s wasn't the best of times."

"If the man is guilty," Preacher said, "what's he doing sitting on the curb, waiting for the cops to arrive?"

That's when Bobby Sorrell slowly unwound from his third-period slouch and put his hand up. Like Molly, Mr. Snowbridge was surprised to see it. "Bobby …"

"Can we go back to your original question?" he said. "Because if that's our choice, I go with murdering manipulator."

"Dude!"

"That's white but it ain't right!"

"Shittttt …"

Bobby was sitting three desks to Molly's right, in Preacher's shadow, giving her a sweet view of his profile as the storm broke around him. Mr. Snowbridge enjoyed the mayhem, then raised a hand to rein it in. "And why's that?"

"The *Vanity Fair* article sums it up," Bobby said. "Mumia had been fired from the radio station. He was unemployed, driving a cab. The police didn't even know who he was until he saw them stop his brother and came running …"

"*Vanity Fair?*" Preacher said, turning toward Bobby with a look of disbelief.

"Buzz Bissinger wrote the story," Bobby replied.

"Buzz what?"

"Bissinger," Bobby said. "He wrote *Friday Night Lights*."

Friday Night Lights? Molly heard the buzz around her. Instant street cred.

"What else do you know about Buzz Bissinger?" Mr. Millner said, making it clear something else was worth knowing.

"A mouthpiece for the man," said Saleem Wright, who was always hitting on Aissiata before class. He owned the most audacious dreadlocks at Lincoln, and a "Free Mumia" button. "He wrote a book about the mayor of Philly …"

"Ed Rendell," Mr. Millner said, "the city's DA when Mumia was on trial. But Bobby, you have the floor. What do you find persuasive in Bissinger's story?"

He didn't answer, not right away, as if his thoughts were still scattered. "Mumia never left the scene," he finally said. "Neither did the witnesses who identified him. There were five empty chambers in his gun. When police arrived, his brother never said a word about another gunman running off, just, 'I ain't got nothing to do with it.' If you don't believe the cop who heard his confession at the hospital, a security guard heard Mumia say the same thing. But that's not the main thing …"

"This should be good."

"That's right. The brother was driving while black! He deserved it."

There were times when Molly wondered if she'd been honest with herself in signing up for this class. Her mother had given her a look, as if she were acting out in some obscene way, adding to the painful legacy of the last three years. Mom thought she should have taken AP Economics and they'd argued for 10 minutes before Molly finally said, "Relax, it'll look great on the resume when I apply to Grambling."

"With your grades," her mother said, "Grambling is shooting high."

She deserved that. She deserved all of this, the self-loathing, the crushing loneliness, the acne and the extra 15 pounds, the sludge-filled moat that separated her from her parents and her sister and the belief that everything turned out for the best. She should have seen it coming. She should have seen *him* coming. She should have dug that moat a little deeper. Signing up for African-American Studies, she'd always thought, was part of that. Just not all of it, she realized when Amir, Terrence, and Saleem went Samuel Jackson on her and, once again, she felt Coach telling her she was wound too tight, too damn tight and she just had to trust him.

"When I read the pro-Mumia stuff," Bobby Sorrell was saying, "it's all black and white ..."

"Damn straight!"

"Pipe down," Mr. Millner said.

"I don't mean black and white that way; I mean, there's no middle ground, no concession the other side may have reason to believe what it does."

"When Officer Faulkner's widow sends a plane and a banner up over Abu-Jamal's publishing house, declaring that Addison-Wesley coddles cop killers, does that sound like a quest for middle ground?" Mr. Snowbridge asked.

Bobby shook his head. "The anti-Mumia stuff can be just as bad. That's why I like Bissinger. He's the one guy who doesn't have this ... agenda, I guess. He doesn't skip the stuff that undercuts his argument. I mean, he says Philadelphia had a reputation for police brutality. He admits the judge was a hard-ass and that Mumia didn't have adequate legal counsel. And ... " Bobby was rummaging through his handouts, searching for a final footnote ... "that 115 of the 130 people on Death Row in Pennsylvania back then were minorities, which sure sounds like racial bias."

"Sounds like chutes and ladders," Saleem said. "Chutes for the black man, ladders for the white man."

"For all that," Bobby said, "Bissinger still ends up thinking Mumia killed Daniel Faulkner. When everyone else is looking to score political points, that's persuasive."

For the next 10 minutes, it was rage against the machine. All the guys wanted a piece of Bobby. The air was thick with ballistics, judicial bias and the inconvenient witnesses who conveniently never testified. This cacophony usually shoved Molly deeper into her shell, out of the line of fire, but the crowd was so energized that she was drawn to the target of their wrath, the slender kid with the great shoulders and bad hair. She wasn't the only one. Aissiata Huston was sitting halfway between her and Bobby, and Aissiata, twirling her beads and braids, was locked in on Bobby as if she'd finally discovered something on the continent she did not expect. It was that absorption, Molly later realized, and not the boys' broadsides, that inspired her to raise her hand for the first time in the semester. She wasn't afraid Bobby couldn't deal with the hand-checks, the moving screens, the full-court press; she was afraid Aissiata would beat her to his side, Aissiata and that flawless skin, those gorgeous lips, that exotic promise.

Mr. Snowbridge, the more reserved of her teachers, caught the movement right away. "Molly?"

"Everyone sounds so desperate," Molly said. "Desperate to believe that Mumia and what happened to him confirms everything they've always thought."

Mr. Snowbridge was whispering to Mr. Millner, but other than that, the room had grown still. Amir turned around at his desk to face her. Preacher removed his Young Life baseball cap.

"What do you mean?" Mr. Millner said. "Don't stop there."

"Girl has a voice," Teisha Outlaw said, not unkindly.

"I don't know what happened," Molly said. "None of us do. I've read the handouts, not the 12,000-page transcript, OK? But it sounds like everyone wants to think that what happened to Mumia proves what they've thought all along. Cops lie. African-Americans can't get a fair trial. Racists still sit on the bench and …"

"You saying none of that is true?" Terrence asked.

"Some of it is. Isn't that what we've been talking about, that sometimes we're biased for good reasons, not bad ones? That's what I like about the *Vanity Fair* story, too." Molly was very aware, suddenly, that she had Bobby's full attention. "Bissinger doesn't seem desperate. He's saying, not so fast. Things did go wrong. Witnesses change their … testimonies. The judge was a jerk, and Mumia is an amazing writer. But that doesn't mean he didn't dash across the street with a gun when he saw a cop hassling his brother. And even if everything we want to believe is true, that doesn't prove Mumia is innocent."

Molly had a hard time keeping her head above the waves for the rest of class. She'd never seen the teachers happier. But given how quickly she bolted for the door when the bell sounded, Molly was surprised when she heard her name and felt the brush on her shoulder before she reached the end of the hall. Turning, she found Bobby Sorrell – was he always that tall? – looking down at her. "And maybe," he said, "we're equally desperate to believe the system still works, that even the dreadlocks get fair trials."

There was so much barnyard noise, so many bumper cars around them,that Bobby had to lean in to make himself heard. She heard the "we." She smelled the morning shower. She felt the heat. My God, she thought. All those nights curled up on the couch, asking Mom if she couldn't find one more afghan. All those mornings in the car, cranking up the heater and leaning against the dash. All those sweaters and flannel nightgowns and leg warmers and hot chocolates before she went to bed. None of which cut through the chill like the heat emanating from Bobby Sorrell.

He had Con Law, she had Choir. There wasn't time to talk, but they were so anxious, both of them, they cut seventh period and walked two blocks to the coffee shop on 15th Street. There were monster scones and wheat-free honey bran muffins in the bakery case but Molly lied about lunch and let Bobby buy her a chai, then lead her to a couch at the rear of the shop.

"Think the office staff ever drops by?" Molly asked.

Bobby shook his head. "We'll say it's our independent study project."

She held her breath when he sat down next to her, terrified she'd feel nothing but the inside of the refrigerator, the dampness of the garage, the same old frigid memories.

"Wow," she said.

"What?"

"Where did you come from?"

Bobby lowered the coffee to his lap. Molly felt the silent vibration of her cell phone in the purse beside her. "Where did I come from? You're the one who only drops in once a week."

"I'm there every day."

"No, you're not. I used to think it was Prozac. I almost gave up."

"Gave up?"

"I'd stare at you for an entire period, and you'd never look up."

"Why didn't you say something?"

"The dead bolts? The bullet-proof glass?"

"It's African-American Studies," she said, slowly. "I don't know if I've earned the right to an opinion."

"So, what's your excuse in AP Gov?"

Her cell was buzzing again. "Who do you know in my AP Gov class?"

Bobby laughed. "I sit two rows behind you."

"Wow," Molly said.

"So, what happened? You raised your hand. You had my back. What changed?"

She sipped the chai, her legs up beneath her, her sandals on the floor at the foot of the couch. "I thought I had something to say."

"Everyone had something to say. I wonder if Snowbridge was disappointed."

He hadn't shaved. Or he didn't need to. He'd worn the Linfield t-shirt before without throwing it in the wash. One look at those legs and you knew he ran in the mornings, gliding through the rain. "Why would he be disappointed?"

"It's the O.J. trial all over again," Bobby said. "White people want to fry the guy; blacks want to hold a parade."

He'd watch her for an entire class? Is that what he said? And she never looked up? She tried to remember the last several months, what she wore, what she'd looked like, when she ever crawled out of bed caring what she looked like. He said so himself. He thought she was strung out, too medicated to wrap her head around a coherent thought, sinking into the deep end of the ...

"Hey," he said, his fingertips on the sleeve of her blouse before she was aware he was reaching for her. Startled, she jerked her arm away, stunned at how quickly the heat had moved from the valley of her elbow to the pit of her stomach.

"... you were disappearing again. I'm sorry ... I didn't ..." Bobby was looking at her lap and she followed him there. The chai stain was blinking at them like a warning hazard on a deserted street.

"I'm such a ..." Molly said, struggling to her feet. Searching for the restroom, she finally located the oaken door in the far corner. Grabbing her purse, she left him on the couch, scuttling into the bathroom, turning on the light, taking in the black porcelain sink, the 60-watt reflection in the mirror, the stupid phone still growling in her purse.

She flipped it open without bothering to see who was stalking her. "What?"

There was a sigh, a light-headed pause, then, "Molly ...?" Laura. Sounding needy and lost. "Why aren't you answering your phone?"

"'Cause I'm in the middle of something. What do you want? Did you forget your key again?" Molly turned on the cold water with her free hand, then made the mistake of checking the mirror. Her hair looked like the straw in the elephant cage at the Washington Park Zoo. What was she doing here? Why had Bobby Sorrell followed her out the door when he could be knee deep in the bliss of Aissiata's braids?

"No, I just ..."

"What?" She jerked a paper towel off the edge of the sink and dunked it under the faucet.

"I just wanted to ask you something."

"I'm listening. Hurry up." She started tamping the stain with the wet towel, wincing as the cold water dripped onto her legs.

"I don't know what to do."

And this was Molly's problem? Laura's squirrelly group of smart-ass friends weren't available? "Where are you?"

"Westlake. In the bathroom. I came in to call you."

There was a puddle at Molly's feet. She had no idea whether her skirt was looking better or worse, so she turned the water off. "How'd you get there?" she asked. Westlake was a mile from the junior high.

"Billy McCay."

The cell phone slipped from Molly's hand and fell clattering into the sink. She snatched it up again. "Are you still there?"

"Yeah … what …"

"Billy McCay?" Billy was a senior, a maniac in his parents' boat, a borderline alcoholic when they were still in school together. "Why are you with Billy McCay?"

"He said he'd give me a ride home."

She didn't have time for this. Her skirt was soaked and Bobby was out there somewhere, convinced she was a basket case. "What are you talking about? Why would Billy give you a ride home?"

"I don't know."

And why did it sound like she was about to cry? "So why are you at Westlake?"

"Because he kissed me. And put his hand … inside my blouse. And I don't know what to do."

She felt the chill climbing her spine, hand over hand, the icy fingertips digging for a better grip. "He kissed you? Where?"

"In his car. I'm sorry, Molly, I've never even talked to him. What did I do wrong?"

What had she done wrong? God damn it. "Nothing, pumpkin," she said. "You didn't do anything wrong. How long have you been in the bathroom?"

"I dunno."

Molly stepped back into the coffee shop, the cell to her ear, looking for Bobby. When she turned toward the afternoon light, she found him, leaning against the wall. "Are you OK?" he asked.

"Do you have a car?" Molly said. Bobby nodded. "Can you drive me?" Unbelievably, she thought, he didn't say anything. He simply nodded again.

"Stay there," she told her sister. "Don't move. I'll be there in …"

"Don't move? I'm in the bathroom, Molly! I can't …"

"I'll be there in 10 minutes," Molly said, moving toward the door. She paused outside, waiting for Bobby to catch up; she had no idea where his car was parked. "Wanna tell me where we're going," Bobby asked as a white panel truck accelerated past.

"Lake Oswego. Westlake Park. Where's your car?"

"Ten minutes away. Who we going to rescue?"

"My sister," Molly said, crossing the street, pulling him in her wake.

"What happened?"

"Some guy groped her on the way home from school. Where's your car?"

"By the MAC. Should we call the cops?"

Molly shook her head. "I know the guy. He's a senior."

"You know the guy?" Bobby was struggling to keep up.

"I used to. He gave her a ride home and ... fuck. This way?"

"Yeah. So, why's she calling you?"

Molly turned on him, realizing all the while that she couldn't remember the last time Laura asked her for anything. "She's 13, Bobby. Eighth grade. He probably weighs 210. She ran into a bathroom to call me."

"Did you tell her to wait in the bathroom until we get there?"

"Yeah, and we're wasting time, dammit. Can we ..."

"Molly." Bobby was anchored suddenly on the street that flanked the Lincoln campus. "May I have your phone?"

"What?"

"Your phone. I have an idea."

If the cell hadn't still been locked in her right fist, she might have argued. Bobby took the phone and pressed re-dial.

"She might not ..." Molly began, but standing three feet from the phone, she still heard Laura's frantic howl: "Why'd you hang up on me?"

"Laura," Bobby said. "Laura, I'm Bobby. A friend of your sister's ... yeah, at Lincoln. Sorrell. Two R's, two L's. Friend me tonight on Facebook ... No, she's right here … That's what I figured. And I have a better idea."

Molly felt out of the loop. Billy McCay. He'd put his hand on her ass during the Autumn Equinox dance, and she couldn't remember what he looked like.

"We're 20 minutes away," Bobby was saying. "And you don't need us, anyway. Go back out and tell him your Mom called, freaking out because you have a dentist appointment and she was supposed to pick you up." Bobby listened for a moment, then nodded. "Yeah. That's why you don't need the ride home. She knows you're at Westlake and she's racing over to pick you up, OK?"

A light rain was falling. "Sure," Bobby said, "a doctor's appointment is good, too. Stay cool. You'll be fine. And Laura? If he argues, call us back, OK? Yeah. Bye."

Us. She heard the 'us,' even if she didn't understand it. "I need to go," Molly said.

"I know. I just thought it might get weird if we roared up like Jason Strathern. Especially in Mom's Subaru."

"I need to go."

"C'mon, I'll give you a ride. Be good if you're home when she gets there." Bobby was already moving west, toward Goose Hollow and the MAC. She couldn't help but follow. He was taking the warmth with him.

*   *   *

She didn't say much on that drive home. He didn't get it. He didn't understand why a sloppy move by your average over-sexed hound had pushed the terrorist threat level to dark red, but he didn't get in the way or interrupt the flurry of texts she and Laura exchanged on the 20-minute drive. And he didn't linger or get weird when he dropped her off. He waved to Laura through the passenger window, and then he was gone, Laura staring after the Subaru as it climbed the hill toward Mountain Park. When they were alone, standing at the edge of the soccer field, two blocks from the house, Laura looked at her accusingly. "I never said you had to come rescue me," she said.

"Tell me what happened."

"I told you what happened. And you told Lincoln High School."

"I told Bobby. I needed a ride."

"Who's Bobby? Your boyfriend?"

"I don't have a boyfriend. Are those my jeans?"

Laura reddened. "You left them in the laundry room, like for a week."

Molly shook her head. The jeans hung on her sister without so much as a wrinkle. "I'm surprised they fit you."

"They've fit for six months. Not like you're ever around."

"Laura …" Tears were running down her sister's cheeks, tears streaking the mascara she'd ladled on with a butter knife, tears she made no attempt to brush away. Molly couldn't help herself. She closed the gap between them before Laura could throw up a defense and hugged her. "I'm sorry," she whispered in her ear. "I'm sorry."

Laura was the first to pull away. "They think you're gay, you know."

"Who thinks I'm gay?"

"Mom and Dad. Well, Mom." Laura hoisted her backpack off the sidewalk. "Dad's a dork."

"Mom thinks I'm a lesbian?"

"She's never seen you with a guy. Me, neither. Where'd Bobby come from?"

They were walking slowly, skirting the plum trees. "I asked him the same thing."

She didn't close her bedroom door that night when she went upstairs to study, and she didn't complain when Laura cranked up the rap and left the lights on in the bathroom. Later, much later, when she was sure Laura was asleep, she called Billy McCay. He didn't pick up, so she left the message on his cell: "My sister is 13 ... and I know the combination to the gun safe in the basement."

Something was different when she returned to Lincoln the following week, at least in African-American Studies. Saleem and Terrence both brought books they wanted her to read, Philip Dray's *At the Hands of Persons Unknown*, and David Bradley's *The Chaneysville Incident*, a novel Terrence said had changed his life. Aissiata sat down with her at lunch and, after 15 minutes picking at her Caesar's salad, confided how lonely she sometimes felt.

"Are you kidding me?" Molly said. "You're like, runway gorgeous. Every time I see you, there are five guys around you."

"When you're from Africa," Aissiata said, "everyone has an opinion about you that's not true."

Bobby kept his distance, which surprised Molly, now that she was taking a shower every morning and digging into a make-up drawer she hadn't touched since freshman year. She thought something had happened between that hallway and the coffee shop, but maybe not. Maybe it was a brief hormonal spike, a harbinger of climate change, a wisp of her imagination. Maybe it was enough, she told herself, that Mr. Millner was looking to her for input, that Preacher gave her a hug one morning in the hall, that her dilemma suddenly was over-reaction rather than no reaction at all.

On the Monday after spring break, Mr. Snowbridge spent the first half of class setting out guidelines for their major writing project. The assignment was to bookmark the African-American experience: to find a metaphor – midst Oprah Winfrey, divorce and incarceration rates, Bill Cosby and the celebrity of Illinois Sen. Barack Obama – that describes where African-Americans fit in the 20th century landscape. Molly's mind was a wretched blank when Bobby found her in the courtyard after school and asked her out.

"Don't look at me like that," Bobby said. "It's not a date."

"It's not?"

"It's an archaeological dig. An adventure. An inconvenience rightly considered."

"What?"

"That's Chesterton. An adventure, he said, is an inconvenience rightly considered. And an inconvenience is an adventure wrongly considered."

Chesterton? Molly stared at him, an embarrassingly thin veil over her confusion. "None of which matters," Bobby said, "if I can pick you up at eight o'clock."

"Is the library still open at eight o'clock?"

"We're not going to the library."

"I thought ..."

"I'll ring the doorbell at eight."

"You don't know where I live."

"OK, 8:05."

He could have pulled the Subaru up to the curb and honked, she realized later, but he volunteered to come to the door and deal with that meet-the-parents thing. It was a tough call: Molly rather enjoyed the idea of her mother at Borders, flipping through Alison Bechdel's "dykes to watch out for," but that was worth foregoing to see Bobby charming her parents in the foyer and hailing Laura when she arrived at the top of the stairs. Molly finally had to shove him out the door, lest he accept her father's invitation to watch the first half of the Blazer game, and she could still feel the cotton shirt and the contours of his back in her palm as she buckled her seatbelt.

"You can relax," she said as he backed down the driveway. "They have no plans to adopt."

"I kept waiting for them to ask where we were going."

"Where are we going?"

"Powell's. Downtown."

"What's at Powell's?"

"More than enough."

They parked a block away, in front of a 'zine shop called Reading Frenzy, then crossed Burnside to the bookstore. Bobby didn't say much on the drive and he seemed curiously remote as he stood just inside the door and just beyond the reach of the Street Roots hawkers. "How well do you know this place?" he asked.

"I don't," Molly said. "I haven't been here since ...."

Bobby snatched a map to the "City of Books" off the information desk and handed it to her. "Just in case. And follow me."

And she did, up a short ramp into the Blue Room, then a small set of stairs into the Gold Room. The Rorschachs of paint on the floor sometimes matched the room's official color designation and sometimes did not. Many of those they passed were toting plastic baskets filled with books.

The third room sported an espresso bar, and a dozen people camped out with books and laptops at small wooden tables. "We're almost there," Bobby said, squeezing between chairs to an empty table against the glass wall that looked out on Burnside. He tossed his sweatshirt on one chair, his backpack on the other. "Think you can find your way back here?" he asked.

"Well, with the breadcrumbs, sure," Molly said, removing a small notebook from her backpack. "Is this where we dig?"

"No, base camp. Do you need another chai for the climb?"

"Ah, yes, the chai joke. I've given up chai. And I've been clean … for 17 days. Why are you looking at me that way?"

It probably wasn't the right question, or at least not the one she needed answered. Molly knew why he was looking at her. She was wearing the sleeveless blouse and decent jeans. She'd washed her face and let Laura braid her hair. She'd scraped off the camouflage and dead skin, the Army-Navy surplus baggage she'd kept wrapped around her for as long as she could remember.

"I don't know," Bobby said, "Your happiness?"

The better question, really, was why that look cut through her like the wind in the Columbia Gorge. Why she wanted to step toward him, not run away from him. Why it made her feel good, not bad. "What's our next move?" she said, her eyes locked on Bobby Sorrell's.

"The Purple Room."

"And what's in the Purple Room?"

"Your African-American study guide. The ultimate search engine."

He was leading her back through the labyrinth of slackers, readers and after-dinner conversations. "They keep Google caged in the Purple Room?"

"Google is for when you know what you're looking for. Powell's is for when you don't. Come on."

As they trekked to the back of the store, they cut through a room riffed with calendars, maps and travel books. Molly slowed to stare at a calendar labeled "Alien Abduction," depicting a Madonna-like figure leaning back in the arms of a robot. When Bobby came back for her, curious about the distraction, she swallowed the lump in her throat and surprised them both. She took a chance. She took his hand.

So many things could have gone wrong. His hand might have been tense or aloof, a pile of leaves or an oven mitt. Her hand might have realized, at the moment of contact, that intuition had led her astray. But before she had time to anguish, to pull away, to run for cover, his fingers interlaced with hers and Molly said the first thing that came to mind: "I forget why we're here."

"It's not much farther."

They passed into the Purple Room – the name was plastered on the book carts and hanging from the numbered aisle markers overhead – and sailed past 10-foot high shelves dedicated to Pre-Tudor Britain and the Weimar Republic. They skirted Italy and the Drug Culture, a half-dozen step-ladders tossed haphazardly against the end caps, and finally reached a small but open alcove bearing the heading:

748
African American Studies
Slavery

Reconstruction
Anthologies
Civil Rights

Black Mutiny. Black Athena. The Hemingses of Monticello. The book titles surrounded her. From Jim Crow to Civil Rights. *From Bondage to Liberation.*

"Your study carrel," Bobby said. With shelves on three sides of the alcove, 1,500 books were screaming for her attention.

"Google made flesh," Molly said.

"Google isn't this selective. It can't tell you how much the package weighs. It can't separate the things that matter and the things that don't. I mean, look at 'em: You recognize right away which ones deserve to be taken seriously. There's a first impression. There's ..."

"Bobby," Molly said, squeezing his hand. "It's OK."

Bobby let her go, and pulled a book on the Black Panthers from the shelf. "There aren't many of these left," he said.

"Black Panthers?"

"Book stores. They're closing all the time. Libraries are going digital. Pretty soon we'll forget what it feels like to hold this in your hands."

He was so damn intense. "Where *did* you come from?" she said.

He returned the book to its shelf. "The '50s. Do you collect stuff?"

"Like what?"

"Anything. Everything. Do you pack stuff away or throw everything out?"

Light-headed, she felt her stomach turn. "I hold onto things way too long."

"So do I. If it survives 'til it gets to me, I want to keep it safe. Especially books." He paused. "You have an idea yet? For your writing project?"

Molly shook her head. "There are a bunch of ideas here," Bobby assured her. "Poke around. Bring a few books down to the coffee shop. I'll be by the window."

"You're leaving me?"

"'I'll see you in, what, a half hour?" As if Molly had any idea.

It took 20 minutes. She only had to circle twice through the black faces studying her with dignity and indignation. Medgar Evers and Frederick Douglas. Cornel West and Vernon Jordan. Martin Luther King and James Baldwin. *Jim* Crow and Kaffir *Boy*.

Where were the women? Beyond Rosa Parks, the slave girl narratives and the various props of Iceberg Slim – *Trick Baby, Mama Black Widow* and *Pimp* – where were the female pioneers, the female mavericks, the female martyrs? Stuck on the plantation? The civil-rights platform only had room for guys? She opened the notebook and began jotting down thoughts, book titles, dust-jacket ideas. Now and then, someone wandered through the alcove – two girls wearing Benson colors, an old man who smelled like the street – but Molly refused to engage. She was three pages along when she heard the in-house PA system call her name. Or part of it, anyway:

"Molly Sorrell: Please come to the Coffee Room to meet your party."

Molly Sorrell? Molly *Sorrell?* Had she heard that right? She checked her cell. It was 10:10, getting late. She didn't put much stock in coincidence.

She had no problem reaching the Coffee Room, but Bobby wasn't waiting at the window table. She started at his sweatshirt, their backpacks, his pile of books, wondering if they'd gotten their signals crossed – *Molly Sorrell?* -- and that's when she saw the yellow 3x5 note card, carefully set atop his open notebook. Written on the card, in careful calligraphy, was a three-digit number: 864.

Molly flipped the card over. Nothing. She swiveled and searched the room, half-expecting to find him peeking out from behind a bookshelf. She sat in an empty chair. He'd gone to the bathroom, she guessed, or set out after a book. She'd wait. But with each passing minute, she felt more uncomfortable. He'd told her to come back. He'd sent a message over the PA system. What had she missed?

864. The number meant nothing to her. She flipped open one book then another, but neither had more than 300 pages. She was staring vacantly out the window – the Benson girls were passing on the sidewalk – when she caught the reflection of the latte-colored sign at the center of the room:

Audio Books: 401-405

Humor: 407-412

Was there a pattern here?
401-405: Audio Books
748: African American Studies.
864?

She had nothing to lose. She needed a minute to get her bearings, to reach the room where she'd taken Bobby's hand, then work her way through the Religion section until she found the right aisle:

864
Christianity
Christian Living
Angels
Prayers

The aisle was empty. Bobby, she thought, why are you messing with me? She drifted between the shelves, studying the subject labels: Creationism. Ethics. Angels. Demonology. What in the ...

Angels? Molly retreated several steps. How had she missed that splash of orange? Another note card. Another three-digit number: 625.

Back at the stairs, a guy with a bandana and ponytail was bent over a computer. "Where can I find 625?" Molly asked.

He didn't look up. "Rose Room. Downstairs. Children's books."

Bobby, Bobby, Bobby ... where are you taking me? This was a children's game. Hide-and-seek.

Capture-the-flag. And since it had been years since she'd dashed around Westlake in the dark, why was curiosity winning out over exasperation?

625
Children's Collectibles
Girls & Boys Adventure
Happy Hollisters
Bobbsey Twins

As soon as she saw the sign board, Molly knew where to go: Girls & Boys Adventure. The telltale note card was poking out of an Annette Funicello hardback like a forgotten bookmark, but this time there wasn't a number, just a sentence:

"The play's the thing."

The play? The stage production or the game they were playing? Molly tucked the card into her jeans, and worked her way back to the ponytail.

"Shakespeare?" she asked.

"Pearl Room. One floor up."

At the top of the stairs, the room opened dramatically: a rare-book room, a small photo gallery with rows of empty chairs, an empty information desk. The Pearl Room directory hung over a table packed with movie-poster replicas and sale books:

Architecture 930-936
Art 922-945
Dance 904
Drama 905-007

Film & TV 908-915
Music 900-904
Photography 916-921

"The play's the thing," she whispered. The last piece of the puzzle. Molly walked slowly toward the drama section. Far to her left, she saw a small man in a yarmulke sitting on a footstool, a large book in his lap. Other than that, the room was empty. She paused at 906, peeking around the corner. There was another 40-foot alley between the 10-foot shelves, at the end of which were windows, belt-high, looking out over the Pearl District. She opened her mouth to say his name, then closed it again. If Bobby was somewhere in the room, he could hear the footsteps. She wanted him to wonder. She wanted to prolong the suspense. She slipped down the aisle, past the volumes of Shakespeare, a menagerie of folios, boxed sets and battered paperbacks, six shelves high. Just as she reached the windows at the end of the aisle, just as she was beginning to think she had the advantage of stealth and nothing could surprise her, a hand reached out from her right and pulled her into the warming oven of Bobby Sorrell.

She yelped. She couldn't help it. "What took you so long?" he said, an impossibly smug grin on his face.

Molly was against his chest, her fists and arms between them. "Lousy clues," she said. "Angels? Boys and girls ..."

That was the last word she got out before Bobby shut her mouth with his.

The kiss took her breath away, rolling over her like a sneaker wave at the beach. For one gut-wrenching moment, it blotted out the light overhead and she pulled away, expecting the stench of the upholstery, the glow of the tape-deck, his Juicy Fruit crooning and the size of his hands to smother her all over again. She didn't even know how hard she must have pushed Bobby away until she saw the surprise on his face, the painful confusion, and she swept it away the only way she knew how, unclenching her fists and reaching for his face, pulling his mouth down to hers yet again.

She was suspended there, on the edge of dizziness, soaking in the warmth that was coming off him in waves, when he set her gently down. Suddenly he was pulling her down a hallway between the rare-book room and the windows at the back of the store, a hallway that ended in a clock, a fire the blinking light on an emergency exit door.

"The alarm will go off," Molly said, convinced he was about to pull her into the darkness behind that door, and urging him on.

"The alarm already went off," Bobby said, leaning back into the corner, kissing her again even as he leaned back into the door frame and slid his hands beneath her blouse, his fingertips working each fissure of her spine, the blouse riding up with his hands. She felt the night air and glanced out the window, at the balconies of the condos floating on the other side of Couch Street. "They can see us," she gasped.

He was breathing into her neck, and she couldn't keep her eyes open. "An adventure," he said, his hands at the clasp of her bra, "is an inconvenience rightly considered."

Ten seconds later, he was still struggling with the clasp, and Molly was laughing. "And an inconvenience," she began …

Off in the distance, she heard the same voice that called her to the Coffee Room solemnly announce, "It is 10:40. Powell's will close in 20 minutes."

"Twenty minutes," she whispered, kissing the rim of his jaw. "What will we do with the time?"

He laughed, gave one more tug on the clasp and then – just as she was about to lend him a hand – pulled slowly back, his eyes never leaving hers.

"You're giving up?"

"No," Bobby said. "There's no reason to rush. Can we just do this until closing time?"

She heard the question, but she *felt* the heat ripple through Bobby Sorrell. At that very moment, she also felt the weight slide off her back, as hope and desire filled her lungs, and Molly knew what she would finally do, whom she would finally call, when – *not yet, not yet* – she was alone again.

While she waited for Shilts and the backup to swing into the Dairy Queen, Detective Cheri Lapchick watched the evening traffic ebb and flow and wondered if she was playing this right. Shilts had pushed the pre-text call pretty hard, just to see what the dip-shit would say on tape, but Lapchick talked him out of it. She wasn't sure the girl could handle it, first off. The girl had waited three years to come forward and Lapchick guessed she was curled up in a ball on her bedroom, not letting anything slip past her iPod. Put her on the phone with the perv and things might bounce off the rails. Plus, Lapchick figured this guy was greasy smooth. The usual antenna for the girls who'd fall for his line. A call comes out of nowhere and he'd disappear in the van. She'd convinced Shilts they couldn't take the chance.

She had dispatch on low. There was a fatal on Highway 30 and the usual barnyard routines at Waterfront Park in the ramp-up to the Rose Festival. She didn't miss those Friday nights. Sex crimes were a bitch but a damn sight better than weekends cruising MLK and the strip joints on Sandy, or watching meth heads beat the crap out of one another in those fleabag apartments along Powell. She'd made it to detective without shooting anybody or otherwise popping up on the chief's radar, only firing her gun once, in that 49-bullet barrage behind the Outsiders' bar. Lapchick would have sworn she'd hit some of that white trash center mass, but forensics and the medical examiner said otherwise. Probably for the best. It had been 11 years since Shilts put one cap in the wrist and two in the throat of a tweaking B&E who came out of a Hillsdale apartment with a DVD player in one hand and a serrated kitchen knife in the other. "Screws up your sleep," said Shilts, who wasn't sentimental.

She'd had options when she came downtown, and she took the usual crap from the bureau's Cro-Magnon frat when she filed for sex crimes. *"Not getting enough at home, Lapdance?"* Shilts ignored her and the hazing for two weeks, then took her to lunch at the Acropolis. They ate rib-eyes at a table well back from the three stages, and in the 20 minutes Shilts grilled her on her background and biases, he never once peeked at the 105-lb Vietnamese stripper with the Catholic school-girl knee socks. Afterwards, Cheri noticed, the Neanderthal noise downtown faded away.

They still had their moments. Shilts was warming up for his third divorce. He was stubborn and profane and deeply cynical about a lifetime monitoring "garbage in human skin," as he put it. He walked through the door convinced everyone on the other side was downloading kiddie porn or propositioning the babysitter, but he got pissed when Lapchick took the pervs seriously. "Take it personal," he said, "and you make mistakes." She didn't argue. She never mentioned her uncle.

An Accord EX swept past, low slung and high beams, early '90s, back before Honda stepped up with the anti-theft device. Three-to-one, Lapchick guessed, it was hot. Two chunky high school kids trudged past her front bumper, deep in Butterfinger Blizzards. She was second-guessing the Frappuccino she sucked down at lunch, when a squad car pulled in, followed by Shilts' true love, a '67 Mustang convertible.

Lapchick stepped out of her car, a dirty, unmarked Chrysler with certifiable kick-ass under the hood. There were two uniforms in the squad car; Jimmy Brownell, an east-side redneck, was behind the wheel. She nodded at him, then Shilts. "Hey."

He was wearing century-old Dockers and a Disneyland tie under his bureau windbreaker. "Washington County know we're here?"

"I invited 'em. More the merrier."

"You do like to make a scene, Lapdance," Shilts said, taking a sip from his Stumptown cup. He was the total coffee snob.

"Can I borrow that?" she asked.

Shilts looked down at the plastic lid and sighed. "It's leaded."

"Good to know," Lapchick said, taking the cup from his hand. It was still warm. She walked over to the squad car, opened the back door on the driver's side and slowly emptied the cup onto the hard plastic of the rear seat.

Brownell nodded approvingly. "I still have my dinner burrito," he said.

"Hold it in reserve," Lapchick said. "Let's go."

Beaverton High was a two-minute drive. According to the Black Tornado website, the championship game had started at 7:30 p.m., so Lapchick was sure she'd timed this right, early second half, everyone settled. She wheeled the Chrysler into the no-parking lane in front of the gym door, the Mustang and the squad car pulling in behind her. Four junior high brats were sprawled on the steps leading up to the battered double doors. "Damn," Lapchick heard the kid in the Seattle Mariners' cap say: "Busted."

Just inside the door, a Carolina blue spandex freak sat at a folding table, guarding the cash box. "Who's playing?" Lapchick asked in an oily Gino Auriemma.

"Black Tornado and Emerald City," the woman said. This close, Lapchick could tell she'd had serious work done on her eyes. "Adult admission is five …"

She stopped as Shilts and Brownell followed Lapchick through the door.

"We're just peekin' in," Lapchick purred. "Won't be a minute." She paused at the door. "Your partner waiting out back?" she asked Brownell.

"Tanned, rested and ready," Brownell said. Lapchick stepped into the gym. You always hoped for SROs for dramatic effect, that hush settling over the congregation when the handcuffs popped out. This wouldn't be one of those nights. She pegged the crowd at 100, searching the gym's upper reaches. Championship banners and little more. The scoreboard read 47-26. Eight minutes left. "One ass-kicking in progress," Shilts said at her elbow, "one set for launch."

Both teams were gathered around their coaches by the scorers' table. Their arrival hadn't sparked so much as a ripple, and that, Lapchick decided, would not do. She was almost at mid-court, angling toward the home team's bench before she realized Shilts and Brownell were skirting the court, still terrorized, 25 years on, by the gym-class prohibition against black-heeled shoes. Thirty feet shy of the Black Tornado bench, Lapchick felt someone hustling in from the right, radiating indignation. "Ma'am! Ma'am! Excuse me, ma'am! You are not allowed on the ..."

Lapchick turned only slightly to confront a balding, overweight dork in a black-and-white striped shirt. When, she wondered, did they start scraping refs off the rubber mats at the retirement home? "Back off," she snapped.

"You can't ..."

"Back off!" Lapchick barked again, and the stack of pancakes stopped, mouth agape. The gym had grown silent. Everyone loved a parade. Lapchick could hear her rubber soles attacking the gym floor. As she reached the Tornado huddle, the circle came apart and the coach stepped forward. Black sweater, black jeans. He looked like he'd gained five baby-back pounds since the weekend, when she'd spent three hours in the Chrysler across the street from his Lake Oswego love-shack.

"What?" he said, his eyes fixed over Lapchick's left shoulder on Brownell, the only one of the three in uniform.

They were so damn young, the girls around him. Their shoulders were slight, their arms so thin, the uniforms as vague as the bodies inside them. She couldn't remember that age without feeling something dark and bitter in her gut, or the bruised hostility that marked them now. And she couldn't imagine how many of them were now fending off the same rapist who'd come after Molly Koertje three years ago.

"Taze Elliott?"

"You're damn right."

"Det. Lapchick, Portland police. You're under arrest."

"For what?"

"Rape. Sodomy. Girls, I want you sitting down, now, on the bench. Mr. Elliott, you need to step forward, put your hands behind your back and turn around."

Shilts and Brownell had fanned out on either side of her. She felt the shudder of his gears turning: fight or flight, words or muscle. Coming for him in public was designed to maximize his humiliation and minimize his options. The girls were frozen in place, confused, trapped between the familiar muscle of his authority and the fresh arrival of hers. That needed to change. "Girls! On the bench! Now!" Lapchick stepped forward and grabbed Elliott by the arm, trusting her assertiveness would start herding the cats. Elliott tensed but she didn't release her grip.

"If you resist," she said, "I will put you on the *ground*."

Shilts moved in, cuffs in hand. "Coach, what are they doing?" one girl asked. Elliott shook his head as Shilts torqued his right wrist to bring it in range of the cuff.

"Same old," Elliott said. "Sticking it to the black man."

The crowd was humming, the shock wearing off, curiosity aroused. As Shilts took Elliott's other arm, a thin member of the Tonkon Torp set, his tie still knotted, arrived and said, "Officers, what's this about?"

Shilts gave him a look. "This is a police matter, counselor, and you're about six inches from joining the douche bag on the ride downtown."

My partner, Lapchick thought. He really gets into these character roles.

"Taze, if you need a lawyer, I'm available," the guy yelled after them.

Elliott didn't respond. His head was down as Shilts and Brownell led him across the court, past Carolina from Club Sport, her hand still at her mouth, and out the door. As they marched down the steps, the slackers drew back, suitably impressed.

"Did he kill somebody?" one of them asked.

"Kiss my ass, boy," Elliott said, suddenly roused from his stupor.

"My, my," Lapchick said. "Always ready to mix it up with another 12-year-old."

"Don't know what you're talking about," Elliott said, stumbling down the steps as Shilts and Brownell pulled him toward the squad car. "What is this rape crap?"

Lapchick desperately wanted him to keep talking. Just not here. "You have the right to remain silent," she said, "Anything you say can and will be used against you in a court of law. You have the right to speak to an attorney, and to have ..."

"I know the drill," Elliott said, "but this is bullshit. Who you been talkin' to?"

"... questioning. If you can't afford an attorney, one will be gift-wrapped ..."

"You let me at my cell phone and I'll call my lawyer right now."

" ... at our expense. Officer Brownell, will you relieve Mr. Elliott ... "

"Ow! Stop twisting my arm! You know I get to call a lawyer."

They reached the squad car; Brownell opened the back door. "Seeing as how you know the drill so well, you must know we're taking you downtown and processing your sorry ass first," Shilts said.

"This ain't right. I didn't rape nobody. And I'm gonna sue your ass ... hey, watch the head ... n' anybody says different. Don't know who you're messing with."

"Yeah, I do," Lapchick said. "Been on your website. You're the second coming of John Thompson."

"I don't know ... shit, man, what is this, a wading pool ... hey, Debra! Debra!"

Brownell slammed the door as a woman in a beige cashmere sweater broke free of the rubberneckers at the gym door and floated down the steps, yelling, "Wait a minute! Wait a minute." As Brownell slid into the driver's seat and punched the ignition, Lapchick turned to meet her.

"Wh-wh-where you taking him?"

"Justice Center. Downtown. Second Avenue," Lapchick said, all the while thinking, damn if she isn't wearing Beyond Paradise at an 8th grade basketball game.

"What did he do?"

Lapchick tapped the squad car's rear door and Brownell pulled out, Elliott's face up against the window, furious and contorted, yelling something they could not hear.

She turned back to the cashmere sweater. "M'am, I'm not the bureau's PIO and you're not ..."

"Did I hear you say 'rape'? *Rape?*"

Lapchick paused, struck by the outrage in the woman. "That's what I said."

"Who? Can you tell me …"

"No, ma'am, I can't."

"Well, there's some mistake. You're making some mistake! I left my daughters alone with him." She grabbed Lapchick's sleeve. "On weekends."

Lapchick reached into her pocket and produced a card. "You need to take a deep breath, ma'm," she said. "And my card. Call me after you've talked with your daughters. Call me later tonight. I have to put Mr. Elliott down, but I'll be up. That's my desk number and I'll stay there until midnight. I want to hear about your daughters."

*   *   *

He was slouched in a scuffed-up, black plastic chair, one of three stationed around the wobbly table at the center of the room. He was numb from lack of sleep and he felt like something soaked in kerosene had crawled down his throat and died.

Taze Elliott wanted to smack someone. Anyone would do.

The room was no bigger than a refrigerator carton, the walls and ceiling an egg-shell white. Twice in the last 20 minutes, a Multnomah County sheriff's deputy had peeked through the 10-inch square glass pane in the door, just in case Elliott was removing his shoelaces. Next time the son of a bitch popped up, Elliott was gonna pick up this chair and …

He checked his anger.   One barbed-wire indignity after another had been shoved up his ass the last 12 hours.   The assholes forced him to wait three hours before letting him make that phone call and damn if Carrie never picked up, forcing him to vent on the answering machine.   All those f-bombs might have been a mistake.   He begged her to get someone to bail his ass out, even though she was clueless as to how she'd kick-start the process.   A lawyer?   Bail money?   What did she know about that shit?   Sometime in the middle of the night, with the drunk cracker in the lower bunk passing gas like a methane bog, Elliott realized he might not have given Carrie much incentive, so he was stunned when the sheriff's deputy – a dead ringer for John Candy – reappeared and said his lawyer was in the building.

His lawyer?   Had Carrie come through, or was someone jerking his chain, given that he'd been sitting here for 20 minutes, listening to the lunatics in the hall, marinating in his own sweat, compiling the list of the assholes who were gonna pay for dragging his name through the mud on this trumped-up, jive-ass, back-stabbing, racist …

The door wheezed open.   Elliott almost came out of his chair.   The new arrival was in his mid-50s, wearing faded jeans and a white button-down shirt with the sleeves rolled up.   He had a double-wide nose, a wild thatch of hair, and an extra 15 pounds draped over his belt as he corralled the chair on the far side of the table.

"Buzz me when you're done," the Candy man said.

"I figure 15 minutes," the guy said. The door closed behind him. He pulled a manila folder from a thin leather satchel, a pair of reading glasses from his shirt pocket, and sat down heavily. Elliott stared at him, waiting for eye contact, a grunt, anything.

"Where'd Carrie find you?" Elliott asked.

The guy looked up over the rim of those glasses. "I'm sorry, Mr. Elliott, I haven't had much time to go over this. My name is Joe Schellenberger. Who is Carrie?"

"My ..." Elliott paused, "... girlfriend. She call you?"

"Debra Giuliani called me at 10:30 last night. An old friend."

"Took your sweet time getting down here."

Schellenberger removed his glasses. "As you may recall, Mr. Elliott, it's a serpentine path that brings you into the belly of this building and your over-night accommodations. I just re-traced your steps and I can promise you that nowhere along the way did I spot anyone else with the slightest interest in advocating on your behalf. Would you like me to go back out and check again?"

Mother had an attitude. "Sorry," Elliott mumbled. "Feels like I've been here for days, and I didn't do shit. Pisses me off."

"Well, I would hope so," Schellenberger said, as he bent over the papers before him. "They're trying to piss you off. That's the point."

"What?"

"What time they pull you off the basketball court?"

"Second half, sometime."

"The real clock, Mr. Elliott, not the game clock. What time was it?"

"Eight, eight-thirty, maybe."

"The witching hour," Schellenberger said. "You can't post bail between 10 p.m. and 7 a.m., so if you aren't processed before ten, you have your involuntary sleepover. Most people can't raise bail over the weekend – how liquid is anyone on a Saturday anymore? – and there are no court appearances until Monday morning."

He checked the signatures at the bottom of the page. "Detectives Lapchick … and Shilts did everything they could to guarantee you'd be here for the weekend."

Schellenberger leaned back and pulled a pack of Juicy Fruit from his jeans, removing a piece and popping it into his mouth. "So, what did you do to piss them off?"

Elliott said nothing.

Schellenberger tilted his head, waiting for something more, then shrugged. "That's the usual starting point. Care to know what they think you did?" When Elliott didn't reply, Schellenberger leaned forward again over his small wad of papers: "Rape. Four counts. Sodomy. Three counts. Unlawful sexual penetration. Three counts. It goes on. They're not messing around, Mr. Elliott."

"Who's accusing me of this shit?"

"They don't say, Mr. Elliott. They don't have to."

"Thought I got to face my accuser."

"Eventually, you do … though if it comes to that, I won't be doing my job. If this were to proceed to trial, your attorney would learn the identity of your accuser through discovery. But the DA won't need to take that before a judge Monday morning. The testimony of one victim, especially a minor, is more than enough to fire up a judge."

Schellenberger scratched one of his eyebrows, which had gone to gray quicker than the rest of his mop. "I understand you're a basketball coach, Mr. Elliott."

"That's right."

"How long have you been coaching in Portland?"

"Six, seven years."

He read for a moment. "What's a Black Tornado?"

"Team name. AAU program."

"How many girls come through the program each year?"

"Enough. More all the time."

"Junior high? High school?"

"Both. Got a 5th grade team this year."

"So you've coached dozens of girls over the years."

"Yep. Got four of 'em playing D-1. You ask any high-school coach in town, anyone you want, I'm the …"

"Mr. Elliott." Schellenberger had his hand up. "I don't need testimonials right now. I'm not verifying your resume. I'm trying to get a rough count of how many potential candidates are out there, accusing you of a sex crime that, under Measure 11, will send you to prison in the high eastern Oregon desert for a minimum of 70 months. You're saying you have no idea who might be accusing you?"

Elliott glared at him. "I didn't rape nobody."

Schellenberger nodded, as if he'd achieved some measure of victory. "Maybe it would help if we established a few things," he said, rising to his feet. "You don't know me, Mr. Elliott. I don't know you. Debra Giuliani's testimony notwithstanding, I don't know if I *want* to know you ..."

"Then, get the hell out of here," Elliott said, his voice rising as he, too, came out of his chair. The anger in his voice and the ragged clatter of the plastic chair legs across the floor brought John Candy's face back into the square peephole, but Schellenberger waved him away.

"Relax, Mr. Elliott," he said, his voice flat. "I'm not trying to establish dominance; I just process things better when I'm pacing." As Elliott slowly pulled the chair back beneath him, Schellenberger did indeed begin to prowl his end of their cage.

"Until you indicate otherwise, I am here in the capacity of your lawyer," he said, "which means everything you tell me is privileged. Do you understand what that means?"

"Our secret."

"Precisely. But even if I'm your attorney, I'm noting that we have no prior relationship. I point that out to put our conversation in context. You may not want to tell me anything that might explain 14 Measure 11 counts. I might not want to hear it."

"Yeah? Why's that?"

"It has nothing to do with whatever revulsion I might have for a youth basketball coach who is preying on his players," Schellenberger said, "and everything to do with hearing things that might compromise my ability to defend you. That said, I want to assure you of several things. First, you continue to glance about the room as if you believe this is an episode of 'Punk'd' and you're trying to spot the hidden camera."

"You mean, like 'Candid Camera'?"

"Precisely. I didn't want to date myself. Let me assure you, I have never met Alan Funt. More to the point, this room is not bugged. You are not being video-taped. Nothing you tell me here will leave the room."

"Bullshit."

"The phones still make me nervous; that's why I requested 15 minutes with you in this broom closet," Schellenberger said. "But this is the proverbial cone of silence. If the Multnomah County sheriff brought recording equipment into this room, he would jeopardize the conviction of every detainee who's passed through here in the last 20 years. You're not worth it.

"Now then," he continued, "as to my curiosity about the identity of the young woman who is telling Portland police detectives that you can't keep your dick in your pants. There are a number of reasons why a young woman might wrongly accuse someone of sexual assault. Perhaps she's bored and craves attention. Perhaps she wants to *deflect* attention from several poor choices that she's made, or wants to wreak vengeance upon the coach who didn't get her that scholarship she was promised. There's even the possibility that she is being assaulted at home by a family member and wants to initiate an investigation without pointing a terrified finger at a loved one.

"There are, in other words, a number of explanations as to why you woke up this morning in the Justice Center, wrongly accused of reprehensible actions. People are wrongly accused every day. But if I'm to prepare a defense that will expose the unseemly motives of your accuser, I first need to understand the background of the young woman we're dealing with. Only then can I proceed to the other questions that are relevant at a time like this: Has the girl cried wolf before? Why did she wait years to come forward? What else in her background might explain this daunting display of her fantasy life?"

"Like ..." Elliott began, edging out onto the ledge, "maybe she had some weird crush on me ..."

"A crush." The lawyer seemed intrigued by the choice of words. "Like ... what, a junior high infatuation?"

"Infatuation," Elliott repeated. "Yeah, that's the word."

"How often does that happen?"

"Hell, man ... you got daughters?"

"No, Mr. Elliott, I never was that fortunate. I do, however, have two nieces."

"How old?"

"The oldest is on the cusp of her 14th year."

"You watch. Something happens. They decide no one at home gives a shit. Not about them, anyway. Like the only words they ever hear are the ones telling 'em how stupid and lazy and selfish they are."

"My partner – at the firm, Mr. Elliott, at the law firm -- says that 90 percent of what parents say to their kids is negative."

"Sounds right. Ask a question about what matters, act like you've noticed they're curled up like a wounded dog, and they come alive. It's like you've turned the hose on that tray of flowers you left out all day in the sun."

"You're good with the hose, I take it."

"Kids ain't rocket science. I have 40 girls playing for Black Tornado one time or another. Different shapes, different sizes. Some girls give you everything they got and some hold everything back. Some won't talk and some don't shut up. They want the ball in their hands in overtime or they're hiding from that ball in the corner. Each one's a trip to some place you haven't been before, but in one way they're all alike."

"And that would be ... ?"

"They need someone to care. When the shit hits the fan, they need to know someone has their back. Most don't care about basketball, not the way I did. Basketball is just another place to hang out with friends and stay clear of their parents. Another place where somebody might tell 'em they're OK and everything else is, too. Girls need to hear that more than the boys. Boys already think they're LeBron. Girls think they're too fat and too slow and too selfish 'cause that's all they ever hear."

"But they know *you* care about them, right?"

"Damn right."

"How's that?"

"I pay attention. All the great coaches know you need to pay attention. Before they care what you say, they need to know you care who they are"

"And it's possible that somewhere along the line several girls have gotten the wrong idea about all that attention."

"What wrong idea?"

"You mentioned a 'crush.' Infatuation. Is it possible one of these girls began to take that attention too seriously."

Elliott slumped in his chair, working the idea over. Schellenberger waited him out. "A lot of things possible," Elliott finally said. "You had daughters and their friends running 'round the house, you'd understand that."

"And is it also possible that you might be able to identify for me the young woman who at some point in the past misinterpreted your attentions?"

"Get me out of here, there's all sorts of things we might be able to talk about."

Schellenberger sneezed into his fist, then wiped the hand on his jeans. "There are several other things I need to review. Who's putting up your bail money?"

"That ain't your job?"

"No, Mr. Elliott, it's not."

"How much you need?"

"We won't know until Monday morning."

"Ain't right."

"As I said, Lapchick and Shilts wanted to make you as uncomfortable as possible. You can't post bail because you won't have a court appearance until Monday. You'll need a lawyer for that. Do you want me to represent you or give you the number of the public defenders' office?"

Elliott felt the bile deep in his throat. "What's that gonna cost me?"

"Debra Giuliani has stepped up for now and guaranteed my retainer."

"She taking care of my bail, too?"

Schellenberger's eyebrows were doing the wave. "I see, Mr. Elliott, that you don't lack for chutzpah. Right now, I can't predict what bail will be. On sex crimes, a judge often gets carried away: $250,000 for touching the left breast, $250,000 for the right, $250,000 for each time your penis saw the light of day. He might reach a million five and ask you to post 10 percent. Do you have $150,000 stashed away?"

Elliott didn't even look up.

"I didn't think so. I am obligated to advise you that if you find someone who will post that bond for you, it should be posted in your name. If they post it in theirs and you take an unexpected vacation in Mexico, they are liable for the other 90 percent."

Elliott said nothing. "That's about the worst of it, Mr. Elliott. Would you like to hear the rest?"

"Whatever."

"I spoke with Debra last night. Understandably, she was most forthcoming about your history in this community and some former players who might be harboring a grudge. She also said she would be willing to step forward when the time comes and write a glowing tribute to the work you've done with her daughters."

"I never touched those girls."

"Debra is desperate to believe that, Mr. Elliott. I understand she has already had intense conversations with the girls on the matter of your libido and truthfulness. Of course, she's in a precarious position. From what I gathered, there were weekends when you were alone with the girls while their parents were away. If she ever saw anything suspicious in the way you interacted with the girls, if she ever considered the possibility you are a scumbag, how could she explain abandoning those girls to your care so she could raft the Metolius?"

Elliott squinted at Schellenberger, his jaw tightening. "Scumbag?" he said. "You considering the *possibility* I'm a scumbag?"

Schellenberger nodded, half to himself, then sat down across from his client. "Do you have time for a story, Mr. Elliott?"

"I ..."

"Yes, of course you do. You're here for the weekend without so much as a copy of the latest *Playboy*. Several years ago, Mr. Elliott, I represented a swim coach at one of the suburban high schools on the east side of Seattle. He was in his late 50s when our paths crossed, and he'd been coaching for years. He was seemingly inoffensive, grandfatherly almost, but he had a very hands-on manner with his swimmers. He always had an arm around one of his girls, encouraging her, consoling her, giving her that loving pat on the back. But occasionally there were girls, usually girls without fathers or girls whose parents missed the practices and those tedious meets, girls with weight or self-image issues, with whom this coach was more familiar. He would reach inside the towel she had wrapped around herself, reach inside her bathing suit, and squeeze her buttocks. He was brazen and unapologetic about it. He had nothing to apologize for. He was bonding with the girls. Tending his flock. Reaching out in ways no one else could.

"I don't know how long this went on before he brought his swim team to Yakima for a meet. On this morning, a father on the opposing team was so shocked by what he saw that he pulled out his cell-phone and snapped pictures of the coach's groping, then took the photos to the local sheriff. The coach was arrested and charged, and I was asked to represent him by the mother of one of his swimmers, a woman who believed in him as passionately as Debra Giuliani believes in you. With her help, I talked to most of the girls and their parents, and it was their testimony, not my closing argument I can assure you, that convinced a jury to clear my client of all charges. I brought one after another to the stand and each one, mothers and daughters alike, put their hand on a Bible and swore they'd never seen this gentle old man touch anyone inappropriately. He wasn't a lecherous pedophile like Humbert Humbert; he was Saint Nick, Father Flanagan and Spencer Tracy. They could not bring themselves to admit they'd ever seen something as wretched as an old man's hand caressing a 13-year-old's ass, and that it didn't register."

"You thought he was guilty?"

"You're damn right."

"You get him off?"

Schellenberger sighed. This was the problem when no one had time to read any more. No patience for good storytelling. Everyone rushing to the last page.

"Not like those young girls did, Mr. Elliott. But, yes, I convinced the jury that this loving grandfather, so falsely accused, deserved robust applause, not a three-year stint at the Washington state pen. Then I expressed my disgust with the man in the only way the system truly allows, by overcharging him on his final bill by 40 percent. Were that the final chapter in my understanding the man, I don't know that I would remember him any more fondly than the other characters I meet in this lucrative line of work."

"There's more?"

"Just a phone call or two. The first came a week after the trial ended quietly and our misunderstood swim coach returned to his captain's chair by the diving board. A woman called my office. She was in her mid-

20s, I believe, but she'd spent two years swimming for my client, becoming quite close not only to him, she said, but to his wonderful wife. Because she had a single mother who worked while she was growing up, she often needed a ride to the swim meet in Walla Walla or Bellingham, and a place to sleep when meets required an overnight stay. On occasion, she said, she slept on a rollaway in the same motel room with her coach and her wife, and enjoyed the sleep of angels, I assume, until the night that old man got out of bed and, with his wife gently snoring 10 feet away, put his hand inside her nightgown and did far more than squeeze her buttocks."

Schellenberger paused, as if waiting for some response. Elliott had his arms folded in front of his chest and his eyes on the empty table between them.

"The second phone call," the attorney continued, "was more disconcerting. A woman called from her home on Lake Sammamish. Several years earlier, she said, her 17-year-old daughter told her best friend she'd been molested by one of her coaches when she was in junior high. Then the young lady went home and sat down in the family's three-car garage with the doors shut and the Aviator running.

"One of her coaches, the mother said, was my client. She understood attorney-client privilege, she said; she'd interned at a law firm before she got pregnant as a senior at Pomona. She just wanted to know if I'd heard anything that might bring her closure."

Elliott shoved back from the table. "Why you telling me this shit?" he asked. "What the hell this got to do with me?"

Schellenberger regarded him silently, then rose to his feet. He walked to the door and calmly pushed the red call button to the right of the door frame.

"I appreciate your passion, Mr. Elliott," Schellenberger said, "and your question. Truth be known, I've occasionally told the story of what happened on that rollaway while Chester the Molester's wife slept six feet away, and my rapt audience invariably asks, 'Why didn't the girl report him? Why didn't the young woman go directly to the cops?' Is it possible you are not similarly curious because you know all too well why a child, violated that dramatically, would stay quiet?"

Surprisingly – from Schellenberger's point of view, at least – Elliott appeared to be contemplating a thoughtful answer. He scratched the over-night bristle on his cheek. "Probably figured no one'd believe her," he said.

Schellenberger nodded. "And who could truly blame her for reaching that cynical conclusion about veracity and human nature?"

He reached down and collected the pages on the table, carefully stuffing them back inside the manila folder, which he slid into his satchel. Then he firmly pushed the red call button to the left of the door frame.

"I'll be honest, Mr. Elliott. In terms of our continued association, you're fortunate I owe Debra Giuliani a favor. I don't know that I'm rooting for you, and that's not a good place for an advocate to be. Among the many things you deserve, however, is a stellar defense and a fair trial. You will get both if I'm in the room. Should I tell Debra that we have an agreement?"

"Don't look like I got options," Elliott said.

"No. You don't. But you've made stupid choices before. You're free to make another one."

Elliott's chin was sinking ever deeper into his chest. "Whatever," he said.

"Fine. I don't know that you will have access to a telephone any time soon, but in the event you do, please don't call me. All calls are taped. Every one. Every inmate. When I have spoken to Debra and done more research, or when I have located the good but misguided Samaritan willing to post your bail, I will call. In the meantime, I encourage you to keep your mouth shut and stay out of trouble. There is nothing to be gained by antagonizing the deputies here or sharing your inner-most feelings with the upstanding citizens with whom you will share a jail cell. Under no circumstances should you explain to anyone, guard or inmate, what you are 'in for.' If the question arises, tell your curious new friend that it's none of his business. Do you have questions?"

Elliott glowered at him. "You're a prick, you know that?"

"Yes. I am. I believe that's why Debra called me. She was under the impression that we would intuitively understand one another."

Schellenberger walked over to the door and leaned against the wall, just out of sight of anyone peeking through the pane of glass. He looked painfully relaxed. The way he was standing there, like one of those guys outside the Rose Garden after a Blazer game, thumbing his nose at the Max 'cause he'd already called his Town Car.

"You gonna push that buzzer again?" Taze Elliott asked.

Schellenberger didn't bother to glance his way. "Every time you do, it's another 20 minutes," he said. "The key is making them think you don't want to leave."

Layla heard her father leave. He was trying to be quiet, she could tell, but he tripped over the recycling bin. Her parents were weird that way. Mom could slip out of the house without making a sound; she just wouldn't see a reason to. Dad had the right intentions but two left feet.

She raised her head just far enough off the pillow to check the digital alarm clock. It wasn't even 6:30 a.m. Too early to be up. Too early for Facebook. Too early for instant messages. Even Chiaro, her hamster, had yet to take a good sniff of the morning. What Dad was doing up she had no idea. It was too early for Starbucks.

She rolled over on her back, listening for another sign that something was out of sorts: a call from Grandma, another airplane into a building, some emergency involving strawberries and Mom's breakfast cereal. She'd heard her brother stumble into the bathroom sometime after midnight. She had no idea where he'd been but there must have been beer because his pee cascaded into the bowl for 40 seconds, easy.

Layla could hear the rattle of the breeze in the plum trees, but no one else was moving. She closed her eyes, listening for the twinge in her stomach, the first gasp in the bundle of nerves, but everything was quiet at Agida Central. If there'd been a basketball game today, she'd already feel the knots and the tiny drops of sweat on the soles of her feet. Soccer was different. Layla didn't know why.

Soccer – the spring segment, anyway – should have ended two Saturdays ago when they played undefeated FC Portland in the first round of the State Cup. Even though they were the defending champs, they knew they didn't have a chance in the game; even Jack and Jill turned down the volume on their Malice cheerfulness. FC Portland had the Tesla twins. FC Portland had Lizzie Geiss in goal. FC Portland had wave after wave of West Hills' prima donnas who would end up at Lincoln or Jesuit and spend the rest of their lives thinking they were better than everyone else. All the Malice hoped to do was pack it in on defense, deny the Tesla twins the ball – fat chance – and root for Mount St. Helens to cut loose before the score became embarrassing.

On the bookshelf beside her father's desk sat a book titled, "How Soccer Explains the World." When she asked, Dad said it was a lot more about the world than about soccer, and a part of the world she'd understand better when she reached high school. Layla thought about that title now and then, wondering if soccer made sense of things in a mysterious, older sister way. So often when she played basketball, she felt lost, as if she were standing at center court of the Rose Garden, waiting to sing the Star Spangled Banner if only the music would start. She never felt similarly exposed in soccer, not even when she and the ball were alone on a breakaway. With so many of her friends on the field, she never felt so devastated by defeat, so set up by victory, so boxed in by threats from the sidelines. When she scored in basketball, it was only a bit of breathing room, another step up on the down escalator. When she scored in soccer, it was a game changer, a group hug, that gasp of fresh air when you came up from the deep end of the pool. Even when you didn't score, and she rarely did anymore, soccer had the means to surprise you the way it did that Saturday night against FC Portland at Delta Park.

Sophie Tesla had lasered two free kicks off the crossbar and the FC offense was having a sleepover in the Malice end, but the game was still scoreless with 90 seconds left in the first half when FC's Amazon sweeper got her feet tangled up, leaving Amanda with nothing but second thoughts between her and an open goal. Well, second thoughts and Lizzie Geiss: Had Amanda entertained the former, the latter might have been more of a problem. As it was, she kept her head, and her head down, and beat Geiss low right.

One goal shouldn't have mattered, but after stewing over halftime, FC began pressing. As FC's annoyance became more pronounced, so did the long dumps into the Malice zone. When those failed to turn the tide, the favorites got chippy, and Lisa eventually bent a 30-yard free kick around Geiss for the 2-0 victory that put Malice back into the State Cup finals.

Well, the semifinals, technically, but that was against Eastside, a 4-0 win. So much for sleeping in on Saturday morning. Layla closed her eyes. She was two weeks into summer vacation. She should be unconscious. She should be hyperventilating about high school. If her father was at Starbucks, Layla decided, he better bring back a grande white chocolate mocha.

* * *

Tomas Keller woke up before Alex was 10 feet inside the gate. He was wrapped in two movers' blankets and tucked into a deck chair. He stretched and yawned ingloriously. Fast food debris was wedged under a shard of carnelian beneath the chair.

"Happy Meals? You're getting by on Happy Meals?" Alex said.

Keller was trying to get out from under the morning's sleeper hold. "Coffee black?" he asked.

Alex extended the Peet's carrier. "Guatemalan. You'll catch pneumonia sleeping under the stars, Tomas."

Keller set the cup beneath his chin. "You know a better way to go?"

Alex glanced around the yard, searching for the still point in the stone garden. He was surprised the outdoor workshop ever pulled anyone off the street. Customers were forced to pass beneath loops of razor wire and weave around two abandoned telephone repair trucks and an old horse trailer rigged with a pulley-and-winch. The work area and the display room were indistinguishable: Keller left his busts and statuary wherever he lost interest in them. A garden table here, a patio fountain there, a slice of verde butterfly marble behind the bamboo screen. If the compression hose was any guide, the old man had spent the night working on a woman's torso, one still attached to a cardboard cut-out of her neck and head.

Alex crossed the yard, fragments of rock squawking underfoot, and sat down beneath the beach umbrella. A paperback sat on the table, dog-eared and coffee-stained. "How long you been reading the McPhee?"

Keller was still steeped in the coffee fumes. "Long as I can remember."

"Ever going to finish it?"

"I'm happier when I'm reading it than when I'm not. What brings you around?"

Alex rubbed his temples. "Anxiety. Stress. A soccer game."

"No kidding. Chelsea-Manchester United?"

"What?"

"Juventus-AC Milan?"

Alex laughed. "Classic soccer, Tomas. Classic soccer."

"My next guess."

"My daughter," Alex said. "The stress is … well, coming between us."

Keller raised the coffee to his lips. He'd stopped listening, Alex was sure. He was trying to remember what he'd been working on before he collapsed in the deck chair.

"I'm guessing the torso," Alex said.

"I dreamed about that girl last night. For dessert."

Alex studied the marble. He thought he saw a hip and a swell or two, but the piece looked surprisingly unfinished. "You still have some work to do."

"Oh, I don't know," Keller said. "The more you touch it, the less you make."

Alex glanced at his old friend. "What?"

"An old Italian saying. The more you handle the stone, the less money you make. All the dough comes from selling the slab. You can polish it to death and not make a dime. So, you quit. You leave it rough. You leave well enough alone."

Alex was staring at the cardboard cut-out of the woman's head. He didn't know why he hadn't seen it before. It might as well have been a teen-age girl.

"The more you touch, the less you make," he repeated.

"The Italians," Keller nodded, "knew their shit."

* * *

She sat in Dr. Dave's office, as she did every month. Emily didn't know if this confirmed her special status or if the invite was his subtle way of introducing her to the trophy wife and the rest of the fam, gathered in three framed 5x7 photos on his desk. The kids were flop-top perfect but – Emily tilted the frame toward the morning light, trying to determine where the wife ended and the Villanova sweatshirt began – the missus was a let down. Elizabeth Shue in that stupid movie where they never stopped drinking.

Emily set the photo down on Dr. Dave's desk. With the office door closed behind her, the room was quiet. She'd left her cell phone in the car – doctor's orders – and her iPod on the nightstand. The morning paper was atop the desk; the headline read "Area girls hoop coach arrested." There were also purple lilacs, the kind you clipped off a bush in the back yard. The fragrance was hypnotic. A ladybug creeping up the stalk, her black wings fluttering each time her weight proved too much for the petal underfoot. She was resting when Emily heard voices in the hall, and the door opened behind her.

"Morning, Emily," Dr. Dave said as he rolled around his desk. He was dressed for Saturday morning, the usual file folder in his hands and reading glasses hooked to the neck of his sweater vest. He smelled better than the lilacs. "I didn't see your parents."

"Dad's in the car, catching up on work. He wanted in but I said …"

Dr. Dave's expression was maddeningly vague.

" … this was no big deal. Housecleaning."

"Housecleaning." He sat down gingerly in his gonzo leather chair, that ox-cart of a desk rising between them.

"Well … "

"I was thinking more of a … remodel. A new kitchen. With a well-stocked refrigerator. You guys win last week?"

"Smoked 'em," Emily said. "Four-zip."

"Way to go. So, you're …"

"State Cup. This afternoon."

The ladybug dropped off the lilac stalk and disappeared, but Dr. Dave was focused on her chart, the one with her blood pressure, the weekly read-out from the scales and, Emily was sure, an R-rated suggestion from the nurse with the Angelina Joli lips. Without changing expression, Dr. Dave closed the folder and set his reading glasses down on top of it. "Nervous?" he asked.

"A little. Maybe."

"You have breakfast?"

"Cereal."

"Captain Crunch?"

She giggled. She couldn't help it. "Smart Start. With strawberries."

"You haven't gained any weight in the last three weeks."

"Seriously?"

Dr. Dave looked right at you when he talked to you. His eyes weren't frisking the room for better options; they were locked on yours, for better or worse. "How serious that is, I don't know. For awhile, I liked what I was seeing. You gained a pound or two each week. Your blood pressure was normal. Your color was back. Then you plateau. We're closing in on that July 4 target date, and your progress stops."

Emily did her best to mirror his frustration. "Are you sure Nurse Red isn't riggin' the scale?"

"Only when Nurse Red is on it." He was staring at the family photos. "What time's the game?"

"Five o'clock."

"Good luck." That killer smile. Emily stared for a moment, then collected herself and turned for the door.

"Oh, and Emily …?" She stopped, waiting. "When you finally hit 115," he said, "I still want to see you. You don't have to stop coming in. You can drop by whenever you want to talk."

"Thanks," Emily said, though she didn't believe a word of it. She breathed purple lilac deep, then exited the office through the empty waiting room. The parking lot was drenched in sunlight and she woke her father when she opened the passenger door.

*   *   *

Eight minutes. That's how long it took. As they stretched, Layla felt one swallow away from throwing up. It was all she could do to slap hands, change direction, get her foot on the ball until eight minutes into warm-ups when the nausea dissolved. Whatever it was that held her down and held her back finally let go, and she could form words, float across the grass, focus on the faces around her.

She spotted Melinda six minutes before Alex and Mick sent Jessica and Emily out to midfield. Melinda was wearing the same number "2" on her Westside green and white. They hadn't spoken since the night of the basketball game. Had they bumped into one another at Michael's, it might have been different, but there was more between them now than 30 yards of turf. You couldn't let on you knew the other team was there. Wasn't that what Colin Welch said? You didn't watch them warm-up. You didn't give them any sign you cared whether they lived or died.

Everyone seemed tight or over-caffeinated. Shots were flying over the bar. Maggie was bouncing off the posts in goal. No one was saying much; there was no point in pretending this was just another game. When Mick finally waved them over to the sideline, Jack and Jill spent 30 seconds frisking them for jewelry and bobby pins, then retreated. Layla stuck one last slice of orange in her mouth, unwilling to glance at her father who, she was sure, was waiting to give her some embarrassing paternal support before he delivered the pointless pep talk. Curiously, it was Mick who finally silenced the nervous chatter with a wave of his hand.

"One state championship? You'd rather win one than lose one, but one State Cup isn't that big a deal," Mick said. He was wearing his Chicago Cubs cap and his Nike sideline jacket. "But two? Two gets everyone thinking. One, and your edge isn't set in stone. Two, and they begin to sweat."

Mesha was sweating. She smelled like Teen Spirit and the watermelon Bubblicious she was chewing to the beat of her pulse. Beads of perspiration speckled Jennifer's forehead; a fine film glistened on Leslie's auburn arms, as if she'd just dashed through the Salmon Street fountain.

"From the get-go," Mick said, "assert yourselves. Pressure them. Knock them off the ball. Rattle their confidence that anything is going right for them here."

However nervous she was feeling, there was comfort in the familiarity of all of this. Amanda was taking deep pre-game breaths with her eyes closed. Madeline was tightening her hair bands. Emily was mouthing silent prayers while Jessica was staring down the sideline at the Westside huddle, trying to convince herself they routinely clubbed baby seals. Lisa was down on one knee, tightening her laces. She'd already tightened them three times in warm-ups. She'd tighten them again at the first dead ball.

Layla looked for her dad. She couldn't help it. He was standing at the edge of the circle, staring out over the field as if he'd lost something.

"I'm sorry, sweetie. I guess I'm nervous. You get to run around out there. I have to sit on the bench and obsess."

"Wanna trade?"

Sometimes Layla asked herself why it mattered so much to him. He didn't have a life? He had nothing else to obsess over? He and Mick couldn't play softball at Westlake Park like all the other slow, fat people?

"We aren't here by accident. We're here because you played with purpose, regardless of who was coaching. We're here because you are tougher than FC Portland. We're here because you figured out how to stick together as a team. We're here because one State Cup isn't that big of a deal."

Her father wasn't checking out the Westside girls or searching for Mom in the stands. He was staring, instead, over the field at something that must be coming by hot-air balloon. She wished Mick would shut up. She wished she was still in first grade, fighting to wrestle the ball from Graham in the shade of the backyard, surprising them both with how easily she slipped inside his defenses, listening to her father whoop in delight from his chair by the fountain. She wished she was still skating across the scorched grass at Lake Grove Elementary, debating – as she flew in for her fourth goal of the game – whether she should chip it over the net so her dad didn't take her out.

"But two? Two State Cups get their attention. Two ruins their summer. Two convinces 'em they had the misfortune to play Oregon soccer when the best they could hope for was to huddle after the state finals and watch Malice storm the victory stand.

"You ready?" Mick asked. There were the usual whoops, Leslie and Emily's war cries rising above the throng. "On two, then," Mick said: "One … two … "

"Malice!"

Layla let the wave roll past her, then slipped up behind her father, who was still pretending he wasn't totally focused on her, and wrapped her arms around him. It was a quick, self-conscious hug and nothing more, but in the curve of his back, in the folds of that old gray hoodie, Mick's words finally got through to her.

One wasn't that big a deal. Two made all the difference in the world.

*   *   *

The Westside offense wasn't rocket science. They set their best player -- #7 – on the right wing and funneled the ball to her. She had the strength to win the ball, the speed to take it down the sideline, and a deft sense of timing on the perfect moment to catapult a crossing pass on a low, hard line into the box. Madeline was dogging No. 7 down the sideline, and Jessica had the wheels to race her to the end line. That left Emily and the mids floating in center field with the butterfly nets, marking the Westside forwards and slapping away the passes that 7 lobbed into the danger zone. It wasn't rocket science.

It was living dangerously. As the first half wore on, Malice struggled to control tempo and the ball. Weird bounces and the frenetic play of Emily's counterpart in the Westside defense – Melinda, that old faithful – kept kicking the ball back into the Malice end, disrupting any momentum. The mids were stumbling about like conjoined twins. Emily wondered if Lisa and Mesha were waiting for text messages to move their ass.

With four minutes left in the half, No. 7 found open field with the ball at her feet. With Madeline leaning toward the end zone, she crossed over to mid-field, even as Madeline, knees akimbo, went down in a heap. Emily had to hand it to the girl. Packing an ass *she'd* never take to the beach, she still had Shannon McMillan speed. In the space of two seconds, Emily realized they were screwed.

As 7 charged, Emily retreated, ready to pounce on her right foot, even as a Westside forward headed dead-red for the corner. Emily knew Jessica had her back long before her sweeper screamed, "Mine," even as 7 slowed for a heartbeat, shoveling the ball toward the corner, then cut hard to the far post.

The pass to the corner was perfect, the forward reeling it in even as Jessica went for the slide tackle, hoping to poke the ball out of bounds. She was a second late and a cleat short: The ball popped up and off the forward's hip and stayed in play, leaving Jessica on the turf and Westside with a clear path to the box. Maggie had moved out to the near post to cut down the forward's angle, opening the goal. Emily wasn't the only one who'd figured that out. Jessica was already back on her feet and closing. The Westside forward was small and quick, with a nice touch. Twenty feet from the box, she planted that left foot and sent the ball airborne toward the far post.

In so many ways, Emily had 7's number. She was fluent in twice as many languages and two years ahead of her in math. She could beat her by a full second in the 100 and at least four sizes at Jessica McClintock. But for all that, 7 had four inches on her ... and four was just enough to get a head on the ball, and flick it into the net.

Jessica and Emily stood together as Westside did the team orgy thing. "Nice head," Jessica finally said, then turned to Maggie: "We'll get it back."

They sat on the end line at the west end of the field at halftime, sucking on fresh orange slices and bottles of water. The quiet was just getting uncomfortable when Emily said, "My fault. Never should have let the water buffalo by me."

"She outweighs you two-to-one," Leslie said.

"Yeah," Emily said, adjusting her shin guards, "but whose fault is that?"

"Do we even have a shot on goal?" Caroline asked.

They reviewed the listlessness of the offense. "Two is all over me," Amanda said, placing her water on the back of her neck. "I can't believe how quick she is."

"Melinda," Layla said.

"2?" Lisa said. "I hate 2."

"Well, we need *two*. Two goals," Amanda said.

*   *   *

Five minutes into the second half, Lisa stepped in front of a Westside pass at midfield, drove hard for five or six strides, angling toward the right flag, then put her heart into a 30-yard blast that, at the last minute, ducked inside the left post.

Tie score. And just like that, everyone got cranky.

The circus began without rancor. Malice was trying to stay aggressive, Westside desperate to regain momentum. It made sense to lurch into that last gasp of the season with a little extra hip if that's what it took to win the ball.

Layla went for another steal and knocked the Westside defender out of bounds. A Westside mid upended Mesha as she rose for a header. Jessica took the same Westside forward down with a slide tackle, and the girl jumped up and shoved her, drawing a yellow. After Melinda stripped her of the ball, Amanda stuck out a foot and tripped her, drawing another card. With each foul and free kick, the scowls got nastier, the theatrics more intense, the spectators more juvenile. With each collision, each whistle, each elevated elbow, one section of the crowd came unhinged as parents rose like the outraged defense attorney at a murder trial to protest the tragedy unfolding before them:

"Are you TRYING to ruin the game?"

"Watch the ELBOWS!"

"Make the call!"

"Thank you!"

Everyone was tired, everyone pressing. Both teams had abandoned the subtle passing schemes for high-risk lobs and quick kicks that sailed 15 feet over the bar. And no one – or so it seemed from Layla's box seat at midfield – was playing with the same dazzling efficiency as Emily. She was tireless, forever in the heads of the Westside mids. And she was the starter's gun on the 40-yard-dash that changed everything.

With two minutes left and the score still tied, Melinda trapped another listless counter-punch near the sideline, spun past Amanda and cut to the center of the field. The Malice defense was retreating, Madeline marking 7 and Jessica drifting right to support her. One would have thought any number of players would have sacrificed heart, soul and limb to separate Melinda from the ball, but after the two mids took feeble swipes at the ball, the field opened up for her like the pizza tray at the post-game party.

In a game that spends an inordinate amount of time contemplating its own reflection, things happen awfully quickly, especially when players remember the ball moves quicker than the girls chasing it. Because Melinda still had open field in front of her, the Malice defenders paused, worker bees trained to react to the most direct threat to the hive, and Melinda didn't, sending a precise lob to 7 racing down the sideline. The Westside offense wasn't rocket science, and Melinda trusted the rocket.

Layla and Amanda were still at midfield, as was Westside's back line. It was a classic overload and it got worse when 7 beat Madeline to the ball, beat her to the corner and left her standing there. As Maggie headed for the near post, she and Jess were outnumbered 4-2 in front of the net, terrible odds when someone with 7's touch was teeing up the 80-degree wedge.

The cross wasn't perfect. It didn't have to be. When the ball fell to Earth, it rattled off several heads and landed at the foot of the blond Westside forward Jessica had twice upended. Maggie was out of position.

The goal was open. The blond kept her head down and played it safe. A quick jab, low and certain, just inside the far post.

You rarely heard the crowd when you were on the field but the net was so open, the advantage so certain, the hour so late that Layla could feel the celebration begin at Westside's end. There were screams and hallelujahs, heck, 21-gun salutes, and the volume was still building, the parents still rising from their seats, when Emily slashed through the wishful thinking and made the best save of her young life.

One moment Westside had an empty goal mouth, and the next Emily was digging for the ball seemingly beyond her reach and her speed, beyond everything but her ability to react rather than reflect, to focus not on where the ball was but where it was going.

She didn't simply clear the ball, knocking it over the end line and into the realm of corner kicks; she intercepted the bouncing ball at the goal and kept it glued to her foot. With the sheer momentum of the game heading west, Emily and the ball were suddenly speeding east. She downshifted and angled left between two Westside players. When she broke into open space, she was still 70 yards from the net.

Layla was not.

Timing is everything. Layla knew she was on her teammate's radar, even if the Westside defense hadn't figured it out, but she had to play the listless spectator until Emily locked in on her target and put those 108 pounds – or was it 110? – into the low, hard rainbow that soared overhead. Unlike the last line of

Westside defense, Layla was ready. That made all the difference. She was already well into her third full stride when the defense heard the alarm clock go off. By then, those defenders were hopelessly out of position.

Melinda was not.

Five yards ahead of the pack, Layla never saw Melinda, only sensed her leading the chase team, but there was no reason to focus on anything but the keeper, rapidly backpedaling, and the goal she could not defend. The keeper's body language said it all. She was dead meat. If she charged, Layla would chip the ball over her head. If she kept retreating, Layla would blow it by her. Either way, the ball was going into the net.

When the keeper finally dug in at the PK line, Layla shifted the ball to her left and set up for the kill. This wasn't altogether different than a PK and there was a good reason she never missed PKs: all those hours of practice, her father daring her to tell him where she thought she could beat him and beating him there anyway. She grew more relaxed on her approach, not less, so it was all the more bizarre when she felt the tug at her elbow, the odd hop of the ball and her clumsy self going down in a heap.

The fall took her breath away and the bounce wrenched her elbow and bruised her chin. Somewhere on the way down, she felt the stab of what must have been Melinda's cleat on the back of her calf, but even when Melinda completed her somersault, even when they both were lying still and she heard the referee's whistle piercing the heavy surf of the crowd, there wasn't the slightest doubt in her mind as to what had happened to her:

A breakaway ... and she'd spazzed out, tripping over the stupid ball. Why the referee was signaling a foul in the box, she had no idea.

Layla was still on her knees when Melinda picked herself off the ground, yelping, "No way!" at the ref. He ignored her, checking to make sure the clock had stopped, then looked for the ball. Melinda took two steps toward him, then stopped, her teeth biting down on her lower lip. Players from both teams were gathering around them. "She never touched me," Layla said to Lisa as she helped her to her feet.

"Shut the hell up," Lisa said.

There was a buzz in the air, the heavy echo at the end of the fireworks show. As the referee gestured for one of the Malice to step forward for the penalty shot, Mick motioned for Layla to finish what she'd started.

She found her father a good 10 yards out onto the field, his hands in the air as if questioning whether she was OK. Layla took two steps toward him and mouthed the words – "She. Never. Touched. Me" – and watched the confusion sweep over him as she was pulled back to the penalty spot. As Layla set the ball, logo up, on the chalk, girls from both squads spread out at the box; if the penalty kick bounced off the post, the ball was live and fair game for the first to the rebound.

At midfield, Mick arrived at Alex's elbow. "What?"

"Said the girl never touched her."

"So what? There are 30 fouls he hasn't called."

"I know," Alex said. "I know."

The ref checked the Westside goalie, then nodded to Layla and blew his whistle. Layla tried to clear her head of everything her father had ever told her. You never look at the keeper. You never think outside the net. You never consider the possibility that she'll even get her hands on the ball if you do what you're supposed to do. You keep your head down, you strike it pure, you do what you've done so many times before.

Layla took a deep breath, surprised by how calm she felt. She knew the drill.

*   *   *

They didn't talk much on the way home. While they were waiting on the on-ramp to the Sunset Highway, Dad tried to say something, but Mom put her hand on his arm and squeezed. KINK was on the radio. Layla didn't recognize a single song.

When they pulled into the driveway, Mom said she was going to poke around the garden before dinner. While Dad pulled the bags out of the back, Layla tossed her cleats into the rectangular plastic bin beneath the workbench. He was leaning against the passenger door as she eased the flip-flops on. "Are you really hungry?" he asked.

Layla thought for a moment. "Cold Stone, maybe."

He smiled. "What do we tell your Mom?"

"Tell her we'll bring her two scoops of Chocolate Devotion."

She brought her sweatshirt so she could ride with the window open. On the way down the hill, she stared past the old couples on their evening walks and into a sky, Caribbean blue, free of clouds. She noticed how slowly her father was driving, waiting at stop signs to motion people forward, as if he was no hurry to reach the ice-cream store.

"Do you think that's a record?" she asked when they turned onto Kruse Way.

"The shootout? I don't know. Twelve rounds?"

Layla picked at a ragged fingernail. A jogger in a Gonzaga t-shirt turned her stopwatch off at the intersection and danced in place. "Maggie was unbelievable."

Her father sighed. "Three or four amazing stops," he finally said.

"Did you talk to her?"

"Yep. Told her she kept us in it 'til the end."

The parking lot was empty. Alex held the door open for her so she could get a running start on the Strawberry Blonde in the sugar cone. He went for the Banana Carmel Crunch – he was a geek for caramel – the chocolate for Mom, and grabbed the napkins. She chased the strawberries in small bites. She kept waiting for her father to fill the gap between them with his overwrought voice but he was still checking his mirrors, coming to a complete stop at the intersections in silence.

"Is Mick mad at me?" she asked.

Alex had his elbow out the window. "Of course not. Why would he be mad?"

"I missed the PK."

"Yeah. And we had 20 minutes of overtime and 12 rounds of PKs. One of which you made. You didn't lose the game, Layla."

It just feels that way, she thought, remembering the shock and bruises on everyone's faces afterward, the sullen tears, the lame-ass platitudes from the LO parents, the horns of the Westside cars in the parking lot. That was the worst. That's when she asked herself what in the world she'd been thinking.

They turned left on Kruse and headed toward Westlake Park. She let another spoonful melt on her tongue. Maybe there was no reaching a safe place, at least not tonight. Maybe the sting was meant to hang around for awhile. Maybe that's what you wanted to remember the next time you stood at the edge of one of those decisions.

When they reached the corner of the park, Alex eased into the left-turn lane. The intersection was empty, but the light remained red and resolute. Layla heard her father's spoon scrape the side of the cup, then the opening call of the Supremes:

> *I need love, love*
> *To ease my mind.*
> *I need to find, find someone to call mine*
> *But mama said*
> *You can't hurry love*
> *No, you just have to wait ...*

"Wow," Layla said. "The Supremes."
"What do you know about the Supremes?"

"I know Graham and I gave you their greatest hits for your birthday."

His spoon stopped moving. Her father, Layla was reminded, had the memory capacity of a 10-year-old laptop. "Wow. That's right. Which birthday was that?"

Layla did the math. "Your 40th."

The light was still red, the intersection still empty. The June coming through the diver's window was warm and quiet, and her father's face was striped with streetlight and begrudging pride. "How do you remember that?

"I was in 5th grade. You were mad at me 'cause I wanted to go to Seaside with Lisa instead of playing in that stupid tournament in Tualatin."

He didn't say anything. At first, Layla thought he'd forgotten that, too, but then she realized he was listening to Diana Ross.

How long must I wait
How much more can I take
Before loneliness will cause my heart to break?

Headlights blinked in the distance, where the light was fading, but otherwise they were alone, the two of them, alone on the cracked wooden sill of a small window in time, a window overlooking everywhere they'd been together.

"I'm not mad at you, either," he said, finally. "You know that, don't you?"

Did she? "I guess."

"I'm just …"

He stopped and took a breath, or lost his nerve or his train of thought, and Layla listened to the seconds drift by until, suddenly, the light on the cross street turned yellow and Layla realized they couldn't stay here forever.

"What?" she said. "What?"

Their light turned green. He set the ice-cream cup back down in the cup holder and their eyes met.

"I'm amazed," he said. "Amazed you knew the right thing to do." Then he took his foot off the brake and they took the long, slow turn toward home.

Mom pretended she wasn't all that excited about the ice cream. Graham, who was watching a "Lost" rerun, said he was sorry to hear about the game. Layla was halfway up the stairs when she remembered she'd left her cell phone in her travel bag in the garage. She retrieved it, then retreated to her room.

There were 12 text messages, five from Lisa, three from Emily … and one from a number she didn't recognize. She called it up. Melinda. The text was from Melinda, and Layla stared at the screen for a long time. All it said was this:

You did good.

after

He'd been out for three weeks when he stopped at Pal's Shanty for lunch. He was living in a garage apartment that smelled like a bladder infection, a mile further east on Sandy, and he was taking long walks to build his wind and lose the ass. The third or fourth brought him to the tavern door. When he checked his pockets, he had enough for the calamari steak, but not the IPA. The indignities kept piling up.

Or piling on. Debra Giuliani and two of the fathers had posted his bail, one of the dads on the condition that Elliott never return to the neighborhood. Taze only made the one trip. When he reached Carrie's place, he discovered his clothes sitting in the side yard, where they'd been taking shots from the sprinkler since the night of his arrest. The house? The house was empty.

The tavern was flush with old farts in fishing hats and grease monkeys from the Chevron station. Like the waitress and the clam strips, they'd seen better days. When the sandwich arrived, he let it sit, staring into the corner he was backed into. He had a court date at the end of the month. He had three changes of mildewed clothes and expired tags. He didn't have change to buy a beer, much less leave a tip, much less hit the gun show for the 30.06 he needed to go after everyone who'd left him high and dry.

He had a hazy flashback of Delroy and that Glock. Last he'd heard, the dude was providing security at the Bellagio. Married to a Venezuelan stripper. Two kids and a beer gut. Elliott reached for the calamari. He'd fought halfway through the sandwich when he realized the guy at the bar – pin-striped shirt and dumb-ass mustache – was sizing him up. He dropped his eyes to his plate, feeling the muscles in his neck bunch, trying to remember if the clown followed him through the door. He gazed the length of the tavern, at the postal clerks in ponytails, then slowed shifted back to the doofus with the Miller Lite. Still staring. Nodding like they were old friends. Sliding off the chair.

Taze was not in the mood. He'd walked a goddam mile so he could sit and enjoy what might be his best meal of the week. He didn't want some ghost from his past to trot over like the chairman of the Oregon Youth Authority reunion committee and …

"You're Taze Elliott."

Taze leaned back in his chair. Cyndi Lauper was on the house stereo. "So what?"

"I buy ya a beer?"

Well. Taze wasn't expecting that. Without waiting for an answer, the guy had the Czechoslovakian waitress pull a Budweiser out of the cooler. He set it down between Taze and the water glass and, without asking, sat down. "We met?" Taze asked.

The guy shook his head. "Dan Morgan. Miller Nash. The law firm."

Taze drained a third of the Budweiser. He could feel the cold in his sinuses.

"Read about you the other day," Morgan said.

Taze picked up one of the sandwich halves, dipped it in the tartar sauce, and stuffed it in his mouth. Then he took another long pull on the Bud, measuring the distance to the tavern's oaken door. "Don't know what we got to talk about," he said.

Morgan turned to his beer glass as if he wasn't quite sure, either. "You happy with your lawyer?"

Taze plucked the feathered toothpick off his plate and jammed it into his right cheek. "He's a smart-ass."

"Probably what you need."

Taze nodded. Morgan was equally out of place here. He had a few bucks. He was fine with picking up the tab. He'd showered. And he had an agenda.

"You still coaching?" he finally said.

Didn't the guy say he was a lawyer? "Court order. No contact with minors."

Morgan shrugged as if to say don't that beat all.

"No place to coach anyway," Taze continued. "Places I used to run don't believe in innocent until proven guilty."

"I have a key to the Riverdale gym," Morgan said.

Years back, Delroy took a run at explaining "entrapment" to Taze and it pissed him off he couldn't remember a thing the man said. "What's that got to do with me?"

Morgan returned to his beer. "A court might be available if you are."

"Available for what?"

"Run my daughter through some drills. See what you think."

"Your daughter."

"Yeah."

"How old?"

"Fifteen. Sophomore at Jesuit. You saw her play a couple months back."

A couple months back. He remembered the night, the Jesuit coach cutting him off when he went after Meleta, the only girl in the gym worth a JV minute at Portland State.

"Blonde, right?"

"Well ... dirty blonde, yeah."

"Tough defender? Quick to the glass? Smooth J?"

Taze could have been describing any one of 80 scrubs in the Metro League, but the guy lit up like a neon beer sign. "That's her. Zoe. Works hard. She's a natural."

Taze nodded. "Ever since she first picked up the ball, right?"

"Yeah. And she didn't get it from me."

Taze drained the Budweiser and felt the familiar glow. "You mind?" he said.

"Sure," Morgan said, signaling the barmaid for another round.

Taze set his elbows on the table. "I don't know," he said, looking all reflective and shit. "Trial coming up and everything, don't know if I can take the chance."

"No one has to know. And I'll be in the gym every minute. Just to be safe."

"Wouldn't consider it otherwise," Taze said.

The tavern door opened and a young woman in her early 20s walked in with the afternoon light and the warm spring air. She had boots and tight jeans and that semi-exhausted look that came with a nooner at the no-tell. She brushed past their table, heading for the changing room behind the kitchen. Until she disappeared, Taze followed each crunch of those jeans, feeling better about things with every step.

When the second Budweiser arrived, he raised his bottle to Morgan in a small toast. Yeah, Dad would be there, vigilant and possessive, watching their every move. But eventually he'd get lazy or busy. He'd relax. He'd blink. He'd give his daughter's best shot at making it big the benefit of the doubt.

Taze took another long pull on the beer. He'd start lifting again this afternoon. Run a lap or two over the weekend. Rethink his whole approach. A great coach learned from his mistakes.

Acknowledgements

Amid all the inspiration and encouragement that made this story possible, the author wishes to express special thanks to Fred Schreyer, a coaching partner through several different seasons; Mike Staropoli, for his long friendship and advice on legal issues; Rachel Bachman and Maureen O'Hagan, for their investigative reporting at, respectively, *The Oregonian* and *The Seattle Times*; Lorna Nakell, for her provocative cover design; Jeff Manning, Emma Rosen and Mike Rosen for the feedback they provided on early versions of the manuscript; and, finally, Bill Kane, whose enthusiasm and shepherding skills at Wake Forest's Digital Publishing have been nothing short of extraordinary.

About the Author

Steve Duin has written a column for *The Oregonian* in Portland since 1984. He has authored six other books, including "Comics: Between the Panels," a history of the medium, and "Oil and Water," a graphic novel about the aftermath of the Deepwater Horizon oil spill.

He has two English degrees from Wake Forest University and lives with his wife, Nancy, in the real Lake Oswego.

Readers may contact the author directly at: stephen.b.duin@gmail.com.

CPSIA information can be obtained at www.ICGtesting.com
Printed in the USA
LVOW10s2132010915

452479LV00004B/254/P